Ignite the Shadows

When Ingrid Seymour is not writing books, she spends
her time working as a software engineer, cooking exotic
recipes, hanging out with her family and working out.
She lives in Birmingham, AL with her husband, two
kids and a cat named Mimi. She can be found on
Twitter @Ingrid_Seymour

Ignite the Shadows

INGRID SEYMOUR

HARPER
Voyager

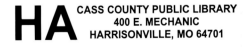

Harper*Voyager*
An imprint of HarperCollins*Publishers* Ltd
1 London Bridge Street
London SE1 9GF

www.harpervoyagerbooks.co.uk

This Paperback Original 2015

First published in Great Britain in ebook format by Harper*Voyager* 2015

A catalogue record for this book
is available from the British Library

ISBN: 978-0-00-812049-8

This novel is entirely a work of fiction.
The names, characters and incidents portrayed in it are
the work of the author's imagination. Any resemblance to
actual persons, living or dead, events or localities is
entirely coincidental.

Set in Sabon by Born Group using Atomik ePublisher from Easypress

Para mi madre
Por todo lo que me ha dado y aún me da

Chapter 1

I try not to look inside the alley. It's dark. Creepy dark.

Really, I don't know what I was thinking when I let Xave slink in there to spy on his brother. He walked between the two buildings until shadows devoured him.

Shadows ...

Crap, Marci. You know better. Don't think of shadows. Sunny days. Think of sunny days.

So I think of my dad and me at the beach all those years ago—his broad hands under my arms as he threw me toward the sky and caught me on the way down. A sad smile spreads across my lips. I push thoughts of Dad aside. I don't want to get depressed remembering him, so I concentrate only on the sand, the ocean, the palm trees. As hard as that is to do in the middle of February in freakin' Seattle, I force the images to stay inside my head. Without Dad, the beach colors come out lackluster, but it's the best I can do.

My hands sweat inside rubbery gloves. The black cloak that fell over Xave's figure as he disappeared inside the alley is imprinted in my mind and fights the sandy haven I'm trying to recreate. He's been gone too long. What if something happened? Clark can only be up to no good on this side of town, and he won't like it a bit if he catches his little brother spying on him.

I wait in the empty street under the cover of night. It's cold. The motorcycle purrs against my thighs, ready for Xave. My rapid heartbeats feel like a drum roll. I don't need this kind of stress. It will trigger me.

No, it won't. Stop thinking about that.

Bright things. Pretty things. Think of that.

The alley looks like a tomb of indefinite depth. I'm trying to tear my eyes away from it when my hands begin to shake. Crap. Not now. There's never a good time for an attack, but right now has got to be the worst. Fear floods my chest, paralyzing my racing heart.

My eyelids grow heavy with that familiar force that always threatens to banish the light. I fight it, biting the inside of my cheek, clinging to the image of that beach. I take a deep breath, trying to stay in control. My best friend's in the dark alley. He's counting on me. I have to—

The attack comes at once.

Shadows form inside my mind, scurrying like teeming spiders. In an instant, they climb one another, forming massive black giants that obscure everything. As they swarm, my very thoughts are scattered like bricks in the path of a wrecking ball. Quickly, the giants break apart and flock to each broken thought, ready to destroy them, like hungry locusts.

I fight to form a new thought, a simple one.

Breathe, Marci.

I inhale. A new specter rises inside my mind. It's amorphous, but my fear gives it a jagged mouth and empty sockets for eyes. It devours my thought to breathe, killing the impulse to fill my lungs, spreading over my consciousness like a whirling oil spill. In the next second or minute—I

2

don't know which—I'm gasping for air, trying to remember why I'm not breathing. Then it comes back to me. I'm under attack!

Breathe, I think once more. I need to let the thought bounce and morph. If it stays in the same place or shape, the shadows will destroy it. Breathing is important. Random thoughts are important.

Air. In and out.

My gloved left hand squeezes the clutch without my permission. I struggle to release it, while trying to hold on to the thread of my precious thoughts.

Stay calm. Don't lose it. Steady. Controlled. Breathe!

With unblinking eyes, I see my hand shaking, torn between gripping the handle and letting it go. The two conflicting commands clash inside my brain, neither of them winning or losing. My hand is in the limbo between the shadows and my will to fight them off. My eyes burn like hell. Tears spill down my cheeks, but I don't blink. I need the light. I need to stay grounded or I'll be lost in the shadows and their ravenous gloom.

I hear slapping footsteps. They echo against the alley's walls, splashing in shallow puddles. I want to turn toward the sound, but the idea is swallowed by a black shroud. Xave's coming, and I'm paralyzed by my demons.

Get a hold of yourself.

"Go, Marci, go, go, go," Xave says as he sprints out of the alley.

More steps echo behind him, heavy and menacing. "Hey, you. Get back here!" a booming voice cries out.

Xave jumps on behind me. The motorcycle lowers a few inches with the added weight. Now that I need to work the clutch, my hand fights back. It stiffens, fingers forming a rigid claw. The shadows mock me, trying to show me they're stronger than me. They want to undo me, but I won't let them. I snap my head to one side, exhale and squint at the alley. Two large figures advance at a fast clip.

"What are you waiting for? Go, go!" Xave urges, thrusting his hips back and forth, as if that will make the bike go.

The pursuers, two men, are almost out of the alley. Xave curses, puts his hands around my waist and shakes me. My bones rattle. Tense and trembling, my limbs respond in slow motion. My foot slowly shifts to first gear. I release the clutch, one finger at a time. My right hand twists the gas, barely making the red needle jump on the rpm gauge. Every one of my movements is painful. God, the men are only a few paces away.

Furious, Xave curses at me.

"Stop right there!" The men are close to the lonely lamp-post on the corner. I can almost see their faces. A faint buzz starts in the back of my head.

"*Marciiiii.*" Xave's earsplitting shriek melds with that of the revved-up engine.

Finally, we lurch ahead. The front tire leaves the blacktop. Too much, too fast. Xave and I lean forward and stay that way even after the wheelie dies. Half of my mind fears the men will shoot at us, while the other fights to keep the bike moving away from danger. We swerve from side to side, barely under control.

"Get yourself together, Marci," Xave screams.

I'm fighting the attack as hard as I've ever fought, but it feels like I'm losing, and I'm scared. I speed through a red light. It's late and there's no traffic. We're getting away. No one's chasing us, but we're not alone.

I'm not alone.

My muscles ache from being so tense, from fighting. Xave's body moves with the twists and turns of the road. He's the one keeping us upright. I'm nothing but an unyielding body, fighting not to be possessed by a sinister, alien force.

"Let me drive," he yells when it seems we're out of danger. "Stop the bike and let me drive."

I want to let him, but my body is still caught in limbo, my mind still cloaked in shadows. Suddenly, we speed up and it's not my doing. My hand twists the accelerator of its own accord. Window displays, stop signs and parked cars are a blur to each side. Downtown Seattle falls behind as we head north. A humid breeze from Puget Sound presses against me like an invisible force field.

"Damn it. Stop, Marci." He kicks my foot off the brake. The tip of my boot scrapes the pavement.

Good, I think, except in the next second my limbs fight him, even though I want to stop. Xave applies pressure on the brake and the back tire wobbles. I give it more gas and we speed onward. My foot kicks back to regain control of the pedal.

Xave gives up, knows we'll splat if he doesn't. "Please, stop." He sounds scared now.

I want to tell him I'm trying, but it's taking all I've got to keep this thing from fully taking over. Then something totally shifts inside my head, and I speed even more. Complete recklessness. As we whiz by a dark street, a blue light flashes, followed by the whine of a siren.

"You really messed up this time," Xave says and his words are carried away by the wind.

The needle in the speedometer pushes above eighty and keeps on. I'm going faster than I've ever dared in the city. If there wasn't something maniacal possessing me, I might even enjoy the ride, the chill in the air and the speed. But I'm terrified.

We speed for a few blocks and I dare hope we've left the cop behind, but I'm fooling myself. He can go from zero to screwing-up-our-lives faster than I can. He'll catch up soon. He's got his radio.

Suddenly, we take a sharp turn. We barely slow down and still we make it around the corner, missing a parked car by a few inches and eliciting a cry from a bystander. This goes beyond my skills. I haven't been riding bikes that long. I learn fast, always have, but this feels like something else.

Something else entirely.

I crisscross through alleys and streets I don't recognize. Some fancy part of town. We've lost the cop. As my panic dies down a bit, I try to regain control of my body. I can do it. I've done it before. I just need to concentrate.

Concentrate!

As I struggle to find myself, everything goes blank. Suddenly, I can't see, hear or feel anything. Panic gains a new level. I try to focus, reaching out for my self-awareness. Nothing happens. Everything feels different, far away and utterly desolate. I can't find myself. I'm right here and I can't find myself. Desperation sets in. I whirl in an empty space, trying to claim my body and my very mind. But everything is gone.

All my senses are gone. Yet somehow, I know I'm here, pushed to a corner where I'm tiny and inconsequential. I'm weightless. A plundered body, a consciousness without gray matter, nerve endings or synapses. A wisp of nothing.

What is this?

Then I understand. The shadows have won. I've lost total control like never before. My brain, my body are gone. I have been … replaced, as if the code that makes me who I am has been erased by a flawless hack. Something else fuels me, and I realize that my lifelong fears are far worse than I've imagined. I'm still alive. This thing didn't kill me. It made me a prisoner, and it's worse than a thousand deaths at the blade-end of a thousand knives.

No, no, no!

Rage boils fire-red in my secluded corner. This can't be happening. Not to me. I'm strong. I'm Brian Scott Guerrero's daughter. I don't give up. He was a fighter, a decorated officer, a doctor in combat. Brave as a mountain against a blizzard. I'm like him. I'm like him.

With what little I've become, I picture a strong body. It has claws instead of hands. I imagine myself tearing through this quiet bubble. I punch and punch until my claws pierce through something. With all my strength, I drag down, ripping, tearing my prison.

Shadows flow into my space and swarm, attacking my imagined claws. But I'm ready for them, ready to let what's left of me morph, fluid like water. My claws turn to knives that stab, guns that shoot, beams of light that cut through the darkness. Shapeless, changing thoughts. That's the key. I learned this a long time ago, before I had enough reason to know what I was doing. The specters shriek as I burst into the light. They grasp for my thoughts, but I force them to morph, concentrating on nothing specific.

Multi-core motherboards ... Roaring engines.

Wile E. Coyote ... Speed.

Cinnamon gum ... Xave.

Ideas fall and rise, turn and twirl. Never the same.

Creaking leather. A dark alley.

A cop!

I break out into the open, gasping and shaking. A million needles prick my limbs. The world seems brighter and every sound louder.

Release the gas. Release it!

I do, but I can't manage much else. Inside, the shadows still threaten to strike, hunkering like thieves in an alleyway. I can taste their gloom, a bitter mouthful of loss and imprisonment.

We're on a curvy road which I recognize immediately. The bike wobbles. I compensate to the left, but so does Xave. We lose balance, the bike tips over and we hit the pavement hard. The weight of the motorcycle clamps my leg and its momentum carries us forward, slipping, scraping, burning. Heat reaches my thigh through my leathers. The side of my helmet scrapes the road. A horrible screech fills my head.

The bike skids ahead of us. I'm relieved to have its weight off me, but we keep sliding after it. We roll off the road into the supple earth that is more forgiving. Branches and bushes scrape and snap, harmless against my body armor. I hear a loud crash. As I roll and tumble amid the brush, I catch a glimpse of the bike smashed against a tree.

I travel downward on my stomach, every rock and bump knocking a little more air out of me. I claw gloved fingers into the dirt. Pebbles hit my visor, but I feel my descent slowing. Finally, I come to a stop. I lay there for a moment, assessing my aching body. Nothing feels broken.

Head spinning, I wobble to my knees and look around. I can't see anything. Horror grips me, then I realize it's too dark to see through the helmet's visor. The bike's headlight must have shattered against the tree. I stand up on shaky legs, take off my helmet and look around under the dim moonlight that seeps through the trees.

"Xave," I whisper.

My eyes search the darkness, and I can't find him.

Chapter 2

Panic sets in. I'm about to scream Xave's name when I'm pitched forward, shoved from behind. My helmet flies off and hits the ground as my arms flail in an attempt to keep my balance. I take two staggering steps to avoid a fall, then whirl and strike a fighting pose, ready for anything. Xave is behind me, apparently furious enough to shove me. His own helmet is on the ground next to him, his shaggy, brown hair matted to his forehead.

"What the hell! You trying to get us killed?" Xave shouts.

My instinct is to jump and karate-kick his ass for pushing me, but I manage to control myself. I need to come up with an explanation for my screw-up and fast. I haven't had one of these episodes in over a year and never in front of Xave. Even Mom thinks I'm over my "epileptic" attacks, as she chooses to call them—even though the doctors never gave that diagnosis.

I take a deep breath and relax my arms. Sensei would be proud of me. Hell, I'm proud of me. I may only be five-foot-five, but I don't let anyone push me around. Never have. Xave's a year older than me and considerably taller, but I can give him a run for his money, if it comes to that.

"What kind of stupid stunt was that, Marci?" Xave sounds as if he's about to pop. "The cops, the freaking cops, were after us."

"Not for long," I say, sounding smug, just the tone I need for the explanation he unknowingly provided me: a "stupid stunt." I abandon my defensive stance and make a big show of dusting myself.

Xave limps in my direction. Uh-oh, did he break something? I'll feel really bad if he did. His black leathers creak with every step. He stops and looks down at me with a kind of anger I didn't know him capable of. I watch him, wary of sudden moves. It would suck if this ended up in a nasty fight.

Moonlight cuts through the trees above and bathes Xave's face. His hazel eyes look nearly black, his high cheekbones sunken.

"I'm tired of your cocky, I-can-do-it-all bull-crap," he says. "If you want to go all Evel Knievel, do it on your own time. Leave *me* out of it, okay?"

"Hey, you were the one who wanted to spy on Clark." I take a step back, trying to put some distance between us.

"All you had to do was be ready to drive off. But you couldn't even do that." Xave's tone grates on my nerves. "Now Clark knows we were there and on his Yamaha."

At the last word, his face goes all Hulk-green or maybe it's putty-gray, I can't really tell in the dim moonlight. He points at the wrecked bike, hand shaking.

"Look, I'll get the bike fixed," I say, using a conciliatory tone—though it's a lame offer, considering that Xave already spent hours working on this bike. He's good at fixing things. I think he got it from his mom. She likes crafts, doing detailed things with her hands. He says he'll be a mechanic after school. "I'll talk to Clark and tell him it was my—"

"Screw you, Marci."

I flinch at the harshness in his voice. What's wrong with him lately? I know I screwed up, but where is all this anger coming from? We've been in bigger trouble than this before.

"Everything's always so easy for you." His tone is mocking. "Oh, I'll tell him it was *my* idea," he mimics me in a whiny voice, which sounds nothing like mine. "We'll lie, steal and cheat. It'll be okay. Just chill out, Xave. You worry too much."

"Hey, you're pushing it," I tell him, feeling a bit injured.

"Am I? And what are you gonna do? Land me in jail when I least expect it?"

I take a deep breath to control my rising temper. I can't get angry right now. Not after what I just went through. "Let's just go home and talk about it later before we regret it. Okay?"

"I already regret it. I don't know why I bother with you anymore." His words hold a venom I can almost taste. "You're selfish and immature. You never stop to think of anyone but yourself."

"You ... don't understand," I say.

"Understand what?" he demands.

I feel like my only choice is to wait for his fury to die down. I can't tell him about the mess inside my head. I've been hiding it from everyone for too long to start sharing now. He'll think I'm crazy, and I'd rather continue lying than face his disappointment. I get enough of that from Mom.

A part of me tells me I'm wrong, that I should trust him, that he'll understand. Dare I listen to it?

I clear my throat and begin in a weak voice, "I ... lost control—"

"You're damn right you lost control." His anger runs unchecked, killing what little courage I'd mustered. "My

11

dad's gonna have my hide and so is Clark. Did you stop to think about that?"

There isn't a good response, so I start toward the bike to avoid answering. When I walk past, Xave grabs my shoulder and makes me face him.

"You didn't answer my question. Did you stop to think about it?" His eyes look darker than a starless universe would.

"No," I say, because a "yes" would mean I did it intentionally. "I just thought we'd have a little fun, that's all."

"Like I said, *selfish*!" The word echoes through the quiet patch of trees.

"Is that what you think?"

"Yes, that's what I think!"

Rage seethes inside me. He has no idea what he's talking about. He thinks he knows me, has me all figured out. Well, he doesn't know the half of it. No one does. Dad was the only one who ever tried to understand, but he's gone and now I have only myself.

Through another deep breath, I manage to stay in control. "Whatever," I say, trying to sound like the brat he figures me for. I look for my helmet on the ground. I can get home on foot from here. We're only a mile away. When I spot it, I pick it up and start walking away.

"Oh, so now you're leaving?" he says sarcastically.

"That's what selfish people do."

"It must be nice to live never having to face the consequences of anything you do."

I whirl. "Shut up, Xave. You don't know what you're talking about." The anger rolls through me in waves. Automatically, my breathing slows and my thoughts shift at a million gigahertz a second. My defenses are second nature most of the time. They have to be. Anger is bad. Anything that can make me lose my concentration can bring the shadows back. That's why my entire life I've felt as if I'm walking on eggshells, always afraid of cracking and spilling out my insides.

"'Course I do. No one ever tells you anything or cramps your style with chores and speeches about responsibility. No one cares—" He abruptly stops.

"Finish, Xave." I dare him.

He exhales, knowing he's gone too far. A car drives by on the road, its headlights flooding our space for a quick couple of seconds. I see no hint of remorse in Xave's face, but he doesn't dare finish his sentence.

"But no one cares about me? Is that what you were going to say? Huh?" I wait for a response. I can feel him teetering. He still wants to get to me, hurt me somehow. But he must know that if he goes there, whatever friendship we've shared will die. We've been through too much together to ruin everything over something like this. I can tell he's thinking the same thing, but maybe his anger will beat his common sense.

Sensing we're at the brink of making a huge mistake, I walk away without saying a word and head north toward our neighborhood. I don't look back. Xave can limp home for all I care, even if this is my fault. Maybe I am selfish, after all.

Keeping to the shoulder, I move at a steady pace. I'm fuming, wondering if I could have handled this better. The air is crisp with winter's bite. It makes every deep breath count. There are no street lamps on this side road, but the moon is full, the sky cloudless—a rarity in this damn city.

I haven't been to this small wooded area in years, but I can see why Xave and I used to like playing here. It's quiet and hidden from prying neighbors and their objections to BB guns, baseballs and fireworks. God, that all seems so long ago. We were inseparable then and now it seems some huge wedge is making its way between us. He's become so moody and sullen with me. I don't get it. I fear things won't ever be like they used to. The thought hurts.

The smell of crushed pine needles wafts in the breeze, bringing back memories of happier times with my friend—many of them in these woods. I huff, thinking of the time he dared me to kiss him. He must have been ten and I, nine.

"Now there's a scary dare," I said. "I'd rather kiss a slug."

"Not so brave, are you?" he said.

"Oh, I'm brave, just not *that* brave."

He smiled wickedly. "All right, here's another dare. Climb that tree." He pointed at the tallest tree in the patch of woods.

I was afraid of heights, afraid of anything that could trigger an attack, for that matter, but I wasn't about to let him show me up, so I climbed the tree. The problem was, once I found myself fifteen feet off the ground, I panicked and lost all my courage. I started crying and fearing my mind would go blank. In seconds, Xave was by my side, perched on a thick branch.

"Don't worry. Don't cry. I'll help you get down," he said.

He tried to tell me where to place my feet and hands, but I was too scared to follow his instructions. When he realized it wasn't going to work, he had me wrap myself around him, a little monkey on his back, and painstakingly climbed down. A few feet off the ground, his arms gave out and we plummeted to the ground. His weight knocked the air out of me.

He hovered above, as I lay there inert. "Are you okay? Are you okay? I'm sorry. Please forgive me. I didn't mean for you to get hurt."

When I opened my eyes, his nose was inches from mine, worry etched on his face. He was making sure I was still breathing.

"You're alive!" he exclaimed. "Thank God, you're alive."

"You silly goose," I said, using the endearment Dad often used with me. "Of course I'm alive." Then I kissed him on the cheek.

His eyes widened in surprise and after that we both rolled on the pine needles, laughing like idiots. I guess things have to change. We're not kids anymore. I just wish we could still laugh about our misadventures. Instead, we're yelling at each other.

After a few minutes walking, I hear gravel crunching behind me. I try to ignore it and pick up my pace. The crunching is followed by a shuffle.

Crunch, crunch, shuffle.

Reluctantly, I look back and see Xave, pushing the bike forward a couple of feet, then dragging his right leg. He repeats the process, looking as pathetic as one of those dogs with wheels for legs.

Damn it.

I stop and hope Xave doesn't make me regret doing so. I wait for interminable minutes for him to catch up. Surely, he's taking his sweet time on purpose. When he reaches me, we say nothing and just stand there looking at anything but each other.

"I'll push the bike," I tell him.

He nods. We walk without exchanging any more words. Enough has been said already.

Chapter 3

Awkward. Awk-ward.

All the way home, Xave and I stare at the ground, mouths zipped. I should apologize, but after he dragged my family into the argument, I'm too mad.

His limping is worse.

He deserves it!

I'm not sorry for him, not when he assumes the worst about me, like everyone else. I expect more from him. I don't care if he has no way of knowing I'm possessed, crazy or whatever it is, he should treat me better than this. He's known me for nine years. "He feels my pain," like he often says. Maybe he doesn't.

Our street comes into view. A few lampposts cast weak light on the cracked sidewalk, but it's mostly dark in spite of the clear, moonlit sky. Too many large trees line the street and few people keep their floodlights on once they turn in for the night. It helps keep the electric bill low, Mom says. I don't argue; it helps me sneak out when I need to.

I slow down as we approach Xave's house. The split-level looks gloomy, spotted with shadows from the nearby trees. A shudder goes down my back, making me wary. I've seen his house in this light before. Why is it spooking me all of a sudden?

I'm contemplating the question when a male figure steps from behind the largest tree in the front yard. His face is obscured, but the silhouette and swagger let me know it's Xave's brother. I stop and exchange a quick glance with Xave. There'll be no lying our way out of this one. We never got our story straight. Besides, Clark's not blind. He saw us from the alley. Why else would he be waiting for us?

Still wary, even though it's just Clark, I look around. A faint buzz begins in the back of my head for the second time tonight. I frown.

Clark plants his intimidating six-three, muscular frame a few paces from us, arms crossed. I can see his face better, and it isn't pretty. Well, it *is* pretty, but in a Dirty Harry kind of way. Intense eyes, tight lips, strong jaw.

"Hello there, *X-avier.*" Clark says the name as if he's referring to pond scum. He pauses at the "X" and says the rest with a sarcastic British accent.

Xave's eyes shift from one crack of the sidewalk to another. He hates being called by that name, has heard enough jokes about gay mutants in tights and will pretty much beat up anybody who dares call him by the full name his comic-book-obsessed father gave him. Clark's the only one I know who still dares call him that. If you ask me, he's just lucky his dad didn't name him Louise instead of Clark.

"You've got some explaining to do, bro," Clark says.

"It was my fault," I say.

Xave gives me a dirty look. I match it. So he's gonna be ungrateful like that? Well, in that case, I hope his brother kicks his ass. Clark turns toward me, very slowly. He shifts his weight from one foot to another, stamping his biker boot down. The heavy heel *taps*. He takes in the full length of my body.

"So what are you saying?" he asks. "That my *sissy* brother has no more sense than a wet-'round-the-ears gal?"

What did he just call me? Not like he's all mature and experienced with only four years on me and three on his brother.

"Told you to stay out of it, Marci," Xave mumbles through the corner of his mouth.

Very slowly, I inhale, closing my eyes until my lungs are full. I let go of the bike and give it a shove toward Xave. It catches him off guard and he scrambles to keep it from falling on him, favoring his injured leg. I'm about to turn and head home when that strange buzzing in the back of my skull gets worse, recognizable. It stops me in my tracks.

This sensation has nothing to do with being spooked, like I thought at first. I've felt this before, except this time it's so intense it sends strong shudders down my spine, totally freaking me out. My eyes dance around the yard, but there's no one else here. It makes no sense. I only get this creepy feeling in crowded places, like the mall or the movies. That's the reason why I hate crowds. But I've never felt it at home, at school with my friends, and certainly not with Xave's family.

I stare at Clark. He's watching me with sudden distrust.

"You should go home, Marci," he says. "My little brother and I have some serious talking to do."

It is then that I sense, more than see, a dark shape moving behind Clark. I take a step back, eyes darting, adrenaline pumping.

Xave spooks at my behavior. "What?!" he asks, looking at me like I'm crazy.

He hasn't noticed the dark shape behind his brother. The shadow advances without making a sound, hidden by Clark's bulky frame, who shows no sign of suspecting something lurks behind him.

I've finally gone crazy.

The shadows don't only live inside my head. They've figured out a way to break free and stalk me in the night. My heart beats in my clenched fists as I dissolve into fear.

Something stretches out of the darkness, reaching for Clark's shoulder. Words of warning rise in my throat, but they die down when a thin ray of moonlight falls upon the shadow, revealing a flesh and blood man. He steps next to Clark and pats him on the shoulder. I've never seen him before. I would remember, because he makes my head drone with a thousand bees. I want to run, but I'm glued to the sidewalk.

"Wow," Xave says, startled by the sudden appearance of the stranger.

"Clark, is this your brother?" the man asks in a deep purr that makes me think of an idling motorcycle engine. His bald head reflects what little moonlight there is. He's several inches shorter than Clark and Xave, maybe five-eleven. He's also leaner, but I have the feeling he could beat up both of them if he wanted. Something in his confident and powerful stance makes me suspect that. I wish I could see his eyes. I've got a feeling they'd tell me a lot, but they're hidden under the shade of his strong brow.

Clark nods, never taking his eyes off me. "Yep, that's him."

The man removes his hand from Clark's shoulder and extends it toward Xave. "Nice to meet you, Xavier. My name is James McCray."

Xave stares at his hand. James's mouth twists into a crooked grin, as he waits for Xave to make up his mind. In the end, he shakes it, encouraged by a nod from Clark. James hasn't looked directly at me, but I feel watched, evaluated like an open book.

"So you were ... spying?" James's speech is calm and reassuring, but I don't trust him at all. "I take it you'd like to know what your brother's up to?" James asks. He smiles, but his voice sounds like a dare, hinting at something dangerous.

Xave puffs up like a bullfrog. "Yeah. Yeah, I would."

Clark called him a sissy. I guess he thinks this proves he's not. It doesn't. The panic that flashes in his eyes gives him away. I don't blame him. Something's going on here. Maybe Clark got himself in a real mess this time. I don't think I want any part in it. Xave shouldn't either.

As if James could read my thoughts, his eyes settle on me. "What about you, Marci Guerrero?"

He knows my name?! Why would freakin' Clark tell him my name?!

"No, thank you," I blurt out. "Whatever you're selling, I'm not buying it." I take two steps back, look straight at my friend. "Xave, you should stay out of it, too."

"Who says he's got a choice?" Clark puts in. "Not after wrecking my bike like that. No, he's got a debt to pay. Besides, he has a right to know what's going on in our neighborhood, our country. Hell, our fucking world!"

What is Clark talking about? And why is James looking at me like I'm to blame for world hunger? There's no way Xave doesn't see through this weirdness. Besides, I'm not a *joiner* and this sounds too cult-ish for my taste.

"Xave." I pull on his sleeve. He pulls his arm back.

I jerk my head to one side. "Come talk to me for a minute."

"Get lost, Marci," he says.

"Don't be stupid. This—"

"I said get lost." His eyes bore into me with anger. He can't stand to be challenged, much less in front of the "guys" and by a girl, no less. God, he so needs to grow up.

I resist the urge to scream and let him go get brainwashed if that's what he wants. Instead, I give it another try. "Please, Xave." I give him big, pleading eyes. His expression softens, but he quickly tries to hide the shift.

He motions with his head for me to follow and walks out of earshot. "Why don't you just go home?"

"Look," I start, but my head drones so loudly I'm having trouble thinking straight.

"What is it you want to say?" he asks.

I focus on his hazel eyes. "Look Xave, I don't think you should go with them."

"And why is that?"

"Do you have to ask?"

"What do you care what I do?" he asks, thick brows pinched in that way that always gives him two creases above his nose.

"I ... I don't want you to get in trouble," I say.

"Right, that's why you wrecked Clark's bike and got the cops on our tail."

"Please." I take his hand. "Don't go."

He looks deep into my eyes. "Why?" His tone suggests that if I find the right words, he'll stay.

I struggle to figure out what he wants to hear. "Because ... I think Clark is up to no good, and you're, um, my friend. I don't want you to get hurt."

Xave drops my hand. Clearly, I've said the wrong thing. Our almost-kiss of three weeks ago flashes through my memory. I pulled away from him that day, surprised and confused. The sudden closeness between us had been an accident. We'd both turned at the same time and ended up nose to nose without meaning to. But accident or not, there'd been something there, hadn't there? And *I*, not Xave, pulled

21

away. Since then he's been getting mad at me for no reason at all. He's always been too tough, too proud to say what really bothers him. In spite of that I was fluent in Xave, up to a few weeks ago, but after the non-kiss, the Tower of Babel has nothing on us.

"Go home, Marci. Go hide in your dungeon. I'll see you later." He walks to James and Clark. I stand there feeling vulnerable and lost. Maybe our friendship won't survive our teens, after all. Red wagons and skateboards may be the only type of rides that'll ever bring good memories back. Frustration floods me.

Fine! He can go get brainwashed for all I care. I spin on my heels and speed-walk home. The droning in my head dies down as I put distance between me and them. I cast glances over my shoulder every few steps.

The first time I look back, all three are staring at me. For an instant, James's eyes reflect the light, putting the image of a wild cheetah inside my head. Ice crawls slowly up my neck, then I realize I'm just imagining things. The second time I look back, James has an arm around Xave and seems to be talking him up. I've got a bad feeling in the pit of my stomach, but what can I do about it? Xave's a big boy. He can take care of himself. I've got my own problems to worry about.

I trudge up my front steps and look back one last time. Xave is walking up the road toward two parked bikes. They look like big Harleys. He climbs on the back with Clark as James straddles the second bike. The engines roar to life in unison. The poor, wrecked Yamaha is left behind by the sidewalk, all battered and broken.

It seems Xave has finally graduated to the big boy club, like he's always wanted. By tomorrow, our friendship may be a thing of the past.

Chapter 4

Inside the house, everything is dark. Shapes dance on the living room wall visible from the foyer, where I stand watching them shift. Blue, white, gray ... the changing frames from the TV screen reflected on the white paint.

I stand there, hypnotized by them, listening to the hum of the refrigerator and Mom's rhythmic breathing. I sigh, weighted down by all the sadness that hangs like a haze inside this house, a haze that obscures everything, even ourselves. Out there, I hide from the world and put on a tough exterior. In here, I hide from Mom and wish for so much more than I'm given.

The only place where I don't have to hide is my bedroom. My sanctuary, where I can listen to heavy metal, read poetry, hack computers and cry my eyes out all in the same hour, without anyone thinking I'm a basket case. I want to run in there, lock the door and, for a short time, just be who I really am, but Mom's been waiting for me. I should at least let her know I'm home.

After a moment, I walk into the living room and watch her sleep on the sofa in front of the muted television. She looks sad, even in her sleep. Her hands are sandwiched between her face and a cushion. Her sandy blond hair spills over the sofa's dark fabric, and her pale skin serves as witness to how little time she spends outside. Her job at a small fashion magazine keeps her tied to a desk. She's still wearing her fashionable clothes and, for some reason, that brings a knot to my throat. She used to model and desperately clings to that prettier, younger version of herself. She takes a deep breath and her face turns my way a little, as if some part of her knows I'm watching. Her long lashes flutter, then her eyes open.

She looks unsurprised by my presence. She sits up, arches her back and rubs her eyes. Aided by the coffee table, she stands and walks toward me.

"You're home," she says. Her tone suggests she wishes I wasn't. Her blue eyes are cold and expressionless, but I can still see the disappointment in them. Why does she wait for me? So I can see in her gaze how much I let her down? She leans in and gives the mandatory kiss. I close my eyes as her lips touch my cheek and wish for so much more than this formality. Mom turns toward the hall, pats my shoulder and heads off to bed.

So much pain, so little to say to each other. She used to yell at me when I was late. It still didn't mean she cared, though. She was only worried the neighbors would gossip. These days she doesn't even care about that.

In my bedroom, I click the light on. The bed is unmade, inviting. It's past 1 A.M. I should crash and get some sleep, so I can make it to school on time. But I want to check my probes, see if they found any unprotected servers when they scoured the web looking for vulnerable targets.

I kick an old motherboard out of the way as I make my way to the computer, shedding my jacket. I sit and rejoice in front of my rig. Three wide-screen HD monitors, the best gaming keyboard money can buy, a laser sensor mouse—all hooked to a blazing-fast, custom-made CPU. I smile, tap the keyboard and enter my password. The monitor in the middle displays a black screen with a few IP addresses written in white. I started the probe this morning, and it's already found some vulnerable servers. I smile to myself. The algorithm is working. Of course. I'll let it run a full twenty-four hours, and tomorrow I'll peruse through those systems.

On the left hand side monitor, I start my heavy metal playlist. On the right, I log into the H-Loop and take a quick look around to see who's online tonight. As I wait for it to load, I slip out of my leather pants and look them over. Several holes run from my thigh to my knee. Great, looks like I'm going to need a new pair. I'm reminded of Xave, so I throw the pants on the floor and push thoughts of my friend out of my head. I can't worry about him. I won't.

After I change into a pair of pajama shorts, I examine my leg. There are a few spots where it looks as if someone attacked me with a sheet of coarse sandpaper. In four different spots the skin's split open, and there's dark, dry blood caked on the wounds. Not too bad. Nothing some soap and ointment can't take care of.

SMASH and Hazard-Us are logged into the H-Loop. Those two never seem to have anything better to do, which is sad because, for some reason, I imagine them as middle-aged men without real jobs. I bet they never take a bath.

SMASH> Late night, Warrior?

I crack my fingers and begin to type.

Warrior> Yep, just got in.

SMASH> Ur outta luck, I'm off. Sleepy. L8r

Hazard-Us> Night, sissy!

Hazard-Us> What u been up to, Warrior?

Warrior> Testing some new probes, u?

Hazard-Us> Unleashing a few viruses here n there, fun stuff!

Hazard-Us and his viruses. Doesn't he get sick of doing the same thing all the time? I play along, though, tell him he should send me the code. He promises he will, but I know he won't. He's a script-kiddie. We chat for a bit before he hops off the loop. The cursor blinks next to my handle name. I need to quit staring at the computer screen and go to bed.

I'm about to log out when Mom screams. My heart slams against my chest. When the burst of panic passes, I sigh. I should have known she'd have one of *those* nights tonight.

In her room, I find her sitting up in bed.

"You okay?" I ask from the threshold. Light from the hall spills on her, revealing a pale face with strands of sandy blond hair matted to her cheeks. Sweat stains the front of her gray tank top in a V-shape.

She shakes her head in response.

"I'll get you some tea." I head to the kitchen.

I pour two cups of water in the electric kettle, open the tea drawer and select the Sleepytime variety for the both of us. Four spoonfuls of sugar later, I walk into Mom's bedroom. Her bedside lamp is now on. Her room is tidy. She sleeps on one side of the bed, as if she expects Dad to come back one day. I wish she'd just use the whole stupid bed and stop reminding me of his absence. He'd be here if he could, but the dead can hardly make someone's bed warm.

She cradles the mug between both hands and I sit by her side, holding mine the same way. We both sip quietly.

"Sorry to wake you," she says, though her eyes are unapologetic, and still seem lost in the folds of her nightmare.

"I wasn't sleeping. Just double checking my math homework."

Her eyebrow lifts, an indication that she knows I'm lying. Homework has never kept me up at night. School's too easy for my overactive brain. Besides, I learned long ago that marginally good grades keep you out of the spotlight, both ways.

My eyes gravitate to the picture on her nightstand. In it, Mom looks radiant with Dad's arm around her and the ocean sparkling in the background. I stand in the middle, a toothless grin on my face, my chubby body stuffed into a pink bathing suit. Hard to believe I ever liked that horrendous color, harder yet to recall ever being that happy.

Dad's wide smile gleams on his tan face. He was tall, handsome and strong, with deep brown eyes that inspired trust. I'm glad I look like him and love those rare occasions when I catch a glimpse of him in the mirror.

Back in those days, my brother's kidnapping never weighed so heavily on Mom's mind. Since Dad died though, it's like she lost her grief compass and went off the deep end. While Dad was alive, she never lit an extra set of candles on my birthday cake and wept as I blew them out. Or told near-strangers she had two kids just to have them ask later why one of them was never around. Or kept a box under the bed full of baby outfits Max never had a chance to wear.

No, when Dad was alive, she was normal.

"We were happy then, weren't we?" Mom asks, as if she's read my thoughts.

The question makes me recoil. She knows I hate talking about it, yet she insists. Maybe to torture me.

"Yeah." I slurp my tea and shift my body toward the door.

"I dreamed about Max," she says.

I clear my throat. Let's not go there, please.

"A memory, really," she adds. "His tiny body whisked away, prodding needles, doctors. He was so small. Only three pounds. He never made a peep. You, on the other hand, came out ten minutes after Max, kicking and wailing." She makes it sound as if I came out with two heads. I can't help but wonder … if I'd been the one taken away, would she hurt Max the same way she hurts me by saying stuff like this?

She must notice something in my expression because she adds, "You had a head full of black hair already, spiky and shiny." This is one of the things Dad used to say when he fondly talked about the day I was born. The words sound empty on Mom's lips.

"It still sticks out if I cut it too short. That's why I keep it long," I say, trying to steer the conversation in a different direction. I don't like where this is going.

Mom puts her tea down on the night table. Her hands fall to her lap, where she worries at a hangnail. Her eyes lose their focus and her expression grows pained.

Oh, no.

"When I saw Dr. Dunn at the hospital and then that horrible alarm shrieked, I knew what had happened. I told everyone, but they didn't believe me. Not even your father. That man took your brother, Marcela."

"I know, Mom." She's told me this story a million times, as if talking about it will make the outcome different.

My teeth grind, as *her* memories swim in my brain. They're lodged in there like a splinter, as vivid as any movie I've seen on the big screen, as vivid as if they were my own. This is why I hate these conversations. They awaken these images, which have no business being in my head. I already have enough in there that doesn't belong. They make me understand Mom's pain all too well and, even if I never knew Max, his loss hurts. Every time Mom brings this up, the splinter digs deeper—so deep that I think it will split me in two one day.

I imagine Dr. Dunn as a balding, short man with small hands and Vienna sausages for fingers. He wears a spotless white coat over an equally white button-up shirt and dark blue tie. He smiles with thick, fleshy lips. He winks at me and my heart skips a beat.

Damn, my overactive brain. I shake my head. "Mom, uh, I think I should ..."

"Why would he take him? Why?"

"I don't know."

Because he was a sick man, I want to say. Why else would he have tracked Mom's pregnancy after doing the fertility treatments? Why else would he have stolen a newborn baby in need of neonatal care?

Mom clings to this hope that Max is alive somewhere. I know because one night she woke up screaming that she had failed Baby Max and now that he was a teenager, we both failed him *every day* by not bringing him to his real home.

Does she really want him growing up with that bastard? I want to shake her, ask her if she's crazy. I pray to God my little twin brother didn't survive after he was taken from his incubator. I pray he's an innocent little angel with wings and a halo, floating on fluffy white clouds.

And like always, as I pray for his redemption, I think: it could have been me, that monster could have taken me.

Chapter 5

Back in my bed, I toss and turn. I keep seeing weird shapes and I can't sleep. Tonight only the H-Loop can keep me sane. I wrap my quilt around me and tread back to the computer desk.

I tap on the keyboard and notice I never logged out. Not smart. The customized console program I wrote to connect to the loop creates a daisy-chain through different servers, so I'm never detected. But still, you can never be too safe.

As I start scanning the list of people logged in, I noticed a new chat window is open. One single line stares at me.

IgNiTe> I know what you are.

The timestamp of the message is now. The cursor blinks. My heart keeps the same beat. I tell myself the words mean nothing. It's just some idiot playing games. I've no idea who this IgNiTe guy is, but I've ran into his kind before. He needs a taste of Warrior's cyber wrath. Just what I need to keep my head free of the ghosts weighing me down.

I rub my hands together, load my tracing program, and type a message to keep the jerk online.

Warrior> Do you, skiddie?

He calls himself a hacker when he's nothing but a *cracker*. I hit enter and just as I'm doing it, a belated sixth sense warns me to stop, but it's too late. All three monitors go blue and white text starts raining down the screen, repeating the same thing over and over again.

I know what you are. I know what you are.
I know what you are. I know what you are.
I know what you are. I know what you are.

Cursing, I drop to my knees and fight to untangle myself from the stupid quilt. I slip and slide in an effort to get traction on the parquet flooring. Under the desk, I'm faced with three CPUs and a tangle of cables swathed in dust bunnies.

Furiously, I push everything out of the way until I find the power strip. I press the button and the LED light goes out, indicating the flow of electricity has been cut off. In the same instant, the uninterruptible power supply kicks in and starts to beep. I scramble to unhook all the cables to the battery backup. Damn, why do I have to be such a meticulous freak?

Finally the hum of the CPUs dies down. I lay under the desk seething, wanting to strangle something. He better pray I don't find him, because I'll kill him, very slowly. No one messes with my equipment, my sanctuary. My ears are hot, and if I was a cartoon character, there'd be steam coming out of them.

When the rage subsides, my mind hits fifth gear. How did he do it? How did this IgNiTe jerk get through my intricate security measures? Everyone in the H-Loop knows I'm the hacker to beat, so it's obvious why he'd want to mess with me. But how did he do it? My system is tight. The hardware, my code ... I don't ever leave any trails. I rack my brain trying to figure it out and come up empty. I've been outsmarted, and I don't even know how.

Suddenly, I feel like crying. I can't even hide in my room anymore. I shake my head. Self-pity isn't something I allow myself. Slowly, I crawl out from under the desk. The clock reads 5:29 A.M. I groan. When the display changes to 5:30 A.M., I walk over to the alarm and turn it off. Time to leave for the dojo. I ponder whether I should go or sleep for an hour before school. The bed looks tempting, but after what just happened my brain won't quiet long enough to let me sleep. Only punching something can help me now. That is ... if I can even stay upright long enough to do it.

I start jogging on the spot, letting my arms hang like a dummy's. They swing from side to side as I turn my head around and bounce on my toes. My body feels supple enough in spite of the lack of sleep. Okay, I guess I'll go. I try to never skip practice. The emotional focus that martial arts give me is critical. It keeps the shadows and the fear away.

Looking back at my desk, I'm tempted to stay to assess the damage to my computers. Tension bites the back of my neck at the simple thought of what that good-for-nothing cracker just did to me. Anger flares again, but I get it under control after a few deep breaths. It looks like I really need to go to the dojo to clear my head. I can't let emotions control me.

This is how my life goes. Every day is a struggle. An endless array of do's and don'ts designed to keep the shadows at bay. And after what happened last night, after discovering the torture I would endure if I let my defenses down, I can't afford to make any mistakes.

If only my worries amounted to no more than what outfit to wear today.

After almost two hours of grueling practice at the dojo, I enter the locker room and throw my sweaty karategi in a plastic bag. I fold the belt and drop it on top. The contrast between the white canvas pants and the black belt isn't as startling as it should be. The uniform has been washed too many times and it's now starting to look more yellow than white.

New leather pants. New karategi. New helmet. New computers? I sigh.

I don't have enough money to pay for all those things. Not after having spent my savings on the Kawasaki. Clearly, it's time for a hacking gig, except for the minor inconvenience of my system being infected by some punk's virus.

I sling my sports bag over my shoulder and wince. I hit the heavy bag too hard while I was drilling and hurt my wrist. Sensei took a look at it, bending it this way and that. It hurt like hell. He said I should ice it and then bandage it at least. I told him it would be fine. It already feels better.

"You're a lucky sucker, Guerrero," he said.

"It has nothing to do with luck," I told him. "It's all about *toughness*."

He laughed and frowned at the same time. "It's gotta be. I don't know how you always bounce back so quickly."

I walk through the dojo, sports bag bouncing against my side. The short, forceful battle cries of the 7 A.M. students fill the air, as well as the flat sound of their uniforms snapping with each of their kicks. I wrinkle my nose at the gym-sock smell and wave Sensei goodbye.

"Nice workout, Guerrero," he says with a quick grin, before turning back to instruct the class. "Check out the tournament website, will ya?"

Steve Yakamoto, your ass is crazy if you think I'm joining that tournament.

"Sure deal, Sensei 'Moto." I wonder when he's gonna give up. He thinks I should care about winning trophies and medals. I don't.

As I walk down the sidewalk toward my bike, I relish the calm left behind after the hard workout. Kicking and punching the bag and pads make my limbs sore and heavy. The physical exertion grounds me, roots me to the pavement, makes me worry about my body. Not my mind.

Sensei 'Moto doesn't understand that this is all I need from karate. He always asks me why I don't want to learn Kata or try meditation again. He says it would improve my technique even more. But Kata, with their repetitious, choreographed moves, require me to concentrate on one thing for too long, while meditation demands that I think of nothing at all. Yeah, like I want that kind of trouble.

I strap the gym bag to the back of the bike, on top of my book bag. Running gloved fingers along the curve of my helmet, I cringe at the scratches from last night. I'd just bought the stupid thing and now it's less than perfect. Man, I'm so glad we took Clark's Yamaha and not my new Kawasaki. Lovingly, I pat the bike's leather seat. My new toy was worth every hard-earned penny, every line of glorious code.

I check my phone. No answer from Xave to my earlier text. I hope the idiot can still think for himself this morning. After putting on my helmet, I straddle the bike and start the engine. It roars to life, putting a smile on my face.

I tear down the street, slipping between two SUVs. The driver of the Blazer screams at me through his open window. I flip him the bird and punch the bike for more gas. Within minutes I'm at school.

Oh joy!

Dragging my feet, I join the throng of equally enthusiastic students. I wish I could skip ahead to trying to find out who hacked me, but I've pretty much maxed-out my absences. For now, I'll hold on to the few I have left, just in case. The way things are with Xave and the virus attack, I have a feeling I may need them soon.

Chapter 6

Classes are a blur. I make sure to sign in and, after that, I pretty much nap. I don't perk up until five minutes before the last bell goes off. Then I head to the gym, where chess club, my only mildly entertaining school activity, meets every Friday.

I enter the chatter-filled gym and scan the floor. Tables are set up in the middle, topped with chessboards and timers. The teacher, Mr. Gallager, walks around, handing out papers to the students.

Small cliques stick together. A few Asians here. Two Hispanics there. Whites elsewhere. I belong to none. I keep scanning, but I don't see the person who makes this activity challenging enough for me to stick around. I start to turn when Mr. Gallager moves a few steps, revealing the table behind him.

"So you *are* here," I mumble to myself when I spot Luke.

My shoulders square off as I take a deep breath and walk toward him, boots clicking on the polished wood.

A few heads turn my way, including Mr. Gallager. "Boots, Marci, boots. I've told you, they scratch the floor," he says, pointing at my shoes with disapproval. He really doesn't care about the floor. He's just supposed to say that.

"There are no jocks here today, Mr. Gallager. They can't stop me," I say with a smirk.

He shrugs and keeps handing out sheets.

"Unless we count you. You're a jock, right?" I say, as I sit in front of Luke, who looks up from the chessboard and lifts a perfect, blond eyebrow.

He reclines back on the chair and bends his head to one side, appraising me. "Didn't think you were gonna show up after your sad defeat last week, and the week before and the week before that one, and the week … should I go on?" His tall frame looks almost too big for the chair. His sandy blond hair slides to the left and brushes his temple.

Luke Smith, the conundrum. Jock by day. Lady's man by night. Straight-A student and chess player extraordinaire. I've known him since kindergarten and he always manages to surprise me some way or another. Like the day he asked me out on a date. Yeah, that was different and totally unsettling for some reason. He's good looking as all get-out, and many a girl would give a lung to go out with him. Me? I got sick to my stomach. Violently. Like never before in my life—not even after that time I ate the street tacos that nearly landed Xave in the hospital and barely made me feel queasy. But, judging by the way I reacted with Luke, you would have thought my own dad was making a move on me. He played it cool, though. Even when I made a beeline for the girls' bathroom, ready to puke. To this day, I still don't know what came over me and I can't stomach the idea of being romantically involved with him. In all, it's a surprise he still talks to me.

I narrow my eyes into small slits and give him a fake grin. I would promise him an ass-whipping, but if I knew I could beat him, I probably wouldn't be here today. No. I'm sure I wouldn't be. I wonder if he would? I wonder if, like me, he comes for the challenge. It's true he has won every game we've ever played, but I make him sweat for it. And I know that pretty soon I'll finally beat him.

As I lean to put my book bag down, he asks, "Had a rough night last night?"

My eyes flash back to him, suspicion rising in me. What does he know about last night? Could Luke be the IgNiTe dude? My mind examines this possibility, weighing in all the variables.

He's certainly smart enough. The way he plays chess and beats me every time serves as proof. There's even a small chance he's smarter than me. Okay, not really, but still. His IQ has to be pretty up there. I wonder if he's into computers. I know he's into football and girls and … parties, but what else? I frown. The truth is I have no idea. We've been class-mates on and off all these years, but, for all I know, every night he turns into a flesh-eating transvestite. Like me, he might have this other life that no one suspects.

"Your eyes are red," he adds when I don't answer. He smiles, crosses freckled arms over the logo of his black Under Armour t-shirt. He sounds innocent. Clearly, I'm just being paranoid.

"No, they're brown," I say.

He leans into the table. "Brown and big and pretty," he whispers, his own blue eyes sparkling. My mouth sours and my stomach flips. I swear he relishes the way his flirtatious tone twists me up into knots.

"Screw you," I say.

Luke chuckles. "Does your bed have two bad sides?"

"What?"

"It's just you're always so … ill-tempered. I figured you wake up on the wrong side of the bed every day."

"Yeah, I'm sure your bed is perfect." As soon as I say this, I cringe.

"Sweetheart, you have no idea. All I can say is you would always get up on the right side of *my* bed." His grin is wide. He looks so pleased at his own wit I could punch him. If it wasn't for the crippling nausea his comment unleashes in my gut, I would do it.

I regain my cool in time to say, "Your foul, slut-ready lair, you mean." I can't hold the acid from my words. Great, I've answered his wit with an insult. I guess he *is* smarter than me.

He puts a hand to his heart. "I refuse to pay back your insult with another. This should serve as proof that I'm a gentleman and innocent of the accusation you lay before me."

"Oh, get over yourself, Luke," I snap.

He laughs and laughs, pleasure brimming in his gold-flecked, blue eyes. My mind churns with nothing but more insults. I squeeze my eyes shut and let it go. The game started the moment I sat in front of him. The pieces haven't even moved and I've already lost.

Checkmate.

After Luke outsmarts me in chess as well as other areas, I ride my bike to Millennium Arcade to look for Xave. Cigarette smoke wafts past me as I open the door. Randy, the owner, ignores the public smoking ordinances. His patrons don't complain.

I find Xave at one of the pool tables, playing with Cameron. He breaks the balls with a quick flick of his wrist and watches as four of them find homes. The way he plays pool should grant him a PhD in physics, if only this ability translated into good grades at school.

"What's up, Xave?"

The smug smile disappears from his face when he looks up and sees me there.

"Had fun last night?" I ask, walking over to get a cue. "Hey," I say to Cameron, who, used to the pool rivalry between Xave and me, gives me a quick nod and finds someone else to play with.

"You could say that." Xave scans the balls, planning his next move.

A fast-paced song plays in the *Dance Dance* machine, trying to entice someone to bust a move. We all have two left feet here. Randy will realize that soon and get rid of the abomination. He'll replace it with a good shoot-'em-up game, if he knows what's good for business.

"So, are you gonna tell me how it went? Or is it some … national secret?" I examine the balls on the table, calculating possible shots. As I glance back at Xave, I wish assessing his mood was as easy as assessing this game.

He returns his cue to the rack, wipes chalky hands on his black jeans and walks away.

"All rightie," I say, "I guess that means you don't wanna play … or talk."

Xave looks over his shoulder. "Let's go out back."

I don't understand what's up with him lately. God, I wish he'd quit acting like an idiot. It's as if all that testosterone coursing through his veins has a negative impact on his IQ. I don't think I can put up with his moody butt much longer. But for now, curiosity gets the best of me, so I play along.

We go into the back alley through the emergency exit. Xave leans against the wall right next to the door, pops a stick of cinnamon gum in his mouth and crosses his arms. I walk out, stand in the middle of the alley, my back turned, and wait for him to say something before making eye contact. He says nothing. I exhale and bite my tongue, trying to control the urge to scream. Maybe he's still mad at me for crashing the motorcycle. If so, he needs to get over it.

My favorite alley cat shows up, purring at my feet. I squat and pet her, relieved for the distraction.

"Hey there." I scratch the backs of her ears. Her round, green eyes squint, a clear sign of pleasure. I smile, almost forgetting Xave stands brooding nearby.

"Come here," I say, picking Alley Cat up and sitting down on an upturned recycling bin. I place the cat on my lap, where she stays content.

Finally, I look up. Xave's staring at me, frowning. I stare back, and for the first time take a good look at him. His light brown hair, usually styled to look casual/shaggy, lies limp like wet noodles. There are dark half-moons under his eyes and stubble accentuates his jaw. He looks tired, but above all, angry.

"So what, you're still mad at me?" I ask.

His eyes are dark, hiding everything but his ill temper. He huffs, a quick exhale through his nose that makes his head go up and down.

You big bobblehead!

"What's the deal, Xave? The *cult* got your tongue?" I chuckle.

Practically growling, he stomps toward the Dumpster like a lumbering bear and proceeds to kick it with the tip of his boot. Alley Cat spooks and jumps two feet in the air, but not before digging sharp claws through my jeans and peppering my face with black fur.

"Ow." I jump up, rub my thighs and glower at Xave. He stands breathing heavily and slouching as if he just ran a race and is trying to recover.

"Look," I say, "if you don't want to tell me anything about your new *friends*, that's okay. But you don't have to act like a Neanderthal."

I understand guys sometimes don't like to talk about feelings and stuff. Hell, I don't like it either. But if he's still mad at me, he needs to spit it out, so we can get past this.

Do I have to be the one who brings reason into this mess? I sigh. "Okay, I apologize about Clark's bike." The words feel like spiked ninja Makibishi going down my throat. I swallow my pride and continue. "I promise to fix it and to never pull a stunt like that again."

He looks at me as if I'm speaking Japanese. I guess Clark's bike is not what's on his mind. I put my hands up in a give-me-something gesture. He gives me nothing but a darker shade of those hazel eyes. Well, I guess we have nothing to talk about. With resolve, I walk past him and head toward the street.

"You know where to find me if you wanna talk." I've taken five steps when he finally decides to speak.

"They call themselves IgNiTe," he says.

I freeze. My eyes grow wide and my hands go as cold as dead fish. I whirl around, a tornado vibrating with the force of nature.

"What?!"

Inhale.

Keep cool.

Don't choke him.

Xave stares at the ground. I wait for him to make eye contact, fingernails digging into my palms. His eyes flicker toward mine for a split second, then fall back down, this time to a broken crate. His anger is gone. He just looks embarrassed now.

With measured steps, I approach him until he's at arm's length. "You told them about me?" As I ask the question, my upper lip twitches, enough that I'm sure he can see my clenched teeth.

Xave sniffs once and flicks his nose with a quick thumb, a nonchalant gesture that he pulls off all too well.

"Did they catch you by surprise, *Warrior*?" he says.

What happened to being embarrassed? I never knew him to feel such … discontent toward me, never knew him to flip emotions so quickly.

"Why the hell would you do something like that?" I ask in complete disbelief.

I don't get it. I know lately things have been squirrely between us, but we've been friends for a long time, ever since he showed up in front of my house wearing red rubber boots and started splashing in a puddle, asking me to join him. We laughed and held hands while we jumped.

Since that day, we've done countless things together and know everything about each other. I sat with him when he got his first tattoo and the first time a girl dumped him—even if I never said a word, he still let me hold his hand. I've even memorized the exact shade of his hazel eyes for his every mood. I wish I knew why lately I've seen plenty of that dark, threatening hue when in the past, I've only seen it directed at others, especially those who mess with me.

"Why would you let them infect my rig like that? All my hard work's probably messed up for good. Why?" I really want to understand.

"Oh, it was a harmless message, Marci. They said it wouldn't hurt anything." Uncertainty crosses his eyes for a second, then he asks, "Everything still works, right?" But it's not a caring question. It's a challenge. He doesn't want to believe they would play him.

I could tell him that I don't know, that I didn't have a chance to check, but I choose to let doubt settle on him. I hope it's heavy. His eyes waver. Good.

"Well Xave, I'd say we're even now. So maybe now you can stop being so mad at me."

If anything, my comment only makes him angrier. Ha! And they say women don't make any sense.

"What do they want with me, anyway? I already told them. I. Do. Not. Join," I say.

At the question, he looks as puzzled as I feel. Then it hits me: he doesn't know what's going on any more than I do. They didn't tell him jack. I chuckle at the irony. The newest member of IgNiTe knows nothing. It's probably part of their cult philosophy.

"It beats me," Xave admits. And there's bitterness in his tone and something else, too. Jealousy?

Oh, man. That's it! He's jealous. I should have seen it before. For months, all he's talked about is discovering what his brother's up to. Ever since they were little, Xave has looked up to Clark, emulating him in every respect. And now that he's finally within his brother's circle, he hates to see the attention shift to me.

The question remains. Why are they interested in me?

I know what you are.

IgNiTe's message flashes in front of my eyes. I try to pretend the words mean nothing, that it was only a stupid prank, meant to get my attention. I hate to admit it worked.

"What do these people do, Xave? What did they tell you? Why are they interested in recruiting … high school kids?"

"If you're so interested in the details, I guess you'll have to join, won't ya?" he says, then walks away rubbing his chin, making a raspy sound.

"Cut the bull-crap. It's obvious they didn't tell you anything. Don't act as if you're with the *in crowd*, now. Tell James and IgNiTe or whoever that I'm not interested."

He lays a hand on the door knob, ready to get back inside. "Whatever you say, Marci." He speaks over his shoulder.

"Oh, and don't worry, I'll stay out of your way, so you can play Bad Boys with your brother without me cramping your style."

Something like regret takes shape in Xave's eyes. He looks as if he wants to say something. His lips part, but as I see he's at the verge of letting the words out, I spin on my heels and walk away.

I'm too mad to even look at him anymore. If I stay, there'll be no hope of ever keeping this friendship or controlling the shadows. It's the latter that scares me the most.

Chapter 7

When I get home, the house is quiet. Mom's not back from work yet. I go straight to my room, fall on my knees under the desk and pull out one of the CPUs. I unplug all the cables and carry the metal box to the opposite end of the room, where there's another electric plug. I go back and forth, snatching a monitor, mouse, keyboard, and cables out of my stockpile.

I boot the machine by itself, isolated from the other computers to avoid cross-contamination. When it comes up with no problems, I still don't trust it. With quick keystrokes and mouse clicks, I fly from one scanning routine to another. After one hour of scouring, using programs written by me and others, I come up empty. There is no trace of any malicious code.

Exhausted, I sit cross-legged on the floor in the deep silence, my back curved, my chin touching my chest. I feel beaten and vulnerable. My eyes lock on an old Cheerio that lies on the floor. For a hair's breadth, my mind goes blank.

Sensing the wasteland of my thoughtless mind, shadows lurk, stalk—like lions crouched amid tall, golden grass. I've become a sitting duck. As a trained response, adrenaline explodes inside me and gets my heart hammering. I smell the threat, sense the hunger, and my own fear threatening to paralyze me.

Stand up.

Breathe.

Bugs Bunny.

Get to work.

I become a moving target—my instincts razor sharp, the product of a lifetime fending off countless assaults. In a frenzy, I check the rest of the computers in the same fashion. When I finish, my frustration is even greater than before. I still have no idea how IgNiTe managed to bombard me with those messages.

I know what you are. I know what you are.

The words resonate with me and I get hung up on a particular one. "What." Not "who you are" but "what you are."

What did they mean? Is it possible that I'm not …? No! I shake my head, unwilling to take any guesses, desperate to find out what exactly IgNiTe is talking about. Could they be aware of the secret I've so carefully guarded all these years? Or is this just some big coincidence? Because it seems unthinkable that they would have an answer to the one question that has obscured my entire life.

But what if they do? Am I foolish enough to hope they can expel the shadows living inside my brain? What if there's a cure? There's nothing I want more than to be free of them, than to live without fear.

My head hangs low again, aware that these conjectures are all part of my madness. Because what else could I be but barking mad? The puzzle never ends. How much of my life is real? How much is a product of insanity? Because the truth is: demons don't exist and possession and exorcism only happen in the movies.

Psychosis on the other hand … they have medication for that.

Not caring anymore whether my system blows up or gets hijacked again, I connect everything the way it's supposed to be and get back online. I don't dare go on the H-Loop today. I'm not in the mood, anyhow, so I decide to check my email instead. I open the inbox. A solitary message awaits.

My heart freezes.

From: IgNiTe
Subject: You are NOT the only one

The mouse pointer hovers over the message. There are no attachments that could contain dangerous files, so I open it. In the body of the message, one simple sentence stares at me in bold and italic letters.

Watch the State of the Union Address.
9:21, 25:58, 43:07 . . .

What the … ?

This game isn't funny. If Xave is behind this new messed-up prank, I'll kick him so hard he won't live to spread his seed. My fingers pound the search words into the web browser. When I hit enter, the first listing is a video of the most recent State of the Union Address by President J.P. Helms.

I click on it. It's one hour and fifteen minutes long.

You've got to be kidding me.

I haven't slept in thirty-five hours. If I play along with this ridiculous game, I'll be drooling over my keyboard in two minutes flat. Forget it. If I'm gonna sleep, I'll do it in the comfort of my bed. I'll get lost in my dreams, where the shadows can't reach me.

The fact that I'm safe when the sandman whisks me away is proof that I am, indeed, off my rocker, because if there was something living in my brain, wouldn't nap time be the perfect time for it to attack me? But what do I know? Maybe dreams are too fluid for the shadows to get a hold of them. Besides, I've trained myself to fall asleep in five seconds flat with music playing in the background to help my mind maintain a base level of activity.

With one longing, backward glance at my fluffy pillow, I abandon the idea. As much as I'd like to forget about IgNiTe and Xave and their games, they've trapped me in their web. I'm a helpless fly.

You are NOT the only one.

I need to know what this is about. And if, maybe, there are others who feel invaded, like a house occupied by a squatter.

I click play.

The president stands in the foreground. The Speaker of the House and vice-president sit behind him, looking as bored as I feel. President Helms talks about the economy, his stately face powdered to perfection, his salt-and-pepper hair as pristine as always.

Yawn.

Blink.

"Nope, don't care about joining your workforce, Mr. Helms." My words slur. "Unless you're hiring hackers who get hacked."

I prop my chin on my hands. The president's words stop making sense. They don't really register.

"Our country ... deficit ... committee ..."

My eyelids close for a few seconds. Then they open.

"Congress ..."

Eyes close again for long, long, long seconds.

Semi-blink.

"Approve ..."

Dreams.

Something shatters. I jump to my feet, look around. I've fallen asleep in front of the computer. The screensaver flashes pictures of road bikes. Slobber shines on the desk. Gross. I'm looking around for something to clean it when I remember the sound that woke me.

Maybe Mom's home. I step out of my bedroom and shuffle through the hall. I peek in her room. She's not there. Rubbing my eyes, I head for the living room. Mom likes to watch the evening news after a quick dinner.

I find her sitting at the edge of the sofa, broken glass at her feet and a large wine splotch on the floor. Her eyes are locked on the TV. She's shaking all over. I follow her gaze. The headline at the bottom of the screen reads: "*Doctor found murdered in his home.*" The frame is frozen. I look back at Mom. She holds the remote in her hand. Why did she pause it? My eyes bounce back to the TV. Above the headline, the picture of a familiar-looking man stares at me.

Puzzled, I step into the living room, trying to figure out where I've seen him. A vague recollection flashes through my memory.

"Oh, my God! I think that's Luke's dad," I say.

I don't recall Mom ever meeting him, but maybe she did. She attended a few PTO meetings during my early school years. Even if she knew him, though, why does she look so stricken?

"Mom?"

Her head turns my way, but she continues to stare at the screen. Then she blinks very slowly, and when her eyes open, she's looking at me, lips trembling. A single tear spills and runs down her cheek.

"It's him." Her voice is a shaky murmur, barely audible.

"Who?" What is she talking about?

"That's the man that took Max," she says. Tears fall freely now, making her cheeks shine.

"Wait." I look back at the TV. The word "Doctor" seems to blink at me. My eyes drift to the small print under the main headline: "*Dr. Peter Smith, Seattle top OB/GYN and fertility doctor, brutally murdered.*" Smith ... Luke's last name.

Mom leaves the couch and walks in my direction. "It's him. It's Ernest Dunn."

I stare at the TV, a slight tremor starting in my knees. "No, Mom." I shake my head. "It says Dr. Peter Smith. I think you're confused."

She's standing right in front of me, her blue eyes huge and fierce. "I would recognize his face in the pits of hell. It *is* him!" she says, the words hissing through her clenched teeth.

My heart pounds like an angry fist against a locked door. "Mom, it's been sixteen years. Maybe you—"

"NO!" she yells—startling me—then points a finger at the TV, even as her eyes drill into mine like I'm the enemy, like I'm the one standing in the way of something monumental. "That man is Dr. Dunn. That man took Max from me."

She can't be right. She can't! There's nothing distinctive about this man's face. Nothing. He looks like any over-weight, balding man out there: round and soft and doughy.

He's forgettable … so *unlike* Luke. I bite my tongue and taste deceit.

Mom's hands drift upward and grip my shoulders. "Marcela, who's Luke?" Her bottom lip trembles and her voice breaks at the name, heavy with something that sounds very much like hope, like a creature I'd thought extinct in her world.

"H-he's nobody."

"Marcela!" Mom's nails dig into my shoulders as she begins to shake me. "Who. Is. Luke?" Her tone is desperate, maniacal.

He's nobody.

He's nobody.

He's nobody.

"What does he look like?" she demands.

A current of frigid air travels from Mom's stiff fingers down my back. My spine freezes, shatters into a million pieces, and I feel I could crumble.

Some part of me has always known this. Luke's blond hair, gold-specked blue eyes, angular nose … so much like Mom. He looks just like her and I've always pushed the knowledge away. It's the reason his flirtatious advances have always bothered me, the reason my stomach churned when he asked me out.

Luke is Max.

Luke is my brother!

I stagger backward, head spinning.

"Who's Luke?" Mom asks again, her nails like claws. I knock her arms away in one swift motion and take another step back.

"It's Max. It has to be Max," she says. Life floods her gaze. Suddenly, her eyes don't look empty and distant the way they have all these years, the way they greet me every time I walk in the room. They have fire in them now.

The burst of light, this flash of immeasurable hope, hurts me deep inside. I've been here all along. Was I not worth a little bit of this radiance?

My chest feels like a too-large cage for my shriveling heart. *Pain.*

"Marcela, it's Max, isn't it?"

Yes, your son.

My ears ring and I take another step back.

My brother.

"Where are you going? Wait!" Mom's loud command makes me realize I'm running, headed for the door. I burst outside into an afternoon that has started to blend with the night colors.

Gray. Dark. Blue.

The wind blows in my face. The motorbike hums as I speed away from home. How did I get here?

Stop. Get off the bike.

I make it as far as the wooded area where Xave and I crashed last night. Almost out of control, I drive off the shoulder, between two bushes and into a small clearing. The bike wobbles. I kill the engine and jump off, letting it drop to the ground. Tottering forward for a few steps, my legs give out and I fall to my knees.

My chest pumps furiously. Shadows lurk and it takes all my strength not to succumb to their attack. My brother is alive. I stare at my hands. They're shaking with the effort of keeping this upheaval from triggering another attack.

Luke is my brother and the knowledge threatens to unravel me, like a wool sweater without the final stitch.

He's been here all along, slipping in and out of our notice, grazing the fringe of our somber existence but never quite touching it. Why? It makes no sense. I always imagined him dead or miles and miles away. Instead that man, that sadist, was raising him right under our noses, taunting us. The sick bastard! To get away with such a monstrous crime. How?!

I slam my fists against the ground, trying to channel the tsunami of emotions that is washing over me. I feel cheated, fooled … replaced. Just like that.

Anger against Mom takes center stage in my private storm. I can only imagine what's going through her mind now, how new, exhilarated thoughts are quickly erasing any trace of me. Clenching my jaw, I let my anger bulldoze the pain that threatens to grip me by the throat. My teeth audibly grind and I feel as if my skull will split in two.

Darkness descends over me, obscuring the world.

Get up! Do something!

I spring to my feet, my eyes darting in all directions.

Rocks. Ants. Wild flowers.

My thoughts shift, hop, morph. They become everything and anything that makes me forget why I'm trying to hide. I take a deep breath. The shadows retreat, like fog being sucked into a giant vacuum cleaner. My jaw relaxes and control slowly returns.

I straddle my bike and ride out of the patch of wood. I drive slowly, reading the street signs and spelling their names. All thoughts of Mom and Luke fade into the background. I'm good at ignoring monsters that I'd rather slip under the rug. As their images grow fainter, Mom seems to become nothing but a vague specter. She feels more absent than ever. Lost.

My heart seizes. I was never meant to have a family anyway.

Chapter 8

After driving aimlessly, spelling street signs until I feel I might have a stroke, I stop the bike and look around. Dr. Smith's face flashes in front of my eyes, fleshy lips mumbling something. His resemblance to the man I'd imagined after so many of Mom's stories is uncanny. My stomach churns as the emotions I've been trying to hold back threaten to rise.

I need to focus my attention on something else. Anything else.

The State of the Union Address!

Straddling my bike, one foot on the blacktop, I take my phone out and browse until I find President Helms's video. As I start watching, groaning at the thought of sitting through a full hour of babbling, I remember the numbers at the bottom of the message. My brain was too foggy with sleep to understand before, but they must indicate minutes and seconds. Impatient, I fast-forward to minute nine and let it play.

Helms is talking about the economy. His words offer zero explanation as to why I'm supposed to be watching this. The president pauses, takes a big breath and widens his eyes, then transitions to a new topic. I skip to minute twenty-five and listen closely. Helms is now addressing foreign policy issues. He might as well be speaking Chinese. I've never cared for politics. Once more he switches topics, pausing, breathing deeply. His eyes do a weird little roll, as if he's tracing a circle with his gaze. It strikes me as odd, but I can't put a finger on why.

On minute forty-three, it's the same thing. Another boring subject, the delay from one idea to the other, the shift of his eyes, the deep breaths.

Then it hits me, like light bursting in front of my eyes. I know why he's not blinking, why he takes deep breaths and looks as if the load on his shoulders goes beyond the responsibility of being the president of the United States of America. I know the weight of this burden. I carry it with me every day.

President Helms also fights the shadows.

Pushing, shoving, ramming any thoughts of Luke to the back of my mind, hoping the shadows eat them for good, I rush into Millennium Arcade. I need to find Xave so he can take me to this James guy.

"Cameron, have you seen Xave?" The noise and lights in the arcade disorient me further. I rode like a lunatic to get here, my mind a fluid continuum of disjointed ideas.

He ignores me as he slides the cue over his thumb. After making the shot, he pushes his layered bangs to the side. "Nope, he hasn't been here today."

I turn on my heels and head out.

"You're welcome," Cameron shouts behind me. I ignore him.

Dialing Xave's cell phone, I step outside, where the sky is now a deep shade of navy blue with heavy clouds starting to roll in. After several rings, the call goes to voicemail. Obviously, he's ignoring me. At home, Selina, Xave's twelve-year-old sister, says he just went out.

Where is he when I need him? I have to tell him about Luke. He's the only one who can understand how I feel right now.

Damn, don't think about Luke! James, concentrate on James. Deep breath.

Logic returns. Maybe Xave is with James and that's why he's not answering his phone. One other place comes to mind where I can look for him. I turn the key in the ignition, put on my helmet and drive toward downtown. I'm not sure going back to that alley is a good idea. My head is too jumbled right now to know which way is up, but I drive there—at war with the shadows. After a million thoughts about trees, siblings, candy bars, jealousy, hamsters, loss … I arrive.

The dark alley lies before me. Shadows loom inside as a light drizzle begins to fall. I shiver. The solitary street lamp barely illuminates the entrance, the huge mouth that may grow teeth to chew me up once I step in. I shake my head, take a deep breath and walk tentatively into the darkness. My eyes readjust, the shadows against the walls become less threatening as I identify the objects that cast them. I pass a Dumpster and a few barrels. A large stack of compacted cardboard boxes lie to my right. Maybe there's a recycling center in the building.

The thought of a legitimate business operating in this place is reassuring, even if gangsters sometimes use garbage-related schemes to hide their illegal operations. Or is that only in the movies?

The hum of an air conditioner and the trickle of water echo with an eerie quality that sends my skin crawling. Stubbornly, I continue forward, throwing glances over my shoulder every few steps, trying to figure out if IgNiTe's lair lies in one of the two buildings that make up this dead-end alley.

The wall on the left is solid, while the one on the right has several windows accessible through a fire escape. They're pitch-black, so climbing the staircase to peek inside would be no use. I doubt IgNiTe's holding a meeting in the dark, although weirder things have happened. If they're here, my guess they'll be somewhere deep inside the bowels of one of the buildings.

At the end of the alley, I spot a door. I approach and twist the knob. When it turns and the door swings open, a cold wave slides down my spine, raising goose bumps on my skin. A dank smell wafts from inside. I face nothing but blackness. I let my eyes adjust, hoping I can make something out. As I stand there, the distinct feeling that someone is watching me from the depths of the passage takes over me. I shudder. I have nothing to light my way, but even if I did, there's no way I'm going in there. I don't need to find Xave that badly. This can wait.

I shut the door and head back slowly, keeping away from the cardboard boxes in case someone's hiding behind them. My heart rate slows when I see my bike, waiting patiently on the street. I pick up my pace, then halt when I notice movement out of the corner of my eye. I freeze. A man's standing past the Dumpster, back resting on the wall. He digs in his pockets and pulls out something that glints in the dark.

He doesn't see me. Slowly, I take a step back.

"Where do you think you're going?" he asks.

My heart slams against my chest and adrenaline ripples through my body. Run or fight?

A flame comes to life in front of the man's face, illuminating his features. A pair of gray eyes shine for a quick second. James!

James comes away from the wall. The lamppost casts a dim light on him. He lights a cigar and speaks with it hanging from his mouth. "Looking for someone, Marci?" He takes a deep drag and turns his head my way. His movements are controlled. He looks me dead in the eye, and I've no idea how he can see me wrapped in these shadows.

To hide my fear, I walk forward, staying as close to the opposite building as possible. A low buzz starts in the back of my head.

"Not very smart going into dark alleys like this, don't you think? You might get yourself killed one day." His voice is a deep rumble, like stones washing down a landslide. He wears a lopsided smile. If his comment is meant to be a joke, it isn't funny. There's enough edge to his tone that it feels more like a threat. I sidestep, keeping far from him, inching my way out while ignoring the insistent hum inside my cranium.

Swathed in shadows, I feel vulnerable. I want to move into the light and erase the possibility of being forced into the back of the alleyway, never to be seen again.

When I'm parallel with James, I look him up and down. He's wearing jeans, square-toe boots, a black t-shirt and leather jacket. Something about him looks too clean-cut for his own clothes, like he doesn't belong in them. I figure my chances of outrunning him are pretty good. I could get to my bike faster than he could get to his, which I now notice is parked on the corner. He looks to be in his mid-forties, probably too arthritic to catch up with me. At least that's what I tell myself, because the vivacity in his gray gaze and the latent power in his lean, muscular build don't give me much comfort.

Before I run, though, there's something I have to know. "How'd you do it? How'd you break into my computer?"

James draws on his cigar, holding it between thumb and fore-finger. Then, with a careless flick, he throws it on the ground, not even halfway spent. He runs a hand over his bald head.

"Those things will kill you," he says. "They're nasty, but whatever helps keep the fog away, right? I'm sure you have your own tricks." He stretches his lips in a smile that doesn't travel to the rest of his face.

The fog? Tricks? Maybe his strategy is to overwhelm me with snippets of information that'll make my questions multiply like horny rabbits.

"So, you got my attention," I say. "I'm here, what the hell do you want?"

James runs a lazy hand over his jaw and sighs, as if disappointed. He watches me through a squint, analyzing me, seeming to ponder a million question of his own. I hold my breath, waiting for the result of his appraisal, mad at myself for caring whether I pass or not.

My patience dwindles. "Why did you want me to watch President Helms?"

"You know why."

James's certainty is disconcerting. Why is he so sure? What does he know?

"You're wondering how come I know what you are," he says.

Great, he's a mind reader. He's got to be, because how the hell could he know? James stretches his neck, tilting his head from side to side, just like President Helms, just like me.

He takes a deep breath. "I know because ... I'm like you. That buzzing in the back of your head, I feel it, too."

Surprised, I take a hand to the base of my skull, where a steady hum hasn't let up since I got too close for comfort.

He rubs his own head. "Annoying, isn't it? But that's how I know. I felt it last night as you drove away from here." He points a finger toward the spot where I waited for Xave atop the idling motorcycle. "You were struggling with it, under attack. Weren't you?"

I nod once, speechless. Never in my wildest hypotheses did I imagine there were others who knew about the shadows.

"Ever been shadowed?" he asks.

"Huh?" It's all I can manage.

He waits, eyes locked on mine. Shadowed?

"I don't know what you're talking about. I—"

"You sure?" he presses. "I know you've seen the world through eyes that should have been yours. But have you ever lost total control? Have you been blind, mute, dumb? Have you been shadowed? Trapped within yourself?"

My horrific discovery of just yesterday comes back to me, pouring its paralyzing shock into my limbs. My throat goes dry, my mouth bitter. The numb, life-without-parole certainty returns with a vengeance.

James knows about the shadows. Truly.

"I'll take that as a yes," he says, tilting his bushy eyebrows.

My helpless expression has given him the answer he wants to hear.

"Very few ever come back." His voice is low and menacing. I feel as if I've dodged an eternity in hell. "Good, that means I can trust you. You're strong." James takes two steps toward me and looks me straight in the eye. "We have the answers you've been looking for. If you're interested, follow me."

James doesn't wait for me to agree. He straddles his Harley and rides off. It takes me a moment to come out of my trance. When I do, I hop on my bike and gun it. The voice of reason screams in my head. No sensible girl would follow a stranger like this. But what choice do I have? All I've ever wanted is to know what's wrong with me.

I would risk *everything* to find out.

Chapter 9

A bar?!

He has brought me to a bar? Does he realize I'm only sixteen? I follow James, looking all around me, expecting someone to jump in front of the door demanding an ID. No one does. In truth, the whole area looks like a ghost town. There's a gas station across the street. Its sign flickers. The gas prices flash with askew numbers. The large metal building on its right looks as if it sprouted out of the weeds that surround it.

The bar itself is the nicest-looking building on the street, and that's not saying much. A blue neon sign of a wolf howling at the moon shines on top of the door, illuminating the cracked sidewalk. James pulls the door open.

"Welcome to Howls," he says, showing me in with an extended hand.

I hesitate, then step inside. The back of my skull—which hasn't stopped humming since James appeared in the alley—vibrates a little harder. I wince and throw my head back a few degrees.

James watches me intently. I feel like he notices everything—reading me as if I was a simple "hello world" program—and filing everything he learns about me inside his bald, shiny head. I can't blame him. I'm doing the same. I'm a lost sock that's just found its match. He rolls his neck to indicate he knows my head feels like it's being assaulted by a million frantic hummingbirds.

"C'mon, Clark and Xave are here, if it makes you feel any better."

I'd already noticed Clark's bike outside. And no, it doesn't make me feel any better. Clark's a punk, and with the way Xave's been acting lately … well … let's say I'd rather drink antifreeze than endure all that drama.

The smell of cigarette smoke mixed with sweat and stale beer makes me wrinkle my nose. A few men sit at the bar, staring at their drinks or at empty space. They ignore us as we walk in. The patrons look like they belong on the bikes parked outside. Faded jeans, leather jackets, heavy boots, scraggly beards. I look back at James and get the impression that he belongs in this place about as much as I do.

He stops at the bar. "Whiskey, on the rocks," he tells the bartender.

The guy doesn't even give me a second glance. After James gets his drink, he heads to the back of the building. We walk through a narrow door and go down a flight of stairs. Posters of women in skimpy bathing suits line the walls.

Before crossing a doorway with a bead curtain, James stops. "Not all in there are like us. I trust you won't say anything about our earlier conversation," he orders, then walks through the curtain.

I bristle. I don't like orders. In fact, I'm tempted not to obey just on principle. But who am I kidding? I'm not about to start telling anyone that shadowy specters live inside my head. I crack my neck and cross the threshold. Behind the curtain, I find myself in a dimly lit room and the center of attention to five distrustful pairs of eyes.

"Crew, this is Marci," James says, then takes a sip of whiskey and makes a face as if the drink isn't good enough.

No one says anything. They just stare. Xave sits on a shaggy sofa to my right, his expression unreadable. My body tightens in response to what feels like open hostility.

A pale woman with jet-black, freaky hair stands up. "Another one?" she asks in an angry voice. "What are we now … babysitters?" She looks me up and down, as if I'm here to force her to give up hair-styling gel. Because really, how else could she have accomplished that Medusa-looking mess on her head? I narrow my eyes and return her gaze, unwavering. I swear she looks like she jumped out of a *Resident Evil* video game, all tight black leather pants and knee-high boots with more straps than an electric chair. A see-through black top rests over a red camisole that stops midriff. She even wears studded arm warmers and it's not even Halloween.

James introduces her. "This is Blare. Spelled B-L-A-R-E, mind you."

She gives James a nasty look. He ignores her.

"Relax, Blare. Marci has skills," James offers.

"You mean unlike this dimwit, here?" She gives Xave a patronizing look.

Somehow Xave manages to limit his anger to a glare and a jaw twitch. No Dumpsters to kick in here, huh? Not in front of his big brother, anyway. He's always had anger management issues that might stem from being the middle child. I keep hoping he will grow out of them, but maybe I should give up.

"What kind of skills?" a guy as pale as Blare and with hair just as black asks.

He's wearing dark slacks and a blue button-up shirt. His tone is forced as if he really doesn't want to know. A tie hangs around his neck, the knot loose. James seems out of place, but this guy clearly is. He'd do better behind a cash register at the local bank. He makes my head hum. We exchange knowing glances and both nod imperceptibly, the way two lions might nod at each other in a den full of tigers. I take a quick look around. He's the only other one making my head feel like a bee hive.

I turn my attention back to James, wondering what skills he's talking about. He opens his mouth to answer, but Blare interrupts him.

"Do they include wiping her own butt and feeding herself?" She barks out a laugh.

I don't know what her deal is. Maybe she feels threatened by other girls. Either way, I'm not putting up with it. "Hey Medusa, *herself* is standing right here."

If you don't stand up to bullies from the start, you're doomed to become somebody's punching bag. I learned that in the first grade when Will Hooper thought it was funny my dad had died and figured pushing me around was a nice way to remind me I was fatherless. Sick little bastard. I brought his bullying days to a halt before he could do any real damage to someone vulnerable.

"What did you call me?" Blare says, her pale face growing noticeably red.

"Ooooh, catfight," Clark says, pushing himself to the edge of his chair and rubbing his hands together.

"You heard me," I tell her in a steady tone.

James sits back, the twinge of a smile resting on his lips, as if he knows something no one else does. I get the feeling that's often the case for him.

Blare marches toward me. When she's two steps away, her hand comes up, ready to shove me. Lightning quick, I step aside, grab her wrist, and pull it behind her back, then wrap my free arm around her neck. She yelps in surprise. I hold her in a lock for a fast beat, then push her away from me.

Xave's eyes twinkle with something like pleasure. When he sees I've noticed his reaction, he looks away. It appears Medusa's been busting his chops, too. But he needs to do his own shoving if he expects to gain her respect. Besides, I would hardly do any shoving for his benefit, not after he told this bunch of misfits where to find me on the net.

He's supposed to be my friend. Some friend.

"Look, I didn't come here to fight," I say.

Blare is fuming, rubbing her wrist and neck and trying to hide her embarrassment.

"I don't even know why I'm here." I turn and step backward to be able to see everyone at the same time. "So unless you've got something to say, I think I'll leave."

"We have something to say, all right." A muscular man sitting next to Bank Teller guy stands up and extends a hand my way. He's of average height, but his torso looks like it belongs on a much taller man. He cracks a wide grin, as friendly as I've ever seen. Our handshake is a firm, brisk squeeze. "I'm Walter, but everyone calls me Oso."

The simple sound of his nickname fills me with a strange sadness. From somewhere in the depths of my brain I conjure the meaning of the word "oso." Amazing how ten years of disuse haven't erased the knowledge that Dad so zealously tried to ingrain in me. Oso is Spanish for bear and, given this man's bulk and hairy forearms, it's easy to understand why they call him that.

"You'll have to excuse Blare," Oso continues. "She can be a bit … feisty sometimes."

Clark rolls his eyes. "To say the least."

"That one is Clark," Oso says, "and that's his little brother Xave."

I try not to laugh. Xave hates being referred to as Clark's little brother.

"We're neighbors, you oaf," Clark says.

Oso frowns, then hits his forehead with the heel of his hand. "Oh, she's *that* Marci. I get it now. Anyhow …" Oso turns and points at Bank Teller guy. "This white-collar dude over here is Aydan." The comment makes Aydan self-conscious, and he loosens his tie further and gives me an indifferent nod. This time I notice his casually mussed hair and the purple half-moons under his dark eyes. He looks like he needs some serious sleep, and probably a transfusion or some sun. He's way too pale.

James points at the chair next to him. "Sit, Marci."

I pull the chair away and sit. My muscles are taut, ready to spring. They may be trying to make me feel comfortable, but psycho Medusa's still staring a hole into my forehead, even as she reclines against the wall, looking nonchalant. Maybe she's trying to turn me to stone.

"Apparently you have more skills than I gave you credit for," James says, eyes darting a quick, mocking glance toward Blare. She crosses her arms and shifts her weight from one foot to another.

"She's been doing karate since she was four," Xave says, sounding proud and amused at the same time. I give Xave a don't-do-me-any-favors look. He rolls his eyes and shifts position in his seat.

"Has she?" James asks.

"My dad wanted me to know how to defend myself." I don't know why I feel the need to explain. So this is how it feels being the center of attention? No wonder I've always avoided it.

James appraises me with a knowing expression. "I'm sure it's taught you much more than that."

I nod and more passes between us than those in the room can understand. The focus karate gives me has been essential in keeping the shadows at bay.

Slapping his palms on his jeans, James shifts his attention to Aydan. "Marci wants to know how you hacked into her computer."

I blink, surprised. Bank Teller was the one who hacked me?!

Aydan shrugs. "You mean she's Warrior? I'll send you the code," he says. "It'll speak for itself."

I wait to hear more, but it seems he's a man of few words.

James fills in the blanks. "Aydan is a programmer. He works for *Sylica Rush*." James says the name as if it explains everything. And well … it does. Getting into Sylica Rush is almost as exclusive as becoming an astronaut for NASA. I'm mildly impressed. Okay, I'm very impressed. Now I don't feel so bad about being hacked.

"He was impressed by how tight your system was. And if he's impressed, then we should all be," James says, giving Blare a pointed look.

Aydan and I exchange a glance. We see eye to eye, even if we're not saying much. He and I share a unique wavelength. Computer bits and bytes could be our language. His code will tell me much more about him than his words could. He nods. I nod back.

"So undoubtedly," James continues, "he agrees our team could use someone with your skills. You see, he has to work for a living and doesn't have as much time to take care of the technical side of our operation. He could use a hand."

Wait a minute, what is this? I look at James and shake my head, trying to show him this is not why I came here for. I followed him thinking he'd have answers to my questions, but it seems he's just trying to drag me into whatever activities they're up to—which no doubt are criminal as all get-out.

"A hand doing what?" I demand.

"All in due time, Marci."

My expression tightens. "Listen, I'm flattered that you're *impressed*, but I don't get the feeling I'm going to like what you guys are up to."

Medusa chuckles, "derisive" written all over her black painted lips. "That's an understatement."

I stand, making the chair screech across the floor.

"Settle down, Marci. This is not the sort of thing you're imagining." James points at the chair with an extended hand.

"Just tell me." I will count till ten. If I don't get a straight answer, I'm out of here. I'm not going to get involved in anything that will land me in jail.

One.

"Good luck with that," Xave huffs, sarcasm wrapped around all four words. They haven't told him anything either. Cult tactics vary, and I wonder if the lure of something enigmatic and dangerous is what they use to entrap thrill-seeking idiots like Xave and me.

Four.

Blare exhales with frustration. "This isn't child's play. And the sooner you two get that into your heads, the better. Besides, it's not the sort of thing that can be told. You have to see it to be able to believe messed-up shit like this."

"Oh c'mon, Blare," Oso says. "You're gonna spook them."

Seven.

"Good! 'Cause this *is* spooky crap." Blare's eyes swivel my way. A pierced eyebrow goes up and her lips tighten for a second before she says, "Crap that'll make you run crying to Mama. Make sure you understand that before you go *joining*."

Ten.

I'm outta here. The only scary thing here is Medusa's hair-do.

"Ooh, I'm shaking in my boots." I snigger. "I don't know about you, Xave, but I need more than just empty talk and *secret meetings*," I draw quotes in the air, "to buy into bogus crap."

That said, I head for the door and invite Xave to follow me with a quick nod toward the door. I'm still mad at him, but I can't leave him at the mercy of this bunch. I can't believe Clark has dragged his little brother into this.

Oso lets out a hearty chuckle. "The girl has spunk. I'll give her that."

Xave's attention shifts from side to side, apparently considering the option of leaving with me. If he's still the smart boy I know, and testosterone and jealousy haven't skewered his brain, he'll come with me. I doubt Clark even knows what's really going on here. "Marci." James stands and takes a deep, deliberate breath, a clear reminder of our earlier conversation in the alley. "Promise me you'll think about it."

He knows he has answers I'd kill to have and he's using them as bargaining chips. The question is: are the shadows somehow linked to what they're doing here? Or are they just bait to suck me into their cult? I'm afraid accepting a deal with James might be too high a price to pay for learning what I need to know. Anger seethes behind my breastbone. This isn't fair. I was so stupid to think I could get something for nothing.

I hesitate and look at Xave. His brow furrows, as his eyes dance from James to me and back again. Everyone watches with interest, even aloof Aydan, who I'm sure understands why James's offer is so tempting to me.

Decisively, I exit the room without an answer or backward glance. I didn't say no. That should let James know I'll at least consider it. No harm in that, I suppose.

Outside, I crank the bike and slide on my helmet.

"Marci, wait!"

Xave runs up to me. I lift the visor to look at him, but he avoids eye contact and looks toward the road instead.

"Um." He bites his lower lip, blinks in slow motion as if his long lashes weigh a ton. Finally, he meets my gaze. His Adam's apple goes up and down. "I …" His pause stretches for a full minute.

I sigh and roll my eyes at his fantastic eloquence. "Want a ride home?"

"Y-yeah, that'd be great."

"Hop on."

Xave gets behind me, wraps large hands around my hips then leans forward until I can feel the length of his torso against my back. My throat locks, keeping my breath captive. My eyes close and I find myself leaning back, pressing closer to him. My body's reaction shocks me.

"I'm sorry," he whispers in my ear, then he pulls away slowly. Cold air slides up my back, making the distance between us feel as wrong as a sixteen-year-old in a bikers' bar. His warm breath quickly turns frigid at my earlobe. I shiver and snap the visor shut. My fingers feel numb. It's too cold to be out tonight.

Chapter 10

Meeting James and the rest of his crew was nothing but a poor distraction. As soon as we drove away from the bar, the brunt of my pent-up emotions hit me like a hook punch. I got us home, fighting the urge to drive in the opposite direction and never look back.

Now, we sit on Xave's front steps. I don't want to go home and face whatever is waiting there. A suddenly joyful mother? A brand-spanking-new brother? A second fiddle? I hate feeling this way, but I can't help it. I was there for her all along, why wasn't I ever as important as the absent son she never really knew?

Crickets chirp and the moon hangs huge and watchful, unobstructed by clouds, even when light drizzle falls from a gray sky. I stare at a water stream making its way toward a drain at the far end of the street.

"What do you think about those fools?" Xave asks.

"Mmm?" My eyes are transfixed by the glittering moonlight as it skims the surface of the little stream.

"What's wrong? You want me to apologize again?" he says a bit grudgingly. "I know I was an ass, and I—"

I tear my eyes from the drainage and the water traveling to its doom. "Luke's dad was murdered." Xave is a grade ahead of us, but everyone in school knows blond, popular, perfect Luke.

"What?!"

I let it sink in.

"You mean Luke Smith?"

I nod.

"Really? Wow, that sucks. Why? What happened?"

I bite on my thumbnail and taste bitterness.

"I gotta go." I stand and take a few steps.

"Why? It's still early. We could … hang out."

I look over my shoulder. "I should go see Mom."

"C'mon. She's probably asleep already."

"Not tonight."

Xave stands and puts a hand on my shoulder. I look at his fingers.

Tears. Are prisoners. In my eyes.

Breathe and go home.

He pulls gently, makes me face him. He knows me so well, reads my face and finds there's something I'm trying to drown. There's no one else in the world who can do that.

"Luke's my brother," I blurt out.

Xave's hand falls off my shoulder. A million expressions decorate his face, surprise, wonder, understanding, shock.

"Are you sure?"

"Yes." A whisper full of regret, anger, uncertainty. "All this time he was right there, and I … I think I knew, somehow."

Xave shakes his head. "There's no way you could've …" His words run out, like sand through a tightening fist. There's nothing to say. Nothing to ever make up for the lost time.

I feel numb and slow like the passing of millennia. I blink and when I open my eyes, I'm in Xave's embrace. His arms

74

passed me by, drew me in, and I let it happen. Now his chest warms my cheek.

I pull away. No words cross between us, only the brush of his lips on my forehead. I dare hope we can go back to normal. I have a feeling my life's about to redefine the meaning of rough, so I could really use Xave's support right now.

Without him, I don't know if I can make it.

"Marcela!" Mom crosses the living room with clipped steps and stops at arm's length. "Where were you? How could you leave at a time like this?"

She takes my hand. Her touch is feverish, intense. I stare at her alabaster fingers pressed against my olive skin, my dad's skin. I wonder if she hates me because I remind her of him, of what she can't have. Or maybe expecting her to compare me to Dad is too much to expect. I've never been enough like him to make her happy. Never been at all like her to make her proud.

I always wondered what my brother would look like—if he would be like Dad, like me. I never thought we could be so different. In every imaginable way.

"Sorry," I say, pulling my hand away. "I ..."

Lie.

Relax.

"I was ... I needed to think."

She exhales and beams in a way I haven't seen her beam in years. She lights up the room and I'm eclipsed, obscured by new reasons.

"I contacted the police. It was him, Marci. It was him. That awful man is dead. And Max ... your friend has to be Max. They'll begin an investigation." Her voice cracks with joy, her cheeks glitter with tears made of hope.

Me? I feel myself go pale. I'm a ghost.

"Tell me about him." Mom grabs me by the elbows, pushes me into the living room and stuffs me in the sofa. It's kindergarten all over again, where eager kids pestered me until I share all my secrets.

"No," I say.

Her lips make a small circle, her eyebrows a crease above her nose. "No? You know him, right?"

"I … don't think so."

"You've had classes together, I would guess. Is he … tall? Smart? Kind?"

My eyes find a speck on the far wall. "He looks like you," I say and after a pause, "can I go? I didn't sleep good last night. I'd like to rest."

Mom stands, frustration painting her face red.

"I don't understand you. Aren't you glad we've found him?"

"I am, Mom." I nod, my voice monotone. "It's good to see you happy. I think you'll like him."

Mom, I don't have to be strong for you now, don't have to pretend I'm okay. You got your heart's desire. And maybe when you've traveled that road you've craved, your regrets will be for me.

Closed casket.

I look away from it, fidget and ignore Mom's restless energy. Her eyes are glued on the blond boy in the black suit. The boy who sits very still staring at the carpet, blue eyes void of the cocky liveliness I'm used to seeing in them.

Mom is dying to talk to him, to spill years of longing onto his lap. But she sits there, smiling and frowning all in the same second, containing her desire to tell it all.

A few brave classmates approach Luke and offer their condolences. He barely acknowledges them. I wonder what I should do; what he will think of my silence once he learns the truth?

Deep breath.

I decide to be brave like the others. I'm about to walk his way, when Luke stands, stuffs his hands into his pockets and walks away. Mom watches his every move.

"Where are you going?" she asks when I stand.

"Restroom," I lie. "Be right back."

As I pretend to go toward the bathroom, my gaze follows Luke. He goes through a set of French doors that lead outside. Unnoticed by Mom, I sneak into a corridor. The funeral home is an intricate maze of dreary halls, parlors and visiting rooms. I find another door that leads outside and step into the quiet evening.

Luke is reclining against a tree, chin on his chest, shadows splitting his face in odd angles. The sharpness of his features, the gloom around him make me shiver.

Be brave.

I don't want to catch him by surprise, so I walk with meaningful steps. He looks up, an annoyed expression on his face, which disappears when he realizes it's me.

Why?

"Hey," I say.

"Hey," he says back.

"I—I hope I'm not bothering you."

Luke shakes his head and shows me a tiny smile.

"Um ..."

Meaningful words.

Don't exist.

"You don't have to say anything," Luke tells me in a quiet whisper.

"I'm sorry," is all I can think to say.

Your father was a thief, but I'm sorry you have to go through this. I'm sorry you'll have to go through so much more.

Luke blinks several times, then looks up at the branches above. A tear spills over, and he slaps it away, quick and proud.

Something beyond my control takes my hand to his arm. He startles a bit, looks at my fingers, then into my eyes. I hold his gaze, sense the iron bars that cage his pain. Too much to bear by himself when he doesn't have to.

More tears streak his cheeks and when he looks away, my arms find their way into a tight embrace I didn't know I had in me to give. In the first instant, his limbs become stone, but they melt quickly, like pieces of ice next to kindling flame. He rests his cheek on my head, but leaves limp arms hanging at his sides.

It's not his fault Mom preferred the idea of him to the reality of me. It won't be his fault if he hates me when he finds out the truth. The truth that will make his life up to this point a lie.

I pull away, feel my own tears building, building.

"I'm sorry, Luke."

He frowns, as if aware my apology is meant for more than it should be, meant for what is to come.

"I'll see you soon."

Brother.

Chapter 11

After the funeral on Monday, the week has been strangely calm. Realizing I've nothing to share about Luke, Mom left me alone. The few times I've seen her, she's been filled with anxious energy, jittery like a rocket ready to blast off into space.

Tuesday, she started to tell me about the social worker handling "Max's" case. When I showed no interest in her efforts to reach out to Luke—a name she refuses to use—she was upset for a millisecond, then the glow of more important matters than me filled her eyes again. She's too far up on cloud nine to notice her insignificant daughter. Her indifference has reached an unprecedented level.

That was until this morning, when she said I had to skip school to go with her to the child protective services office. She informed me that today Luke would hear the truth about his abductor. The social worker would then ask him if he'd like to meet his real family. Mom wants to be there, waiting for him to come out and meet us. It seems she expects him to come running into her arms as soon as he hears the news. I wonder if she's considered the possibility he might not?

I wait in my room, reading in bed. Gently, I hold Dad's copy of a Neruda book of poems between my hands. Dad's full name is written on the first page in his beautiful rolling script—*Marcela Victoria Guerrero* is spelled in my third-grade, blocky letters right underneath.

I treasure the book, treasure the words of the poet my father so admired. He grew up reading Neruda's work with Grandpa Roberto. They both liked him for his skill with words and for the fact that Neruda was from Chile, Grandpa's homeland. This book has love poems, mostly. The rich language and word-play challenges my mind. Every time I re-read them they evoke different feelings and conjure new meanings.

My foot shakes nervously. I don't want to imagine how Luke will react, so I shift my thoughts to James and his crew. As promised, Aydan sent me the code he used to hack my system. The jerk did it to boast. There's no other explanation. Not when he named all his routines things like "ProbeKiddieCode," "ChildsPlay," and other condescending stuff like that.

The program told me a lot, especially the fact that leaving a way to access my own system remotely—a feature I used only once—was monumentally stupid. It also told me that Aydan is a thorough, methodical, smart son-of-a-gun. Man, I can't wait to show him up. I hope I get a chance. Other than Aydan's code, I've not heard another peep from IgNiTe, which is oddly comforting and disquieting at the same time.

Putting down the book, I heave a sigh and decide to check my email for the hundredth time. I push away from the bed and sit at my desk. I've been so bored that when I notice a new message from sender IgNiTe, I double-click it in a rush.

James, Aydan, whoever, has sent me a small challenge. The message is encrypted. I relish the game and the tiny clues they've given me to help solve the puzzle. It takes me fifteen minutes to crack the message. When I do, I'm almost disappointed.

Answers. Saturday night. Midnight. The bar.

A knock at the door startles me.

"It's time," Mom says.

I cringe at her beaming smile. Doesn't she realize this won't be easy?

"Is that what you're wearing?" she asks.

Ripped jeans. Boots. Tight olive t-shirt with black strokes of the Chinese symbol for "serenity." Yep, that's what I'm wearing. What does she expect? A skirt? A grin full of teeth?

"Luke's seen me a thousand times, Mom. He won't recognize me if I go in disguise."

"I don't understand your attitude," she says, turning on her heels and clip-clopping down toward the kitchen. She wears a dress I've never seen before. It's white and it hugs her slender body tightly. A thin black belt encircles her waist. Her normally straight hair curls at the tips and bounces as she heads for the door.

My feet shuffle forward. I give myself time to build some patience. When I enter the kitchen, Mom waits with a hand on the knob of the open back door.

"Hurry, Marcela. I don't want to be late."

We ride in silence, a silence loaded with Mom's expectations and my dread.

She thinks Luke will be delighted to learn he has a family.

I think she sees the world through rose-tinted glasses.

The question is: who will be proved wrong?

*

We sit in a claustrophobic office, waiting. I've been staring at a dusty plant in the corner, sure it's fake or it would have choked by now.

The door opens. Mom and I look up.

"Mrs. Guerrero?"

Mom jumps to her feet, a nervous smile on her lips. For once her expression seems to match the situation.

"Mrs. Peters." Mom shakes hands with the social worker.

"Luke was here," Mrs. Peters says, a cautious expression on her lean face. She's petite, with a pixie haircut and long lashes.

Mom's smile holds and she doesn't seem to register that Mrs. Peters used the past tense.

"I explained the situation in full detail. He took the news very well, in my opinion. However ... he has decided to take some time to let it sink in before considering a meeting with you. I'm sure you can understand."

Mom's face breaks into a thousand pieces. "Why? Why doesn't he want to meet me? Did he agree to do the DNA tests? They *will* prove I'm his mother."

"You have to understand this is a very difficult time for Luke. I warned you this could happen. The best thing we can do is give him time to come to terms with everything."

"I'm sure if I could just talk to him, he would—"

"Mrs. Guerrero, this isn't something we can rush."

"But he's alone, and he doesn't have to be. He has a family. Besides, he already knows Marcela. They're friends. I think this is ridiculous." Mom sounds like a spoiled child. I hide my face behind my hand.

Mrs. Peters sighs. "I assure you he's well taken care of and I'm certain he will come around. We just need patience. I'm sorry. Your eagerness is understandable, but Luke's wellbeing should be the priority. For all of us." She says the last few words with emphasis, reminding Mom that Luke should be her priority as well.

Before Mom can say anything else, Mrs. Peters extends a hand forward. "I'll be in touch with you."

Mom looks heartbroken, her face a clear indication that the situation isn't computing in her brain. She can't fathom why Luke doesn't share her eagerness. She sees only her gain and not his loss. I feel sorry for her, but more sorry for Luke.

Her eyes cloud over and I shiver. She will probably start walking like a zombie again and the nightmares and box under her bed will renew their scheduled program. I'd better make sure we have enough Sleepytime tea at hand.

It's Friday, and I'm late for class. I speed-walk down the hall, turn the corner in a hurry then freeze. Luke is standing by the door to my classroom, waiting.

For me? He looks up and his blue eyes sparkle with the answer. Yes, he's waiting for me.

"Hi," he says.

This is the first time I've seen him since the funeral, since he learned the truth. The anger I expected to find on his face isn't there. What I find in its place is something I have no name for. There's too much there. Confusion. Disappointment. Doubt. Sadness. Hope?

"Can we talk?" he asks.

He doesn't wait for my answer, just walks away, knowing I will follow.

We get into his Land Rover SUV and drive away from school without saying a word. I inhale the brand-new car smell and think of awkward things *not* to say.

After a few blocks, he parks the car by Boeing Creek. A man plays Frisbee with his dog, several joggers run on the outlining path. We watch them through the windshield.

"At the funeral, you already knew, didn't you?" Luke asks.

"Yes," I murmur.

"Why didn't you tell me?"

"It wasn't my place." I'm staring at the glove compartment, and even if it grew teeth and threatened to bite me, I wouldn't tear my eyes from it.

"And you left it up to a stranger?"

I can't argue with that one. He's right.

"You should have told me." An undercurrent of anger rides his tone.

"I wanted to, but I wasn't … brave enough," I admit.

Luke chuckles. I look his way, surprised. He seems genuinely amused. "*You* weren't brave enough? That's a first."

His amusement dies and he lowers his eyes, lost in a new thought. A curtain of golden lashes hides the sky-blue of his gaze. "Don't do that again, okay? If we're to be in this together, just tell it to me how it is. I promise to do the same."

I'm not in the habit of being open and neither is he. I guess he intends to change that. That should be interesting.

Without waiting for an answer, he continues, "They say that since I'm only sixteen, I can't live alone. I'm staying with a foster family. They're all right, but it's weird," he says.

Outside, the Frisbee flies across a patch of white clouds. The golden retriever jumps high in the air to catch it. Sharp canine teeth flash for a brief instant before they snap closed. It feels as if they just pierced through the fragile membrane of my reality. I know where this is going. Luke lived by himself with that man, no mother or other relatives in the picture.

I guess that explains why no one came forward when "*Dr. Smith*" became an overnight dad.

"They said I could move in with you." Luke clears his throat, as if the words left a lump there. "What do you think?"

"I … um … it'll make Mom happy." My answer sounds forced and shallow, but I don't know what else to say. It's the truth. Yesterday, after Luke refused to meet with us, Mom went back to moping and fell asleep in front of the TV following one-too-many glasses of wine.

"I'm asking you, Marci. What do *you* think about it?"

"I don't count. Haven't for a long time."

My skin tingles. I can feel his eyes scrutinizing me, trying to figure out what I mean. I stare at the cloud that looks like a broken heart.

"No one else counts. Not to me," he says.

I find myself examining his face, trying to figure out if this is the same person I've known since kindergarten, wondering if I ever really knew him. His usual pretense is gone, his words are straightforward, sincere. I guess he does intend to change things.

Is it possible that, like me, he puts on a different façade to hide the real Luke? If so, maybe this affair will turn out all right.

"Well," I say, "I think it would be … awkward."

"Amen to that … *sister*."

Slowly, a smile stretches across Luke's lips. His eyes twinkle and the smile grows into a grin, which turns into a hearty laugh. Soon I'm laughing with him. And we hold our stomachs, like five-year-olds tickled by a silly joke. When our giggles die out, the air between us feels lighter and full of possibilities. I have a brother and maybe there's still hope for our broken family.

Chapter 12

As Xave and I dismount his bike in front of Howls, my clock reads exactly midnight. Riding side-saddle has made my butt and legs stiff, not to mention the cold February air. I shake my limbs and rub my backside.

Xave snickers. "Very ladylike," he says.

"Shut up." I smack his arm. "We had to go and get involved with criminals who ask you to dress up. How very James Bond."

"Clark swears they're not bad guys."

"Yeah, and I was born fully clothed."

"If you were born wearing anything like that dress, then I have no complaints." Xave gives me a look similar to the one he gave me when he picked me up. My skin tingles as if his eyes were feathers traveling down the length of my body. I smack him again because I can't insult him. My mouth has suddenly gone dry.

I hate dresses. With a raving passion. I have no idea where James is taking us, but it has to be somewhere fancy. So much so that he, himself, provided the clothes Xave and I are wearing to make sure we look the part. How he knew my exact size is disconcerting. I have to admit that whoever picked the dress has good taste, even if the plunging V-neck line is cut too low for comfort. I would have never picked white, but it makes my olive skin pop in a really nice way.

Xave looks *different* in his tuxedo, and if someone were to twist my arm I might even say he looks handsome. But I'm not about to mention that and risk stretching the awkwardness that has plagued our relationship lately. The way he's been stealing glances my way, making comments about my appearance and, worst of all, acting like a moody toddler at the drop of a hat has been unsettling enough already. I'm afraid I know where this is headed, and the idea just doesn't compute in my brain. Xave is like a cousin to me, right?

I take a few steps away from him, half-smile at his comment and wiggle my toes. "I really, really hate high heels." A country song plays inside the bar, its muffled sound drifting outside, loading the air with its sad melody. I clear my throat. "Where are they?"

"Over there." Xave points to the road ahead. Under the canopy of a large tree, a van sits almost unnoticed in the darkness.

We approach at an unhurried pace. When we reach the van, the side door slides open. Oso waves us in. He wears a long-sleeve black t-shirt, black jeans and black boots. I frown. Is this a joke? Why are we dressed up and he's not?

He shuts the door behind us. My eyes take a few seconds to adjust.

"Glad you decided to join us," James says.

I blink and stare into the back of the van. It's crowded, filled with people and what looks like surveillance equipment. All the blinking lights, knobs and computer monitors mesmerize me.

Aydan sits at the controls, wearing jeans, a turtleneck sweater and a beany—all black. Across from him, Clark looks like his twin.

I'm about to protest when I notice that James is also dressed up, sporting a tux that fits him like a glove and actually makes me think of Bond's sophistication and good looks. I grin, itching to ask him if, by the way, he's truly *Bond ... James Bond*. My grin dies when—for some weird reason—an image of Dad flashes across my eyes, the way he looked in his wedding picture. He would have been about James's age now, if not for that freak car accident.

I shake myself as Oso squeezes into the driver seat. Blare sits next to him, wearing a blond wig and ignoring us. The seat hides the rest of her body, but if the hair is any indication, she must be dressed up too.

James invites us to sit in the back seat. As we pass, Clark pulls on Xave's jacket and wolf-whistles.

"Don't touch me, you perv." Xave slaps his hand away.

Xave and I stuff ourselves in the narrow seat and end up hip to hip. I squirm.

Oso starts the van. As we drive away from the bar, James explains, "This is a reconnaissance mission. You and Xave have two simple tasks. One, do as you're told. Two, pay close attention."

"Above all don't freak out," Clark offers with a sarcastic grin.

"What you will learn tonight," James continues in a serious tone, "is nothing to joke about." He gives Clark a disapproving glance that sobers him up. "This is serious. A matter of death and survival. If you aren't prepared to be ... terrified out of your skin, then we can stop. Right here, right now. You don't have to come. Do you understand?"

Xave and I nod.

"Do you understand?" James asks, louder this time.

"Yes," we both respond.

James's eyes burn holes into mine, into Xave's. He stares us down for what feels like five whole minutes. Then he asks, "If you saw a monster, would you scream?"

The quiet, deep rumble of his voice and the intensity of those gray eyes—which right now look black—put my hackles on end. Xave fidgets, tugs his shirt and smooths nonexistent creases.

"Xave?" James asks pointedly.

Is James really expecting an answer to this ludicrous question? Where is he taking us? Hannibal Lecter's mansion? Are we invited to be someone's dinner? What the heck?

"What do you mean … a monster?" Xave asks.

"Frankenstein, Dracula, Predator," James whispers.

Xave blows air through his nose, smiles. "Um, I guess if I saw something like that I'd think it was a dude in a costume. So no, I wouldn't scream. I'd laugh … or something." His smile dies, as James's expression appears anything but amused.

"What about you, Marci?" James's eyes turn to me.

The humming in the back of my head intensifies. My stomach roils, as if a snake has made its lair in there. I've suspected for a long time that there's more to the shadows than meets the eye. But monsters? Is James joking? Nausea tightens my insides. Fear floods me. Somehow I sense that what James wants to show us is real, and I won't like it. Silence festers like an incurable disease.

Finally, I say, "I—I wouldn't scream. I would … bite my tongue."

James nods. Clark, Aydan, Oso and even Blare stare at me, tight-lipped.

"You follow her lead, little brother," Clark tells Xave. "You follow her lead."

Chapter 13

Oso pulls the van over. In the back there are no windows, and it's too dark to see through the windshield. I have no idea where we are, or why we've stopped.

Aydan swivels his chair and beckons James. With quick hands, he attaches a small pin to James's lapel, then turns back to the computers and punches a few keys. One of the four monitors comes to life, displaying an image of Aydan's back.

"Okay," he says, "try to point the thing at as many faces as possible. I'll record everything. And Blare," he reaches for a small box, "these earrings are for you."

Blare takes the box. "They're hideous!" she exclaims.

"Sorry, darling. They didn't come in crossbones. I did what I could," Clark says.

She gives him the finger. "Screw you."

When another monitor comes to life, showing an image from Blare's perspective, Aydan rubs his hands together. "It's showtime."

"C'mon." James slides the door open and gestures for us to get out.

"Be careful," Oso admonishes.

Once outside, I look around. We're in the almost empty parking lot of a Mexican restaurant. If we had disembarked in China, it couldn't be more bizarre. The restaurant is closed and there isn't much else around.

Blare steps out through the passenger door. When I see her, I do a double take. She looks stunning, nothing like the Medusa monster I met the other night. Her every curve is revealed like an individual art piece; her dress fits as if a master artist painted it right on her skin. She has long, well-toned limbs, and a graceful air I would have never suspected. Her blond wig falls onto naked shoulders in loose curls and—if I didn't know better—I'd say it was her real hair. The brow ring is gone and the black lipstick has been replaced by a deep red tint, creating a dramatic effect on her pale features.

My hands self-consciously tug at my dress and I feel like an ugly duckling. I'm taken by surprise by the ridiculous reaction and even more by the surge of anger that electrifies me when I notice Xave ogling her.

I want to ... slap him. Instead, my eyes shift to James, the retreating van, and the restaurant's neon sign that reads "Casita Mamita."

James pulls a set of keys out of his pocket and clicks the remote control. The sound of popping locks directs my gaze toward a black Lincoln LS. Blare and James walk toward the car with purposeful steps. Xave and I just stand there, watching like a couple of idiots. With a nasty backward glance, Blare says it all. We snap out of it, follow and get in the car.

As James drives out of the parking lot, he checks his watch. "When we get there, the others will be nearby in the van." He looks at us through the rear-view mirror. "The party is by invitation only. Everyone is expected to bring a date, so a little bit of acting will be required on your part. Do you think you can handle that?"

Blare huffs. "For these two? It should be effortless."

The heat of a blush ignites my cheeks. My stomach turns upside down. The passing buildings and lampposts become terribly interesting all of a sudden.

Cool it.

I dare turn my head a little toward Xave and catch a glance out of the corner of my eye. It seems he's developed a passion for lampposts, too.

After a fifteen-minute drive, the view outside changes considerably. Dark alleys and dingy bars aren't everything IgNiTe has to offer. We're in some fancy neighborhood. The kind I've only seen on television. There are huge iron gates, security cameras, impeccable landscapes in every house … or I should say mansion. No wonder we had to ride in this car, except now I'm not sure it's fancy enough.

Xave and I elbow each other, point and gawk. When James comes to a stop at a huge gate guarded by two mean-looking guys in suits, we compose ourselves and act cool and collected.

James rolls down both front windows and gives a small wave. The two ogres on either side practically stick their heads in and peer at each one of us with narrowed eyes. Their noses flare like hound dogs' and the humming in the back of my head picks up a couple of notches.

Inhale. Once. Twice.

The one on my side gives me a smile full of complicity, as if we've known each other for ages. I smile back, doing my best to match his expression. They wave us in, just like that. I thought James said the party was by invitation only. What did the guards do? Sniffed the fancy stationery to make sure we have an invitation?

As we move up the long driveway, bumpered by two rows of perfectly trimmed hedges and many strategically placed spotlights, James turns and says, "Good job." It seems like a harmless comment meant for both Xave and I, but—from the way his gray gaze lingers on me—I know there's a deeper compliment in there meant just for me.

Blare shakes herself and rolls her shoulders, as if chilled. "Disgusting." She sounds as if someone just poured a bucket of slug slime down her impossibly tight dress.

The driveway takes us to a majestic mansion, capping the top of a hill. The place is gigantic, and even though I understand squat about architecture, I know you have to have some serious money to own a place like this. Not just any "Joe Blow Millionaire" can afford this type of luxury.

Xave and I exchange puzzled looks. I know he's thinking the same thing I am. How does James and his miserable, shabby posse fit in with this filthy-rich bunch?

As we step out of the car, a man wearing a white coat and black bowtie takes the Lincoln and drives away. James pulls me aside. Xave and Blare look surprised by his hand at my elbow, leading me away from them. Begrudgingly, Blare takes the hint and pulls Xave with her, walking with slow, easy steps toward the main entrance.

When they're out of earshot, James grabs my hand. "When you walk in there, the droning in your head is going to feel like a million killer ants eating your brain."

His eyes are dead serious and the hard line of his lips uncompromising. My heart takes a leap and runs, scared like a jackrabbit. James takes my hand and puts a wide ring in my palm. The ring is pretty, with red stones inlaid in three rows. I stare at it, rendered speechless by surprise and confusion.

"When that happens and you feel you're about to lose control, you can use this, if you need to." He presses a button on the side of the ring. Little, sharp needles spring out on the inside. "Pain is your friend, Marci. Remember that. I'm taking a big risk bringing you here, but I have my reasons. I wish I could have prepared you better for this, but lately time has become a luxury. Don't worry, you'll learn everything soon enough. For now just remember, I need you on board. There's something that makes you special. Being here will help you understand that. And I *need* you to understand. Fully. I know you're strong. You can do this."

Putting an instant smile on his face, James loops his arm around mine and ushers me along. We fall in step with the others as they're about to enter the house. I slip the ring on my index finger, sparing a frightened glance its way. James just handed me a tiny and beautiful torture device. He's crazy if he thinks I'm going to use it.

Nuts.

Relax.

Totally cracked.

Blare leaves Xave's side and gives me a look plastered in ice. James nods slightly toward Xave. I know how to take a hint too and rush to my friend's side.

"What was that all about?" Blare asks James between clenched teeth.

James's answer to her question is lost to me as we step inside and the sound of voices, classical music, and wine glasses clinking in toasts fills the air. I barely have time to register all these details before the back of my head explodes into a maddening buzz. I grip Xave's arm, my knees turning into rubber. My vision blurs.

"Are you okay?" Xave asks, putting a hand around my waist.

Calm down.
Connive. Fractious. Incisive.
Breathe.

My eyelids grow heavy and I fight to keep them open. Shadows spread over my thoughts like never before. They take macabre shapes that make me want to weep in terror.

"Marci, what's wrong?" Xave is holding most of my weight now.

I can't … lose control. There … are … no—

Suddenly, James is at my side, grabbing my hand and pressing the button on the ring. The needles spring out and stab my finger, sending a jolt of pain up my arm. My eyelids shoot up and a fierce clarity floods my brain, shining a brilliant light over the shadows and breaking them apart. Surprisingly, no one notices, and I even have enough presence of mind to choke the cry that wicked pinprick kicked into my throat.

Now I'm very much in the moment, wrapped in layers of extravagance and luxury. Yet, as I stare into James's intense, gray eyes, I realize I'd rather be in hell.

Chapter 14

Xave frowns at James's hand over mine. I pull away and try to look calm and unaffected.

"What's going on?" Xave asks. "You've gone pale."

"I'm fine." My voice comes out cracked. I clear my throat and make a show of looking around the room, when what I really want to do is run, run, run. "L-look at this place. It's ... huge."

Reluctantly, Xave unlocks his gaze from mine and checks our surroundings. A hard line forms between his eyebrows. "I don't like it," he says. "Not one bit."

In a place like this, there should be nothing to dislike. Every wall, every piece of furniture, every single detail spells opulence. Crystal chandeliers, marble floors, exquisite art work, a grand staircase. Wealth drips from the ceiling like rain from a leaky roof. It's despicable. The vibe is all wrong.

As people mingle, toasting each other, gossiping, laughing, my head drones and my skin crawls with a million spiders. Xave feels something, too. I can tell by the muscle jumping on his jaw, and the sweat building on his brow. Whatever it is, it hangs thick in the air, like the stench of road-kill right against our noses.

James motions for us to move deeper into the crowd. My knees lock, and I consider bolting, forgetting him and his gang and even my intense desire to find answers and a cure. But who am I kidding? I'd sooner click the ring's button again than lose this chance.

I square my shoulders. I'm strong. I'm my father's daughter, and I don't give up. I will stay here with my throbbing finger and buzzing head. I will find out what this curse is, and I will free myself.

Xave's feet are glued to the ground. I try to pull him along, but he doesn't budge. Leaving him behind, I follow James and Blare.

"Hey!" He catches up and takes my hand in his. "You're not going anywhere without me." A crooked smile touches his lips, but not his eyes. He's just as scared as I am, but he's also brave.

I let my eyes travel over the room. Everywhere I look it's the same. Men and women hanging out in couples, feeding each other, locking arms, dancing, kissing. It's like Saint freakin' Valentine's day. A tall brunette walks beside me, wearing so many diamonds she literally sparkles. She's dazzling, but the sight of her kicks up the hammering inside my head. I look into her companion's face, a man with angular features and the most perfect eyebrows I've ever seen. The droning quiets down one degree, and I can think again.

As I assess everyone, I realize my head hums for one member of each couple, but not the other. It puzzles me, then—as I remember what James said in the car—it begins to make sense. "Everyone is expected to bring a date." My gaze darts around the room, validating the pattern. The more couples I evaluate, the more certain I become. They're all like Xave and I, like James and Blare.

One of them has shadows eating their brains out, while the other is normal and unaware that their companion is a freak. They're happy and carefree, laughing, making conversation, nuzzling each other's necks and laughing again. I feel like I'm going to scream, lose it, ruin this whole plan that I've not yet begun to understand.

Just when I think things can't get any worse, the sound of leather soles against the marble floor enters my awareness. Each step beats in the back of my head, as if I'm being carved out of stone and the sculptor stands behind me pounding away with his tools, moving the chisel a tiny fraction after each blow and hammering with all his might over and over again.

Sweat slicks Xave's grip in my hand. I've gone cold and my knees refuse to hold my weight. I'm at the brink of collapsing.

The ring.

Pain.

My thumb fumbles for the release. I look up and find my gaze locked on a pair of golden eyes. They seem to float toward me before I realize there's a face that goes with them, the face of the person whose steps are pounding my brain into mashed potatoes. Those eyes narrow and fix on mine. Flecks of copper surround pupils that seem to be nothing but pinpricks. Their strange, animalistic quality terrifies me to the bone. He smiles at me.

I push the button. A thousand piranha teeth pierce my skin. It takes all my willpower to stifle a cry along with the panic that begs me to check if my finger's still attached to my hand. Instead, I smile back at Golden Eyes, return his gaze and act as if this really is Valentine's Day and blissful chocolate is about to start pouring from the ceiling.

"My dear James," the man says in a thick English accent. "What a delight to have you here tonight. So glad you could make it."

"Hello, Elliot. Back from the motherland?" James says, shaking his hand.

The man smiles with so much English charm, I feel like puking. I lean on Xave as I take the man in. He's in his early fifties and wears a dark tailored suit and some sort of silky mess around his neck. What *posh* name do they call those things? Cravat? Oh heck, I don't know, but the pattern looks like cat puke and the whole style is just too effeminate for my taste.

I blink several times to clear my head. I should be scrambling out of here and this is what I'm thinking about?! Obviously, random thoughts have taken over as my default self-preservation mechanism.

Elliot takes Blare's hand. "And Veronica, as staggering as always." He plants a kiss on her hand and nothing but the smallest tightness around her eyes reveals any emotion besides pleasure.

Veronica? I wonder if that's her real name.

"Same to you," Blare says.

"And who do we have here?" Elliot turns.

His eyes, those iridescent, spell-binding eyes, land on me. I feel hypnotized by them and their strange, inhuman color. My breathing quickens, and suddenly I need pain to ground me, to stop the incessant droning that beats to a new, unprecedented rhythm.

Pain!

I bite the inside of my cheek, until my teeth mash together. My mouth fills with blood.

Awkwardly, James steps in front of Xave, jolting my attention to his gray eyes. "This is Marci and her friend Xave. Guys, this is Elliot Whitehouse."

Elliot frowns and his nose flares like those of the guards outside. One of his eyebrows goes up, appraising me, revealing a small hint of suspicion. I know I must pull it together. Something big is at stake here, even if I don't know what.

I shed pounds of repulsion and put my hand out. I open my mouth to speak and, for a second, I fear nothing will come out. Yet, my voice is steady, pleasant even.

"Elliot." The name rolls off my tongue, as if I'm savoring it, but it nearly gags me. "May I call you that? I'm Marci ... Milan. I hope you don't mind, James took the liberty of inviting us." I pull what I think is my most enchanting smile.

Xave gapes. Blare reevaluates me. James smiles with what I know must be relief. Elliot inclines his head and gives a slow nod. A smile stretches his lips, revealing perfect teeth, erasing the suspicion that never quite materialized.

He takes my hand in his and says, "Not at all. Any friend of James is welcome in my humble home." He leans a bit closer and inhales, as if I'm some sort of flower and he a proud gardener. "Ah, such youth. A new generation full of promise. Well done, James." He pauses, then releases my hand at last.

He spares a curt nod for Xave before his attention shifts back to James. After all that charm and manners, I feel like protesting his rudeness toward my friend, but that would be a mistake. Those eyes need to shift their attention elsewhere. The quicker, the better.

"A nice new addition to your small circle of friends, James," Elliot says. Then he turns to Blare. "Now, if you'll excuse me, Veronica, I will borrow your date for a few minutes. In the meantime, enjoy the party. My *entire* house is at your disposal."

Elliot walks away, and in spite of my little performance, he leaves me feeling desolate. I take two ragged breaths, trying to pretend the world keeps on turning outside this nightmare.

"I'll be right back," James says. "Don't go far."

We stay behind, our body language screaming for James not to leave us.

Xave clears his throat. "Is that the monster James was talking about? What does he do? Kill you with … charm?"

Blare spins around. "I need a drink," she says, walking toward a large table laden with hors d'oeuvres and champagne.

"Me, too." Xave turns and follows.

I stay planted like a sapling, weak and new to this cruel world. My forefinger throbs and it feels as if I've grown a second heart. I squeeze it with my other hand and feel the wetness. When I examine it, I discover thin streaks of blood decorating its full length and am reminded of a candy cane.

Wincing, I search the crowd for James and find him standing with Elliot, his back turned. Elliot looks past James and locks his gaze to mine. They're talking about me. I know it. Suddenly, I want to hurt him, to rip that ridiculous thing off his neck and stuff it down his *bloody* throat. I never knew there was hatred at first sight, but there you have it.

Elliot gestures to a waiter, who brings over a tray with drinks. James takes one and brings it to his nose. He closes his eyes and smiles. After a few sips, they walk over to a painting on the wall and examine it. Bored and disgusted, I look away and go back to face-surfing. I study the crowd, wondering what all these people are doing here.

A blond man dances with a brunette.

She's petite and curvaceous.

He is one of them.

One of me.

A middle-aged woman with cruel features leads a younger man toward the grand staircase. She looks delighted as they ascend.

He's barely thirty and average looking.

She's one of them.

One of me.

I shiver. Fear brews inside my ribcage, turning dark and viscous, like spent motor-oil. I think of my bedroom, nestled in whirring computer equipment and my father's old books. There's comfort there, safety. I look toward the entrance and imagine myself walking away, turning my back on IgNiTe and this place. I can go home to my sanctuary—the only place where I can be myself.

Be myself. Be myself. Be myself.

Looking at all these faces, the lie echoes louder than ever before. How can I be myself if I don't know who—no, what—I am? No, I can't run. I can't hide from this no matter how terrifying. I have to know and, maybe then, I will be free.

Suddenly I notice James at my side. He's saying something, but his words float away before I catch their meaning.

"Here, take this." He hands me a handkerchief.

For an instant, I wonder about its purpose, then, cottoning on, I use it to clean the blood on my hands.

"Who's that guy?" I ask.

"Elliot? A man with exquisite taste in Scotch and art, but terrible respect for others."

What is that supposed to mean?

"C'mon," he urges.

"Are we leaving?" My question is really a plea.

"No, Marci." Sympathy flashes across his gaze but it's quickly replaced by determination. "We haven't done what we came here to do."

Chapter 15

We find Xave and Blare by the banquet table, each holding a glass of champagne.

Xave spits something into a napkin and says in a muffled voice, "It's disgusting."

Blare laughs, but grows serious as soon as she sees us. Her eyes snap to James's arm around my waist as he offers me his support.

"Let's go upstairs," James says.

Blare takes Xave's glass and sets it on the table. "Help your *girlfriend*," she orders him.

James and Xave switch places.

"Time to do that bit of acting," Blare says.

As we head for the staircase, James leans toward us and whispers, "Don't drink anything up there." He turns his attention to Blare. His large hand runs down the length of her back and he whispers something in her ear. She laughs and looks into his eyes with something like hunger, then kisses him on the mouth with exaggerated, soap-opera passion.

I blush and look away.

Mid-stairway, a warm caress travels down my neck. The tender touch startles me. Xave plants a kiss on my bare shoulder and pulls me close to him.

"You look beautiful tonight," he says in a deep voice. His hazel eyes twinkle with mischief.

He's acting. At least that's what I tell myself. I'm supposed to do the same.

"You really think so?" I flirt.

At the top of the stairs, James takes Blare's hand and leads her down a hall as wide as my house. Both smile and chatter, as if on a real date.

I try to act as if I know what I'm doing, but I have no clue. I've never been on a date. Not when every time I get close to a boy, the nervous fear sends the shadows over the edge.

We're behind James, walking down the carpeted hall. The padding under my feet is so soft it feels like walking on pillows. Huge flower arrangements decorate the way, filling the air with nauseating sweetness. The road to hell couldn't be more deceiving. I'm sure of it.

There are many doors at every side of the corridor. I get the impression I'm in a grand hotel and expect to see numbers on the doors and card readers to allow entry. Of course there aren't any, but my idea, it turns out, isn't ludicrous, because there are "do not disturb" signs hanging from several door knobs.

A couple walks behind us. The woman giggles, unaware that this place is all wrong and she should be running, getting as far away as possible from whatever is behind those closed doors. But she doesn't suspect a thing. How could she?

She's not one of them.

Not one of me.

If I die in the next few minutes, I deserve it. I know better than that poor woman and I'm still here. Every nerve in my body urges me to flee. My feet are restless, the back of my head tolls like a bell, and my heart thunders. Yet, I press forward, and I allow Xave to keep walking into the gaping jaws of this unknown beast.

We walk deeper into the hall, as James surveys each door. To our left a man with gray hair steps out of one of the rooms. He has an arm around a young woman, whose legs seem unable to hold her full weight.

He gives us a rueful smile. "One too many cherry martinis," he says, leading her forward, supporting her limp, scarecrow body.

"What kind of place is this?" Xave whispers in my ear. "I'm pretty sure whatever's going on here ain't legal."

He's on to something, but I doubt they even have a law for what's really happening.

James comes to a stop in front of a door without a "do not disturb" sign.

"Have fun," he says, directing his pointed gaze toward another vacant room next to theirs. The couple behind us picks the room past James's.

Xave gets the hint. "You too." He wraps an arm around my shoulder and ushers me into the room.

An admiring whistle leaves his lips as we walk in. "Look at this place."

I don't know what I was expecting. Torture devices? A wormhole? But the room is just normal. Well, not normal. It is ... exquisite.

I don't think I've ever used that word to describe anything before, but that's the only adjective that comes to mind. The place *is* exquisite, and I feel like I'm going to vomit. The ambiance is subtle, with warm lamps glowing in each corner. At the far end, sheer curtains cover a large set of floor-to-ceiling windows. Heavier drapes made out of something that looks like golden velvet hang at each end. Luxurious, yet comfortable and utilitarian furniture is placed strategically throughout. Museum-worthy art hangs from the walls. A massive bed commands the eye to the middle of the room, its duvet silken and embroidered in golden thread.

The door is still open behind me. I know I need to close it, but I'm afraid the room will swallow us whole. With a deep inhale, I find the little "do not disturb" sign and hang it outside. I push the door with one finger and watch the open gap get thinner and thinner, closing in on my unwitting past. After this, there'll be no turning back. After this, I'll know things I'll want to forget. But even with this certainty, I brace myself and turn the deadbolt.

It clicks with finality.

Chapter 16

"Oooh, cherry martinis," Xave says.

I whirl, lightning fast. "Don't touch that!"

His hand freezes midway toward the glasses. He backs away as if the drinks are nuclear warheads. "O-kay, so ... what then?" He looks toward the bed and wiggles his eyebrows.

"Don't be stupid, Xave."

A lopsided smile tips his mouth. He's trying to get a rise out of me. I ignore his smug expression and walk around the room, examining every corner, every piece of furniture.

"What is this place?" Xave asks, fingering the chocolate that rests on one of the pillows. "How about this, can I eat *it*?"

"I wouldn't touch anything," I warn him.

"Um, am I missing something here? I mean, that Elliot guy's creepy, but he's just a dude. I don't get what James and Clark keep going on about."

I look behind a mirror, wondering if it's one of those two-way contraptions. I really can't tell.

"I admit it's weird," Xave continues. "This place is like some sort of rich, fancy cathouse or something. But I don't really see what's so scary about that. I always figured they had places like this for rich people who are into … you know … that sort of stuff."

I examine the ceiling looking for cameras. So far I've spotted nothing out of the ordinary.

"Why are we here, anyway? What are we supposed to do?"

I shake my head. "I don't know, but I have a feeling it's not what you're thinking."

Xave stands in front of me and looks down into my eyes. "What happened out there? I noticed your hand is bleeding. How did you hurt yourself?"

Balling James's silk handkerchief up in my hand, I try to hide the evidence, even though it's too late. "It's nothing."

"C'mon, let me look at it." He's serious, nothing like the careless boy I've grown used to.

I've yet to reconcile the two sides of him, especially since I never know which one I'm going to get any given day. This new, budding Xave scares me and throws me off balance with his intermittent flashes of maturity. Who said boys are simple? I could take up astrophysics and understand it a lot quicker than I'll ever understand him.

He puts a hand on my elbow and slowly slides it down my forearm. Stopping at my wrist, he lifts my hand and examines it.

"Where'd you get that ring? You didn't have it earlier."

"I …" I can't think of what to say.

A small knock at the window makes us jump.

"What the …? Stay there," Xave orders me.

Staying close to the wall, he sidesteps toward the window, then peeks outside through a gap in the curtain. My shoes are glued to the floor, and I'm ready to kick them off. I'd be in trouble trying to fight in this dress. The least I can do is be ready to run.

"It's James," Xave says. "There's a balcony out there. He wants us to come out."

Xave pulls back the curtain and opens what turns out to be a set of glass doors, not windows. James steps in, a finger pressed to his lips. I won't be making any noise. Even if I knew what to say, the knot in my throat would choke my voice.

"There's no way I can prepare you," James whispers. "But if you don't feel ready, we can go."

"We didn't go through all this just to quit," Xave says.

"How about you, Marci?" James asks. "Can you handle it?"

No.

"Yes."

My fear is an avalanche, but Xave is right. I've come too far to chicken out now.

"All right. Follow me and be quiet." James exits the room. Xave and I follow. I look right and left. The balcony seems to wrap around the entire house. The soft glow coming from the rooms reveals several lounge chairs and potted plants. The floor is a checkerboard of dark and illuminated patches. We're overlook a large garden with sculpted trees, a fountain and a greenhouse that sparkles like an ice house.

James stays in the shadows and we follow. Blare is not out here, and when we pass James's room, I spot her silhouette behind the sheer curtains.

We move past and approach the next room, backs pressed to the wall. James leans in and takes a cautious look through the window, peeking with one eye. He nods, satisfied with whatever he sees inside. With one hand, he beckons for us to take a peek, too.

Xave gives me a meaningful glance and shakes his head, indicating there's no way he's going to spy on anyone's private *business*. It's cute, really. He's worried about his morals when the priority is getting this over with and making ourselves scarce.

I push past Xave, pretending I'm wearing armor and I'm a brave knight. After a deep breath, I peek inside. The couple with the giggling woman occupies the room. She sits at the edge of the bed, holding an empty martini glass. She sways as her eyes fight to stay open. Her partner is sitting next to her, watching her intently.

Xave puts a hand on my shoulder and makes me jump. He presses against me and peers in over my head. I push against his warm body, finding that I'm a bit braver with him by my side.

The woman looks about to pass out. The guy takes the glass away and sets it on the night table. Her eyes roll backward and, a moment later, her body goes limp. He catches her and, after some pushing and shoving, settles her against the headboard. With a smile of pleasure on his face, he stands and removes his jacket. Back to us, he proceeds to unbutton his shirt.

For support, I put my hand on top of Xave's, where he grips my shoulder. Slowly, the shirt slides off the man's back and the first glimpse of James's monster is revealed. Xave's fingers dig into my clavicle and I welcome the pain. Breathing becomes a struggle as my heart drowns in panic. My eyes are frozen wide, my mouth open as I gasp for air, my brain struggling to believe my eyes.

I try to form a reasonable explanation for the patterns on the man's back, and come up with "tattoos." These vivid red, black and yellows, however, are nothing like any tattoos I've ever seen. I know what ink looks like on someone's body, and this is nothing a mere human artist can create.

This is ... *alive*.

The man's right side is covered in iridescent, bright colors that smoothly blend from one shade into another in a strip pattern. As my brain tries to fit what it sees into a category, it comes up with the word "snake." Where there should be skin, there are ... scales? Large red, black and yellow sections that seem to have life of their own, breathing, accommodating themselves as he flexes his muscles. His left side has similar patterns, but they are uneven, incomplete somehow, as if they were an afterthought or the tattoo artist forgot to finish them.

He sits on the bed in front of the woman. I see only their profiles. She looks numb. Him, pleased in the extreme. He tilts his head back, closes his eyes and takes a deep breath. His chest expands and his eyelids flutter in something that looks like ecstasy. The scales wrap around his chest but there's something else there, something I can't distinguish.

My skin crawls with the knowledge that this is the moment, the point of no return. I want to hide my face on Xave's chest, but I go on gaping, eyes burning with my inability to blink anymore.

Something moves on the man's chest. It throbs to life like a second heart, then unfolds, tasting the air. A cry jumps to my throat, but I bite my tongue and I bite again. I will not scream. Even as blood pools inside my mouth, I will not scream.

Two tentacles covered in tiny hairs reach toward the woman, making me think of roach legs. At the spot where they sprout from his chest, the appendages are wide, then taper into sharp, needle-like ends made out of something like bone.

Vomit burns behind my sternum. Xave's chest thumps on my back. His hands grip my shoulders and tremble. My heart hammers in time with his. My body shakes against his rigid frame.

The tentacles elongate and move in waves, reaching, hungry for the woman. They're millimeters away from her nose, then undulate their way to the back of her neck and wrap her in a hug. My mind goes through a hundred possibilities of what her end will be. They're all horrific, worse than any nightmare I could have imagined just five minutes ago.

Why has James brought me to see this? What is he trying to tell me? He can't mean that I ... Terror surges from my gut and explodes inside my head, ripping my feeble control to shreds. As the implications shake my core, the cry still lodged in my throat suddenly becomes a living, earsplitting reality.

In an instant, the tentacles are sucked back into their slimy hole. The man's head whips toward the window. Black eyes rimmed with wide strips of yellow search the dark night beyond the sheer curtains. I scream again. His gaze isn't human.

James is beside us, urging with frantic gestures to get back in our room. I spit blood, wishing I had bit off my tongue. Xave pulls me back, arm around my waist, dragging my wilted body. The sound of a thousand steps and voices fill the house.

Chapter 17

We're inside our room. Xave lets go of me and James looks madly around. Someone bangs on the door.

"Is everything okay? Open the door."

We look to James for an escape. His eyes are wide and hold no answer. I think about jumping off the balcony, but it's a long fall and I would have no idea where to run. There seem to be acres and acres of grounds around this house. They would catch me.

More banging on the door, more shouts.

James's eyes alight and, in the next instant, his hand is in his pants' pocket. He pulls out a knife, unfolds it and snatches my left arm. Without hesitation, he slides the blade across the back of my arm. My scream is muffled by James's quick hand on my lips. Blood seeps out and runs down my fingertips, staining the carpet crimson. I feel faint from shock.

"Are you crazy?!" Xave goes for James, but the man is too quick. In an instant, he's at the bureau, sweeping the martinis onto the carpet. The glasses fall, but don't break. A cherry rolls under a chaise longue. The smell of alcohol impregnates the air.

I know James says he had good reasons for taking this risk with us, for bringing us here, but I think he's simply insane! He should have never brought us here, even after he made us swear we wouldn't scream.

Outside, the sound of keys jangling signals imminent entry.

James rushes toward the balcony. "Make the best of it," he urges in a soft tone, then closes the sliding door behind him.

"Shit, shit," Xave curses.

The knife is at his feet, covered in red. We look at each other, our lungs going through more oxygen than they should. When the door opens, I stare in panic. My mind reels, trying to figure out what James expects us to do.

Two large men burst in. They look like bodyguards, bouncers, and criminals all rolled into one. The first one to barge through the door is massive, tall and wide as a server rack, and has a thick, leathery face with deep grooves that should make him look old, but instead make him appear tough and impervious. A dozen more faces peer in from the door.

"What happened?" I hear James call out from the crowd. "Let me through. That's my friend in there."

My friend. Not my friends?

"Ma'am?" Leather Man says, looking from my arm, to me, to Xave.

I have to do something, but what? Why did James cut me? My brain goes into warp speed, as it always does when something complicated lies before me, then it comes to me. There's no way I should know what James wants me to do, but I think I understand, and it's horrible.

Oh, God.

I look into Xave's eyes.

Forgive me.

"H-he went crazy," I say, pointing at Xave.

His jaw drops.

"Marci, are you okay?" James runs in. He's not wearing a jacket anymore and one side of his shirt hangs outside of his pants.

Everyone outside murmurs and moves closer to the door.

"He just went crazy," I repeat hesitantly.

James whirls, charges Xave, grabs him by the neck and pushes him against the bureau.

"What are you? Some sort of psycho?" James asks, squeezing Xave's neck.

Outside, the crowd goes quiet and shuffles out of the way. Elliot waltzes in, one hand stuffed in his jacket pocket, nose up in the air. He surveys the room with a critical eye.

"What seems to be the matter?" he pointedly asks.

James starts to speak, but when Elliot ignores him, he shuts his mouth. The creep's golden eyes survey every millimeter of my face and trembling hands. I tell myself my tremors are normal for someone who's just been assaulted, that there's no way he can figure out I'm not one of them. I'm not!

Never.

"He went crazy," I say, offering the explanation that seemed to have sufficed for everyone else so far.

One of Elliot's perfectly trimmed eyebrows goes up. "Crazy?" he says as if he's never heard the word.

I lose it then. "Yeah, you know, nuts, psycho, wacko." I'm crying, hyperventilating. "He cut me, he just … pulled out a knife and cut me."

James manhandles Xave, shoving harder, making the bureau hit the wall. "You'll pay for that, you little bastard. I've got just the thing for you." He smashes his fist against Xave's jaw. Xave staggers and falls to his knees.

Elliot addresses the curious crowd. "Everyone, things are under control here. I'm afraid there's nothing noteworthy taking place. Please continue enjoying the *party*."

They all leave, except the bodyguards, who look at Xave with hunger in their eyes. Leather Man closes the door. My knees finally give out and I collapse on the bed, a hand pressed to my wound.

Xave keeps his eyes on the carpet, his body tense and quaking, a volcano ready to erupt.

"We can take care of him for you," Elliot says, as if he's referring to a pesky rodent problem.

James acquires the same tone, same look of disinterest. "My girl's fine," James says. "Just a little shaken. Right, Marci?" I manage a nod.

"Nothing came of it," James continues. "You can have him," James says.

Elliot smiles, relaxes a bit. I'm at the edge of the bed, exchanging alarmed glances with Xave. This can't possibly be James's plan. I won't allow it. My fear burns, gives birth to a pyre of anger. I stand from the bed.

"Unless ..." James gives me a meaningful glance. "Marci would prefer to take matters into her own hands?"

As I process these words, I turn my anger into something useful. "I would," I say, voice low and gravelly. "No one cuts me, no one messes with me. Not without paying for it."

I move forward.

Firm steps.

I'm in front of Xave, looking him in the eye.

Be convincing.

"You little piece of scum. You'll regret this." I grab his face with bloody fingers, squeeze his cheeks until his lips part, then push him down. Xave topples backward, breaks his fall with one arm. There's hate in his eyes, and I hope it's all part of the act.

"It's good to see the new generation taking charge and fighting for themselves. Very promising," Elliot says, pleased. Gold glints in his gaze and something in their strange color reminds me of the man in the next room, those dark irises outlined by a bright yellow rim. The eyes of an animal, a monster. I look away as I imagine tentacles sprouting from his chest. Bile rises to my throat.

Keep it together.

Elliot heads for the door and right before leaving he adds, "Whatever you do, not on my property." He turns to the meatheads. "Help them get that vermin out of here."

Chapter 18

James drives away from the mansion at a normal speed. I squeeze my eyes together and concentrate on breathing. Once we're a few blocks away, he pulls out a handheld radio from the glove compartment.

He breaks our stunned silence by talking into the receiver. "Location?"

Oso's voice crackles through the small speaker, giving the name of an intersection unknown to me.

"Copy." James puts the radio down.

"I knew it," Blare bursts out. "I knew we shouldn't have taken them. They could have gotten us killed. I don't understand why you would take such a risk. They're snotty kids, for crying out loud, James. They've got no business in this."

James looks straight ahead, drives for a few seconds without responding, then finally says, "This is *everyone's* business."

Blare pulls off her blond wig and throws it down. "Maybe, but risking everything like this just makes no sense."

"I had to see Elliot while he was still in Seattle. The party was my only chance. Also the best opportunity to get Xave and Marci on board. Two birds with one stone. You know time is of the essence."

Blare huffs. If I was her, I'd feel the same way. James's secretiveness and MO isn't reassuring. Xave stares out the window. He hasn't looked at me, not even once.

The sight of my own hands covered in dark, dried blood makes me dizzy. I try to worry about trivial things to take my mind off of it.

Ruined dress.

Ugly scar.

Terrifying answers … like those unearthly, black eyes and probing tentacles whose images will be stamped in my cerebral cortex forever.

The car comes to a stop and I snap out of the mental anguish caused by the automatic movie playing in my head. James ushers me into the van's back seat and slips the ring off my finger. No one notices.

"Oso, first aid," he orders like some sort of general.

Oso hops to it, a regular soldier. He grabs a small metal box from under his seat.

"Where are you hurt?" he asks after a quick glance at all the blood.

I point at my arm and cringe from pain and shame. I cracked. Things went wrong because of me. Blare gets in the van. Xave follows, squeezes into the back, and slides away from me, as far as he can.

"You okay, bro?" Clark asks him.

Xave ignores him, leans his head on the side of the van and closes his eyes. Aydan looks pale and breathes in and out in measured rhythm. Oso's dexterous hands work quickly, cleaning the wound and uncovering the gash.

"How bad is it?" James asks.

"Not bad. A bit of skin glue will hold it together." Oso pulls out a small tube and gets to work. "So … what happened?"

119

he asks as he glues me back together, like a broken toy. "It was all so fast on those tiny cameras, we couldn't make heads nor tails out of any of it. Next time we need sound. We were so jumpy we almost crashed in there to help."

James opens his mouth to explain, but Blare beats him to the punch.

"She freaked!" The words come out accompanied by spit. "That's what happened. You owe me ten bucks, Oso. She didn't bite her tongue like she said. She screamed like a little schoolgirl."

Oso gives her a nasty glare at the mention of the bet. At least he was betting on me. "But nothing came of it, right?" he asks.

James shrugs and looks at Xave.

"It could have," Blare says. "And it still could, if we keep acting like we're running a pre-school. Xave better not show his face around anymore or it's 'game over'—unless we're planning to kill him for real."

"Shut up, Blare!" Aydan bursts out. Everyone jumps, even Blare. Until now, Aydan has seemed the quiet type and—judging by everyone's surprise at his explosive words—this isn't typical behavior.

"So says the one who also freaked," Blare mocks.

Aydan's hands twist on his lap. He answers in a barely subdued tone, like the price of keeping his anger in check is too high. "It affects everyone differently for *different* reasons."

James puts a hand on Aydan's shoulder, a warning not to say more. Aydan stares at the floor, clenching his jaw. But there's no way Blare will ever understand his meaning. She isn't one of us. The horror she experienced can't be anywhere near what I just went through, what Aydan and James must have gone through. It's one thing to see the monster, and quite another to realize that you're *it*.

A whimper escapes me without my permission.

This is what I am: a monster, a real freak of nature.

I want to cry. I want to die, want to bash my skull against the ground and kill the thing that lives in there.

I. Am. A. Monster.

Tears roll down my face and I keep whimpering like a sad puppy.

"She's losing it," Blare says.

"Leave her alone," Xave growls, suddenly alive after I thought he'd died of resentment and hatred. "You've no idea what she just went through."

"Same thing as all of us, jackass," Blare growls back.

"Wow, why don't we just chill it, everyone," Oso says. "We can just—"

"No, not the same thing," Xave interrupts, looking like he's gone from a dying ember to a raging bonfire. "She had to pretend she didn't really know me or care about me. She had to convince those freaks she intended to do away with her best friend. She was brave." Xave looks at me. Our eyes lock, and his gaze shines on me, giving me strength.

"And whose fault is that?" Blare says with an upward twist of her mouth and eyebrow. "That wouldn't have happened if—"

"Just shut up." Xave points a menacing finger at Blare.

"Listen, you—"

"*Enough!*" James shouts.

Blare looks injured, betrayed.

"Blare," James's voice is quieter now, conciliatory. "I don't understand why you're so angry."

She seems to shrink a few inches, looks outside through the windshield.

James rubs his forehead. "We're all in this together. We'll talk about it later. This isn't the best place—"

"Fine," Blare says and moves away from James as his hand approaches her shoulder. She slips into the front passenger seat with a grunt.

Oso shakes his head, then removes his bloody latex gloves. "There you go. Hopefully that won't leave a scar. It wasn't as bad as it looked at first glance. It never is."

The bandages are comfortable. My arm still hurts, but it feels much better. Numb somehow.

"Change the bandage for two or three days. After that you can uncover it. Keep an eye out for swelling or redness. Okay?" Oso wipes a tear off my face. "It'll be all right," he says in a tender voice, too tender for such a big guy like him. "It gets better."

I appreciate his effort to cheer me up, but he doesn't understand. Things might get better for someone like him, but for me they won't. I don't see how I'll ever get over being whatever the hell I am. I've seen what James wanted me to see. I've been a victim of his experiment. Maybe I wouldn't have believed him if he'd just told me what I am, if I hadn't seen it with my own two eyes. But this was cruel.

I wish I'd never agreed to come. I wish I'd been happy with thinking I was crazy.

Chapter 19

I'm in my bed, blinking at the ceiling. My tongue is a cotton ball. When I sit up, a serious headache pounds in my temples.

It's raining outside, a thousand drops tapping at my window. After shutting my eyes for a few seconds, they snap back open. How did I get to my bed? The last thing I remember is sitting in the van, seething, staring at James, telling him with the intensity of my gaze that I needed answers. Real ones. My body quaked with rage and I felt ready to explode, sickened by what he put us through.

Now, I'm in my room and I don't even know how I got here. Was there something in that bottled water he insisted I drink? Anger tightens my chest. I've allowed him to make me a pawn in his cruel game, and now he thinks he can make decisions for me. Even if they involve drugging me and turning me into a monster.

Well, I've had enough.

I go in my small bathroom, determined to take a cold shower. As I undress, I'm surprised when I notice the bandage around my forearm. I'd forgotten about the cut. I make a fist and release it. The pain is gone. Oso said to change the dressing, but I don't have gauze or surgical tape. I look in the medicine cabinet and all I see is a box of SpongeBob Band-Aids. They'll do. In one swift motion, I rip the bandage off.

"Ouch." I stare at the tiny hairs stuck to the white tape, then look at my arm. Wow, the cut looks almost healed. Oso really did a great job patching me up. I wonder where he learned to administer first aid so well? Maybe he's a doctor, like Dad. He always fixed my skinned knees and elbows and—no matter how bad the scrapes, even the time I fell off my scooter and left half my knee smeared on the asphalt—they never left a scar.

Aydan is a programmer for Sylica Rush. Clark is a welder. Oso could very well be a brain surgeon for all I know. I wonder what James and Blare do? Thinking of them reminds me of the wicked pinpricks in my index finger. I examine it. Black blood is crusted around it. It looks nasty. I curse under my breath. Why didn't I ask Oso to dress it, too? The last thing I want is an infection.

I run warm water over my hand, expecting it to sting, but I don't feel anything. I rub the dry blood away to reveal a ring of small white dots wrapping all around my forefinger. I stare at them confused. They're completely healed over which seems impossible after the way those freakin' spikes from hell speared my finger. It certainly hurt more than what these scars lead to believe. I stare at them for another moment, then shrug. I guess self-harm turned me into a wimp. Who knew?

After a quick shower, I use four Band-Aids to cover my wound. It looks silly, but at least I can say I've followed Dr. Oso's directions. I put on skinny jeans and a form-fitting black top, then shuffle out of the bedroom and into the kitchen.

"How do you feel?" Mom asks when I enter. Her eyes are shining.

I frown. "Um, I have a wicked headache." I start digging for acetaminophen in the junk drawer.

"Judging by the state Xavier delivered you in, I'm not surprised." Her tone is preachy. That gets my attention. Since she stopped caring, I've come home in worse conditions than last night. I've had a few wild nights here and there. She can't possibly be pulling the reproachful parent card now, can she?

"Uh, hi," a deep voice says from behind me.

Startled, I look back toward the foyer and drop the bottle of pills. Luke stands there in all his blondness, wiping his hands on frayed jeans.

The pill bottle rolls to his feet and he picks it up. "Here you go."

I snatch it and give Mom a look. I hope it says it all.

Him? Here?

So fast? So wrong!

How? Why?

"Honey, Ma—" Mom catches her mistake. "*Luke* came to talk to us last night. I tried to call, but your phone went straight to voicemail. He had a proposition for us, so I asked him to join us for breakfast, so we could talk."

"A proposition?" I say as if I'm waiting to hear a death sentence instead. I can't deal with this right now. Not after last night.

"Yes. And I think it's wonderful." Mom looks at Luke and beams as she sees herself in his eyes. I look back and forth between the two. Seeing them together is unsettling. He looks like a male version of Mom.

"Why don't you tell her about it?" Mom tells Luke.

"Um, I thought we were just having breakfast." Luke has the look of a snared rabbit. "Maybe you two should discuss it by yourselves." His blue gaze sparkles with innocence, even

125

under the faint light of this rainy morning. His eyes look achingly familiar, the way Mom's used to look all those years ago, the way they do now.

My gaze keeps jumping from one to the other. Mom radiates, hangs on Luke's every word, and I can't help but wonder why she's never beamed this way in my presence. She loved Dad, and I look just like him. His same black hair, brown eyes, tan skin. Why didn't she ever see the sun setting in *my* eyes? Why doesn't she love me the same way?

My heart breaks with a thousand emotions, and my mind reels with just as many questions. I want to understand, but it makes no sense. I want to know if it would have been different if I looked like Luke. If he hadn't been abducted by that man. If Dad hadn't died. If all four of us had been together. If *anything* had been different, would I still be the last one to cross her mind when she wakes up in the morning?

But Luke and I *are* different. So different. And suddenly, it hits me. He's my brother. My twin brother and we look nothing like each other. I look just like Dad and he looks just like Mom.

He's not like me.

There's no droning in my skull.

He's my twin brother and he's nothing like me. Nothing like me!

I'm the only monster in this place, and suddenly it all makes sense. Even if Mom doesn't know what I am, she must sense it. That's why she can't love me. Something in her nature, some deep-buried instinct in her gut prevents her.

Who could love a monster?

I'm gasping for air. They're staring at me as if I'm crazy, as if ... as if ... they know what I am.

"I—I'm not hungry." I turn and leave.

It takes all my strength to walk to my room and gently shut the door, when all I want to do is slam it against their ... *sameness*. I collapse face first on the bed. The pillow chokes my sobs, shoving my pain and disappointment back into my throat.

My pillowcase is soaked in tears and my eyes tired and dry by the time a knock sounds at the door. I sit up, ready to tell Mom to leave me alone, but the face that pokes through the crack is not hers. It's Luke's.

"Is it okay if I come in?" he asks. "You can tell me to go to hell if it's not." He smiles sheepishly.

I bite my lower lip, hesitating for some odd reason. I do want to tell him to go to hell and take his *proposition* with him, but I've never been able to resist Luke, and it's nice to finally know why. I've heard twins always share a sort of connection, even after they go separate ways. I think it's true. It feels true.

He sits on one corner of the bed, occupying a space too tiny for his tall frame.

"I'm sorry," he says in a quiet whisper. "She ..." he points toward the door to indicate Mom, "took me by surprise last night. I thought I'd be the one surprising you guys, but," he raises his eyebrows, "she just overwhelmed me with ..."

He doesn't know what to call it, but I do. The word he's looking for is *joy*.

I straighten. "She's been waiting for you for a long time."

"Yeah," Luke says in a breathy, bewildered sigh. He swallows, shakes his head. "Listen, I understand how hard this must be for you. I never expected her to ... go along with my idea so easily. And not just that, but to take it to a whole new level." He laughs an uncomfortable laugh, stands and paces the room, shaking his head from side to side.

Luke's eyes take in the room: the corner where my dusty computer equipment litters the overcrowded desk; the bare walls from which I ripped the music posters of bands I used to like and the wads of tape left behind. The room is in twilight, windows covered by black curtains. A lone lamp with a dirty t-shirt and a bra hanging from its shade offers the only illumination.

I squirm, feeling exposed and bare like a newborn. Luke clears his throat, looks at the worn rug by the foot of the bed and stuffs his hands in his jean pockets.

"I know this is too much to take in all at once, so I'll leave. You need to talk it over with her and make sure you guys agree. I ... I don't want to get in the way of ..."

"Why don't *we* talk it over? You promised to tell it to me straight, remember?" I say as I start picking up clothes from the floor and shooting them into the dirty bin. I'm trying to look like I don't really care, like it's not a big deal and this part of my life isn't caught in a whirlwind, too.

"I don't think it's ... *my place.*"

We exchange a quick glance, smile at the personal joke. I remember telling him it wasn't my place to mention he was my brother. I was wrong.

"Mom and I don't really ... talk, not since..." I can't finish. The pain of losing Dad resurfaces too easily, like a huge whale starving for air. I inhale. "Really, it'll be better if you tell me about this idea of yours."

I plop on my desk chair and shake the mouse to awaken my cyber haven. The three monitors come to life, adding a bit more light to the room. I turn my back on Luke and pretend to check my email.

"O-kay." He clears his throat. "I told you they don't want me living by myself since I'm only sixteen and all. So,

I thought maybe I could start by spending a few weekends with you guys. You know, to get to know each other and see if there's something there."

My hand rests on the mouse and the cursor blinks, blinks, blinks. "That sounds ... reasonable." Then I want to know. "So, I take it Mom loved the idea and ran with it. How far did she take it?" I think I already know the answer, but I ask anyway. I swivel the chair and face him.

Luke sits on the bed again, his back turned, facing the opposite wall. "She wants me to move in. Right away."

I hate that I can't see his expression. I don't know how he feels about the idea. Hell, I don't know what *I'm* supposed to feel about it. I didn't have time to give it much thought since we last talked about it. This is all happening too fast. My life as I know it is disintegrating like sandcastles in a windstorm. If he moves in it wouldn't just be awkward, it would be yet another aspect of my life becoming unrecognizable.

Suddenly I'm protesting, unable to hide the irritation in my tone. "But that wouldn't work. Where would you sleep? This house's a shoebox." I need control over something. I can't let James, Mom, Luke, turn my whole life over on its head.

My anger echoes against the walls, and its irrational quality slaps me as it bounces back. Luke is graceful enough to ignore it, maybe even understand it. Who knew he could be such a stand-up guy when I always figured him for an ass?

"What if there *was* enough room? How would you feel about it then?" he asks, finally turning to face me.

His calm question takes me by surprise and throws a bucket of ice water on my anger, an anger that I realize is misdirected. It's not Luke's fault. He's the victim here, taken away from his family before his mother even had a chance to hold him in her arms. I was born last, strong and wailing at the top of my lungs. Luke was first and had to be whisked away and put on a respirator. It seems impossible, considering how tall and muscular he is now.

Then that man used his doctor's badge to gain access to the NICU and steal Luke from under everyone's nose. And most ludicrous of all, he raised him as his own, with no one the wiser to the twisted criminal living in our midst.

A criminal. What does Luke think of that? He seems well-adapted—not like someone who was raised in a dark basement, but you never know. Before I can help myself, a question I should keep to myself flies out of my mouth. "What was he like?" I hold his gaze even though I want to crawl under the desk and hide behind my high-performance CPU.

For a moment, he just stares at me, face expressionless, but twitching a bit with the effort of keeping it blank. He looks like someone trying to choose his words very carefully. "He ..." Luke stops, then stands and begins to pace along the bed. "It's hard for me to reconcile the man I know with this ... new person." He rubs the back of his neck. "You may not want to hear this, but he was a good father. We had a good thing going, just the two of us. I had no reason to doubt his stories about a mother who abandoned us shortly after I was born." He huffs bitterly. "But she wasn't even real. No matter how good he was. None of it was real."

My throat burns as if the air between us is charged with fire. With his head bowed low, he reminds me of a lost child, and I wish I hadn't asked him anything. Then he looks up from the floor and gives me a quick sideways glance that makes my body tense. His eyes flick quickly away, like he was just trying to figure out what I thought of his *story*, to see if I was *buying it*. Is he lying? I bite my bottom lip. I dare not ask and can only hope I'm wrong. Who am I to pry? We all have secrets and mine are big enough to rival half the world's.

I steady myself with a deep breath. "I—I'm sorry. I shouldn't have ... Look, about your proposition, maybe you and Mom should decide." I can't think straight anymore.

"I disagree. Don't take this the wrong way, but your opinion matters more to me than anyone else's."

My eyes must betray my surprise. Luke's fair face blushes. His golden lashes fall over his eyes, disguising his embarrassment.

"I've known you since pre-school, Marci. And ever since I first saw you, I've felt this ..." he chooses his next word carefully, "affinity to you."

"*Humph*, and you showed it by being an ass to me half the time?" I cringe at my own comment. He's opening up and this is what I tell him?

Luke chuckles. "What can I say, I'm only human." He puts a hand on his chest and smiles that disarming smile of his.

I straighten my already straight mouse pad and smile a little.

"I know Karen is supposed to be my mom, and how could anyone deny it? It's creepy how alike we look." His eyebrows meet above his nose in a puzzled expression, and I'm glad I'm not the only one who feels this way about their resemblance. "But I don't really know her and she ... makes me uncomfortable. Please don't tell her I said that."

"I won't."

"You, on the other hand, it's like you were always there. Even when you weren't. I know it sounds stupid, but it's like I could ... sense you."

"Yeah," I say in a quick exhale of breath. If he only knew how many times I guessed he was about to walk into the gym, the classroom, the cafeteria. "Must be that twin link people talk about," I offer lamely. I flinch. God, he's being so open, so honest, and I'm so used to giving people scraps, hiding who I really am for fear of being dubbed insane. I wish I could do better by him. But who am I kidding? It'll never get better than this with me. Surely monsters are no more articulate than the mentally imbalanced. Funny how I always thought I was simply crazy—"lock her up, hide the key, bring the electro-shock" kind of crazy—and, now, it turns out it's way worse.

How, with this knowledge, could I ever allow anyone to get close to me? How, when I could end up hurting them, the way that monster at Elliot's was about to hurt that poor woman?

I put a hand on my chest, feeling a strange lump there, fearing my ribcage might split open the second the shadows overtake me.

My hands begin to tingle. I need to get out of here.

Outside.

Rain.

Splashing my face.

I walk to the closet, take out a jacket and slip it on. Luke's eyes follow my every move. Under the bed, I find my ankle boots, zip them up and buckle them securely to my feet.

"Look," I say, pocketing the keys to my motorcycle, "what-ever you and Mom decide is fine by me." I'm trying very hard to keep my voice leveled, uncaring. It's not easy. I can still hear a tremor and a trace of regret in my words. I'd like to get to know my brother, try to have a real family. Maybe he could give us that much. But what else am I supposed to do? I never knew the nightmare I was keeping at bay. And now that I do, I can't risk hurting anyone if it finally manages to overwhelm me. "It's not like it'll affect things all that much. Mom already loves you. You're perfect in her eyes. I'm still the same screw-up. That's not gonna change—"

"Marci." He says my name in a don't-call-yourself-that tone.

"It's fine. Mom and I have never gotten along. I was never … enough for her, especially after Dad died."

A shadow falls over Luke's blue eyes, and I wonder if he's thinking about Ernest Dunn or if he's struggling to reconcile himself to the idea that his real father is also dead.

"Anyway, I have other plans for breakfast. I'm sure you and Mom will get along fine without me." I turn the door knob, knowing I should just walk out without a backward glance, but I can't help it. I look over my shoulder and the expression in Luke's eyes makes it infinitely harder to walk away. It's an expression I'm very familiar with: the perfect picture of someone I've just let down.

What else is new? Welcome to my world.

Chapter 20

Under the light rain, I walk across the street and around the back of Xave's house. I have to tap on the glass three times before he peeks through the curtain and slides the window open. I climb in. He's wearing nothing but flannel pants and a deep frown. His pectoral muscles flex when he shuts the window. I stare, trying to figure out when the scrawny kid I used to know turned into such a sculpted boy. Something strange flutters in my stomach.

He turns to me. His hazel eyes are dark and he looks ten years older. I look away, embarrassed at the untimely stirrings. I stand there, avoiding his gaze for a long time, thinking of his weariness. I wonder if I've changed, too. Whatever innocence was left in Xave is now gone. I can tell.

"That water James gave me had something in it, didn't it?" I ask, reclining against his dresser.

Xave sighs, breaks eye contact, and finds a t-shirt riddled with holes. As he lifts his arms to slip it over his head, the flames of the tattoo on his back ripple and lap his toned muscles.

"Yeah, probably," he answers, facing me. "You feel okay?"

I lower my gaze and shake my head.

Xave walks up to me and—for the second time this week—I find myself in his arms. My head is on his chest. The dampness on my cheek soaks his t-shirt. His hand smooths the hair down my back, and his heart taps a rhythm along with the headache between my temples. Before this week, we hadn't hugged since kindergarten and it feels so good, I wonder why we waited this long. It feels safe. Right. A home in the storm.

His warmth seeps into me. Or is that me? My own body responding to this closeness? My head swims, so I focus on the posters on the wall. There are muscle cars, motorcycles and even an engine block.

God, I'm so glad he's here.

"I think they would've killed you. I'm sorry," I whisper. "It was so hard to ..."

"Shhh, I know. You did what you had to do."

"I bit my tongue. I tried ..." I can't finish. The image of those tentacles reaching for the woman plays in full color before my eyes. "It's a nightmare."

"It's worse," Xave says, resting his cheek on my head. "James explained everything."

I pull away, look into Xave's eyes. "You mean, he told you ..."

"Everything. He has a name for what they are."

"A name?"

"Yes, he calls them *Eklyptors*. He said it was up to you whether you wanted me to explain everything, or whether you wanted to hear it from him."

I walk away and sit on the unmade bed. "Neither. I think I'd rather have some more of that drugged-up water," I joke, desperately trying to hide my panic.

For once James has given me a choice, though it isn't much of one. He's trying to protect me, pretending to know what's best for me. He thinks it's better if I hear this from a friend, but I don't see the difference. Whether a doctor or your own father tells you that you have a brain tumor, it's still a brain tumor.

Slow, deep inhale.

"Rip the Band-Aid off, Xave."

"Okay. Well … the party was crawling with their kind," he begins with a gravity I've never heard in his voice before.

Tell me something I don't know.

"But half of them were just regular people. You might've noticed that all the couples had something in common."

I think back to last night and shiver as the image of that huge hall appears in my mind. The only pattern I noticed had to do with the buzzing in my head, but—since James is keeping secrets from his crew—that's something Xave can't know about. I didn't pick up any other patterns and didn't need to. One was enough to send me into a tailspin.

Using this puzzle as a way to make my mind busy, I think back to all the couples there, then it hits me. "Their age differences," I say.

Xave's mouth quirks in a knowing smile. "I figured you would've noticed. I never did."

"I didn't then, but now that you mention it. So the … Eklyptors were the oldest ones in each couple, right?"

"Yeah." He raises one eyebrow. "How did you know that?"

"Um, you know …" I can hardly tell him I feel their presence in the form of a droning in the back of my head, so I offer the next, most logical explanation. "That man with the … tentacle things." I put a hand on my chest, both to contain the rising bile and to make sure I haven't grown my own set yet.

"Not tentacles. They're something else," Xave says with a shiver.

I imagine those hairy appendages with their bony, sharp ends. My hand makes a fist against my stomach.

Swallow. Hard.

So glad I didn't have any breakfast.

"What are they, then?" I ask, not really wishing to know. "What do they do? And why is the age relevant?" I squeeze my eyes and tell myself to be strong.

"Um, maybe let's start from the beginning, with Elliot." Xave sits beside me and rubs nervous hands on his flannel pajamas.

Elliot. Yes, I guess it all begins with him. "Why does he let them use his house? Is he one of them?" I ask, knowing the answer full well.

"Do you have to ask that?" Xave shakes his head. "He's a creep. James says he holds those parties often. Yeah, he's one of them all right."

"And what exactly is that? What they are?"

"No one's sure, but James says Eklyptors have been with us for a long time. They could be another species that has been evolving for millions of years into what they are, just like we have. Or they could be aliens brought in a spaceship. Or demon spawn."

I choke at the words.

"You sure you're okay?" Xave rubs my back. "We don't have to—"

"No. Go ahead. I need to hear this."

"Okay, so that dude we saw. Underneath it all, he's basically human, but he's been taken over by an Eklyptor. James said that as soon as they're in you, they start learning your patterns and within days they can be in control of *everything* you do. Your speech, your movements, your whole body."

My lungs are paralyzed.

Patterns.

137

I have none.

Xave continues. "You know how people say we only use a fraction of our brain power?"

I nod.

"Well, Eklyptors can tap into all of it. And with the extra brain power, they gain higher control over body functions, down to the atomic level. That's how they're able to change the appearance of their host. Like that freak and the scales on his back and those fucked-up eyes. They can do what-ever they want. Some grow cat eyes, so they can see in the night. Others grow fangs and have poisonous bites. That dude started growing scales just for the heck of it, just … just to look different.

"James said some of them live hidden away, because they don't even look human anymore. But the process takes time. They can't just change overnight. That's why at the party the Eklyptors were the older ones in each couple, 'cause it takes them a long time to transform themselves and to grow *those* things. You remember how that guy's back looked half-finished?"

I remember all too well.

"Well, he's in the process of … transmuting. That's how James put it, anyway. So growing those tentacle things took him *years*. But it's their most important transformation, because of what they do with them."

My need to scream is strong, but I clench my fists and armor myself.

Xave's Adam's apple moves up and down and he runs a hand across tense lips. "Those things are their … birth canals."

At his words, my stomach roils. I cover my mouth with both hands, making gagging sounds, and manage to keep from vomiting.

Xave presses forward. "They drive those fang-looking things into your spine, like a lumbar puncture, then they inject …" He trails off and swallows audibly.

"A—an egg?" I dare ask.

"No. It's not an egg. It's some sort of adult parasite."

I shoot up to my feet, electrified. "Wait a minute, a parasite? So there could be a cure, a vaccine maybe?"

"Uh, James didn't mention anything like that, but I guess."

A bit of hope returns. There is something in my brain, something that—ever since I can remember—has been trying to replace me. But it's something separate. It doesn't belong there. It could be taken out and killed. I could really be cured.

Cured!

Unaware of my inner revelation, Xave goes on. "Marci, the damn things go up through the spinal fluid and into your brain." Xave's gone pale and finishes in a broken voice. "Then—in a matter of days—they take over and become you. James says we don't stand a chance against them once they're inside."

I frown. This last part is a lie. Why would James say that? I've had one of them inside me for sixteen years. Or at least eleven. I was five the first time I became aware that something was wrong with me. I remember that day as if it was yesterday. It was my fifth birthday, the first one where I had a real party, a princess party with tiaras, pink tutus and all the girls from my kindergarten class.

We were playing "pin the scepter on the queen." Mom blindfolded me and, after only a few steps, shadows seemed to crawl up my eyes and into my brain. I started screaming, pulling at my hair, cursing with words I'd only heard grown-ups say. Dad scooped me up in his arms, tore the blindfold from my face and asked what was wrong.

When I saw all those pink tutus running away, ushered by their mothers, I lost it. I started crying, gasping for air. Dad stuck his face in front of mine. He steadied me with his eyes and calm, reassuring words.

"Breathe, breathe, breathe," he repeated over and over again. And as I did what he said, I noticed shadows all around me, trying to strip my mind of every conscious thought I was able to conjure.

I was so angry at them for ruining my party. For the spectacle they made of me. For the fear and repulsion in the retreating eyes of all those little girls and their mothers. I had to fight back, so I did. With all the fury of a betrayed five-year-old, with all the love and concern brimming in my father's eyes and the hurt and embarrassment twisting my mother's face, I fought and won. From then on, I remembered each battle I waged not to lose myself.

Dad stood by me more than once, aware of my affliction. He hid it from Mom most times. I don't know why—maybe because he didn't want to worry her. I didn't care. I was just glad I didn't have to face her shame. Dad was trying to figure out what caused it when that freak car accident took him away. Since then, all I can remember are all the times when I had to fight alone.

I worry at a hole in my jeans, lost in my memories and what they could mean. It's true that sometimes I've felt possessed by a foreign entity, by shadows. But mostly, I thought that whatever was wrong with me was genetic. I figured I'd been crazy since I was born and that all it took to unleash it was a hideous princess-themed party. Now it turns out I was infected.

But how? When?

Who?!

Who would do that to a little girl?

Xave stands and paces the room. "James said the hosts have to be young to give the Eklyptors time to grow the tentacles to reproduce. No one knows exactly how many people have been infected, but it's no small number. Most of them look like normal people, just … walking around." He's getting agitated, his words shooting at a rapid rate. "Others are like that man, they've been in their hosts long enough to change them, to grow the tentacles, so they can multiply.

"Then they change their appearance because they think humans are boring and useless. They hate us and want to take over the world. How crazy is that? They think we're weak and don't deserve our *elevated* status on Earth, 'cause we don't even know how to exploit all the things our bodies and minds can do."

Xave's eyes are full of a combination of fear and anger.

"They're everywhere, all over the world." He shakes his head. "And few people know they exist. James has been recruiting here and in a few other cities, but he says it may already be too late. Marci, he says he thinks senators, congressmen and even the president may be infected. They have leaders, too. That Elliot guy is one of them. According to James, he's been infected for a long time. Apparently, he has people here and in Europe, all working to increase their numbers."

Xave slumps on the bed again, arms drooping, back curved. His energy seems spent and his crumpled shape makes me want to scream in rage. I kneel on the floor in front of him, put a hand on his knee. He slides to the floor and takes me in his arms. I take in his scent, so familiar and yet so new. I allow my hands to wrap around his neck and rest my head on his shoulder. The tip of my nose grazes his neck.

"What are we gonna do?" he asks.

I pull away, clear my thoughts. There's only one thing I know to do, only one thing that's kept me free all this time. "We have to fight, Xave. We have to fight."

Chapter 21

Lake View Cemetery is a peculiar place for a meeting. Before coming, I had to read James's text message several times to make sure I understood correctly. Now I stand by the virgin statue he gave me as a marker, wondering if I got it right. It's Monday, right after school. The place is eerie, cold and empty. Only the rustle of leaves teased by a light wind disturbs the silence, along with the cawing crows that stand starkly on white tombstones.

Standing here, I'm reminded of Dad and the fact that I haven't visited his grave in a long time. My heart shrivels just at the thought of his name engraved on cold stone, of pounds of dirt covering a body that wasn't done living.

A black BMW with tinted windows pulls up by the curve behind my Kawasaki. The window rolls down and James gestures for me to get in the car. I climb into the passenger seat and shut the door. James is wearing a coat and tie. I'm taken aback by how different he looks and I realize this is the first time I've seen him in daylight. Fine laugh-lines surround his eyes, which are a lighter shade of gray than I'd previously thought.

"Hello, Marci," he says as he presses the button to roll his window shut.

"What happened to you?" I ask, looking him up and down.

James shrugs. "This is me when I'm not trying to save the world." He gives me a sad smile.

"What are you? Like a CEO or something?" I ask as I examine the car's fancy interior and decked-out navigation system.

"Yeah, something like that. How are you holding up?"

"Fine," I lie.

An unamused chuckle sounds in the back of his throat. "You're a bad liar."

"It must take a good one to know a bad one. Why did you lie to Xave? Why did you tell him we don't stand a chance once we've been infected?"

"Because I can count with one hand the ones I've encountered who are like you and me. Most people succumb to Eklyptors within days. A few are able to fight for a short period of time, but never for long. It takes a very strong will to resist for as long as you have, Marci." James shifts the idling car into gear. "I know you must have a million questions. Let's take a ride. I have something to show you."

"Where are we going?"

James slips on a pair of sunglasses. "You'll see soon. In the meantime, you can ask me whatever you want. Xave knows most of it, but there's a pressing question I'm sure you're itching to ask."

"Why do you lie to the crew?"

"Do you really need to ask that?"

I look out the window, notice we're headed downtown, and try to pretend I don't know what he means.

"Okay, I'll answer. I lie because if they knew what I am, they would never trust me." James's voice is low, sobering. "And that's not an option. I need them to trust me. *They* need to trust me. The knowledge I have is invaluable to our fight." He laughs with no real amusement. "They can't afford to doubt me, fear me, hate me, because, believe me Marci, that's exactly what they would do if they knew what I am. What you are."

"So Clark, Blare, and Oso know nothing about you and Aydan?"

"That is correct."

"And they don't suspect?"

"Not to my knowledge."

To our right, we pass the Space Needle. Tourists snap pictures. A group of Goth kids hang in one corner, laughing and pushing each other in jest.

As I watch, I think about James's words. It seems impossible for no one to suspect.

"How?" I ask. "That party was full of them. You and Blare went in together. How can she not suspect?"

"I think you know the answer to that, too," James says, as we wait at a busy intersection on Broad Street.

I think out loud. "Xave said *most* couples." Then it clicks. "Blare and the others think that some of the couples are made up of two regular people. They have no way of knowing." Their heads don't drum in the presence of Eklyptors.

James nods.

"How do you explain Blare? Shouldn't Elliot be suspicious she's not one of them yet? He'd met her before, right?"

"You notice everything, don't you?" James laughs. "Elliot thinks Blare is … my pet. Many Eklyptors keep humans as such. The way you might keep a dog. It's cruel, really."

"Bastards," I mumble. I have so many questions there's barely time for me to be shocked about any of it, so I move on. "How do you know Elliot?"

145

"Because I made it my objective to meet him. He's one of the Eklyptors' most powerful leaders."

"Yeah, Xave said that. I didn't realize they were so organized."

"They have been, for a long time, now."

"How long?" I ask.

"It's hard to tell, but with certainty since the seventies when they came up with creative ways to infect more people, faster."

"What ways?" My hands are shaking and I'm not sure I want to hear anymore.

Deep.

Smells like teen spirit.

Breathe deep.

James offers me a concerned look. "Are you all right?"

I roll my neck from side to side.

"Relax," James says in his gravelly voice.

"I'm fine."

"Tell me something, Marci, when was the first time the fog came over you?" James asks with interest.

"The fog? Oh, you mean the …" I tap my forehead. "I think of them as shadows."

"Most happen to associate them with shadows, actually. But I started thinking of their presence as a sort of fog and old habits die hard."

I tell him the story about my fifth birthday. He listens with care. Then asks me if I know who may have infected me. I tell him I suspect an old babysitter. He recommends I check into it and let him know what I find out.

"What about you?" I ask.

"I have no idea. We're here," he announces, turning in a parking deck next to a tall building. I look out the window in hopes of spotting a name on the front entrance. There isn't one. I recognize the Fourth and Madison Building nearby, but I've never really noticed this place. It's inconspicuous.

A light, humid breeze blows from Puget Sound. It's a beautiful afternoon with the sun setting in the west in a burst of color. We don't have many days like this in the year.

After flashing a card on a reader, we are allowed entrance to the parking deck. James takes a left and heads toward the underground levels. We descend, going round and round. I notice there are fewer cars in each level the further we go.

We arrive at another barrier and James flashes a second card. Then he drives around the corner and we find ourselves in front of a large metal door. This time, he places the palm of his hand on a small screen.

"Welcome, Mr. McCray," a computerized female voice says, as the metal door lifts open, revealing a parking lot with spaces for ten or so cars. All are empty except for one, which is occupied by a silver Porsche.

"Nice car," I say.

James smiles. "You can take it for a ride any time you want."

"Really?"

"Yeah, really."

"Cool," I say, but my tone reveals a certain lack of enthusiasm.

What is wrong with me? I've just been offered a ride in a Porsche and I'm not excited about it. I must be dying a bit every day and, today, I'll just die a little more.

Chapter 22

As we exit the car, I follow James, paying close attention to my surroundings. Bright lights shine overhead, revealing the most pristine parking area I've ever seen. There are no oil marks on the ground and no smoke stains or grime on the walls. Everything looks as if it's just been scrubbed with a toothbrush. There are cameras in every corner. The Porsche license plate reads "IgNiTe."

When we reach the elevator at the far end, James presses his thumb to a small pad and gets a face scan.

"Mr. McCray," says the computerized voice, "it looks like you have a visitor today."

"I do. Her name is Marcela Guerrero."

I'm staring, dumbfounded by all the high-tech security measures. Impossibly the questions inside my head multiply. In the end, they all boil down to one: who in the world is James McCray?

"Would you mind stepping up to the scanner, Marci?" James asks.

I hesitate. "Um …"

"It's the only way you'll be allowed entry, if you come by yourself later," he explains, eyebrows raised. "You don't have to, if it makes you uncomfortable. But think about it this way, *I* trust you enough to bring you here."

"Honestly, James. I don't even know what this place is, or who you are. So forgive me if I'd rather not leave any identifying information behind."

Besides, what makes him think he can trust me? He really doesn't know much about me. How can he be sure I'm not a ... real Eklyptor? I'm about to ask him when he gives me a wry smile.

James chuckles as he rubs his thumb and forefinger together. "You already gave me some. Fingerprints in the car. Blood on the spiked ring. But no worries, you'll change your mind later."

I feel like an idiot, but I stubbornly stand my ground. His cocky certainty rubs me the wrong way.

James talks into the small microphone. "Allow guest entry."

"Access allowed," the computer voice says.

The elevator door slides open. Inside, the panel has only three buttons. Two to either open or close the doors, and one that reads "Alarm." The door slides shut and the elevator starts moving on its own. A downward arrow appears in a small rectangular screen. We're already three floors below ground level and we're going further down? I run a hand across my forehead, feeling claustrophobic.

"Some place you have here," I say, trying to appear calm.

"You've seen nothing yet," James says with a wink. I'm taken aback by this light mood. The menacing aura I've associated with him since I first met him is replaced by a natural confidence. He loosens his silky blue tie and removes his jacket. His chest rises and falls with ease. There's no visible tension across his shoulders. He's relaxed. It helps *me* relax a little too.

"So who are you? What do you do?" I ask.

"I own this building, and the business that operates here."

Wow, that has to mean he has serious money.

After what feels like many, many floors, the elevator dings and the doors slide open. We step out into a narrow hall fronted by a glass wall. James walks up to it. I follow hesitantly and stop after two short steps. I look to the sides. To the right, there's a dead end. To the left, the top of a staircase leading downward.

"What do you think?" James asks, looking beyond the glass wall.

I join him and follow his gaze. My jaw falls open at the sight of the place. We are overlooking a large, open area, as big as two basketball courts. Below, the rectangular floor plan is surrounded by white walls and divided by clear partitions into four quadrants. Everything looks pristine, even under the halogen hanging lights.

In the top left quadrant, there is an assortment of laboratory and medical equipment. A redhead sits on a stool, her eyes pressed against the viewer of huge microscope. Under that quadrant, computer equipment fills the space. Racks with servers in every slot, cables, laptops, handheld devices, motherboards and more. My mouth waters. A dark-haired man, wearing what looks like a lab coat, is working in front of six computer monitors, analyzing graphs and a vast array of images I can't quite make out from here.

In the top right quadrant, a young woman in gray coveralls stoops over a small engine. A motorcycle sits propped on a stand, gutted like a fish in Pike Place Market. Next to it, the van we drove to the party rests atop a hydraulic lift. The rest of the area is occupied by spare tires, massive red and yellow toolboxes, motor-oil containers, everything a regular auto-repair shop could need. I look around, trying to figure out how they got the van down there, then notice a massive metal door in the far corner.

The last quadrant on the bottom is a gym, outfitted with all kinds of workout equipment: mats, benches, free weights, knotted ropes that hang from the ceiling, medicine balls, treadmills, elliptical machines, all brand-new and expensive looking. No one is in that area.

"So? Do you like it?" James asks.

My eyes return to the man with all the monitors. "I'm … wow … it's very impressive, especially the computer area."

"We call the entire area 'The Tank.' Those four sections down there are the fish pods. So that would be the computer pod." He laughs. "Rheema's idea to call them that," he adds, pointing to the girl in the "auto-repair pod" or whatever it is. "She says she feels like a stupid goldfish when someone watches from up here."

At that moment, the redhead comes away from the microscope and notices us. She waves and says "Hi." The faint sound of her greeting reaches us. The young girl and the man at the computer turn from their work and look up, too.

"Is that Aydan?" I ask, surprised.

"Mm-hmm."

"I thought you said he worked for—"

"He used to, until he joined the crew. Sylica Rush is his cover story, now."

Aydan dismisses us and turns back to his computers. Nice to see you, too. What a jackass!

"So the others don't know about this place?" I ask, wondering how many more secrets James is keeping from everyone and fearing the ones he's keeping from me.

"That's correct. What goes on here is too important to risk telling too many people."

"You're telling *me*, and you barely know me," I challenge.

"I know all I need to know about you, Marci. Everyone here is like us. Everyone here wants to find a cure."

"A cure?" My heart does a weird flip and my voice holds the hope of a thousand condemned death-row inmates. There's nothing I want more.

"Yes, a cure. It's not an easy task and it won't happen any time soon. But we're doing everything we can." James gives me a tight-eyed glance, one that says "don't get your hopes too high."

Something breaks inside of me. *It won't happen any time soon.* The words ring in my ears, breaking my hope, smashing it into fine dust.

"Don't look so sad, Marci. Everyone wants a cure. But you'll come to terms with the fact that it may not come soon enough for our benefit."

What is he? Nuts? Who could ever come to terms with that?

"C'mon, let's go down there." James ushers me toward the staircase and we descend. At the bottom of the steps he takes a right. I stop, take a deep breath and try to push my disappointment aside. Looking around, my eyes focus on a dimly lit corridor to my left.

"Are you coming?" James asks.

My head snaps back. I squint at the bright lights. "What's that way?"

"Sleeping quarters," he says. "Everyone's been burning the midnight oil for the past year or so. This is a big place. There's more. Hospital wing, kitchen, conference rooms. I'll show you around later. Follow me."

As I turn and face the large open space to my right, I'm overwhelmed by the sight once more. I face clear cubicle partitions. Through them, I can see all the way to the opposite wall. The openness and the lack of privacy are a bit unsettling.

For the first time, I notice oil paintings hanging on the outer wall. Their frames are gilded, their images glossy and depicting landscapes, portraits, flowers and vegetables. Really? How weird! They look entirely out of place inside the modern space.

"They're part of my collection," James says when he notices me watching. "I have a weakness for classic art." He should be embarrassed—instead he looks proud.

Whatever.

He turns and walks toward the lab pod. I follow and try not to stare at the redhead as we make our way toward her.

"Hi, Kristen," he says.

Kristen turns her stool toward us and gives James a huge smile. He beams back at her. I stare at the polished wood floor and pretend not to notice their over-happy greeting.

"I brought you someone," James tells her. "Marci, this is Kristen Albright. Kristen, Marci Guerrero."

She rolls my way on her stool, right hand outstretched. "Nice to meet you."

As we exchange a firm handshake, her light green eyes take me in. My head buzzes and our chests rise and fall in unison as we take deep, calming breaths. We exchange a knowing smile.

"Kristen has been doing a lot of research," James says. "She's trying to understand how Eklyptors take residence in the human brain, and also what makes it possible for people like us to resist them. She's a biologist and a medical doctor. A very smart lady."

Kristen pushes stringy bangs away from her green eyes. Her hair is a sharp shade of red in a pixie style that screams

153

high-end salon. Her slender, delicate features are not beautiful, but her face is pretty enough, made more so by a certain confident air, much like James's.

"Are we immune somehow?" I ask, immediately interested in Kristen's research and what it could mean for the discovery of a cure.

"I wish I could say we are," she says. "That would make my life a lot easier, because then I could find a vaccine, like those for polio or tetanus. But no. We're not immune."

"Yeah, I guess not. That was a stupid question, given we're under constant assault."

Kristen nods. "Yes, sadly, we *are* infected. But there's something that allows us to fight back, to control instead of being controlled. I'm trying desperately to understand what that is."

"Control?" I ask, looking from Kristen to James. I feel anything but in control.

"Yes, control," James confirms. "Believe it or not, even if you feel under constant threat and barely able to keep your agent at bay, you've learned to control it and take advantage of it."

"Agent?" I echo.

Kristen explains. "That's what we call the organism that lives in our brains—much like a virus is called an infectious agent. They're not exactly viruses, though. They're far more complex, like a combination of a parasitic *and* viral infection. They're unlike anything known to us."

"What do you mean I've learned to take advantage of it? You're kidding, right? I'm the only one being taken advantage of here," I say, bewildered.

"You're wrong," James says. "Take your elevated IQ, for instance."

"What?" I shake my head in disbelief at the implication.

"Or your mastery of martial arts and the tremendous agility it requires. Oh, don't look so surprised. Xave brags about you all the time." James chuckles and sits on a stool.

I ignore the tidbit about Xave bragging. I'd like to hold on to that piece of information and imagine what it could mean, but, instead, I find myself livid about the first part of James's spiel. He's got to be pulling my leg.

"What are you saying exactly? That without this thing inside my head I would be retarded and clumsy?" My voice is strained, barely disguising my outrage.

"No, I'm saying you would be *average*," James says.

"Is this your idea of a joke?"

James shakes his head. "No. I have no doubt you've learned to take advantage of your agent's positive qualities."

"Positive qualities? There's nothing positive about this." I tap my head with one finger. "There's a parasite living in my freakin' head! I'd rather be average, if what you're saying is true. I'd like for my only concern to be whether to wear lipstick or lip-gloss."

Kristen watches our exchange with a combination of amusement and sympathy.

"You don't really mean that." A simple statement from James.

I try to protest, to deny his words, but I can't. I don't want to be average. Still, I refuse to believe the agent plays any part in who I am, in what makes me Marcela Victoria Guerrero.

"I understand how you feel at the moment," James adds. "I see that—for you to believe everything—it'll take even more proof than I've already given you. Remember I said you were special? Well, this is the reason. It's why I brought you to Elliot's house. So you could see with your own eyes what it is you're keeping under control. So you could understand how strong you are. That risk is minor if I can recruit more people like you. You'll come to grips with it soon and you'll also come to appreciate the meaning of the word *symbiotic*."

"I don't think so." My teeth are a cage, making my words a hiss.

"Then let's agree to disagree ... for now."

He's wrong. He has to be wrong.

"I believe a little bit of training might be in order, James," Kristen says, watching me from under raised eyebrows.

"Yes, it'll help her see clearer," he says.

I clear my throat. "Listen, I'm tired of you making all these choices for me. I'm not a puppet." I keep my voice level as I say this.

"Of course not, Marci. I'm sorry if that's the impression I've given you. I was hoping you'd be my pupil." His eyes are full of understanding and patience as he says the words.

Suddenly I feel like a brat.

"But I realize that for things to work, I need your trust. And that's why you're here. That's why I'm showing you all of this." James's eyes make a wide circle around the place.

Great, now I'm embarrassed by his apology and the fact that he's not pointing out what a brat I am.

"What goes on in this place is a secret to everyone, except the few you see working in here. I brought you because I know you're ready to join our tight circle, because there are so very few like us. You've been looking for answers, and I can offer some. I can help you make the most out of your situation. You're hiding the truth and fighting alone." He pauses, leaves the stool and looks me in the eye. "I stand— here and now—to let you know that you don't have to do that anymore. You don't have to do it alone. You can fight with us."

There's a knot in my throat and my eyes burn as if some-one's put lemon juice in them. I swallow, hold James's gaze, bravely. He smiles, puts a hand on my shoulder.

"You're courageous. You will find it's refreshing working with … like-minded individuals." He chuckles.

I nod once, an acceptance to his offer to join him.

"I have so much more to share with you, but there never seems to be enough time." He sighs. "But we'll get there. Patience is key." James removes his hand from my shoulder. His voice grows serious, his face stern. "Do I have your trust?" he asks. "I will require it. Unconditionally."

The fear that this may be a mistake gnaws at my bones. I'm at a clear disadvantage. James holds all the cards, and I have little to offer. But I've got no one else to turn to. It's not easy to relinquish my independence and put my trust in someone. It never has been. Still, I nod again.

"Great!" he says. "Kristen will require your cooperation, now. I have things to discuss with Aydan. Expect an email tomorrow with details on your training." James takes a step back, looks at Kristen in an intimate way. Something passes between them that I can't understand. The air is loaded with their silent exchange. I feel like a third-wheel and fidget until James whirls and walks away.

Kristen gives me an appraising look. I feel like a piece of paper inside a scanner. Without the weight of their word-less conversation, however, I can stand taller. I examine her in turn. Her serious expression changes in a split second. A huge smile parts her lips, revealing a set of teeth worthy of a toothpaste commercial.

"I like you, Marci." Her grin grows impossibly wider.

I feel like she's making fun of me, though she seems genuine.

157

"But …" she adds, her smile shrinking a bit, "you're going to have to lighten up a bit. It's not like you have terminal cancer. Look on the bright side."

"Seriously?" If she grew a second nose right now, it wouldn't seem any weirder than her comment. "We've got real-life monsters walking around. Excuse me if I don't see the bright side of that."

She shrugs. "We, humans, have grown used to being on top without being challenged. Now we have to prove that we really deserve it. Only good things come out of a little competition."

"This is not economics, lady. This is live or die."

"Yeah, and it makes the former more fun for me. Don't you like a little challenge every once in a while? And by the way, you can call me Kristen."

"All right, *Kristen*. Well, I do enjoy a good challenge, but I'm not suicidal."

Kristen laughs, a hearty chuckle that borders on being contagious. I work on deepening my frown.

"Ready for some more tests?" she asks when her laughter finally dies down.

"More tests?"

"Yes, I tested the blood on the ring already. Made sure you aren't a full-fledged Eklyptor." She winks.

"Oh," I say lamely. I don't like the sneaky way James got my blood, but I guess I can't really blame him. He had to make sure before bringing me here. "You mean there's a test?"

"It's not conclusive, but most Eklyptors have elevated levels of melatonin and hCG. It depends on how long they've been infected. It's part of my research. Maybe it'll lead somewhere."

I can do nothing else but nod. I have an idea of what melatonin and hCG are, but science has never been my forte.

"So, ready for more?" she asks again.

"Okay."

"First, I need some more blood. Then we'll do a CT scan and a few other things," she says with another friendly wink. I walk behind her as she leads the way.

A crooked grin shapes my lips of its own accord. Maybe I'll come to like Kristen, after all.

Chapter 23

I toss and turn in my bed, unable to stop thinking about my conversation with James this afternoon. Sitting up, I click on the lamp in an attempt to shake all the questions that are keeping me from sleep. There's a particular one that flashes in front of my eyes more than any other.

Who infected me?

Pressing tight fists against my eyes, I mull the question over in spite of my effort not to. My first recollection of the shadows is from my birthday party, so it's logical to think that I was infected before I turned five and started kindergarten.

Could Mrs. Contreras be responsible? Dad used to drop me off at her house every day. She babysat several kids in her house, and I was one of them for over a year. She threatened to wash my mouth with soap if I talked back. She gave me nightmares in which my mouth filled with thick suds, while she watched, laughing, her eyes glowing like embers.

Could she have infected me? The threat to wash my mouth and the nightmares seem silly now, but she's the only person that comes to mind. I press my temples and shake my head. It's ridiculous. Mrs. Contreras was just an overwhelmed woman, trying to scare us into behaving properly in an attempt to keep her sanity.

I throw myself on the bed and pull the covers over my head. I need to sleep or I'm going to lose my mind. When sleep finally takes me, I dream of my mouth foaming with soap.

"Someone sent you a hate text?"

I look up from my phone to find Luke. "Hey," I say, slipping my phone into my front pocket. I've been frowning at it all day, waiting for an email from James. After a full battery of tests with Kristen yesterday, I haven't heard back from them. It made school a complete drag today.

The late afternoon sun shines behind Luke. I squint, watch him radiate like a fallen angel. He's so handsome it hurts to look at him. At the thought, my stomach shrivels to the size of a prune. I recognize the queasy feeling. It's the same one I used to get before I knew he was my brother and thoughts like this entered my mind. It seems, deep down inside, I always understood we shared the same blood.

"Missed you during breakfast Sunday," Luke says, sitting next to me on the last wooden step of my front porch. Or should I say *our* front porch? I've no idea what Mom and he decided to do, but it isn't hard to guess.

"I had somewhere to go."

"I think you're just ... avoiding us," Luke says bluntly, looking me straight in the eye. This new Luke is really throwing me off. I think I'm starting to like the snide, smart-aleck version better.

Okay, let me try irony with a dash of sarcasm. "Of course not. I love nothing more than to start my day with a heart-warming family breakfast."

161

He frowns. "I don't understand you, Marci. At the funeral home and that day we talked by the park, you seemed so different. I thought you wanted to give this ... family thing a try, but I guess I was wrong."

I did, but then I found out there's a sentient parasite stuffed in my brain. Thank you very much. Out of the corner of my eye, I watch his chin drop to his chest.

"I'm not trying to become a wedge between you and your mother. I just wish I could understand you better," he says.

"Look, I have nothing against you, Luke ..."

"But?"

"It won't work. I have nothing to offer. I'm not ... sister material."

"Oh, great!" he exclaims, throwing his hands up in the air.

Surprised, I stare at him from under a frown.

"The 'it's not you it's me' speech." He huffs and slaps his hands back down on jean-clad thighs.

I bite my tongue. Nothing I can say will fix things. This is the best I can do and—whether he believes me or not—it's the truth.

"So you really don't care what we do? Whatever we decide is fine with you?"

"Yeah," I say with a shrug.

"In that case," he says with finality as he stands and dusts his butt, "you won't mind the fact that we're moving." With that, Luke walks off.

"Moving?!" I scream.

To say I'm angry is to call a python an earthworm. My fists are clenched, my face is a smoldering ember, my heart a lump of betrayal.

Mom looks up from her fashion magazine, her expression as impassive as a surgeon's at the sight of a paper cut.

"Finally," she says, "an acceptable display of emotion."

I ignore the comment. I'm not a fish and do not take bait.

"I'm not moving!" I yell and cross my arms over my chest. I've never been even mildly stubborn. On this I will be dogged.

I. Am. Not. Moving.

I will not leave the place in which I saw Dad for the last time. I will not leave the home he gave me, even if now I only live off the memories of what a real home should be.

"Why am I not surprised?" she asks, setting her magazine on the coffee table.

Again, I'm not taking that bait.

"I can't believe you would consider leaving Dad's house." She isn't disturbed by this comment in the least. Her eyes are too full of Luke to dampen with sentimentalism. "I'm not moving." I repeat, this time without screaming, which strangely carries the ring of my determination way better than the high-decibel version.

"We will buy a bigger house that accommodates all of us. End of story. If you had bothered to join us, we could have listened to *your* suggestions." Something in the set of Mom's mouth insinuates it might be too late to hear my ideas now. Fine. I don't care.

"I have none," I say. "All I came in to say is that I'm not going anywhere." I spin on my heels and head out.

"Oh no, you don't," Mom says, stomping in my direction. Some of the old furniture rattles with her every step. "You don't get to ruin this for me." She stops in front of me, the true spark of indignation flickering in the golden specks of her eyes.

We stare at each other. The words she's not saying form an insurmountable wall between us. I've always known the barrier was there, I just never knew it was a hundred feet tall and just as thick. I'm ready to add a hundred more.

"Say it, Mom. Get it all out. Tell me how I was never the daughter you wanted. How my clothes were never pink enough. How a trip to the nail parlor should be *my* idea of fun. How my *epileptic* attacks ruined your life."

She flinches imperceptibly. So subtly that I'm not sure she actually did. I guess the truth leaves no room for surprises. She looks no more taken aback than if I told her one plus one is two.

"Get it in your head," I continue. "I'm staying right here. The house is mine."

Her eyes turn the size of jeep tires.

I take in her surprise and feel even more betrayed. I harden my expression, resolved not to show how much this hurts. She was working on the assumption I didn't know the house was mine. She was willing to omit that piece of information to get her way.

"What?" I ask. "You think I didn't know that?"

Dad told me a long time ago that he'd named me the house's sole owner in his testament. Maybe he was worried Mom might remarry if he died. Maybe he was even worried about what would happen to me if he wasn't here to protect me. Or perhaps he simply wanted to keep a tradition. The house has been in the Guerrero family for two generations, since my grandfather moved to the States from Chile. I'm not about to sell a piece of what little heritage I've got left.

"I could fight you in court," she says, her voice wavering with doubt.

My brain is spinning, as if her cruel words have actually slapped me on the side of the head. My eyes sting. I make sure not to blink. I won't give her the satisfaction of my tears.

My eyes are dry. A barren desert.

"Even if it's possible, I wouldn't risk it if I were you. Luke …" I waver, trying to decide whether I should stoop as low as she has, whether I should tell her he cares more about my opinion than hers. It takes a lot to hold back, and when I do, I do it for Luke's sake, not hers. "Luke might not like this side of you. The side that would take her own daughter to court. Not a very pleasant one."

Mom deflates as if I've pricked her with a needle. The same slack disappointment I'm used to seeing returns to her face. Once more I'm the bane of her existence. Her disillusionment. Her biggest letdown. Great! She's gone from a mega coaster of emotions to her run-of-the-mill, flat highway. Again.

Chapter 24

The rumbling sound of my bike's engine echoes within the confines of the parking deck. I flash my card in front of the reader and the barrier lifts. The hand scan works, too, as does the facial scan and voice recognition. I feel oddly relieved and concerned at the same time. Relieved because I was allowed entry. Concerned because, after all the biological data Kristen took, she could probably clone me.

I ride the elevator and when I step out, James is waiting for me. He's wearing a pair of black slacks and shirtsleeves.

As we walk downstairs, he asks, "Ready to start?"

"I guess." I've no idea what this training requires. As always, James is keeping me in the dark.

"It's difficult work, but I think you'll do just fine," he says, as we reach the bottom of the stairs.

James leads me toward the area with all the gym equipment, and as we pass by the glass cubicles I wave at Kristen and ignore Aydan. He needs a taste of his own medicine. Rheema, who I met last time, has her hands inside a huge engine block. She pulls one out and waves greasy fingers our way.

"Hey there, Marci." Her smile is friendly, but again it makes me pause and look closer. There's something strange about her teeth. Her canines are narrow and pointed, with gaps at their sides. Weird.

"Hi, Rheema," I say.

She blows a lock of straight, dirty blond hair off her face. "Good luck on your first day."

"Thank you." I turn to James, starting to feel tense. An admonition from James and good luck wishes from Rheema can't be good. "So, what are we doing today?"

"Let me see." He rubs his chin.

We step into the gym pod. Like the rest of The Tank, this area has clear walls, and I can see everyone else at work. Worse yet, they can see me. James sits on a workout bench, still thinking.

"Why are there no real walls in this place?"

James looks up. "Is the reason so hard to imagine? You notice it's also bright?"

I nod.

"We fight the fog enough every day as it is." He sighs, then stands. "I think we'll try meditation today."

"You're kidding, right? You want me to *meditate*?"

James raises one eyebrow. "Have you tried it before?"

"Uh, no," I lie. I don't want to admit that I have and that I'm terrified of trying again.

I tried meditation once at Sensei's insistence, and all it did was bring on one of my infamous "epilepsy attacks" in front of the whole class. As soon as I tried to clear my head, the shadows went crazy. They burst out like hungry hounds, finding my almost empty mind a far easier target than one full of fluid thoughts. The whole experience was awful, not to mention embarrassing. It might work for James, but I know for a fact that, for me, meditation is a terrible idea. Still, I don't want him to think I'm weak, so I act nonchalant.

"I don't see how some New Age foolishness can help."

"You don't risk anything by trying."

I swallow my pride, which is no easy matter. It feels like a grapefruit going down my throat. "I guess not."

"Good." James removes his shoes, sits on a padded mat and crosses his legs yogi-style. "Take off your shoes and sit there." He points at the mat in front of his.

Cursing inwardly, I do as I'm told. James's eyes lock on mine, serious, way too serious. I feel ridiculous and terrified.

"All right, before we begin, tell me something, Marci. What works for you? What helps keep the fog away?"

"Um ..." The question makes me squirm. I should feel comfortable talking about it with James, but, for so many years, it has been the most private and terrifying secret I've kept. Spilling it all out now doesn't come easy. "I ... uh ..." I sound like an idiot.

"It's okay. You can tell me." James's voice is gentle, almost dreamy.

"I keep my thoughts fluid," I say in a quick stream of words.

"Thought-jumping. That's what we call it," he says, nodding. "Okay, what else do you do?"

Thought-jumping? Good name, I suppose. "Um, I don't know. Martial arts, I guess. Punching, kicking, they're a release. They relax me."

"Good. Anything else?" James asks.

I shake my head and shrug. "That ring trick you showed me worked. I didn't care much for it, but it worked when nothing else would. So pain too, I guess."

"Thought-jumping is common among everyone here. Pain isn't as widely used, but fairly so. Focus on physical abilities, like martial arts, is another. All Symbiots use one of these or a combination of them," he explains.

"Symbiots?"

"Yeah, that's what we like to call ourselves. Although, I have a feeling you won't like that name. In any case, it's what we are. The agent gets a place to live in. And we've learned to reap the benefits."

I roll my eyes. Whatever. I don't buy that I'm smarter and more agile because of this parasite. I don't care what James says.

He chuckles. "As I said before, you'll change your mind soon enough."

I hate his amused expression. I don't see how something like that can make him happy in the least. "O-key doke. If you say so."

"So tell me, thought-jumping, how do you do it?" James asks.

"Huh?"

"How do you keep your—what did you call it?—oh yeah, how do you keep your thoughts fluid?"

"Um, I just do."

"Give me an example," he says.

"Well ..." It's hard putting it into words.

"When Aydan hacked into your computer, that must have been a pretty stressful time for you. Maybe *shadowing* became a threat. How did you keep it at bay?"

"Shadowing?"

"I forget you're not used to our terms. We like to give everything a name."

"No kidding."

"It makes talking about it easier, if we all give things the same name. Anyway, shadowing is what we call that moment when you sense the darkness coming over your mind, ready to steal your thoughts. The moment when you feel you might lose yourself. It's like a shroud descending over you."

James's voice is low and ominous, like that of a child trying to describe the boogeyman.

"Oh," I say in a quick breath of realization. The description is somehow perfect. I clear my throat, try to answer his question in hopes of dispelling the gloomy atmosphere. "All right, so I guess the best way to describe how I deal with the *shadowing* is to say that I ... weave random thoughts with my normal ones. I've found it works best when I think about off-the-wall stuff. Like old memories, song titles, favorite foods, odd words, street signs, cartoon characters, anything."

"Good," he says. "Notice anything interesting about that?"

"Sure," I say. "It's nuts. Not trying to be sarcastic or anything. I really believe it's completely messed up. I used to think I was crazy," I admit.

"We all did at some point," he says in a matter-of-fact tone, before continuing. "What's interesting about thought-jumping is what happens in your brain when you do it. Memory storage is complex. There's been research showing the hippocampus and prefrontal cortex are involved, as well as other parts of the brain. No one really understands the whole process."

I wonder where this is going and how long it will take because it already feels like a million ants are crawling on my butt. Yogi-style isn't the most comfortable position. I shift, trying to relieve the numbness.

James inclines his head. "Do you follow?"

"Sure."

He narrows his eyes, looking skeptical.

"Keep going," I say. The sooner we finish this, the sooner I can stretch my legs.

"When you think of your favorite cartoon character ..."

Wile E. Coyote.

"… You're essentially recalling an image that has been imprinted in your memory. Same with song titles, street signs, etcetera. Those memories are strewn about, tucked away in different corners of your brain. Thought-jumping forces you to exercise different brain cells. If we were to do an MRI while someone is doing it, we would see different areas of the brain come to life. Does that make sense?"

"One hundred percent," I say. "So how does that prevent the agent from taking over?" And how does meditation, which is supposed to leave my brain as empty as my bank account, work better than thought-jumping? Besides, I can hardly drop into yogi pose in the middle of a stressful situation, which is when the shadowing kicks into full gear.

"Our best guess is that agents need a train of thought to latch on to, A to B to C and so forth. Due to the nature of these connected thoughts, they can predict what will come next. They would know that D will follow C, and E will follow D."

Um, I know the freakin' alphabet, James.

"When a person is first infected, no matter by which method, the agent—"

My ears perk up. "You mentioned a different method of infection before, what is it?" The idea of finding out still makes me queasy, but I need to know. I have to resolve the question of how I came to be possessed by another life form. Right now, my best guess is Mrs. Contreras, but I should know all the possibilities in case I'm wrong. If it turns out to be that soap-toting woman, though, I'll make sure she never infects anyone again.

"We'll go over those another time."

"But—"

"We don't have time today. Let's see, what was I saying? Oh yeah, when somebody is first infected, they don't realize it.

171

Eklyptors make sure of that by drugging their victims, as you well saw in the party. After a few days, the host may notice its effects, but by then—for ninety-nine point nine percent of the population—it is too late. The agent has already figured out the host's thought pattern, and it's ready to take over. Then one morning, the poor bastard wakes up, punches the alarm clock, brushes his teeth, takes a shower and by the time he's eating breakfast he's been shadowed. What is worse, from our own experiences we know the host is aware of it."

James twists his neck from side to side, visibly angry. He takes a deep breath and his eyelids flutter for an instant. Then he continues. "Thought-jumping breaks the pattern the agent expects. It makes it difficult for it to guess what your next thought will be; in other words, it makes it difficult for them to supplant you. After each attempt, you probably notice a fairly quiet period. It's possible the agent gets tired or maybe it's just biding its time for when your guard is down. We don't know."

For all I know, there are holes in James's theories, but they ring of truth and I find myself nodding.

James rests his hands on his knees. "This finally brings us back to meditation and how you can use it to control your agent."

"You really mean that? I'll be able to control it?" It seems impossible.

"Yes, Marci." Then he adds with contempt, "I'll teach you to control the bastard. It's a promise."

Chapter 25

The gym pod is cool and quiet. James gets comfortable on the exercise mat.

"Let's give it a try and then I can explain. It may be easier for you to understand what I mean after you've done it. I warn you though, it won't be easy. You need to be strong. You'll come under attack."

No kidding.

Funny guy.

My eye twitches.

James squints at me. "I'd understand if you don't think you can do it."

I want him to believe I'm strong. Hell, *I* need to believe I'm strong. "I can do it," I say.

"Okay, put your hands on your legs," James instructs. "Good, now let your shoulders relax. Take a deep breath."

I fill my lungs, slowly. One, two, three times until I feel an unnerving calm falling over me. My eyes spring open. James's eyes are patient. I try again.

"Your arms are tense, Marci."

I realize my fingers are curved, fingernails biting into my knees through the holes in my jeans. With difficulty, I let my arms wilt, till my hands slide limply to my thighs.

"Better." James's voice is calm, soothing and encouraging. "Now think only about your breathing. Inhale. Visualize the way your lungs fill with oxygen."

I feel the air traveling from my nostrils, through my windpipe and into my lungs. They expand, pushing my ribs outward. I hold my breath for a couple of beats, imagine little oxygen particles traveling to my heart and exploding into my bloodstream to find homes in inaccessible corners of my body.

"Excellent. Now picture the way your lungs expel carbon dioxide as you exhale."

My eyelids flutter with an intense feeling of relaxation and wellbeing. I let my lungs contract, squeezing out the spent air. My shoulders fall an inch or two, as my chest empties. Goose bumps roll down my back and sides. I feel like I could fly. Maybe I can do this.

"Good job. Keep breathing the same way."

James lets me breathe for a few minutes. My imagination runs wild, picturing friendly oxygen particles floating in and winged CO_2 flying out, ready to find homes in the depths of some faerie-haunted forest.

"Keep breathing, but now when a thought enters your mind, acknowledge it, then dismiss it."

Immediately, my body turns into a taut bundle of nerves. This is where things went south last time. I wait for James to snap at me. Instead, his voice grows softer, sweet even.

"It's okay," he soothes. "Get your rhythm back and try it. Don't be afraid. I'm right here. I won't let it hurt you."

Yeah, right! What is he going to do to stop it? Perform a lobotomy?

I try again until I'm flying once more. Then, when my heart steadies, I bravely go for it.

I hope I don't end up ...
A cup of coffee would ...

A shadow rises like a dark ghost in a dusty corner of my brain. My breathing changes. James's voice pierces through the thickening veil of panic that's beginning to envelop me.

"Relax. Re-lax."

Quiet inhale.

You won't break me, I'll ...

Exhale.

The reason you ...

More air.

I'm not ...

Suddenly, a dark swarm of hungry locusts seizes my mind. Every single one of my neurons shrieks like terrified sheep pierced by hungry wolves' teeth. Off in the distance, I sense a flailing body, tingling skin. I think it's me. Shock and survival instincts jumpstart me into my usual defense mechanism. Thought-jumping.

Bugs Bunny.

Hazy smoke multiplies inside my mind, spreading, obscuring everything it touches. I feel as if a belt of heavy fabric has been strapped around my head, covering my eyes and ears.

No! No! Purple laven ...

The shadows take solid shapes. They're strong. I sense their mocking, satisfied pleasure and, for the first time, I hear their thoughts.

– Fighting is futile.

Tart jelly bea ...

– Hush, weakling.

Xa ...

– You are ours.

*

I'm screaming, writhing and kicking. My breaths are shallow, quick, painful. What should have been a scream leaves my throat in a hoarse moan. There's a coppery taste in my mouth. The right side of my face feels wet. My body's compressed by a three-ton rhinoceros, my mouth blocked by something hard.

"You're okay. You're okay," a voice says. "Shhhh." The gentle air stream of a shushing sound brushes my ear. "Don't cry. You're safe."

A warm hand rests on my forehead. My stiff limbs release, turning into limp wastelands. Slowly, I curl my body, caving in, wrapping weak arms around worthless legs.

When I realize I'm keening, I try to stop, but it goes on for a few minutes before I manage. Meanwhile, the tender words continue, the reassuring touch grounds me, makes me feel a bit safe. No one's ever talked to me with such tenderness. No one except Dad. It's been so long, so long, so long ago. I had forgotten.

Tears tiptoe past my lashes in silence, sliding from my left eye onto my right eye, and from there past my temple and into my ear. I feel so lonely, so unloved. I never knew I craved this warmth. I never knew I needed it.

"You're all right, sweetie." A female voice. Kristen's. "You're safe. Do you think you can stand?"

I swallow. It sounds like a frog got stuck in my throat.

"Here," she says, removing the obstruction from my mouth. She hands it to someone else. It's a brown leather wallet. James's.

They hoist me to my feet and deposit me on a workout bench. There are two other people nearby. White spots dance across my eyes. I blink, try to clear my vision. Kristen's face comes into focus. She's kneeling next to me, holding my hand, searching my gaze with concern. James stands to my left, a deep scowl on his face. Rheema stands next to Aydan who holds a red cup with a straw.

"Would you like some water?" Kristen asks.

I nod. The taste of metal is on my tongue. I want to get rid of it. Suddenly, I realize my lower lip is throbbing. I must have bitten it before they stuffed the wallet in my mouth.

Aydan hands Kristen the cup. She holds it in my direction, steadying the straw as I lean into it. The water is ice-cold. It feels good on my lip. I sip and every time I stop the metallic taste returns. My lip's still bleeding. It feels like I bit right through it.

"I'm sorry." I hang my head and stare at the rubber mat.

"Don't be silly," Kristen says, as she hands the cup back to Aydan. "We all went through the same thing. What you're trying to do isn't easy. You were very brave." She gives me a small, sincere smile.

"Rheema, would you mind finding something for Marci to eat?" Kristen says.

"No problem." The oil stains on her coveralls jump up and down as Rheema jogs away.

"I don't want anything to eat," I say. My stomach feels like it's the size of a pea. If I try to eat, I'll throw up.

"You'll feel much better if you do," James says. "Trust me."

I'm too tired to protest.

A moment later, Rheema comes back with a little basket. Inside, there's a banana, an apple, a few cheese sticks, and several chocolate bars.

"I didn't know what you liked, so I brought a bit of every-thing," Rheema says with a friendly smile. "I also brought an ice pack for your lip and this rag to clean the blood."

She hands the rag and ice pack to Kristen, then holds out the basket and urges me to grab something.

I settle for a small chocolate bar. Rheema takes it out, unwraps it and feeds me a bite. I feel like a baby. As I chew at sloth speed, Kristen cleans my face. The rag comes away bloody. She folds it in half and dabs once more. She keeps folding and repeating the process until it comes away clean.

"Hold this to your mouth." Kristen's green eyes shine under a worried scowl. She presses the ice pack into my hand. As the icy surface touches my skin, I flinch.

Rheema feeds me the chocolate until it's all gone. As soon as a bit of my energy returns, everyone's concerned gaze registers, turning my stomach into a pit of embarrassment.

A tangy sweetness lingers in my mouth. "What kind of chocolate is that? It's good," I say, trying to drive attention away from me.

"Oh," Rheema says as she looks inside the basket and pushes the banana out of the way. "It's Belgian. My favorite. It has a hint of orange in it. Here's another one." She hands me a perfect, thin square wrapped in fancy silver paper, stamped with a simple logo and no words at all. I peel it, pop it in my mouth and decide the luscious, rich taste is almost worth the embarrassment.

"Wow," I say after a forced laugh, "I think that could cure just about anything."

Kristen and Rheema smile. Aydan stares with his trademark scowl.

James pats me on the back. "The first time is always hard. You were brave and proved your strength."

"Um, I guess I should be going." I wobble to my feet.

"Not smart. You shouldn't get on that bike till you rest for a while," Aydan says, sounding like someone's father.

I take a deep breath ready to argue, but Kristen cuts in.

"This isn't an easy trick to learn, Marci. We all struggled with it and found it is best to rest afterward," she explains in an understanding tone.

I look at her perfect red hair with her perfect high-end haircut, avoiding eye contact to conceal my displeasure. I don't need her to tell me it's okay to flail on the floor like a dying fish. It's not. I've been able to keep this from happening since I was nine, since the day my mother filled the last prescription for a pill I pretended to swallow, since I stopped carrying an extra pair of underwear and pants everywhere I went. I'm not going through that again. Never.

"Meditation kicked all our butts," Rheema says.

I meet everyone's gaze, search for the lie. I come away empty handed. They're telling the truth. It isn't just me being weak because of my past and what I went through. They've all been through the same.

"After I found out I would be in control, though," Kristen adds, "I never gave up. You'll get it, but it won't be easy. No one's gonna lie to you about that. Just remember, you're here because you're strong. Because you beat your agent every day. You'll master this thing all on your own. We're only here to let you know there'll be no more big battles after you succeed. You'll be in charge."

At the moment, I feel anything but in charge, so I cling to her words and pray she's telling the truth.

Chapter 26

After they made me rest and warned me not to meditate alone—as if I was crazy—I leave The Tank and head home in a daze.

I've almost made it there, driving my bike through busy roads, when I remember the fight with Mom and the way Luke seems to pop in and out when I least expect it. My day has been bad enough as it is. Right now, after being brought back from the dead, I feel too vulnerable and in need of comfort and a bit more of that tenderness Kristen bestowed upon me as she laid a hand on my forehead and soothed me. For years, there's been only one person who's offered me that.

I turn the bike around, knowing where to find him.

As I drive, I can't help but think of how, over time, I've pushed everyone away, friends, family, teachers—all those who ever tried to get close, including Xave. Especially Xave.

Something tightens in my chest as, for the first time, I look inwardly and recognize the way I've driven him away. He's supposed to be my best friend and half the time he doesn't even talk to me about what he's thinking and feeling. And it's not all him being from Mars and me from Andromeda or wherever. No, it's *my* fault. I'm an idiot. How didn't I see that before? How did I expect him to have the warm-fuzzies about our friendship when I've given him so little? The more I think about it, the more I wonder how he has endured the way I've treated him all these years. It's amazing we're still friends. I really need to change that, especially now that we're in this mess together.

I turn on my blinker and take a right. After a few blocks, Millennium's neon sign comes into view. The pinball travels around the edge of the sign's frame and its colorful pool balls light on and off, one at a time.

Leaving my helmet hooked to the handle bars, I walk toward the front door, feeling unexpectedly lighter. A few steps past the front door, I stop and look around, assessing the crowd. Regulars mostly, including the one I'm looking for. A smile touches my lips.

The smell of junk food hits me like a heavenly slap. Rolo's manning the food counter tonight. Unusually ravenous—a meditation side-effect, I suspect—the idea of a greasy dinner at Millennium Arcade seems like a good excuse to be here while I search out Xave's company.

"Heya, Rolo," I say, slapping my palm on the counter.

He takes his eyes away from the deep fryer. "Marciiii, what'up girl?" He tips the baseball cap that sits on his bald head.

"Not much. Hey, you got something good cooking back there?"

"Nah, not tonight. Just the regular stuff," he says, giving the fries a good shake before setting them back down in the hot oil. He wipes large hands on his white apron. He's so tall and wide, he makes all the appliances look like toys.

"No Cajun fish tacos? Crawfish etouffee? Gumbo?" I plead. His Louisiana-inspired concoctions are the best. I really was in the mood for one of them.

"Nope, can't get a hold of any cheap seafood lately," he explains.

"Cheap, huh?" Cheap seafood can't be good by any stretch of the imagination. It's a wonder I haven't suffered from food poisoning yet.

Rolo grins in response.

"All right then, I guess I'll just have my regular *regular*."

"Regular *regular* coming up," he says as he sets to work on the grill to prepare me a jalapeño ranch cheeseburger.

As I wait, I lean back on the counter, elbows propped up. Xave's playing pool, watching the table and his contender, Cameron, with his usual intensity. Trent and Henry occupy the table to their right. George and Twitchy the one to the left. A couple of twelve-year-olds are shooting away at the *Paradise Lost* machine, imparting a level of carnage too high for their age.

To the opposite end, and to my surprise, someone's actually using the *Dance Dance* machine, and really rocking it with well-coordinated moves, making it look like total fun. Who knew? I watch with interest. The girl's feet move at staggering speed, crisscrossing and jumping back apart without missing a beat. She wears black skinny jeans, pink Chuck Taylors and a matching polka-dot top. I groan inwardly. You'd never catch me dead in that getup, especially the cute ponytail that bobs up and down as she shakes her petite goods. To each her own.

The girl's back is turned, so I can't tell who she is. Yet I have a vague feeling of recognition. I'm thinking hard when suddenly, she jumps and twirls. Her feet press opposite corner pads, then leap again as she twirls to hit a mirror pose. The quick second she faced my way was enough to help me identify her.

Judy Pratt.

No wonder she looks like a dang choreographer, dancing on top of that torture contraption. She's been doing ballet since she was in her mom's womb. I've heard the doctors freaked when a tutu and satin ballet slippers were the first things to pop out.

"Ranch cheeseburger. Jalapeño sauce on the side. Fries sprinkled with chili powder," Rolo announces, sliding two red and white cardboard plates across the counter.

My mouth waters at the sight of the glistening fries. After paying, I carry my food to a small two-seater booth that offers a clear view of the pool tables. It looks like Xave's game is almost over, so I want to be able to wave him over before he starts a new one.

I eat a fry. It's crisp and spicy. Perfect. After licking my fingers, I unwrap a plastic knife to cut my huge burger in half. As I finish, I notice Xave shaking hands and bumping shoulders with Cameron. From the crestfallen look of his opponent, it looks like Xave won. Again.

I put a hand up and wave, but Xave turns and walks toward the exit. I'm about to call his name when he veers toward the *Dance Dance* machine. As he approaches, Judy hops off, quitting mid-dance, and joins him. My arm freezes mid-air, plastic knife in hand.

Xave gives her a small smile and stuffs his hands inside his pockets, towering over her petite frame. She looks up at him, beaming like a pocket-sized flashlight. As she talks, her lips move slowly, forming each word in a suggestive manner easy to spot even from where I'm sitting. She pulls out a small red packet from her pocket and offers it to Xave. Cinnamon gum, his favorite. He takes a stick and pops it in his mouth.

Something Judy says makes Xave laugh out loud, a sound I've not heard in the past few weeks. I put the knife down. The grilled meat taste turns acrid in my mouth.

Is Xave on a date with Judy Pratt?! The same girl he and I have shredded to pieces in vicious conversations since I can remember? Has hell frozen over? It must have. There's no other explanation.

Has he forgotten her ever-present elementary-school pigtails? The massive middle-school bows that used to decorate the top of her head, making her look like a birthday gift? How about her snobbish attitude about our torn sneakers? And her haughty comments about our peanut-butter sandwiches, as opposed to her organic carrots, Greek yogurt and homemade entrées?

I've always told Xave she fixated on us, criticizing and gossiping, because she was attracted to him. He never believed me, or so he said. Now, from the idiotic look on his face, it seems he's totally bought into it.

My appetite disappears. I push the food aside, wrinkling my nose, and stare at it, as if it could explain why the world has gone inside-out.

Xave, the skater/biker boy, is hanging out with Judy, the color-coordinated, sickeningly popular ballet diva. Next thing the president of the United States will deliver his State of the Union Address sporting multi-colored scales all over his face.

"Hey," a voice says.

I flinch and tear my eyes away from the nauseating food. Bizarro Xave has decided to honor me with his presence.

Chapter 27

"I didn't see you come in." Xave slips into the seat opposite mine, dusts his hands from the cue chalk, steals a French fry and pops it in his mouth. "Mmm, these are perfect." He takes another one and dips it in jalapeño sauce. "What happened to your mouth?"

I forgot I'd bitten through my lip. "Karate practice."

Xave nods, easily accepting my lie. "What you been up to? I called to see if you wanted to hang."

"I was busy." I take a deep breath, try to bite the mean question that is making my tongue feel like a viper's, the question that involves Judy Pratt.

"Busy, doing what?" He appraises me, probably wondering if I've been doing anything IgNiTe related.

"Oh, just stuff," I say in a suggestive tone, trying to make him suspicious about my whereabouts.

His eyes flicker to one side and go dark for a nanosecond. Then he does an introspective shrug, as if he's decided he's not interested in anything me or IgNiTe may be up to. He flashes me a smile and eats another French fry.

"What's wrong?" he asks, pointing at the burger with the long fry. "You're not hungry?"

"Oh, I'm hungry, all right," I say, taking a huge, messy bite. Ketchup squeezes out of one side of my mouth, dribbles down my chin and splats on my chest. I dab at the spot, rubbing so hard the paper napkin starts falling apart. I give up, crumple the stupid thing and throw it on the table. Xave laughs at my failed attempt to remove the stain. Great!

"It's not funny," I mumble. "And get your own damn fries." I slap his fingers away as he reaches for another one. He jerks his hand back, an injured and confused expression on his face. We've always shared our food. It's never been a reason to bicker.

"What's wrong with you today?" he asks.

"Are you on a date with Judy?" I ask before I can stop myself.

Xave's eyes grow wide, wide and wider. Yeah, my question to his question is not what he expected. What's wrong with me today is Judy Pratt and, clearly, the revelation is making his wheels turn.

I can see his face go through a rainbow of emotions. Surprise, confusion, doubt. The emotions seem to be attached to churning thoughts inside his mind. Several times, his mouth moves as if to ask something, but nothing comes out. He looks as if he's trying to settle on the best question possible and he's discarding them before they make it through his lips.

He finally says, "Why do you care?"

"I—I ..." Any other question would have been better than this one. I can't answer it. Not to him, not even to myself. "I really don't care. I'm just ... puzzled. That's all," I whisper, because it's the easiest, most cowardly thing to say.

"Puzzled?" He ponders. "And why is that?"

"C'mon, Xave. This is Judy Pratt we're talking about. We hate her. We always have. And, by the way, *she* hates *us*."

He gives me a sad smile. "Aren't you always the one telling me to grow up once and for all? Always saying I'm ... how did you put it?" He makes air quotes. "'Perfectly irrational'? Hmm?"

Xave waits for me to say something. But what is there to say?

He continues. "For once I'm trying to see past my narrow, judgmental views. I'm ... expanding my horizons. Breaking stereotypes. And you don't approve?"

I cross my arms over my stained t-shirt. "Is that what you're calling your *sexcapades* now?" There's a twist of bitter lemon on top of my comment.

"Again ... even if that's what this is all about, why do you care?"

I wish he'd stop beating on that drum. It makes me feel hollow inside.

"You've never cared before," he says, having found a more bitter substance than mine to make his point.

Our eyes lock and the silence between us swells and swells with an absence of words that need to be figured out. But I'm dry as a bone. I have nothing to give, nothing to offer. I'm the one who's perfectly irrational. It takes one to know one, after all.

"The world is going to hell, Marci. I may as well enjoy it while it lasts. I can't ... *wait forever*." His last two words are loaded with meaning.

Is he trying to say that he's ... waiting for me? I shrink away from the thought. That can't be what he's trying to say! Why doesn't he just tell me what he means? My mouth hangs open, a mute "O" of incredulity. Is this the way he chooses to let me know? A way that is, by no means, clear.

"We should talk. There's something I should tell you and maybe something you'd like to say to me?" Xave tells me in a sweet, inviting tone. He leans closer, hazel eyes drilling mine with heated intensity.

His hand—up till now resting on the table—moves inches slowly toward mine. His fingernails are blue from the cue chalk. I see the Celtic tattoo between his middle and fore fingers. It's so small I always forget about it. My body tenses and I instinctively pull back a bit. And even though my fingers retract only a few inconsequential millimeters, the distance feels insurmountable, because Xave's eyes darken with the knowledge that I've recoiled from him. Again.

What does he expect? He seems ready for something I've only begun to contemplate. And even if somehow this spark in my heart could ignite me, what could I ever give him? He doesn't even know what I truly am. My soul aches. One person at a time, I'm carving a path toward loneliness.

Mom, Luke, and now …

I swallow, blink, ignore the fire in my throat.

"No, Xave," I croak, somehow holding his gaze as I pronounce each word. "There's nothing I'd like to say to you." *Because there is nothing you have ever said to me. Because even if you did, I can't go there with you. Not anymore.* But I can't add this, because even if he poured his heart onto my lap, there'd still be nothing I could give him back. It's better if I don't let him say what he wants to say.

All expectation collapses out of Xave's chest in one big exhale. His eyes fall to my unwilling hand. Our fingers may as well be on opposite sides of the Atlantic.

Xave's moist lips part, as if they've lost the strength to stay together. Air fills his lungs very slowly and his eyes suddenly brim with sickening resignation and finality, as if he's seen everything clearly for the first time.

"I didn't want to believe it," he says, nodding sadly. "But I guess I always knew."

I'm breathing rapidly, holding back the tears that burn in the backs of my eyes.

I have nothing to offer.

Emptiness.

Nothing.

Xave stands, pats my petrified hand with something like longing. He takes a step forward, without removing his hand. My shoulder aligns with his hip. I stare at the fries, don't even know if he's looking down at me. It doesn't feel like he is.

"I can finally let you go," he says, then walks away, leaving behind the ghost of what could have been.

Chapter 28

I sneak into my bedroom through the window, which I always keep unlocked for such occasions when I don't want to run into Mom.

After kicking off my boots, undressing and donning an over-sized t-shirt, I lie in bed staring at the ceiling. Sleep is impossible with all the conflicting ideas in my head and similar feelings in my heart. Or is it my stomach? I'm not sure. The general area feels tight, like the day Sensei accidentally kicked me in one of our class demonstrations.

A dark shape moves in the heavy drapes by the window. My eyes snap to the spot. Nothing's there. I'm seeing things now. A sad smile visits my lips and I'm reminded of Grandma's old saying, which never translated quite right from Spanish to English.

"Smile when you don't want to cry."

Why do I want to cry? Why, all of a sudden, do I care about who Xave is dating? It never bothered me before, and he's dated plenty, has even asked me for my advice once or twice. Not that I'm qualified to give anyone advice, not when I've never even been on a date.

Am I only upset because he picked Judy Pratt? Or is

there something else behind this portentous weight on top of my breastbone?

The slight squeak of hinges takes me away from my thoughts. I look toward the door and find it tentatively swinging open. I squint, trying to make out Mom's features in the dark gap. Instead, I find Luke. What the hell?! What is he doing here at—I look at the clock—10:30 P.M.?

"Can I come in?" he whispers.

He's in already. I get my naked legs under the covers.

"I thought I heard you come in," he says, shutting the door behind him.

I find myself speechless as I try to work this out. Is Mom still up? Were they perhaps talking, *bonding* like the most perfect mother and son duo? What is going on here?

Luke sits on one corner of the bed. Wait! Is that pajama bottoms he's wearing? What?!

Noticing my puzzled gaze, Luke pinches his checkered pants. "Um, I'm sleeping in the living room," he says with a rueful smile.

"Wait a minute," I say, fidgeting, disguising my discomfort by rearranging the covers and pillow. "You're sleeping here, on the sofa?"

"Futon," he says, chagrined. "We replaced the sofa."

"Replaced the sofa?" My voice rises from whispers into a normal tone.

"Yeah, and we were thinking that … since we're not moving, maybe we could build an addition. You know … another bedroom."

Unbelievable! I stand and start pacing the floor along the opposite side of the bed. "I like how you two make all these *decisions* and inform me after the fact." I try to make it sound like a joke.

191

"What else are we supposed to do?" Luke asks seriously. "You're never here."

Hmm, I wonder why?

"Mom and I—" he starts.

"Mom?!" I don't know why but the word is a sharp dagger right through my heart. I give a sad laugh, feeling strangely deflated, numb. I slump on the desk chair and stare at my bare feet.

"Marci, I never had a mother." I can feel Luke's earnest eyes on me. I want them to turn away and take their accusation with them. "I just—"

"It's fine, Luke. You don't have to explain. An addition is fine. Maybe, if you wait long enough, you may not even need one."

Luke slides across the foot of the bed, reaches the nearest corner and leans tentatively toward me, until I can't bear the closeness. "What do you mean?"

I don't know where the thought came from or if I'd be allowed to do it, but suddenly, I'm considering moving into The Tank. They have bedrooms where Kristen, Aydan and Rheema spend the night most of the time. I could do the same and I probably wouldn't even have to ask. There, among the other Symbiots, is where I belong—the only place where I don't have to hide who I am. Mom doesn't care what I do. I bet she'd actually be relieved if I leave.

"Nothing," I say with a shrug. "Just thinking out loud."

"If my presence here makes you want to leave, I'll go." Luke's voice is quiet. Straight blond hair hides his eyes as his chin dips low. "I won't be responsible for interfering between you and your mom. I couldn't stand that."

Damn Luke! Now he's got me feeling sorry for him and something tells me he's just playing me. None of this can be for real. This is not the same boy I've known since kinder-garten. He was never meek or touchy-feely. He's faking it. He's gotta be.

Yet, I can't bring myself to call him on it, because it's possible the "Before Luke" was just a façade. And this—without the cool, cocky exterior—is really him. I know all too well about living different lives.

"It's okay," I say. "I'm not going anywhere." A short snort punctuates what feels like a lie. "I'll stop causing trouble. You make yourself at home." As hard as I try, I can't leave the sarcasm out of my last few words. "Like you said, I'm hardly ever here, anyway."

Luke locks his gaze with mine. He looks deep into my eyes, as if he's searching for something. A strange chill runs the length of my back, and having him here—in my room at this hour—suddenly feels way off.

"Um, I need to catch some sleep or I'll be worthless tomorrow."

"Me, too." He smiles and walks to the door. Before leaving, he says, "Thanks, Marci. I know this isn't easy for you. I promise you I'll do everything I can to make this work out."

His hand rests on the door knob for a few seconds as he seems to ponder what else to say. I can tell there's something else in his mind, but he doesn't say it. He simply says good night and leaves me wrapped in shadows.

Chapter 29

A pit-bull barks at me, straining its chain to the breaking point. I ignore it, concentrating on the houses, trying to find the right one. They all look the same. Shabby lawns with more weeds than proper plants and grass, mildewed front steps, sagging window shutters and peeling paint. I don't remember it looking like this ten years ago. Maybe it didn't, but I guess it doesn't take too long for a neighborhood to go to the dogs.

A chill trickles down my spine. I shake it off and look up and down the street. There's no one outside. I tell myself someone is watching me from behind one of the many windows. But I know that's not the reason for my jumpiness. I've been like this since my failed meditation, seeing shadows in every corner, paranoid that something will come out of nowhere to snatch me away.

At school, at home, in the very sanctuary of my bedroom, I feel threatened, helpless, with nowhere to hide. I had to do something, so I turned my fear and weakness into anger, an anger I plan to unleash on Mrs. Contreras, if she turns out to be responsible for infecting me.

I've passed ten houses and I really haven't the faintest idea which one's the right one. I'm about to start looking in the opposite direction when I notice someone leaving one of the houses across the street. I jog to the other sidewalk and approach the woman.

"Hi," I say, staying several paces away. My face feels like a mask of fury, and I don't want to scare her.

The woman stops and gives me a hard glare. She looks to be in her late twenties. She says nothing.

"Uh, I was wondering if you could tell me where Mrs. Contreras lives?"

She frowns and stares me up and down. "I'm Ms. Contreras. And you are?" She keeps walking toward a blue Sentra, her black heels clicking against the sidewalk in quick succession. She seems to be in a hurry. The skirt she wears is so tight around her shapely thighs and knees that each step is only a few inches apart.

"Well, the Mrs. Contreras I'm looking for would be a lot older than you. She used to babysit me when I was four or five."

The woman relaxes a bit and searches my face with curiosity. "Did she?" She touches the corner of a red, glittery mouth with her tongue, squinting at me, then her eyes grow wide. "Marcela Guerrero, right?" she asks, but it's more a statement than a question.

"Yeah," I say in surprise.

"You don't remember me, do you?"

I shrug one shoulder, feeling guarded.

She puts her hands out demonstratively. "I'm Consuelo."

I examine her face. "Chello?" I ask, remembering the pimply seventeen-year-old that used to help Mrs. Contreras when there were too many of us to handle. This woman looks nothing like that girl. Her curvaceous figure holds no trace of the chubby playmate that once gave me piggy-back rides. Her black hair cascades around a pretty face with flawless skin.

"The one and only," she responds. "I thought you meant me when you said Mrs. Contreras, but only my students call me that. All that babysitting was good for something," she continues with a smile. "I'm an elementary school teacher now."

"Oh, that's great." My tone is flat.

"What brings you around looking for my mama? You didn't win the lottery and want to repay all the wonderful life lessons you learned under her care, did you?" Her eyes glint with mischief.

Threatening to wash my mouth with soap and giving me nightmares about red-eyed monsters hardly count as wonderful life lessons.

"No, I haven't," I respond.

"Yeah, didn't think so."

"I was just in the neighborhood and wanted to stop by and say hello."

Chello unlocks the passenger door of her car and throws her purse inside. "Sorry to disappoint, *chica*. But my mother passed away three years ago."

"Oh, I'm sorry to hear that," I say, suddenly interested in a patch of weeds.

I thought your mom might be an Eklyptor and she bothered to babysit kids just so she could infect them with disgusting parasites. That's what I want to say, but the whole idea seems ludicrous now. Chello is normal. My head isn't droning in her presence. If Mrs. Contreras was an Eklyptor her daughter would be one as well, wouldn't she?

"Nothing to feel sorry about. She was old and she's with Jesus now. Probably happier than you and I put together." She gives me a genuine smile. "Well, it was good seeing you, kid. You're still just as pretty as you were when you were five. I have to get going now. I have a date." She wiggles one eyebrow and walks around to the driver seat.

Before she gets in, she says, "Hey, do you remember Mickey Ricky?"

I think about it until the cute face of a blond boy pops in my head. "Yeah, I remember him," I say, feeling a bit lighter at the memory.

"You had such a crush on him. Remember you used to chase him and give him kisses?" She laughs, throwing her head back.

"I did?"

"Yep. He hated it. It was the cutest thing. Anyway, he works at the convenience store, one mile down that way. In case you want to … finally *catch* up with him. I'm pretty sure he wouldn't run now." Laughing at her own joke, Chello gets in the car and drives away.

I walked back to where I parked my bike, staring at the ground and shaking my head about Chello's bubbly person-ality. How would it be to feel that light-hearted? I always feel weighed down by so many things that ever being that way seems impossible.

Looking back the way she left, I start wondering if perhaps Mrs. Contreras's Eklyptor had a conscience and didn't dare infect her own daughter. But what if she *did* infect Mickey Ricky and the rest of us? Maybe I should visit him just to make sure he's not infected. Hell, for all I know, it was him who gave me this hellish case of the cooties.

I straddle the bike and drive to the convenience store. I've no idea if it's Mickey Ricky's shift, but it's worth a try. I wonder at the silly name and can't remember how it came about. I doubt he goes by that still. Mike or Rick are more likely names.

My hands are sweating by the time I reach the store. I park my bike next to one of the pumps and lower the kickstand. Maybe I shouldn't go inside. What if my kindergarten crush is one of those mutated humans by now and he attacks me or something?

I come away from the bike, dismissing my ridiculous fear. Before I knew what the buzzing in my head was, I ran into many Eklyptors. They gave me knowing glances that I didn't understand, but they never attacked me. It should be harmless to go in and out of the store. He's probably not even in there anyway.

I move forward. My steps aren't as firm as I'd like to pretend. My thoughts jump.

Twinkies. Yellow Skittles.

And cherry sodas.

I swallow hard.

Accompanied by an electronic *ding-dong*, I enter the store and step right up to the counter.

"Five bucks on pump three," I say, holding out a ten-dollar bill. The kid manning the register is blond. I look down at his name tag. It reads "Michael R. Buckley."

"Thank you," I say, taking my change.

"Hey, don't I know you from somewhere?" he asks, pointing at me and holding his head at an angle. His forehead is sprinkled with acne and his nose is a red knob.

"I don't think so." I walk outside.

Two things I know, Mickey Ricky is not cute anymore *and* he's not an Eklyptor. I'm oddly relieved by the discovery, but now a gnawing uncertainty builds inside me. If neither Mrs. Contreras nor this guy turned me into a monster, then who did?

Chapter 30

After the failed search for answers, I drive to my training appointment with James. I step out of the elevator expecting to find him waiting again, but he isn't there. I go downstairs and find Aydan at the foot of the steps. He's wearing his medical lab coat over black jeans and t-shirt.

"What's with the coat? Aspiring to be a lab technician?" I snicker.

"You're late," he says, ignoring my question. He looks paler than ever. He seriously needs some sun.

"Where's James?" I try to ignore the buzzing that started inside my head as soon as I saw Aydan.

"He had to go out of town, so you're stuck with me." He exhales with discontent and I'm sure he means *he's* stuck with *me*. "Anyway, James said we should try meditation again." He starts walking toward the gym pod, looking as if he'd rather be headed to the dentist. His jet-black hair is a mess in the back. It looks funny.

"After the way it turned out yesterday? You must be kidding."

He glares at me over his shoulder. "Look, I've got better things to do than listen to you whine. So if you think you've got nothing to learn, why don't you do us both a favor and go home?"

What is wrong with this guy? One minute he's defending me from Blare, the next he's ready to kick me out on the street. What is he trying to prove? That I'm weak? Whatever it is, I won't give him the satisfaction. I swallow my anger and follow him. His lab coat swings from side to side.

As soon as we enter the gym pod, he kicks off his shoes and sits on a yoga mat. "Okay, let's get started. And if I hear any complaints or snide comments I'll go back to doing *real work*."

Cursing inwardly, I take off my shoes and sit in front of Aydan.

"Let's start with some breathing," he instructs.

His clipped tone puts me on edge. This isn't going to work. To be able to meditate successfully, peace is indispensable. Aydan makes me want to go to war. Besides I don't want to embarrass myself in front of him. I have my pride to consider.

"Um, I don't really think this whole meditation thing is gonna work for me. Thought-jumping and exercise work, but I'm not on board with this whole *New Age* approach. It's counter-intuitive."

"It'll work," Aydan says with irritation as he watches me with unnerving, dark eyes. "You just have to practice."

"Do you do it?"

"Every. Day," he says, pronouncing each word with emphasis. "We all do. That is how James, Kristen and Rheema control their agents."

I take it he doesn't have his own agent under control yet, but I don't ask.

"You don't have to be afraid of it because it's new," he mocks.

"I'm not afraid." My voice cracks with the lie.

Aydan's unwavering eyes soften a little, showing me a glimpse of that other side of him, the side that defended me from Blare, the side that knows too well what I'm going through.

I clear my throat. "I realize new things might help. I mean, James showed me that ring trick. And, even though I didn't care much for it, pain worked when nothing else would."

One of Aydan's eyebrows makes a steep arch and he leans away from me slightly. He looks defensive, but maybe I'm misreading him. Maybe he's passing judgment. Maybe the use of pain is considered shameful. I stare at the edge of my mat for a moment. It's bright red. Perhaps he just finds me unimaginative. He makes me feel dumb.

"What about you?" I challenge. "What did you used to do before James showed you meditation? Or did you figure that one out all on your own?" I can't help the sarcasm in my voice. I don't know if Symbiots have some sort of etiquette and this kind of question is rude, but I want to know why he's judging me

"No. I had never tried it before," he responds with such honesty that I'm taken aback. "I was like you. It never occurred to me that something like meditation might work. How could it when thought-jumping did the trick most of the time? Meditation brings an absence of thought that couldn't be farther away from that," he says with dry amusement.

"I also wrote code, tons of it," he continues. "Hacking challenges are great brain exercises. It's a form of thought-jumping on steroids, I guess. You know what I mean. Whether you realize it or not, you've been using coding, too."

"Yeah," I say, thinking back to all the complex hacking routines I've written. "I guess I have." Aydan's expression is more open now. Maybe he's not as bad as I thought and he just takes time to warm up to people.

Benefit of the doubt: granted.

Aydan runs a hand across his forehead. For the first time, I look at him openly. The contrast between his pale skin and jet-black hair is startling. I wondered why I never noticed? His lips are full and pink, his nose almost perfect. There's a certain sadness in his eyes that makes him look wise, somehow.

"I also used pain when everything else failed," he says, lifting his chin high as if waiting for me to disapprove of this method. He holds my gaze defiantly.

As I try to understand his demeanor, it occurs to me that he wasn't passing judgment on me for using the spiked ring. He was being defensive since I said I didn't care for using that method, even if it worked. I suddenly wonder if Aydan is a cutter and feel embarrassed for the thought. It's none of my business.

"Yep, pain kicked my butt into shape," I say, trying to sound nonchalant.

Suddenly, his face looks old and tired. The circles under his eyes are darker than before and deep frown lines cross his forehead. I never stopped to wonder how old Aydan is. He can't be that much older than me. Eighteen? Nineteen?

"Can we start now?" he asks, looking so tired I want to invite him to nap on the mat.

I grit my teeth, still skeptical the process will work. "No. I'm sorry, but I need more than vague explanations to buy into this. James is so … frustrating all the time. He hardly ever tells me anything. It's like he's feeding me tiny pieces of some huge secret that I'm ready to swallow whole. Like the whole Symbiot thing. I don't believe this parasite is responsible for any of my skills. Who buys into that crap?"

"Oh, I buy into it, all right. You will too, as soon as you see what James and Rheema can do."

"What can they do?" I ask, puzzled, trying not to let my imagination fly with it, especially if it's anything like what I saw that guy do at Elliot's mansion. At the thought of the man, an ice cube settles in the back of my neck. I roll my shoulders to dispel the chill.

"That's up to James and Rheema to divulge."

"O-key doke. I guess everyone around here subscribes to the cryptic club." Aydan doesn't laugh at my joke. Maybe the agent ate his sense of humor. I wonder if that's possible. What if I've lost pieces of myself and I don't even know it?

"Look, Marci, James has been doing this longer than you and I. He's lived with secrets for a while now. You know how that is, don't you? It's in his nature to be like that. Don't think it's anything personal."

I cross my arms. "You tell me then."

"I told James I don't have patience for this," he says, exasperated.

"Okay, just answer me one question and I'll get out of your way. I promise."

"I'll answer anything," he says, leaving no doubt as to how badly he wants to get rid of me.

Good. His company is a thorn in my side, too.

Benefit of the doubt: revoked.

"If I'm to put myself through meditation again," I begin, "I need to know how it'll help me control the agent."

Aydan stands and reaches for his shoes. "I know it's hard to believe. I didn't believe it at first. But you'll learn to take advantage of the agent. It *is* a symbiotic relationship."

Again with that. I roll my eyes but he doesn't notice. He's too busy fighting to stuff his foot inside the tied tennis shoe.

"The only benefit for the agent is having a place to subsist. You, on the other hand, will benefit in ways you can't even

203

begin to imagine, ways that will surprise you. And while you're at it, you'll also put the bastard behind bars. And once you have it there, it'll do *your* bidding. It will serve you. Not the other way around."

There is satisfaction and deep hatred in each of Aydan's words, and his eyes shine like someone bent on revenge. His entire expression, I realize, is a living portrait of the exact way I feel inside. All I've ever wanted is to be rid of this thing. Hearing James say that he saw no possible cure any time soon broke something inside me. But maybe I understand what he meant when he said I would come to terms with it.

If I can't be rid of the agent, I'll definitely settle for controlling it, for making it my prisoner. If James and the rest can teach me how to do that, if that is the only way I can make the agent pay for what it's done to me, my childhood, my family, then I will control it and jail it. And I will do it until the day I'm able to kill it or the day I die trying.

Aydan gives up trying to stuff his foot inside the shoe. He picks it up, sits on a nearby workout bench, and pulls on one of the strings.

After a deep breath, he says, "Now, to understand how some New Age om crap is going to help you—especially when you rely on methods that overwhelm the agent with random thoughts—you have to understand what the agents *crave*." He says the word with intensity, teeth bare, eyebrows tight, eyes fierce.

"What is it?" I say, drinking in every bit of information.

"They want the sights, the sounds, the smells, the tastes that the human body can experience, and they want them desperately. Think about it. Without a host, they have nothing. They've no limbs, no mouths, no ears. They're nothing without us.

"That's why they *crave* to be you, so they can experience what it is to be truly alive. Try to imagine yourself deaf, blind, mute, unable to feel, all at the same time. Imagine you were born that way and you're fully aware of those impediments. How do you think you would feel?"

I know exactly how I would feel. I don't have to imagine it. Doesn't he know I've been shadowed?

"Imagine never tasting tea or spicy food," Aydan says.

Odd choices, but I approve.

"Or never being aware of colors, like in a sunset or the aurora borealis," he finishes wistfully.

I think of being unable to see Xave's hazel eyes and that special shade of green they acquire when he's happy. The thought is so sad and random, it makes me cringe.

Living like that would be freakin' torture.

Torture?!

Suddenly my thoughts are an avalanche, overwhelming me with their speed. The agent craves the sensations we humans take for granted. They're nothing but smart … rocks that can't experience the world on their own. And Aydan said they're aware of it.

"I see it clicked," Aydan says, watching me with interest. "Do you understand now why painting your mind into a blank canvas is the perfect way to teach the agent to obey you?"

"Yes," I say with fire in my voice. If I empty my mind, the agent would have nothing. It would be trapped inside a desolate, torturous hell. The realization is perfect. Exquisite, really.

"That's why you must master the skill. It's indispensable. Think of the agent as a … toddler that you're trying to teach not to misbehave. Once you can meditate without losing control, you'll begin using it as punishment. As a form of time-out, if you will. Very quickly, the agent will learn that if it tries to shadow you, you'll torture it by depriving it of all the things it craves. Before long, it'll resign itself to living vicariously through you. When that is done, the real training will begin."

I nod as I stare at my mat, mind reeling with possibilities. Most of all, I find myself filled with immense pleasure at the idea that I can torture the agent the way it has tortured me all these years.

Aydan finishes lacing his shoes. "Now, get out of here. I've no more time for you."

After my eye-opening conversation with Aydan, he rushes out of the gym pod back to work. I sit for a moment, contemplating the possibility of torturing my agent. A smile creeps up my lips, a clear sign of the pleasure this idea gives me. I stand and walk to the water cooler, still smiling.

"Had a good session?"

I turn and see Rheema walking in, a yellow squeeze ball between her greasy fingers.

"Yeah, I think so."

She throws the ball up in the air and catches it. I pour water into a cone-shaped paper cup.

"It's good to have another girl in the team," Rheema says.

"What about Kristen?" I ask.

Rheema shrugs. "She's always too busy. Plus," she whispers, placing a hand by her mouth, "she's old."

Kristen isn't old, old. She's probably in her mid-forties like James, but I know what Rheema means.

"Aydan is young," I say, guessing they're both probably around eighteen or nineteen.

"Hmph! In case you haven't noticed, Aydan has a stick up his ass."

I throw the crumpled cup in the garbage bin. "Oh, I've noticed."

"He thinks he's smarter than everyone else and acts as if the rest of the world is a nuisance or a burden he has to put up with."

I walk closer to Rheema and speak in a hushed tone. "What's with the lab coat?"

Rheema laughs openly. "Ah, the lab coat. Don't get me wrong, the guy's smart, but just like many people with high IQs, he's a little touched." She puts a finger on her temple. "I think the coat has something to do with the pictures he's taped to the server racks, but who knows?"

"What pictures?" I ask.

"I dunno. Scientists, physicist. All geniuses, I think."

Pictures of geniuses? I roll my eyes, thinking how conceited he must be. Yep, I have to agree with Rheema; he has a stick up his ass.

"What about you? How long have you been with James?" I ask.

"About a year. Aydan about five months ago and now you. James and Kristen have been at it longer—not sure how long, though."

"Was James secretive with you, too?" I ask. "He won't tell me anything!"

Rheema sits on a workout bench and bounces the ball between her legs. "Yep. That's just how he is. I don't sweat it anymore. He doesn't even do it on purpose. It's just in his nature."

"I'm getting a bit tired of it," I say in the understatement of the century.

She shrugs as if to indicate that's my problem, which I guess it is.

"How long have you been ... ?" I fidget, unable to add "infected" at the end of my question. It feels too personal.

Rheema stands, squeezing the ball in a tight fist. "I don't like to talk about it," she says, proving that indeed I've crossed a line.

Shame makes my cheeks feel hot. "Sorry, I—I'm not sure how long it has been for me or who did it. I've been trying to figure it out, but the only clues I had led me nowhere."

Her face has gone from open and happy to remote and grieved. I bite my tongue wishing I hadn't said anything.

"Trust me, Marci," she says, her eyes dark with hatred, "sometimes it's better not to know."

And with that, she walks out, leaving me to ponder whether ignorance would be my best bet.

Chapter 31

"A mocha latte, please," I say to the snooty coffee shop attendant. I look at the pastry display and wonder if I can afford a cookie, but the prices are a travesty, an outright insult to my scant pocket. I can barely afford the coffee, except I need the stuff if I'm to survive a meditation session with Aydan today. At school, I thought non-stop about what he told me yesterday. The possibility of torturing *and* controlling the agent has me ready to endure the fear and humiliation I know this session will bring.

As I wait for my drink, I look out the window, hoping things go smoother this time. Men and women in fancy business suits speed-walk across the street, enter the coffee shop, get in line and order grande this and tall that, then rush back to work, looking smart and totally miserable. I take a silent vow never to sell myself to Corporate America. Somehow I'll figure out how to be independent and work doing my own thing. If I don't first sprout scales or hairs all over my body, that is.

I pay for my mocha and walk to the counter to doctor it up. Ten sugar packets should get a good buzz going through my veins to help me hold on to my senses when I inevitably flop on the floor like an over-sized trout. I stir and stir, watching those fools run back to their offices. I guess their breaks don't allow them more than a quick trip to the coffee shop.

I'm contemplating my options after high school when I notice a black Bentley pull up to the sidewalk across the street. A guy—whose name must be Jeeves because he wears a black suit and tie, white shirt, and even one of those stupid chauffeur hats—gets out of the driver seat, runs around to the other side and opens the back door to let someone in.

Looking around, I try to spot the lucky bastard who gets sidewalk service in nothing other than a three-hundred-thousand-dollar car. When I recognize the man, the drink almost slips from my grip.

Elliot Whitehouse.

I would know those sharp, cruel features anywhere. Limbs frozen, I stare at his face, experiencing the same gut-stabbing fear from that night in his house. He's yards away, but he may as well be right here inside the coffee shop, analyzing me with those cold, golden eyes. I hide behind a promotional sign and will the man to hurry up and get in his car.

My eyes are glued to him, watching his every step. The closer he gets, the more I'm convinced there's a slight buzz starting in the back of my skull. I shake my head, sure I must be imagining it. Eklyptors have to be within a fifteen-foot radius in order for me to sense them. I take a quick look around the room; no one in here is infected.

When Elliot finally reaches the car, there isn't any doubt. My head is droning as if he was standing right in front of me. He pauses, looks this way. I peek around the corner of the small sign, wondering if he can sense me too, trying to figure out which way I would run if he crosses the street. He puts a hand on the car's roof, frowns as his eyes search for something.

Suddenly someone steps next to Elliot, someone I now realize has been walking beside him all along, but who, in my trance, I hadn't noticed. Elliot turns, although his gaze lags behind for another instant before he faces the person waiting for him. It's James.

My stomach contracts. James is with Elliot, wearing a sharp business suit and a sickening smile. James shakes the creep's hand, tells him a few things. After a small nod, he hands Elliot something that looks like a leather folder.

Elliot turns to the driver, barks what looks like an order, and faces the open door. As he lowers himself into the seat, he spares one last glance this way. I shrink into an empty armchair and watch the Bentley drive away. James runs up the front stairs of his office building. My cup is dripping mocha latte on the floor. I've poked a couple of fingernails through it.

I clean the spilled coffee with a few napkins and dump the untouched, dripping cup in a garbage can. Sinking back into the armchair, I prop elbows on knees and rest my forehead in the palms of my hands. Staring at a large drop of mocha that I missed, I try to understand what I just saw.

James is supposed to be out of town, but instead he's here, exchanging pleasantries with Elliot. I understand that they are civil with each other on some social level, but whatever was going on between them didn't look social, it looked official, like some sort of business transaction. What was that all about?

Could it be that Aydan's been lying to me about James's emergency trip? Or is James lying to everyone else? No. That would be stupid. The Tank is in the same building, any of the other Symbiots could spot James like I just did.

I stand and shake my head, trying to dismiss my mounting doubts. Marching with purpose, I leave the coffee shop and straddle my bike. A car door shuts behind me and suddenly my head begins to buzz.

"I thought that was you," a chilling voice says from behind.

I freeze, helmet halfway to my head.

Elliot's cruel features come into view as he takes a few steps closer. "Do you remember me, dear?" He inclines his head and offers me a perfectly manicured hand. His unnatural golden eyes analyze me with intensity.

Swallowing the rigid lump in my throat, I hook the helmet back on the handle bars and extend my hand to Elliot. It takes a great effort to keep it from shaking.

"Sure, I remember you," I say, feeling like I'm going to puke inside my own mouth.

Elliot takes my hand, gives it a squeeze, then pulls me, gesturing for me to get off the bike. I sling one leg backward, stand on the sidewalk, then pull my hand away and stuff it in my back pocket.

"A motorcycle," he says, looking at it as if it's a mangy horse. "How ... unconventional for a pretty girl like you." He looks me up and down, his regal nose flaring at the sides. "This is a far cry from the elegant attire you wore the other night, but it suits you, somehow."

I stare at the holes in my jeans. Next to his immaculate dress shoes, my muddy boots look like shoewear for the homeless. Elliot and his *compliments* can get stuffed.

"Thank you," I say, but really it sounds more like "screw you."

"Did your friend have a ... *pleasant* end to his evening?"

His meaning almost escapes me, then I remember we were supposed to "take care" of Xave after we left his house. Exactly what he means by *pleasant* though, I don't want to know.

"Yes, he did," I say.

"Well ... ?" He lifts an eyebrow.

He can't possibly want details. I examine his face and find with disgust that he does. With curious pleasure in his piercing eyes, he waits for my account of what happened.

Maybe I'm supposed to feel like he does about torturing and killing regular humans. Maybe all Eklyptors are monsters, but I'm not about to jump into some gruesome story about how we tortured and murdered my friend, even if it isn't true. I don't have to stand here humoring this guy. I'm not in his creepy house anymore. I'm out in the middle of the street where I'm free to do whatever I please.

"I'd love to stay and chat with you," I say, trying to copy his fake-pleasant, arrogant English tone. "But I have to run. I've got far more important things to do than stand here discussing ... trivial matters."

Elliot looks at me, taken aback. His eyes dart around as if trying to see if someone heard my disrespectful tone. Then he shakes his head and laughs in a fuddy-duddy sort of way.

"You young Americans," he says. "So crass and straight-forward all the time. But you're right, we both have better things to do. I understand you have chosen a faction already, and that is all right."

A faction? What is he talking about?

"Just know this, *Ms. Milan* ..." The way he says the fake last name I used in his party leaves me with the certainty he knows it isn't my real name. "When my faction rises to the top, I will remember you could have *humored* me and, instead, you disrespected me." And with that he strides toward the coffee shop with sharp steps, inclining his head to gawking passersby who don't know that this man and his kind are our worst nightmare.

What was all that? What does he mean by "faction"? Is James part of Elliot's faction? Or another one? I understand that IgNiTe's leader lives a triple life, but now it seems that it may actually be a quadruple one.

"James Number One" owns and works in the building across the street—probably holds an important position, judging by his uptight, executive fancy suits. That man is nothing like version number two, the Harley-riding badass I first met, a dude that heads a group of misfits called IgNiTe, whose purpose I've yet to figure out. Then there's "James Number Three," a Symbiot heading yet another group, just as mysterious as the first one. And now "James Number Four." What does *he* do? I don't even want to imagine it, not if it involves that creep, Elliot.

When I decided to trust James, I didn't realize he was such a skillful chameleon. Maybe I made a mistake. Maybe this whole meditation deal is just a ruse to make me vulnerable, to make me lower my defenses so the agent can take over and turn me into a proper Eklyptor.

Stupid. Why didn't I think of that before? Maybe every single person in James's Tank crew is a full-fleshed Eklyptor and there aren't such things as Symbiots. James and Elliot are nothing but friendly with each other. What if they work for the same side? One infecting healthy humans, the other releasing agents trapped in reluctant hosts?

My head feels like an over-sized melon, full of all the things I've witnessed, of all the things I've been told, and all the unanswered questions everyone keeps telling me to stow away until James decides to spill the beans. Well, I've had enough. I can't trust blindly anymore. Someone's gonna have to shed some light on this dark labyrinth of lies, half-truths, and unproven theories. No more compliant Marci.

Chapter 32

When Elliot leaves, I get back on my bike and drive it across the street and into the parking garage. A few minutes later, I'm in The Tank, standing behind Aydan who is sitting in front of several large monitors. It is my first time in the computer pod. A thousand LED lights blink on the server racks. They distract me as much as the pictures taped to their sides. In them, I recognize Albert Einstein, Charles Babbage, and Stephen Hawking. The rest look familiar, but I don't know their names.

"You're late. Again," he says without looking back at me. "Come back tomorrow. On time."

"I've decided to stop," I say. "It's not going to work."

Aydan swivels his chair and looks at me as if I've just insulted his mother. He looks me up and down and says, "I figured you would."

What?! Is he serious? He must be saying that as a sort of reverse psychology. Well, I won't fall for it.

"For all I know next time I try, the agent will take control. Not me."

"I knew I was wasting my time trying to help you. You really are dense. Suit yourself." Aydan turns toward the computer and starts typing again.

Forcing words out of this guy is like trying to make lemonade out of lettuce. Impossible. I decide to push. "I've yet to see any proof that meditation actually works. I'm tired of just taking everyone's word for it."

Aydan looks over his shoulder for a brief moment. "Look, I don't care what you do. You'll put us in an awkward situation if you don't learn to control your agent, but I'm sure we'll figure out how to ... deal with you."

"What is that supposed to mean? Are you threatening me?"

He looks annoyed, as if I'm a fly stepping on his leftovers. "I'm busy. Take your drama somewhere else."

A flash of anger makes me imagine my hands around Aydan's condescending little neck. He's absolutely infuriating. My arms are stiff rods, trembling with rage. How dare he threaten me? I feel ready to erupt and it takes all my will-power not to launch forward and hit him. Suddenly, the glass of water next to his computer catches my eye. It seems to be vibrating. I blink, feeling my anger turn into confusion. I shake my head. The glass looks perfectly normal now.

Deep breath, Marci.

I snap back into the moment and find Aydan staring at me as if I've completely lost it. With my anger gone, I remember his threat. It gives me pause, and suddenly I feel like I owe him an explanation for my behavior.

"How do I know I can trust any of you? I just saw James with Elliot up there. They were practically smooching. For all I know, they play for the same team."

Aydan gets up from the chair in one abrupt motion. There's a coffee stain on his ridiculous medical coat. He seems ready to lash out at me, but he stops short. His eyes lock on a spot above my left shoulder and a satisfied smile tweaks his lips.

I blink. James is standing right behind me. The double droning in my head didn't register before. I was too angry to notice.

"Hello, James," Aydan says, enjoying the situation way too much.

"Aydan," James acknowledges in his deep voice. "Threat of mutiny?" he asks.

Maybe there's a geological fault under my feet and soon there'll be an earthquake. I can only wish the earth will swallow me whole. I bite my cheek, mad at myself. Why do I feel this huge sense of shame when what I want is to go ultra-nuclear on James?

"Yep," Aydan says.

I look over my shoulder to gauge James's expression. He looks as serious as I've ever seen him. I feel like I've let him down somehow. I don't know why I care what he thinks. He should understand my doubts, given the scraps of information he's offered. I know I promised to trust him, but I still want answers, feel the right to demand them. Yet I fear the idea of James being displeased with me. My stomach complains with the familiarity of this feeling. Suddenly, I see myself as a little girl, eager to make Dad smile. I never could stand it when he was cross with me.

"How's meditation going?" he asks.

I lower my gaze, step to one side, trying to meld into a server rack.

"Not going," Aydan says, all trace of his earlier satisfaction gone.

James nods once, as if that explains my misbehavior. "I see. We'll have to make it work, Marci. If we can't, I'm afraid you will become a … liability for us. Do you understand?"

I can't move my lips to shape words. Nodding isn't working either. I think I understand, but I'm paralyzed with fear. He's

217

deadly serious, and I know it because of the way he looks at me with regret, as if I'm a cute, helpless puppy he'll have to put down.

"We've trusted you with very sensitive information," he explains as he meets my frozen stare. "If you *refuse* to do as we instruct, I'm afraid things won't … work out."

I swallow and manage a small nod, my previous anger suddenly diminished. Not by fear, but by James's stout confidence and mere presence. He's the grounding force for this team, and for me it seems.

"Good. I'm glad we understand each other."

Still, the rebellious side of me stirs. All I understand is that he just threatened to kill me. I don't understand anything else, and it doesn't seem like that'll change any time soon. It hardly seems fair, but I don't dare ask James any questions. For that, I hate him almost as much as I fear him. And yet, I'm befuddled by the fact that I also admire him.

"Aydan, call a meeting in ten minutes. Make sure she's there." James hooks a finger in my direction. Aydan looks displeased but doesn't argue.

"Conference room A," James says.

Before he leaves, he looks over his shoulder. I follow his gaze to the glass of water by Aydan's computer. After a moment, his eyes lock with mine and tighten with interest, then he exits without a word.

"Need a pair of clean panties?" Aydan sneers.

"Screw you," I say as I leave his cube and head for conference room A. I don't want to miss a single word.

Chapter 33

I stuff myself in the back corner of the room. Everyone trickles in after me. Kristen, Rheema, and Aydan. There are no chairs, only a few beanbags strewn about. No one sits down.

When James strides into the room, exactly ten minutes after calling the meeting, he's not wearing his fancy suit anymore. In fact, he looks nothing like the snooty businessman and more like he just went through a boot-camp makeover.

A tight t-shirt, cargo pants, belt and boots—all black— make him look like GI Joe incarnate. He walks to the front of the conference room and stands, back to a large dry erase board. His eyes search the room and land on me.

"Try to keep up, Marci," he says. "We don't have time for long explanations, but I'll fill in where I think it may be helpful." He clears his throat before continuing. "I'm the owner and president of *Zero Breach*, a company that engineers state-of-the-art security systems. For the last couple of days, I've been on a business trip in London, a trip for which my staff and I prepared for almost a year.

"Zero Breach and two other worldwide heavyweights staged showrooms for our latest, most advanced security systems. There were many prospective clients there, but there's only one we really care about and that is AR-Tech."

AR-Tech?

"Assisted Reproductive Technologies," James explains, anticipating my question. Aydan heaves a sigh. Clearly, this is all for my benefit. Everyone else seems frustrated. "AR-Tech's clinics in the US have been using our security systems for over two years now. The purpose of the London demos and board meetings was to try to expand our coverage to AR-Tech's clinics overseas.

"We felt pretty confident we would be able to negotiate a deal. But the fact of the matter is that we did not. AR-Tech is not interested in going international with us." The muscles in James's jaw jump and his gray eyes grow dark. After a slow breath, he continues, "We thought it was a done deal. We're the best in the industry, so we didn't see that one coming. Worse yet, they're also terminating our US agreement."

"What?!" Kristen exclaims.

Everyone exchanges shocked glances. James confirms with a simple nod.

Kristen starts pacing. "But why?"

"AR-Tech's board members offered no real explanation. However, Elliot just paid me a visit and offered one. He said he felt *bad*." The last word makes it sound as if Elliot felt no such thing. "He said that the least he could do was explain why the members decided to terminate our contract."

"Ha! As if we didn't know he's the one calling the shots," Rheema sneers.

James gives her a small resigned smile. "He said 'one breach is *not* Zero Breach.' Said they can't afford to have another clinic ransacked."

I'm trying really hard to keep up with the information deluge. The conversation is faster now, as if they've forgotten there's someone clueless in the room. The facts pour into my brain and I try to organize them. Something about this whole conversation is causing an itch in the back of my mind, as if a particular piece should be clicking but is not.

"So what? They're going to a second-best competitor?" Kristen asks with incredulity.

"No. He says they've *acquired* their own security company. They'll be home-growing their own systems."

"Are you serious?"

"Elliot says they have a brilliant staff, working tirelessly to come up with a system that can't be hacked."

"Any idea how long we have before they switch over?" Kristen's still pacing, staring at the floor and looking as if the gears in her brain are on warp speed.

Impossibly, James's expression grows ever darker. "At the end of the month."

"No way!" Kristen's voice is so high-pitched it doesn't even sound like her. "They must have been planning this for a very long time."

"It looks that way."

"That's only two days away," Rheema points out.

"Great, Rheema. Thanks for the amazing display of mathematical skills," Aydan says.

Rheema gives him a rude hand gesture.

"So, all that work, all those hours were for nothing?" Aydan's frustration shapes his every word.

James offers him an inquisitive glance. "Well ..."

"Well what?" Kristen asks.

James rubs the back of his neck. "It might still be possible to take advantage of the work we've done."

"How?" Aydan plops on a beanbag, clearly skeptical about whatever James has in mind.

"I was hoping we could hit Riverbend tonight."

Aydan laughs, throwing his head back and holding his stomach in exaggerated humor. "Very funny."

"Are you saying it's impossible?"

"Pretty much," Aydan sneers, then gets up and gives a huge yawn, stretching his arms toward the ceiling. "I guess I can finally get some sleep."

"How about tomorrow night?" James challenges as Aydan heads for the door.

"Nope."

"Wait," Kristen says. "Don't leave. We can't give up just like that."

"Just like that?! There are two different devices I have to trick. I haven't even started on that. We were supposed to have two weeks to finalize everything. And even if I was able to get it all done, wouldn't it be a tad obvious if we break in after they terminate the contract and right before they switch over? It would reek of insider job. For all you know, Elliot is baiting you."

"Very likely, but we can't hide forever, Aydan. We knew that sooner or later they would find out we're here," James says.

"Maybe, but I think it's suicide. They'll figure out right away that you're involved, James. And you know what they're capable of when they feel threatened."

"I'm ready to take the risk." James's face could be carved out of stone. His eyes are fixed orbs, his expression cold and hard. He means it.

Aydan shrugs. "Still, it's not enough time. And what about you, Rheema? Could you pull your part of the plan on such short notice?"

"Sure can," Rheema says.

"I can also get everything ready on my end," James says.

"Great. I guess it's all on me," Aydan complains.

"What if I help?" The words sprint out of my mouth before I can stop them.

Four heads swivel my way. Eight eyes drill holes into my own.

"Or not," I say, running a finger along my eyebrow.

Aydan huffs and gives me a disgusted look.

Yeah, you too, jackass!

Why is he so infuriatingly haughty? Man, I could smack him. I can almost see my fist punching him in the nose. I think it's actually written in the stars and I must be clairvoyant.

James approaches. "Do you think you could do it?"

"I ... can try." What else can I say? I haven't the faintest idea what I just volunteered for.

"You're kidding, right?" Aydan looks at James as if he just asked a goose to play a symphony.

Okay, now I won't just smack him, I'll kick him till he sings soprano.

"No, I'm not," James says. "It took you hours to hack her computer. I remember your frustration *distinctively*. And also how self-satisfied you were after you did."

"That's bull," Aydan says. But he must be lying because he avoids everyone's glances and his pale cheeks get red.

Kristen's mouth twitches as if she's trying to repress a smile. This couldn't get any more awkward. Although knowing that my code gave Aydan such fits qualifies as a virtual smack.

"Marci could work on tricking the in-vitro lab device while you work on the entrance one. We've got nothing to lose," James says.

At the word "in-vitro", my heart sputters. Facts fly like hummingbirds across my mind, and then it clicks. Assisted reproduction technologies, AR-Tech, ransacked clinic, in-vitro. They're talking about breaking into a fertility clinic, a place where couples who can't have children go for help, a place like the one my mother and father went to become pregnant with Luke and me.

My knees turn to Play-Doh. I put a hand on the wall for support. Something in my stomach roils, makes me take a hand to my mouth. I wasn't infected by Mrs. Contreras or anyone else. This thing has been in me before I even had a brain for it to prey on. Even when I was just a handful of cells, I was already a monster.

God, I never stood a chance.

Chapter 34

"Marci, are you okay?" James is right in my face. One of his arms wraps around my shoulder. I'm on the floor. Here we go again.

"Get her something to drink," James orders. Rheema runs out at his command, as he deposits me into a beanbag.

James, Aydan and Kristen kneel around me, concern on their faces. I take deep breaths.

"Good, good," James says, squeezing my shoulder. "Breathe."

"I'm sorry," I say, when I find my voice.

"It's okay." He rubs my arms reassuringly and pulls me closer until my head rests on his chest. "Too much pressure?" he asks gently.

"Um, no."

"Were you shadowed?"

"No."

"What happened then?"

A sigh leaves my lips, taking every bit of humanity I thought I possessed. I chuckle because I don't want to whimper. *Smile when you don't want to cry.*

"Turns out I was never human," I say.

"Here." Rheema has a handful of my favorite chocolate and a bottle of water. She offers them to me with a smile. "These worked charms on you the last time," she says, giving me a quick wink.

"I'm fine. Really."

I pull away from James. They all get to their feet and look at me with question marks etched on their brows. I stand and straighten my shirt.

"I was an in-vitro baby," I blurt out. "It seems I've been a *freak* since I was just two microscopic cells. I guess I never stood a chance."

Wide eyes replace the furrowed brows. Rheema's jaw hangs loose. Kristen's head moves from side to side in an almost imperceptible sign of incredulity. James's astonishment hangs thick in the air. Only Aydan seems to think I've said nothing shock-worthy and allows his features to return to his I'm-too-smart-to-lose-my-cool expression.

"Are you sure?" he asks, looking bored.

I laugh. What a stupid question. Am I sure I was conceived in a Petri dish?

"Well, let me see, I was there, so I guess I should remember. Um, funny how I don't, though. I suppose I'll have to trust my mom's word on the matter."

Aydan gives me an icy stare. I tell myself it doesn't bother me and try not to start keeping count of how many times and in how many different ways I'd like to smack him.

"Look, I'm sorry I freaked. I thought Mrs. Contreras had infected me. It just came as a surprise. That's all." I try to shrug it off, try to pretend I'm over it already.

"Who's Mrs. Contreras?" Rheema asks, unwrapping one of the chocolates and popping it whole in her mouth.

"It's not important," I say.

"I thought it'd be impossible," James says, still in shock. He steps away, turns his back on me and runs a hand over his shaved head.

Kristen walks up to him, looking as excited as a kid in Disneyland. She talks a million miles an hour. "I can't believe it. How do you suppose she's been able to keep the agent at bay? I always thought in-vitros stood zero chance. I'll have to run more tests, different tests that take this into consideration."

"Hey, I'm right here," I protest. "Try to remember that as you discuss turning me into a lab rat."

Just as I finish saying this, Luke's face pops in my mind. Like fireworks, questions explode against the dark backdrop of this new revelation. Was mine the only embryo infected as he and I were deposited in Mom's womb? Or was he also infected and somehow managed to escape my fate? Or better yet, is he immune by some freak genetic reason? I realize that if there's anyone they should be testing it's him. Not me.

Not me?! Could that have anything to do with why that man took Luke and left *me* behind? My head spins.

I bite the inside of my cheek. I know I should tell James about Luke right away, but the truth is, I can't. There is no way I can drag him into this. He's already been through a lot and probably already hates being part of my family. I can only imagine how he would feel if he found out it's actually worse than he thinks. I doubt he'd be so filial if he realized half of his new family could inspire a B-rated horror movie.

At some point, I know I'll have to tell them about Luke, but not before I, myself, understand all the implications. Bringing my brother into this, when there's so much *I* need to learn, would be a terrible judgment call. I have no right to alter his life without knowing where this leads. I just hope Xave or Clark don't bring up the fact that I have a brother. For once, I'm glad James keeps so many secrets.

"We don't have time for tests right now," James says. "We need to get to work, if we're to have a chance at breaking into Riverbend by tomorrow night. I'm sure Marci will cooperate later with more tests. Won't you, Marci?"

I nod. Kristen already owns every bit of bio-data I can possibly give her. A few more tests won't make a difference. For now, I'd rather get my hands and brain busy on tricking the device they're talking about. If I don't get my thoughts away from Xave, Luke, embryo spawns and the such, I'm going to lose it.

James turns to Aydan. "Give Marci a crash course, so she can get started."

"Yes, sir." Aydan heads for the door, looking as if he'd rather jump off the Space Needle.

"Why does he have to be such an ass?" I throw the question out there, expecting no particular answer.

Rheema laughs and exits the room, shaking her head. Kristen follows suit but stops at the door, a curious expression on her face. "You really don't know, do you?"

I shake my head and shrug once. Maybe Aydan is a lunatic. Maybe his agent makes him grumpy. Perhaps there's medication for his problem. I don't know and I don't care. I've got enough problems of my own to worry about his.

"Youth is wasted on the young." Kristen sighs and leaves the room.

What is that supposed to mean? I looked at James for understanding.

He puts his hands up in a don't-ask-me gesture. "C'mon, we have work to do."

When we get to the computer pod, Aydan's busy clearing a workspace in one corner.

"She can use this area. I'll set up another workstation here," Aydan says without looking back at us.

"Just tell me where the stuff is, I can do it," I say.

Aydan heaves an exasperated sigh. "Fine. You can scavenge any monitors and cables you can find around here. The CPU is over there." He points at a large, dusty box in one corner, plops his behind on his ergonomic chair and starts typing furiously on the keyboard.

I feel like I'm back in elementary school. Next Aydan will stick his tongue out at me, right after calling me ugly names. I shouldn't, but I give James a *rescue me* look. He stares at the ceiling and grabs his chin in annoyance.

Yep, I'm back in first grade. Mrs. Kline always conjured that same expression when she didn't want to intervene in one of our kiddie brawls. James goes over and murmurs to Aydan as I make a huge racket moving and setting up equipment. When I'm done, Aydan looks mollified. Somewhat.

"You kids will do okay?" James asks. "I have a few things of my own to prepare. I'll come back in an hour or so."

"Yeah, we'll be fine," Aydan says, sounding as if we'll be anything but.

"No problem," I tell James, giving him a confident smile. After my hissy fit followed by a nervous meltdown, I want to show him I'm not a kid. Haven't been one for a long while. I can take care of myself and can definitely be trusted to carry my own weight around here.

As I squat to plug in the monitor in the back of the CPU, James leans in. "If there's time, I'd like to do a training session. Okay?"

I nod. When he leaves, I'm left there, wondering what is in store for me next. I run my hand over the dusty CPU and wipe it on the side of my pants, lost in thought. Aydan startles me by jumping into a quick explanation of the device I'm supposed to hack. A replica sits on the desk. It is a fancy piece of equipment that includes a thumb scanner and a keypad.

Aydan explains that Rheema will take care of the bio-data and all I have to worry about is finding the six-digit keypad combination, which happens to be encrypted and stored in one of AR-Tech's databases.

He points me to the encryption algorithm—developed by Zero Breach—and to a way to hack into AR-Tech's database. Then he explains that to cover our tracks we need to make the whole thing look like a hack, that there should be no trace left behind to indicate that insider information was used.

After Aydan's snappy explanation, he sets me loose to see what kind of damage I can do. I'm itching to show him he's not the only one with some IQ around here.

I spend thirty minutes just getting my bearings, making sure to leave no trace of my perusing in AR-Tech's servers. Once I feel comfortable with their system, I take a look at the algorithm and try to think of a way to backward engineer the encrypted password using the code. After another half hour, I have a massive headache. Trying to figure out someone else's code is a nightmare.

A brilliant idea hits me. Of course, it involves ignoring Aydan's advice, but what the heck. I have to do this my way. It'll never work if I don't.

After a while James returns. "How's it going?" he asks. "Any luck yet?"

"Some," Aydan says.

"Almost there," I say, as I type furiously.

I sense Aydan swiveling his chair my way, probably to give me the evil eye. As I tweak the last line of code, I rub my hands together.

"All right, I'm ready to try this," I say.

"There's no way you backward engineered that password in just a matter of hours," Aydan says. He couldn't have sounded more skeptical if I'd told him I was birthed by a motherboard.

"That's right. I didn't." I don't even try to keep the smugness out of my voice.

James and Aydan exchange glances, looking puzzled and incredulous, which I find a bit insulting. But no matter, I'll make believers out of them.

"You said it should look like a hack. Well, instead of faking a hack, I hacked it for real."

"You what?!" Aydan and James exclaim at the same time.

"That should have taken even longer," Aydan argues.

"Um, not really. I don't know who wrote that code, but it was easier for me to write my own than try to weed through that mess."

They don't buy it. I can tell.

Talk is cheap, so I run my program instead. Soon it flashes a six-digit code on the screen, which I enter on the keypad. When the LED light on top signals the device is unlocked, they can't argue. The expressions on their faces make me feel good. Everything is topsy-turvy at home with Mom, and at school with both Xave and Luke giving me black looks. The realization that *somebody* is pleased with me is a good one, a feeling that I've experienced very rarely since Dad died.

James grasps my shoulder. "That is outstanding, Marci!" A huge, satisfied smile shines on his face. "She's something else, isn't she?" he asks, looking at Aydan and nodding repeatedly.

"Yeah, quite a gem." Aydan's tone is derisive, but his deep dark eyes can't hide the admiration and surprise he feels. He turns back to his work. "I'll be done with my part on time. Sooner, if I can have my sanctum back to myself."

Sanctum? I guess Aydan and I have more than a few things in common. Clearly we could both worship at the altar of Holy Microchip.

"No problem, Aydan. Get back to work." James says. "Marci and I will use this time to … have a little talk."

Suddenly, I don't feel so smug anymore. I wish I'd kept my big mouth and my temper under control.

Chapter 35

I head toward the gym pod but James points in a different direction. "Let's try one of the conference rooms instead."

I match his firm stride, but it's all for show. I feel anything but firm. I doubt my hacking feat will be enough to trump both my outburst and meltdown. James leads us to conference room C and closes the door behind us. There's nothing but a table, a dry erase board and an oil painting occupying the area. Bright white lights hum overhead.

James stops in front of the painting and stares at it, hands clasped behind his back. The image is abstract, resembling a thick forest set ablaze. The tree trunks are twisted slashes of black and blue; the flames angry strokes of yellow, orange and red. Heaving a sigh, he moves away from the painting. Full of curiosity, I peer at the signature in the corner of the canvas. It reads "J. McCray." I blink.

"You painted that?" I ask, incredulously.

He ignores my question, lays his hands flat on the table and leans his weight forward. "That was some impressive computer work," he says.

"Thank you." I sense a *but* and I brace myself for it.

He's quiet for a long moment, assessing, probably trying

to decide how to best handle me.

"I thought we had agreed to trust each other." James walks to the dry erase board, takes a red marker from the tray and twirls it between thumb and forefinger.

I don't want to justify myself, but I can't help it. "Yeah, well, it's not easy when you aren't the one holding the aces under your sleeve. You don't give me enough to go by."

With measured steps, James walks back to the table and stands the marker on the wooden surface, its red tip pointing toward the ceiling.

James rests his right elbow on his cupped left hand and taps an index finger on his temple. "True. But that doesn't change the fact that you'd agreed to trust me."

I've nothing to say to that.

James nods and says, "I hope it won't happen again. I hope you have no more doubts."

"Um, I guess not, but it would've been nice to know all about Zero Breach and AR-Tech, who Elliot is, who you are, the attacks on the clinics and all that."

"I won't always be able to tell you everything, Marci. I wish we'd had more time to prepare you and tell you more, but these past few days have been very demanding on everyone. I'm sure you realize that."

"I know. I just saw you with Elliot and lost it. I'm sorry. It won't happen again."

James put his hands out and says, "Just what I wanted to hear."

"I do have a question about something Elliot said to me."

James frowns. "Something he said to you? When?"

"Just now, outside by the coffee shop."

"He saw you?"

I nod. "I waited inside the coffee shop until I thought he'd left. When I got on my bike, though, he was waiting for me. It was like he'd sensed me from far away." I scratch my head. "Maybe it's just me. He did go in to get some coffee. I think I'm just paranoid."

James appears very confused for a moment. He blinks his puzzlement away before asking, "What did he tell you?"

"Well, he wanted details on what we did to Xave. He must be some kind of sadist or something. Anyway, I told him I had better things to do than sit there talking about trivial stuff. He didn't like the fact that I didn't humor him. He said when his faction rises to the top, he'll remember I chose to not be nice to him."

With a deep breath, James changes his stance, placing both hands on his hips. "Two stupid things you did, Marci. Going into that coffee shop and falling into Elliot's bad graces."

What?! He can't be serious. I was just getting coffee and telling some creepy stalker guy to buzz off. How is that my fault?

Before I can defend myself, James adds, "But I guess that's my fault. I should have warned you against both. At any rate, I suppose you want to know what he meant with that comment."

I nod.

"Elliot is the leader of the biggest Eklyptor faction in the world. There are others, of course, and as soon as they are in a position to do so, I'm sure the different factions will fight in a quest for power. Elliot plans to be victorious. As you can imagine, he doesn't take anything he finds suspicious lightly. He's very paranoid and has spies everywhere. He has infiltrated corporations, the police, Congress. He already distrusts me, so you have to be careful. Besides, other factions have their own moles everywhere, too."

Holy crap! If I had any doubts this wasn't a game, now they're gone.

235

"I'll be careful," I promise.

"Good."

"James," I say, unable to look him in the eye. "What did he mean by saying I already chose a faction?" I think I know the answer, but I'd rather ask than jump to any more conclusions.

"He thinks I'm the leader of one such faction. He has no clue there are those who can resist infection. He's asked me repeatedly to join him. I have refused enough times for him to be resentful and suspicious. That's why I feel it's time to make ourselves known."

Oh crap, this is worse, way worse than I've anticipated. What have I gotten myself into? This hole keeps getting deeper and deeper.

We stay quiet for a minute, then James says, "With that out of the way ..." He lets the words linger, giving the red marker on the table a suggestive look. I follow his gaze and wonder if he expects me to write something on the board.

"Move it," he says.

"Excuse me?"

"Move the marker."

"Uh, o-kay." I take a step forward.

"No. Without touching it."

I laugh, a quick burst of air through my lips. "You're kidding, right?"

James's face is impassive. "No."

"I—I can't."

"You did it to the glass by Aydan's desk," James says.

"I didn't ... do that," I protest without conviction.

James smiles. "Has this happened before?"

I blink repeatedly, unsettled by what he's suggesting. There's no way we're having this conversation.

"Look …" I want to say I hallucinated the whole thing, because there's no way I made that glass move. But if James saw it move too, that shoots that theory down. "I don't know what you think you saw, but what you're suggesting is impossible."

"Is it?" James smiles with calm satisfaction. "How about this? Is this impossible?"

I stare at him as if he's gone crazy, wondering what he means. He goes on staring at me for five long seconds … then he disappears! I yelp, my heart losing its rhythm, eyes widening in alarm. As I start to turn to look around, I hear the light switch behind me flip. Utter darkness fills the room.

My breathing kicks into high gear. I try to control it.

The Invisible Man.

H.G. Wells.

Impossible!

I inhale and count to five with each deep breath. I walk tentatively toward the door, arms outstretched in front of me.

"A little bit to the right," James says. I whirl, startled, desperately trying to control the irrational panic that pounds in my chest. He's to my right, but I can't see a thing.

"Relax, Marci." His voice is soothing. The same voice he used in our meditation session. "There's no reason to freak out. It's just me."

"I'm going to turn on the light," I snap.

"Not yet," he says, still in that calm voice.

He didn't just disappear. He didn't. I repeat it over and over. But if that is true then how did he get to the light switch without me seeing him? I struggle to keep the irrational fear from driving me to tears. This can't be happening. People can't just dematerialize and put themselves back together in a different spot.

"Can you see your hands?" James asks.

"No. It's pitch-black in here. Of course I can't see."

"Ask me how many fingers you're holding up," he says.

I flip him the bird.

"Oh, very classy, Marci. No need to be rude."

"You saw that?" I ask with a slow, incredulous blink.

"Yes, and I can also see this red marker."

I hear steps and then a snap. The sharp smell of dry erase marker hits my nose. The squeak and *tap-tap* of the felt-tip against the laminate surface are unmistakable. James must be writing on the board, except it sounds as if a hundred different people are doing it at the same time. A second later, the lights burst on, stinging my eyes. I blink, willing my sight to adjust. When it does, I gasp. The board is completely covered in red blocky letters.

The phrase "IgNiTe The ShAdOwS" repeats over and over and over, probably a hundred times, from the top left corner to the bottom right. I stare at James's handiwork in disbelief, my heart no longer racing, panic no longer pounding in my breastbone. I am numb with awe.

I turn on my heels. James reclines against the wall by the light switch, arms crossed over his chest.

"Move the marker." His eyes shift back to the table where the marker lays on its side. "It's not impossible."

After what I just saw—or didn't see—James do, it's easier to buy into the whole idea that I can actually move it. With tentative steps, I approach the table and place the tips of my fingers on its wooden surface, eyes glued on the marker. I concentrate on moving it, imagine my forefinger pushing it slightly. Nothing happens. Just like that, I lose what little confidence I had, regaining the sense that this is ridiculous. No one can move things with only their minds.

"Focus," James whispers in a quiet, deep voice that soothes away my doubts.

I concentrate on nudging the marker with an imaginary finger. I try again and again, but nothing happens. Frustration builds up and I'm at the verge of slapping the marker off the table. I try a few more times until my head feels like it will implode from the wasted effort.

A sudden growl escapes from my lips, as in a desperate attempt I imagine my hand sweeping across the table, sending the marker crashing against the wall.

In the next second, time freezes. The marker doesn't fly across the room. It's still there on the table, except … it's rocking back and forth. My gaze snaps to James's for confirmation.

He nods and smiles crookedly.

"I didn't just … ?" I can't finish the sentence.

"Yes, you did."

"Holy crap! How? I—I've never done anything like that. That's just insane." I press my hands against my temples. I bite my tongue to stop the *big* expletive burning on my tongue.

James picks up the marker. "One meditation session was all it took to unlock that talent. Think what you could do if you stopped being so … hard-headed."

"But … but …" I sputter, "how does it work?"

"The exact details are anyone's guess. All we know is that punishing the agent through meditation causes *benefits* for the host. The more you meditate, the more you'll understand how to use the agent to your advantage. You will even be able to develop the skills that you'd like to acquire. Telekinesis has come naturally to you, which is amazing. I had to work very hard to gain the skills I have."

There's got to be hallucinogenic gas coming from the vents. Yeah, that's it. I'm high. Freakin' high. "People don't just …

disappear or move shit with their mind!" I feel I'm gonna lose it. Cursing is the first sign.

James laughs and pulls away from the wall. "Calm down, Marci. I didn't disappear. I just moved very fast."

"Wow, I think that's even weirder."

"It's not really weird if you think about it. There's a vast amount of untapped potential in our brains. The agents know how to get to it—something we humans seem to have forgotten over the course of our evolutionary path. Meditation will help you learn from the agent how to exploit all that undeveloped brain power. Once it realizes it can't take you over, it will resign itself to making the best of its situation. Your intuition will grow, your instincts will sharpen, your body and mind will become one. You will be aware of every organ, every cell, every atom that makes you who you are. When that happens, the sky is the limit."

"The sky's the limit? You must mean the nut house?"

"Trust me, it's nothing to freak out about," James says, looking a lot like someone trying to convince me that eating insects is a sensible idea. "Once I understood the mechanics, I actually began to enjoy making the changes. Don't get me wrong, it's very hard work and takes a long period of time. It took me three years to modify my anatomy in order to develop my skills, but it was worth it, I think." He twirls the marker at the speed of light.

Show-off.

"With the agent's help," he continues. "I've mapped every last cell in my body. More than that, I've learned to harness the necessary *ingredients* to make new tissue, bone, hair, teeth, whatever I need to alter my physiology. I wanted to be faster. So I modified my tendons, skeleton, muscles. Even my eyes are able to see in the dark. The process isn't easy.

It takes time and energy. It's why Eklyptors take years to be able to reproduce. Growing those things is no easy matter."

My head is spinning out of orbit. I rest a hand on the table to steady myself. So this is what James really meant when he said I'd learn to appreciate the meaning of the word *symbiotic*? I can have … super powers?

As if being infected since conception isn't enough, now I can also become a freak of nature if I want to. The thought of knowing the molecular composition of my every organ makes me nauseous. All I ever wanted was to be normal. Now I may need a cape and tights.

What a stupid dilemma! Doesn't every human being dream of having super powers at times? Shouldn't I be excited about this? I shake my head. No, I'm certainly not excited.

I'm scared.

I've only had one meditation session and something has already changed inside me that could land me a *Mindfreak* show on TV. What else could change if I keep on this path? My chest tightens. I take a step back.

"What's the matter?" James asks.

"I don't wanna change," I say in a trembling voice. "I didn't ask for this!"

James takes a step closer, hands up in a pacifying gesture. "Calm down, Marci. It's nothing to be afraid of."

"Is that right? How do you figure that?"

"You're still in control, aren't you?"

"Am I? Something flipped in here." I point at my head, shaking all over. "I didn't do that, so how am I still in control?"

"Because you're here, talking to me," he says, as if it's the most obvious thing on Earth. "You're not afraid of your high IQ, are you? Or your agility? So why be afraid of this?"

I take a few more backward steps, heading toward the door, toward an escape. "I don't think I'm ready for this," I say, shaking my head over and over again. The urge to crash through the door assaults me. I fight the restlessness in my legs, the need to scream, struggling to keep it together.

Then James shrugs and says, "Okay, that's fine." He picks up the marker and puts it back by the board. His mouth is turned down in an expression that suggests it doesn't really matter what I do.

Wait! I thought I would become a liability if I don't try to get my agent under control. Was that just a lie to intimidate me?

James walks past me, opens the door and, with a backward glance, says, "I won't make you do it, Marci. But you'll come around." And with that he leaves me behind, while I welcome the serenity that washes over me. I *don't* have to do it.

Good! He can believe whatever he wants. Halley's comet will come around sooner than I ever will.

Chapter 36

After I sneak past the living room and notice a pillow and a mess of covers on the empty futon, I check the kitchen, thinking I'll find Luke there. Nope. Bathroom, then.

At the bathroom, the door's ajar and the light off. I scratch my head. Where is he? My eyes flick to Mom's bedroom door—it's closed—then to mine. A sliver of light escapes through a crack and makes a line on the floor. I stomp forward and push the door open. Luke is sitting in front of my desk, poking around on my computer.

"What are you doing?" I demand.

Luke spins in the chair. "Hi!" He stands. A large smile stretches his lips. He seems so glad to see me that my annoyance at seeing his hands on my keyboard dissipates.

"I was checking my email. You're home," he says, a childlike delight on his face. "Mom went to bed hours ago."

Mom hits the sack at nine every night, which in my book is a plus. Odd how Luke makes it sound as if it's a bad thing. Why isn't he out with his friends? And on a Friday night?

I drop my keys inside a bowl on my night table and proceed to pull off my boots. "What's the matter? Heartthrob Luke's girlfriend *du jour* isn't available tonight?"

He laughs. "Heartthrob Luke? I don't think I like it. It sounds cheesy."

"Isn't cheesy your middle name?"

"No, it's Maximilian."

My fingers freeze on the shoelaces. I look up to see if this is his idea of a joke.

"What?" he asks, still looking happy to see me.

"That was … the name Mom had picked for you."

"Oh." The corners of his mouth fall and make an unhappy arch. "I—I didn't know." He collapses on the chair, shoulders slumped, back caved in, as if Truth has fists and just punched him in the gut.

He must be wondering if his middle name is a coincidence or if that twisted man gave it to him knowingly. I'd bet on the latter. Mom must have mentioned the names to him. I can picture the bastard doing an ultrasound on her belly, and Mom rambling in excitement about what she would name her babies.

Whatever cheerfulness Luke felt when I first walked in is gone now. I feel awful for telling him.

"Um, I'm sorry. I shouldn't have—" I start.

"No. It's okay. It's not your fault, and I guess I'd rather know."

"You sure?"

He nods and smiles again as genuinely as before. Man, he recovers quickly. That or he's a good actor.

His demeanor changes yet again. "Hey, Payton's having a party tomorrow night. Would you like to go?" He's Cool Luke, now. The popular boy no one can resist.

Except his sister. "I can't. I've … got a thing with Xave."

"What thing?" An undercurrent of displeasure creeps alongside his coolness.

"None of your business." I resume undoing my boots.

244

Luke sits beside me on the bed. "Nothing I should be worried about, right?"

I laugh. "Don't tell me you're gonna be one of those over-protective brothers."

He puts a hand on my forearm. I look up, startled by the touch. His fingertips feel warm on my skin. When my gaze finds his, I feel a sudden connection. Our worlds lock. Gentle concern flows like a stream down his fingers and up my arm.

"Maybe Xave isn't ... the best of influences," he says. "Some of my teammates think he's a bit of a criminal."

I pull my arm away. I'm sure those jerks think anyone who's not a football jock is no good. I shouldn't forget Luke is one of them, despite this other side he's been showing me. True, Xave is known more for skipping class than being a model student, but he doesn't smoke or drink which is more than I can say about Luke and his *friends*. More than that, he does odd jobs in his free time, fixing lawn mowers and things for the neighbors. While I'm sure Luke has never worked a day in his life.

"I bet they do," I say sarcastically. I have no time for this. I need to catch some sleep, even if only a few hours. "Look, I'm going to bed, you need to ..." I jerk my chin toward the door.

He stands, looks apologetic. "Man, that was stupid. I ..." Luke shakes his head and laughs. "I guess I *may* be one those over-protective brothers; who would've thought?" He seems truly puzzled by his own behavior. He runs his fingers through tousled blond hair. "I'm sorry. Trust me, I'm not being nosy. It's just genuine concern. That's all." He looks embarrassed, as if he wishes he hadn't stuck his foot in his mouth.

"It's okay, Luke. It's nice for someone to worry about me for a change. It's been a while since..." My throat is unexpectedly thick.

Luke mock-punches me on the shoulder. "No worries, *sis*. I got your back when you need me. All you have to do is ask." He winks and walks out, whispering "Nighty-night" before closing the door.

When I rest my head on the pillow, sleep envelops me in an instant, ushered in by a warm feeling of safety. It's ridiculous, considering what awaits me in a few hours, but Luke seems to have soothed a part of me that's been restless for a long time.

We stand under the opaque light fixtures of a crowded warehouse. The faint smell of wood mixes with the strong punch of varnish and saturates the air. No one seems to mind the odor. Their gazes are intense, determined.

The whole IgNiTe crew stands in a semicircle around James, waiting to hear whether we'll proceed with the Riverbend mission or not. Yesterday, Aydan and I worked tirelessly to finish everything. I caught three hours of sleep before James called me back to The Tank to help Aydan, who ran into unforeseen security road blocks. Presumably we've all been working hard preparing, though I've no idea what everyone else was doing.

The lack of sleep combined with the moral torment I've been going through have exhausted me. I'm still trying to come to terms with this mission and its purpose. In the heat of the moment, I volunteered to help, not knowing what I was getting myself into. Now I know my hack will allow entry to the cryo lab, where the crew plans to blow up all the embryos with plastic explosives.

I feel like we're playing God, deciding who lives and who doesn't. I try to tell myself the embryos are just cell clusters. They don't feel or know anything. More than that, they're infected. Any babies born out of those embryos would be doomed to a miserable existence. I try not to think of Luke and the fact that he's not infected, in spite of being conceived in an Eklyptor Petri dish. How many healthy embryos will we be blowing up? How many of them like me? I swallow hard and try to distract myself by worrying at a hangnail. I've come too far to let morality condemn me.

I shift my weight from one foot to the other, trying to guess what James's words will be. Part of me wishes he would call the whole thing off. My own hacking adventures are covert and small in scale, which allows me to stay unnoticed and in control of every detail. But this is something else entirely.

Notwithstanding the moral implications, this also qualifies as a major criminal activity, and trying not to think of what could go wrong to land me in jail is taking some serious delusional exercises. I should be more worried about going to hell, but I guess that's a given. Jail, on the other hand, I'd like to avoid. Way to have my priorities straight. But really, putting everything on the line—going all heist with a bunch of people I barely know—doesn't speak highly of my judgment in the first place.

The fact that I don't know if everyone did their part and if they did it right makes me extremely nervous. I know a single individual would never be able to pull off a thing like this, but having so many people involved drives the probability for error way high. I must be crazy trusting my future to this bunch. If anyone makes one mistake, we're all screwed. The thought makes my heart skid into my stomach. I trust James; I just don't know about the rest.

But what else can I do? It's not like I have another choice. Not after James explained how important the fertility centers are for Eklyptors and their plans to take over. Infecting embryos is way faster than growing nasty tentacles. So even if one part of me is scared to death, there's this other side that wants to attack them where it hurts the most.

We're all dressed in dark outfits. The IgNiTe uniform, I suppose. I stand at one end of the semicircle, followed by Aydan, Oso, Xave, Blare, and Clark.

Xave's eyes stay on me with unusual intensity. Every time I look his way, that hazel gaze locks with mine for an instant, until I turn the other way and pretend not to be interested in his insistent stare. We haven't talked since that dismal conversation about Judy, one that I've seriously come to regret, especially after seeing them all cozy and nauseating all around school.

"Now that we're all here." James turns toward the open van behind him, and pulls out something. I try to identify the object but can't see what he's holding until he whirls and starts setting it up—a camera on a tripod. He adjusts it, lens pointing in his direction, and pushes a button. A small red light begins to pulse. He takes three steps back.

"Well," James starts as he lets his eyes travel around, acknowledging everyone. "I want to thank you all for being here and for all the work you've put in these past few days. Um ..."

Um? That's gotta be a first. Seeing James hesitate weakens my legs and makes me realize how crucial his confidence is in helping me stay sane. Judging by everyone's puzzled looks, I think I'm not the only one taken aback by this unusual lack of certainty. I wait for his next words, trying to shrink the pit forming in my gut.

"I have a confession to make," he says.

Oh crap! Aydan and I exchange nervous glances. This is not wasted on Xave who is—in spite of James's commencing speech—still fixated on me.

"Uh, maybe we should get going before it gets late," Aydan interrupts.

"We have time," James responds with a reassuring smile. "Up until tonight, you have believed yourselves members of a … small resistance against the vicious invaders that threaten to make humans their slaves. Your lives have remained mostly unchanged by your involvement in our *cleansing* activities. After today, however, I'm afraid that won't be possible anymore.

"You see, this fight is bigger than I've let on. For ten years, I've been working on building a resistance. We have remained hidden because our numbers were few and our resources scarce. Up to this day, our approach has been covert for these reasons."

He calls attacking clinics covert? His definition of that word doesn't match mine at all. Maybe I'll get him a dictionary for Christmas.

"Today, however, we find ourselves at a crossroads. IgNiTe is not a mom and pop operation any longer. There are thirty-eight more cells out there. Eighteen in the US and the rest overseas."

"Holy cow!" Oso exclaims.

Everyone else remains quiet, too shocked to speak, too eager to hear all of what James has to say.

"Besides our members, our resources have also increased considerably thanks to a good number of what we like to call *true philanthropists*." He laughs at the joke with sad amusement. The irony is not wasted on me. It isn't hard to love humanity when its survival is at stake.

"Recent events have made it clear we cannot remain an underground movement anymore. AR-Tech—the parent company of all the clinics we've targeted in the past and a company ran exclusively by Eklyptor board members—has decided to revamp their security at all locations. The insider information that allowed us to break into the first clinic with relative ease will no longer be available.

"After some investigation, we've concluded that they've been planning to do this for some time. AR-Tech will be implementing their new security system tomorrow. It's a well-orchestrated, company-wide conversion, at a cost of billions of dollars.

"The probability that they suspect foul play is high. I see no other reason why they would go through such costly, secretive measures to replace the current security equipment."

James looks to the camera now and takes a deep breath.

"I hope all these reasons will explain why IgNiTe has decided to act tonight. We have all, across the country, been preparing attacks on different clinics. For some of us, all those hours of work are lost. Several of our partner cells were unable to finalize their plans on such short notice. I know it's difficult and frustrating, but I assure you, we will regroup and we will fight harder." James says the last four words with fervor, making my confidence return.

"Not all is lost, though. Some of us will be able to strike tonight and, in the end, we'll all be better off after destroying their embryonic abominations and the means to create more. After tonight's simultaneous attacks, however, Eklyptors will know for sure that someone has taken notice. After tonight, it is war. That is why ..."

James pauses and takes a deep breath, as if what he wants to say is terribly difficult.

He clears his throat. "I want to extend everyone an offer. If any of you wishes to leave, this is your chance. Think it through carefully, for we're about to become a militia."

James's eyes cut from the camera to his crew. His expression holds a question for each of us. "Are you with me?" his gaze asks.

In spite of all my fears and doubts, I nod without hesitation. Aydan, Oso, Blare, Clark and Xave do the same. We are as one, our eyes alight with the desire to fight for our survival. Screw morality. I will follow James to the end. I will fight by his side.

James's shoulders lower slightly, as if he's just let go of a huge weight. Maybe he thought there would be deserters. Not here. I wonder if it's the same in all those other cells. I hope so.

With a nod toward the camera, his expression grows in intensity and determination. His face is a pillar of strength, a mast of confidence. Eyes shining, he speaks to us and to those beyond this cramped warehouse. I assume the other cells will be watching the face of their leader on a television screen and will decide to keep on fighting. For how could anyone decide anything else?

"This cell remains complete," he announces proudly. "I trust out there it is the same and we'll continue to fight the intruders together."

Now James looks down and takes a hand to his chest. His fingers pick at something, a small patch over his black leather jacket. With one swift motion, he tears it off, revealing an insignia.

It's a triangular shape. Red and orange flames rise up from its wide base, devouring dark, ghostly figures as the fire spreads toward the pointed top. James puts a hand over his heart and pats the spot twice.

"It's time to IgNiTe and FiGhT," he pronounces, eyes alight, shining with passion, ablaze with their own brand of fire.

The intensity of his gaze and the conviction in his voice let me know I've made the right choice. With James in charge, there's no other outcome but victory against the Eklyptors.

Chapter 37

James turns off the video camera and hands it to Aydan.

"Send this to Kristen," he says in a low voice. "She'll know what to do with it."

Checking his watch, he walks back to the van and, this time, retrieves a large cardboard box. He pulls a Swiss army knife out of his pocket and cuts the tape.

"There are jackets here for everyone. Your names are stamped on the collar," James says, leaving the box and walking toward the table where the maps and plans for the mission still lay sprawled.

"What? We have to wear a uniform now?" Blare sneers.

"You don't have to, but you'll want to," James says without taking his eyes off the table.

Clark starts digging in the box, trying to find the jacket with his name on.

"Oso, here's yours," he says, throwing one to the big guy.

"Wow, cool," Oso says, shrugging into the jacket right away. "It fits like pantyhose on the legs of a hot babe." He laughs.

Clark's still digging, tossing jackets right and left. Mine flies across the air and hits me in the face. After impact, it slides down my chest and lands in my cradling arms.

Its leather is smooth in my hands. I turn it around and find the insignia. Up close I can see all the minute details outlined by different colored threads. Rich reds, oranges, and yellows for the flames. Black and many shades of gray for the shapes of screaming shadows. I have the feeling it's James's design. At the bottom, I can now make out the small letters woven with golden thread. As I look at each perfectly delineated character, Aydan's voice cuts through my trance, repeating the words written on the insignia.

"IgNiTe and FiGhT."

"I like it," Oso says in a contemplative tone. "It's catchy."

I like it, too. I slip the jacket on, roll my shoulders and move my arms to test the fit. Its leathery scent brings memories of Dad. He used to have a brown leather jacket that smelled just like this. It feels light on me, molding to my body perfectly as if it's custom-made. Curious, I check out everyone else. All except Blare are wearing their jackets now, looking tailored and shiny.

Oso examines everybody critically. "Look at you lot. You clean up real well, if I may say so." He nods repeatedly, displaying a huge smile that seems to show every single one of his teeth. "We look pretty damn awesome."

I catch James looking back at us, his mouth slanted by a small, satisfied smile. He looks like a father observing his kids after giving them a brand-new toy. My heart warms as if the insignia is seeping heat into my chest. James is a true leader. I have a feeling he and Dad would have been great friends, if they'd met.

With a sheepish expression, Blare puts on the jacket. The frown disappears from her face and I dare say she's smiling, too.

"The man's a genius."

I jump. Xave is standing next to me after sneaking up unnoticed. I look up at him. His eyes are on James. "Don't you think?" he asks, gazing back at me.

"Yeah, he is," I agree and look at my hands. I didn't realize Xave and I were back on speaking terms. He's pretty much ignored me since that day at the arcade.

Cracking my knuckles, I try to hide my embarrassment. After the way I acted, I should have been the first one to try to break the ice. I feel selfish, but mainly, I feel dumb. Why was I even mad at him? It's not like we could really be together, anyway. We know too much about each other, even if he doesn't know the most crucial part about me: the part about being infected by one of the creatures he's sworn to annihilate.

I sigh. At least it seems he still wants to be friends. I'm thankful for that.

"So … how did you hear about tonight?" he asks.

Oh, so this is why he's talking to me. The last time I joined an IgNiTe meeting, Xave was the one who told me the time and place, right after Clark told him. Given that today I got here without his involvement makes it obvious that my connection with IgNiTe is now more direct than his. If he only knew.

"From Aydan," I say.

Xave's jaw tightens. "Aydan, huh? I see."

"Since they were pressed for time. He and James … asked me to help with hacking one of the security devices."

"Oh. You got an important job. Not just a lookout, like me."

"Everyone's job is important, Xave."

He makes a skeptical sound in the back of his throat. "Sure. Well, enjoy it. I know that's your element."

Xave starts to turn away. I put a hand on his arm. He stops and stares at my fingers on his tense bicep. I snatch my hand away and something like disappointment flashes behind his hazel eyes.

"Um, be careful," I say.

We exchange glances. More passes between us in the ensuing silence. Regret. Concern. Longing.

"You, too." His voice is soft, with real concern behind it.

"I'll be fine. Just sitting in the van in case something goes wrong with my code."

"Good."

Xave takes a few steps backward, holding my gaze. My lower lip trembles with words that need to be spoken. I bite them back and swallow hard. I have to keep reminding myself that I have nothing to offer him. Lies are not a good foundation for any type of relationship. And if I offered the truth, things would be far worse than they are now.

I break eye contact. I let him go.

Chapter 38

Aydan and I sit inside the van parked off-road under the cover of trees. We left the warehouse around 3:20 A.M. and drove west on I-90 for forty minutes or so. After Oso exited the interstate, I lost track of where we were. He took several secluded roads. And all I know now is that we are in the boonies, surrounded by mountains and lots of trees. I can't see much else. It is dark and cloudy outside. Eerie, if you ask me.

We stare into four monitors that display different perspectives. The first one shows Rheema's car's dashboard with her hands at the steering wheel. The second, jumpy images of bushes and trees rushing by. They come from James's camera, who—accompanied by Oso and Blare—left the van ten minutes ago and ran up the wooded hill toward the clinic. The third and fourth monitors show two empty roads where Xave and Clark are serving as lookouts.

A speaker crackles to life and Rheema's voice resonates through the van. "All right, we're here," she says.

On the first monitor, her car slows down as it approaches a thirty-foot-wide metal gate.

"Okay, working on it," Aydan responds through a tiny microphone attached to an equally small earpiece. He types on the keyboard at a prodigious speed, running the program that will allow Rheema and her companion entry to the compound.

When James described the place, I started thinking about it more as a compound than a fertility clinic. Located in a remote area, surrounded by tall stone walls, protected by a high-security system, it's hardly a place that makes me think of cuddly babies. Apparently, Riverbend caters to Seattle's elite. People who pay top dollar to receive advanced fertility treatments in anonymity and extra comfort. If they knew what they were getting, I bet they wouldn't feel so special.

Rheema pulls over and turns slightly to her left. A hairy arm appears on the screen: the gate guard. He moves closer to the car.

"No signal yet, Rheema," Aydan says as he continues to smash keys like a mad man.

I grind my teeth, a fist pressed against my lips. Oh please, please, work.

"Your card," the guard asks Rheema in an unfriendly tone.

"Good night, or I guess I should say good morning," she says in good humor, trying to make time.

"Your card," the guard repeats after an annoyed grunt.

"Sure." Rustling cuts through the speakers as Rheema pretends to dig in her purse. "It's here somewhere," she adds with a nervous laugh.

Aydan mashes the enter key with an index finger. "Got it!"

"Ah, here it is." Rheema hands the guard a white plastic card.

Aydan explained that, when the guard flashes the card with his handheld device, Rheema's picture will appear on his screen indicating whether she's authorized to enter the facility at this time. During normal business hours, she would have no problem getting in. It turns out a few months back, she snatched a proper job as a lab assistant, and since then she's been gathering information about the clinic's operations.

Just now, Aydan managed to intercept the mobile's signal and download all the required data to get Rheema and her companion through the front entrance. They didn't have approval to be here today at this early hour, but Aydan's program took care of adding them to the list on the fly.

I hear a beep. I assume it's the guard running Rheema's card through the security check. There's a long silence, during which I bite my nails, hardly noticing what I'm doing. The computer monitor shows Rheema's hands squeezing the wheel.

"Here," the guard says. His face appears as Rheema turns to retrieve her card. The square-jawed man peers in to check the empty back seat then the person in the passenger seat.

"Your card," the guard orders.

A hand holding a security badge crosses in front of the camera. It belongs to a man, a fertility doctor named Dr. Schmitt, who also works at the clinic.

The guard grabs the card and puts it through the same test. Aydan sits, hands on his lap, jaw working with a nervous tic.

Rheema's job was to fool Dr. Schmitt in to accompanying her. He has clearance to enter the vitrification lab, something Rheema doesn't possess. The doctor is in charge of readying embryos before implantation. Rheema, his clever lab assistant, has access to all medical records and informed him that one of his patient's hormonal levels indicate the woman will be ready for implantation at 7 A.M., which is why they had to be here so early to prepare the sample.

Apparently, this is a common occurrence. It turns out fertility isn't an exact science and women's bodies will do whatever they want, whenever they want to, no matter how many pills and injections they push on them. So Dr. Schmitt came along suspecting nothing out of the ordinary.

"You're clear," the guard says, opening the massive metal gate. As the car enters the compound, both Aydan and I breathe a sigh of relief. We switch our attention to James's monitor. It shows a dark backdrop punctuated by even darker shapes. Bushes, I guess.

"She's in," Aydan announces after pressing a button to switch audio over to James, Blare and Oso.

They have finished trekking up the steep hill behind the clinic and are now stationed outside the fortress, waiting for Aydan's signal to climb the wall. The guards' shift ends at 5 A.M., at which time they perform a patrol. If all goes well, the crew should have enough time to do what they need to do.

On the computer screen, Aydan pulls up the next piece of code. It will disable the various cameras and alarms that monitor the perimeter, giving James, Blare and Oso two minutes to scale the wall. This is a small window of time, but more than two minutes would cause a failover systems to activate, giving away our presence.

"Ready?" Aydan asks.

"Ready," James's deep voice rumbles through the speakers.

Aydan clicks on a button labeled "X Perimeter Security" and says, "Go, now!"

The images coming from James's camera start moving as he runs toward the wall, which looms like a giant. Seconds tick by, flashing on Aydan's computer screen.

"One hundred seconds," Aydan informs James.

Oso gets ahead of James and drops to one knee a couple of feet away from the wall. He looks as if he's about to propose. James doesn't slow down. Instead, he leaps, uses

Oso's bent leg as a step stool and propels himself upward. In a blur, the wall passes by on the screen.

Once at the top, he secures a rope and lets it drop. James doesn't wait for Blare and Oso. Instead, he jumps down on the other side and starts running toward the main building. His camera reveals a place that looks like a mansion, not a clinic: a perfect hideout for the rich and famous to get their little spawns implanted. AR-Tech's tactics are scary. They target the wealthy, where Eklyptors seek to place parasites in positions of power.

"Sixty seconds," Aydan announces.

James runs through an almost empty parking lot. I spot Rheema's car already parked there. When he's only a few paces from the building, he slows down, looks back and confirms Oso and Blare are right behind him. They soon catch up.

"No sign of guards," James says.

There are supposed to be guards that patrol the grounds, but they're probably sleeping, too confident in their state-of-the-art security system to care. One can never underestimate the complacency of an underpaid employee, Eklyptor or not.

Instead of going straight to the front entrance, James and the others approach from the side and walk along one of the walls. These are blind spots, so if the cameras activate again they'll be in the perfect place to remain unnoticed.

"Forty seconds." Aydan presses mute and glares at my hands. "Stop that!" I've been cracking my knuckles and hadn't even realized it.

"Sorry," I say.

James comes to a halt and presses his back against the wall. Slowly he peeks around the corner. In his camera, I see Rheema and the doctor standing in front of a huge glass door. Rheema's monitor shows the same door, except up close. The palm, retina and voice scanners are in front of Dr. Schmitt, who lets the device take his bio-data.

A big thumbs-up from James lets Oso and Blare know everything is going as planned.

"Twenty seconds," Aydan says.

"Welcome, Doctor Schmitt," a computerized voice echoes through Rheema's audio feed.

As soon as the thick glass doors slide open, James and the others rush in. Rheema walks into a large lobby, followed by Dr. Schmitt. After a few steps, she whips around, takes two quick steps, and stands only inches from the doctor.

James is quietly entering the lobby. From his perspective, I see the doctor's back and Rheema wrapping her arms around the man's neck, as if she's going to … kiss him?

I look to Aydan, wondering what's going on. I'm about to say something when Dr. Schmitt falls to the floor like a limp rag. Oso and Blare come in just as he falls.

"What did she just do?" I ask.

"Neurotoxin," he says.

"Huh?"

Aydan looks at me as if I'm incapable of adding two and two together to save my life. "They made it in with time to spare. Too easy."

"Shut up. You're gonna jinx them," I snap.

"Jinx them? You don't seem like the superstitious type."

"I'm not, but still."

"Now to the lab," Aydan says to no one in particular.

My hands have already been sweating, but the thought that this part of the mission depends on my hack makes them feel as if I've dipped them in a pot of drool.

All four rush through long, expertly decorated corridors. When they reach the lab, Oso, who's been carrying Dr.

Schmitt over his shoulder, lets James grab the man's hand and place his thumb on a little scanner. After the thumb print, it's time to enter the six-digit number my program deciphered. They dump the doctor on the floor next to the door.

My gut clenches as Aydan pulls up the number onto the screen and starts calling it out. "Seven …"

Skipping beats, my heart makes itself noticed. My back tingles and a strange sensation rolls in waves down my spine. James's hand goes up to the keypad.

"Wait!" I yell.

"Marci says to wait," Aydan blurts out.

James's hand freezes. "What's wrong?"

Aydan gives me an incredulous look.

"I … what if the code changed?" I ask.

"Changed in the last couple of hours?" Aydan asks, sounding annoyed. We ran my algorithm more than once and got the same six-digit code every time. I don't quite understand why all of a sudden I'm freaking out. But something feels funky in the pit of my stomach, like a swarm of bees buzzing their way up my esophagus.

"Yeah, it could have," I say.

"Didn't you check for maintenance programs that could change the code on us?"

"Of course, I did. There weren't any."

"Sooo?"

"What if they changed it manually?"

"I guess they could have, but that's stupid and error-prone. So, not likely," Aydan says.

"What's going on?" James asks through clenched teeth.

"One sec," Aydan tells him.

"I knew we shouldn't have trusted her with this." Blare's voice breaks through in a growl.

I ignore her. "Let's run it again. Let's see if it comes back with the same six numbers."

"Marci, we don't have time for that," Aydan growls.

"It'll only take five minutes," I plead.

"Five minutes that could make all the difference. The guards' shift is in half an hour."

"Please, just run it again. I don't know why, but I have a *bad* feeling about it. Please."

Aydan sighs. "James, Marci wants to run her program again. She says she has a bad feeling about it, thinks the numbers may have changed since the last time we checked. It'll take at least five minutes to rerun."

"Shit, shit," Blare curses.

"Quiet," James says. "Put Marci on."

Aydan hands me his headset, digs for another one and puts it on.

"Marci, we have no time to waste," James says.

"I know, I know, but something doesn't feel right. I don't know why, but I think we should run it again."

"Are you sure?" James asks.

"Yes," I say firmly.

"All right, do it," James orders.

Aydan cracks his neck, then clicks on the button that runs my program. I watch, chewing on my lower lip. The computer screen shows an hourglass as my code flies through the list of possible six-digit combinations, checking them against the encryption algorithm.

The minutes drag by and I'm drenched in sweat, tasting blood from biting so hard on my lip. Blare curses, spewing expletives like a public toilet spews bacteria. Aydan stares at the screen from under tense eyebrows and taps on the keyboard's edge using all ten fingers. I want to yell at him to stop, but instead I bite harder and draw more blood. The last few seconds are more than physically painful. My body is so tense that my muscles are literally working out.

When the last few seconds tick down, I feel myself relax. A brand-new set of numbers appears on the screen. Aydan curses.

"The numbers are in. They're different," he announces.

James clears his throat. "Marci, can we trust these new numbers?"

"Ha, if you run that stupid program of hers again, you'll probably get a different answer." Blare voices what I'm sure everyone else is thinking.

But the weird feeling I had before is now gone. I know my program is foolproof. I know the numbers are good. "You can trust them. They will work," I say with as much confidence as if I was stating my name.

"Call them out, Aydan," James says.

Aydan begins, intoning every number with a question mark at the end, as if he expects each one to be the last one before the keypad auto-destructs. James punches the buttons with confidence, though. He either trusts me or his nerves are made of steel. It's probably the latter, but I can't help but hope to have earned some of his trust.

When James enters the last number, there's a collective sigh of relief as the door clicks open. I feel like standing and doing a little dance, but a gasp from Rheema and a few choice curse words from Blare keep me in my seat.

"What the hell?" Oso exclaims.

Rheema enters the room. Her camera suddenly shows revolving walls as she turns round and round. I feel dizzy as I try to make sense of what seems to be an empty room.

"It's all gone," Rheema says, coming to a stop. "Everything was here just yesterday morning. I don't understand. It's all gone."

Chapter 39

James approaches one of the walls, stares at a set of electric plugs and a few loose cables. "Where did they take everything?" he asks in a low, rumbling tone. He whirls to face Rheema. "Think, Rheema. It's still in the building, right? It has to be."

"I ... I don't know."

"Think," James repeats in a lower tone.

"Um ..." I hear Rheema's deliberate intakes of breath. "Wait!" Her face lights up with an idea. "I've seen some activity in the north side. A few weeks ago, I noticed some new people in that area."

"Let's go." James runs out of the room. "Which way?"

"Left," Rheema calls out.

After rushing through a few more corridors, going deeper into the guts of the building, Rheema leads everyone to a locked door. "Maybe here," she says, sounding unsure.

James tries the handle. "It's locked." He examines the door carefully. "Are you sure, Rheema? This is just a normal lock."

Rheema doesn't respond. I imagine her shrugging.

"I can pick it." Oso says.

"This is messed up! Nothing is going as planned. What if when you open that door it triggers an alarm?" Blare says.

"It's possible, but that's a risk I'm willing to take. We have to get to the cryo freezers!" James responds.

Blare punches the wall with her fist. "They knew we were coming. It's a trap."

Man, I wish she would shut up for just one minute. Every comment out of her mouth is nothing but demoralizing.

"Uh, so ... what do we do?" Oso asks.

Through Rheema's camera, I see James rub his neck, his face grim as he considers what to do. "I'll pick the lock. Aydan, keep your eyes open on the outgoing messages, alarm, gate status, the roads, anything to help detect any movement right after we get past this door. Understood?"

"Understood," Aydan says. Our eyes flick to the monitors that display the clinic's adjacent roads, shown from Xave and Clark's cameras. Both streets look clear, dead actually, since 4 A.M. isn't exactly a time of the day the reproductively-challenged rich and famous even know exists. I doubt any of them get up before 10.

James drops on one knee and gets to work on the lock. After a few seconds, he stands, takes a deep breath and turns the knob. Complete darkness greets him on the other side. He fumbles for a switch and finds one. White fluorescent light floods the space, revealing a flight of stairs that heads down.

"The basement," James says. "Any activity on the cameras, the gate?"

"None," Aydan responds.

"C'mon, let's hurry." The crew runs downstairs, skipping two and three steps at a time.

At the bottom, they encounter a cramped space filled with building materials and tools. Several piles of metal sheets, bars and assorted parts litter the floor. Most interestingly, there's a huge, thick steel door leaning against a side wall.

From the looks of it, they're in the middle of installing what appears to be a huge-ass bank vault.

After a quick glance around, both monitors focus on a wide metal door set opposite the building materials. James approaches and examines it up close, first the right side then the left. When he straightens, he laughs one short, ironic laugh.

"What?" Blare asks.

"Cylinder locks. Two on each side, meant to be open in sync, I'm sure," James says, shaking his head.

"So what's the big deal? Oso also knows how to pick a lock, he can help you," Blare puts in.

"These aren't just any type of lock. They're the best that company makes and they require a special key. Have you ever picked one like this, Oso?" James's voice is doubtful, yet hopeful.

"Uh." Oso bends forward and examines one of the locks. "I don't think so. Sorry." The big guy's face twists with guilt.

"It'd take too long to show you how." James presses two fingers in between thick eyebrows and screws his eyes shut. "The irony is just ... too much. Two temporary locks stand in our way."

I'm holding my head between my hands in disbelief. We came this far to be thwarted by some ancient technology. Whatever happened to leaving sophisticated computers in charge of things? Computers that allow genius hackers to unlock any door from the comfort of their vans? This is ridiculous.

Blare takes off her backpack, drops it on the floor and gets on one knee. "Let's just blow it up then."

"It's no use." James pounds on the door. It sounds as solid as concrete. "The door looks pretty thick and heavy. And if I know anything about Elliot and the way he and his *people* do things, if we blow the locks up, the door will seal from the inside, triggering an alarm that will give away our presence before we're able to destroy what we came here to destroy."

"How about the walls? We could blow *them* up." Blare's hands are busy, pulling out tools from her pack.

"No, Blare. They've built this whole area as a vault. Look at the door they're getting ready to install."

"I know." Oso puts a hand on the huge hunk of metal that looks like a huge submarine hatch, rather than something you'd find at a medical facility. "You'd think this is Fort Knox."

James continues, "The walls have to be reinforced concrete. We would need several charges to do any real damage. By then, the guards would be on us."

"What if we drill through them first? Huh? What about that?" Blare looks up at James, her voice sounding more desperate with each question.

"It won't work." James's tone is steady, even though we face defeat.

"So we came all this way for nothing?!" Blare yells in anger. "Is that what you're saying?"

"Shit!" Aydan exclaims. "You mean two stupid, low-tech locks are going to stop us? You've got to be kidding me." He slams a fist against the side of the van.

It has to be a joke, a big fat joke the cosmos is playing on us. What kind of criminal doesn't know how to pick a lock, no matter what kind?! But I guess that's just it, we're not criminals. We're just a bunch of regular fools trying to save the world. If only Oso or Rheema or … wait a minute.

"What type of locks are they?" I ask.

Aydan looks at me, annoyed. His expression asking *Does it matter?*

"Evva," James responds.

Oh crap. "I—I think I know how," I say.

"What?" Aydan is shaking his head, probably thinking that I'm full of it.

James points his camera to one of the locks. "Take a close look at it," he says. "Have you picked one like this before?"

The sight of it conjures old memories. "Yes, a similar one," I whisper.

The image of Dad's desk takes shape in my mind. One of the drawers had a lock that looked very similar to the one on the monitor. After Dad died, I got obsessed with finding out what was inside that desk. I searched the house for the key but was never able to find it. Later I discovered Mom kept it in a safe deposit box at the bank.

I begged her to let me have it, but she refused, said she was thinking about selling the ugly old thing. I pleaded with her not to do it. She refused me that, too. Before she got around it, though, I taught myself how to pick that lock. I cried all night after I found the drawers empty. Mom had taken everything out, and I can't help but think there was something in there she didn't want me to see. Some piece of Dad that was meant for me, something she was too selfish to share. I suspect his will and testament was there, spelling in clear legal terms that the house was mine—also some of his medical files. I distinctly remember him puzzling over charts and numbers, especially after he ran lab tests on me, trying to figure out what ailed me. If he'd only known.

"Aydan," James's voice is clear, full of command and poise. "Get her in here."

Chapter 40

"I can't let her in," Aydan protests. "I can only deactivate the cameras twice. I—I didn't plan for more than that."

"You mean your hack is *fixed, hard-coded*?" I can't help but laugh. Aydan shoots me a poisonous stare.

I know it's wrong to call him out. This is a tough spot for all of us, but still. I'm tired of his pompous, there's-no-hacker-better-than-me attitude. I can't believe he didn't plan for hiding more than four minutes of camera activity. Two minutes to get in and two to get out would have sufficed if everything had gone as planned; but really, when do things ever go as you expect? Has he even heard of Murphy's Law? I don't know what he had to do to accomplish even those two small time windows, but it seems to me he should have planned for more. One can never be too cautious when it comes to hacks, especially those that put people's lives at risk.

Quick to understand, James starts calling the shots. "Marci, are you up for coming in here?"

"Yes, I want to help." I don't know where this bravery is coming from, but it's too late to back out now. I may as well go all-in.

"Can you scale the wall?"

"I think so."

"I don't like this," Blare growls.

"Do you have a better idea?" James asks her.

Blare throws down the tools in her hands and paces around the room.

"All right. Aydan, deactivate the cameras for her."

"You realize that on your way out—when I deactivate them a third time—the alarm will go off and you risk getting caught?" Aydan argues.

"We knew this mission would be different. There's no turning back. We'll take that risk," James says.

"Okay, I'll deactivate them, but don't blame *me* later."

James tells me where to get a lock-picking set, rope and other supplies.

When I'm ready, Aydan pins a camera to my jacket. "The longer we stay around, the greater our chances of getting caught." He shakes his head. "I personally think this is pushing it. But I guess I'm not the boss. Anyway, just keep running. Don't stop. I'll deactivate the perimeter as soon as you get close to the wall. Okay?"

I nod and turn to leave.

"Marci." Aydan puts a hand on my elbow. "Be careful." His voice is a low whisper and it breaks a little, as if it's too hard to show that he cares somehow.

I leave without a word and move toward the wall at top speed. My heart pumps hard as my legs trek through heavy undergrowth and over uneven terrain. I try not to think about what I'm doing, and what would happen if we were to be captured.

Closing my mind to anything else, I concentrate on my body. I relish my agility and strength until the wall comes into view. Then I focus on the task ahead. Quickly, I judge the wall. It looks about nine or ten feet tall. Without stopping, I run straight toward the barrier, building momentum.

When I'm only a few feet away, I jump toward it. As my foot hits the brick, I use the built-up force to propel myself upward. Arms extended straight over my head, I reach for the top. The force of my jump is enough to take my fingers past the target by a couple of inches. When gravity claims me and I start coming down, I grip the edge. I move my feet fast, walking up the wall, using the remaining energy to scale the obstacle.

Muscles rippling, I clamber to the top and, without stopping to think, I jump down. Ducking my head, I roll over my back and keep spinning until I'm on my feet and running away.

I head straight for the front door, looking in all directions. Suddenly, I spot a dark shape next to one of the lampposts on the west end of the building about forty yards away. I duck and hide behind Rheema's car, by one of the back tires. My lungs are pumping and I struggle to take deep, silent breaths.

One inch at a time, I slide up and peek through one of the back windows. On the other side, I can see a man smoking a cigarette. I freak out for a split second, wondering if he can sense me. But my head isn't droning, so he's either too far or he's not an Eklyptor. I pray he doesn't walk this way, hope he's almost done with his cigarette.

Time is ticking down and the man continues sucking away on his cancer stick. Anger brews inside me. *Hurry up!* I've no idea how long he's been out here or what he will do once he's done watching into the night through the billowing cloud of smoke. I take another peek, try to determine how long his cigarette is. I curse under my breath. It looks as if he just got started.

"Marci, what are you doing?" Aydan says through the earpiece. "Only twenty seconds left."

I take a deep breath and decide to go for it. Staying low, I tiptoe from my hiding place, tentatively at first, my eyes glued on the man's back. I'm only about twenty yards from the entrance, where a wall recess will provide the perfect hiding spot.

Halfway there, I notice Oso waiting for me behind the glass door. He holds his hands palm-up in question, wondering why I'm skulking about. From where he stands, he can't see the guard. Getting braver, I pick up my pace. When I reach a pathway lined by immaculately hedges, a voice reaches my ears carried by the wind.

"Got another one?"

I look to the left and notice a second guard walking toward the first one. The smoker starts to turn and I know he will spot me if I don't do something. Panicked, I drop to the ground in a sort of drop push-up. The bushes hide me from view and give me a perfect path to sneak to the entrance, which I do in a military crawl.

After reaching the recess, I stand and press my back to the wall. I point and mime the word "Guards" to Oso. He nods in understanding, then drags the still unconscious Dr. Schmitt to the thumb scanner on the inside. The door slides open with the smallest whooshing sound.

Oso and I exchange no words. He simply drops the doctor and takes off at a clipped jog. I follow right behind. Once at the basement door, he waves me in and I trot downstairs with a surprisingly purposeful gait.

The doubts that gave me pause before seem to be gone now, and I'm not really sure why. Perhaps it's seeing what lengths AR-Tech goes to protect its spawn creations. Or maybe it's finally having the opportunity to act, instead of just sit on my ass. Could be that it's easier to judge others when one isn't an active party. No doubt I'm involved now. I'm here to help, to be a real part of IgNiTe's war against Eklyptors.

Suddenly, the possibility of failure is unthinkable. I must succeed, because the thought of innocent babies coming into the world without ever standing a chance at being human twists my gut into knots. If I had set out to imagine the most wicked, despicable thing possible, I could never have come up with this nightmare. Human minds trapped, aware of their imprisonment every second of their existence. It's like being born an eagle but never allowed to soar across the sky. Worse yet, what about those *lucky* few who might escape that fate to end up just like me, haunted by shadows, pain and loneliness?

There's no doubt, now. I'm meant to be here. This fight is my own.

Chapter 41

Blare looks up from a crouching position on the floor, her backpack's contents scattered in a semicircle in front of her. She offers me a quick, contemptuous glance and continues her work. I stare at her hands as they deftly prepare what looks like enough explosives to blow up Mount Rushmore. And for the first time, I wonder if Blare is a nickname. I remember Elliot calling her Veronica at the party. Is that her real name?

James walks up to me and places a hand on my shoulder. His eyes look both proud and sad at the same time. "Great job getting in, Marci."

I nod and give him a faint smile.

"All right, here's the deal. There's little chance we'll undo both locks exactly at the same time. We'll be lucky if we can do it at all. But if we manage, I'm certain the alarm will go off." James's words spill out one after another. "We won't have time for anything else besides setting the charges on the cryo freezers. Blare, are they ready?"

"Yes," she answers.

"Good. As soon as the explosives are in place, we run out of this damn building. Marci, you'll go last. Oso and

I will go first." James takes a moment to look everyone in the eye, then says, "Try not to get shot."

"I'll go upstairs and stand guard by the door," Oso says. "Just in case." He leaves without waiting for an answer.

I swallow. James is making me go last to protect me, and I'm reminded again that, to him, I'm just a child who needs to be safeguarded. Still, what sense does it make to protect me above everyone else? He's far more important than me. I'm just a foot soldier. He's the commander-in-chief.

James extends a hand toward the first lock. I approach it as if it was a deadly insect.

"Take your sweet time. We have all night," Blare says sarcastically.

James gives her cold, scolding eyes and puts a finger to his lips. "Shhh, she's our only hope of rescuing this mission."

Rheema steps quietly to one side and gives me two thumbs-up. Her eyes tell me she trusts I can do this. I hope I don't disappoint her.

Kneeling by the lock on the left, James encourages me to get by the one on the right. I take a knee in front of the door. As I take deep breaths and examine the set of small lock-picking tools, Blare's expletives—it's like she has freakin' Tourette's syndrome or something—become a faint buzz.

Inhale.

Ketchup stain on my shirt.

Exhale.

I pick two of the tools and insert them one by one into the keyhole. My lungs expand and collapse, moving more rapidly than I intend them to. One of the small tools slips from my grip and makes a clinking sound as it hits the concrete floor.

"Relax, Marci. If you can't open it, it's okay. Just give it your best shot," James says as he slowly works on his lock with steady hands.

I pick up the tool and try to ignore Blare who has started pacing up and down like a caged lioness … or maybe a hyena. Wiping my hands on my black cargo pants, I twist my neck from side to side. I can do this, if only to shut Blare up.

Putting the tools back inside the lock, I set to work, letting instincts and memories steer me. I move the pick in my right hand up and down. Eyes closed, I listen to the small clicks to guide me. Sweat drips down my forehead and becomes lodged in one eyebrow. I ignore it even as it begins to itch and makes me want to scream.

"How's it going?" James asks. "I think I'm almost done."

"I—I'm doing okay."

But it's a lie. Panic is welling up and I'm starting to feel as if I'll drown in it. On the outside, this lock looks like the one in Dad's desk. But on the inside, I can't make heads nor tails out of its mechanism. My chest feels tight, and I'm afraid I might start sobbing like the kid everyone figures me for.

Squeezing my eyes shut in an effort to quell my rising despair, I try to clear my mind of all thoughts. It may be a terrible idea at this moment, but something tells me that's what I need to do. Far away, I can hear an annoying *yap, yap, yap.* I think it's Blare running her motor mouth. I dismiss her, shove her deep down in the not-at-all-important mental drop box. Every fear and every doubt that enters my mind gets stuffed into nowhere-land with Blare.

A sudden peace sweeps through me and, without preamble, the lock's complex mechanism materializes in front of my eyes like a 3D image. The clear-as-daylight picture in my mind should freak me out. Yet the image of the small, interlocking disks and bars that can only be arranged in the right order by a special key seems like the most natural thing.

I should be panicking, losing my mind. This isn't right. This isn't me. I never asked to change, to be able to do inhuman things. But instead, it feels right. It's just what we need right now to avoid failure. It's what may save us all. So I take a deep breath and accept it.

When my mind is settled, I become keenly aware of the fact that James is almost done picking his lock. If I hurry and catch up, the door will open without activating the alarm. I work frantically, using the picture in my mind to move the pick in the right direction. I want to tell James to slow down, to give me a few seconds to catch up to him, but I know if I speak my trance will break and I'll lose the lock's image.

A grinding sound distracts me for a second, but I realize it's just my teeth. I ignore it.

"You can do it, Marci." James's soothing voice echoes in the depths of my spell. "Just breathe." Precious air fills my lungs. I didn't know I had stopped breathing.

Seconds pound like hammers inside my ears. James is a couple of steps away from finishing.

Hurry!

My heart seems to explode time and time again. My fingers feel like lead sausages, too clumsy and heavy to succeed, to get us out of here without being noticed. Suddenly, my thoughts jump ahead. They don't just show me the motion my fingers should perform now, but the next, and next and next.

Of their own accord, my hands stop. Yet the insides of the lock continue clicking, aligning themselves in the right position. Things fall into place at a staggering speed. James is almost there. I have to hurry. I have to catch up and

278

prevent the alarm from going off. I can't let the Eklyptors trap us in here.

Anger builds up. I urge it to climb higher and higher. I hate this pathetic obstacle. I hate what lays behind it. This small thing in my hand is nothing. My heart beats faster. The lock clicks and clicks, turning, whirling. I'm only five steps away from James, four now, three, two ...

Something sharp cuts through my throat and eardrums. I open my eyes to see my arms flailing. I'm screaming so loud my voice is hoarse, my larynx burns. A strident, intermittent noise drills inside my skull. The alarm is blaring.

James helps me to my feet. "You did it, Marci."

I look at the door. It looks the same.

Noticing my confusion, James explains, "The bolt clicked, then the alarm went off. Here." He shoves a piece of chocolate in my mouth. It's bitter, not sweet at all.

I give him a nasty look. "Yuk," I say, holding my head between shaky hands, worried that I blacked out again, and mad about not being able to prevent the alarm from going off.

James ushers me out of the way toward Rheema. She wraps an arm around me and rubs my shoulder. "Good job, girl."

"We only have precious seconds," James says. As soon as the last word leaves his mouth, Aydan's voice bursts through my earpiece.

"Guards headed your way. Hurry!"

James pulls on the door. It opens with the moan of heavy metal to reveal an expansive area as big as a tennis court, full of state-of-the-art medical equipment. I press closer to Rheema, my jaw slack in awe.

Suddenly, shots erupt upstairs. James's attention flickers toward the exit for a split second, then back to Blare. His intense gray eyes say it all. I imagine the guards rushing in, shooting at Oso, peppering his thick chest with a thousand bullets. The thought of that mellow, cheerful guy being shot makes my mouth go dry.

We're trapped, and it's my fault.

Chapter 42

Without a word, James nods to Blare and then takes the stairs two at a time, pulling a gun from inside his jacket, rushing to help Oso. I know it must kill him to have to move that slow to hide his powers from Blare.

She wastes no time, rushes past the metal door and is soon standing in front of a vast array of strange-looking equipment. I don't know what I was expecting, but inside looks like some sort of spaceship, full of stainless-steel cylinders that must be used for embryo vitrification. There is a sharp chemical smell in the air and not a speck of dust anywhere, in spite of the fact that the place is under construction.

Blare's hands move at a staggering pace, sticking plastic explosives to the sides, tops, and bottoms of cryo freezers, cabinets, microscopes, tables. Everywhere. As she sets each charge, she punches a button and seconds start ticking down on clock displays. They all read the same. Two minutes.

She's done before I have time to get over the shock of having actually unlocked the door. She takes the stairs, pulling out a weapon of her own, a huge automatic gun that looks like it could blow anyone's head into oblivion. Rheema follows, armed with not one, but two guns.

I stand there dumbfounded for a second too long, feeling defenseless without my own weapon. Maybe this is why James wanted me to go last. I snap out of it and rush upstairs, trying to ignore the repeated gunfire and the scent of spent ammunition clogging the air.

When I reach the top, I crouch and peek around the door. Rheema, Blare and James are standing with their backs against the opposite wall, clutching their weapons, muzzles pointing toward the ceiling. James is further up, where the hall intersects with our only exit. He takes a quick peek around the corner, aims and shoots. A bullet whizzes by and strikes the back wall, sending pieces of drywall in all directions. James pulls back.

I search for Oso, and I'm relieved when I see him kneeling at the other side of the intersecting hall. He sticks a hand out and shoots around the corner without looking.

"Rheema, what's the quickest way out?" James asks, after sending another bullet down the hall.

Three consecutive loud cracks make me flinch, as more drywall erupts and sprinkles the dark carpet with fine, white dust.

Rheema closes her eyes, thinking hard. "Second right, then a left," she says. "There's a fire exit."

"Okay, I'll take care of the guards. At my signal, run for it."

"James!" Blare calls out in a panicked tone. But it's too late, he's already turned the corner, disappearing from view amid a battery of gunshots.

"You crazy bastard," Oso says.

Blare moves up and looks around the corner. A bullet hisses by her head, and she pulls back, looking impossibly paler than she already is. She curses under her breath.

"He's gone," she says, perplexed. She has no idea how fast James can move.

"I can't just sit here and wait," Oso says, and with that he rushes into the hall, too.

Gunshots redouble, and suddenly I'm thought-jumping at a staggering speed. I shut my eyes.

Oso.

Pink sucks.

James.

Okay. They'll be okay.

Rheema nudges me with one elbow. My eyes spring open and meet her dark brown gaze.

"They'll be okay," she says, as if she's read my thoughts.

"Now!" Aydan's voice echoes faintly through my earpiece, almost imperceptible in the din of gunfire.

We sprint into action. Blare goes first, walking cautiously with her huge gun at the ready. Rheema does the same, both guns pointed to the floor. The hall is empty, walls punctured with a spray of bullets.

"Keep going," Rheema says when we get to the first corridor that intersects with ours.

The fight continues ahead of us, but the crack of exploding bullets is further away. James and Oso are flushing the guards out of the building.

"Shit," Blare exclaims at the sight of a puddle of blood on the floor and splatters on the wall. "Is James shot?"

My stomach clenches. I wish that is Eklyptor blood.

Please. Please.

"James and Oso are fine," Aydan says through the earphone.

We all breathe a sigh of relief.

"Is that where we need to turn?" Blare asks as the next intersecting hallway comes into view.

"Yes," Rheema says.

"C'mon, I think it's clear."

"It is. Go, go, go," Aydan says.

Abandoning all stealth, we run into the passage, then take a left. Ahead, the exit sign flashes red in time with each shriek from the alarm. Blare pushes the door open and we break into the crisp, clear night. We look in all directions, trying to regain our bearings.

"Go right, around the back," Aydan instructs.

"Screw that," Blare snaps, sprinting left, the glint of her silver gun moving up and down as her arms pump.

Left leads toward the front, where Oso and James are fighting the guards. Blare seems determined to get in the middle of things. Rheema shrugs and follows Blare. I know it's stupid, unarmed as I am, but I'm right behind them.

When Blare reaches the building's south edge, she skids to a stop, digging her feet into the supple ground of a large flower bed. Rheema and I stop just in time, inches shy of crashing into each other.

"James and Oso are still inside, but the guards left the building and—wait!" Aydan stops mid-sentence, a note of extra urgency in his voice. "Xave reports reinforcements speeding down Rachor Road. He says he'll try to stop them."

"No!" I yell in a rush of panic. Xave can't hear me and no one in the crew will tell him not to. We all have our parts to play now. We had our chance to leave IgNiTe. From here on out, we're one hundred percent in. Still, what can Xave do by himself against a group of Eklyptors?

Blare looks at her watch and says, "Boom!"

A huge explosion erupts in the back of the building, rattling the ground and walls and shattering windows with its shockwaves. The sound of debris raining down on the parking lot and top of the building makes me wrap my arms around my head. My skin crawls as I imagine a brick splitting my skull in two.

"Aydan, where are the guards? How many are there?" Blare asks.

"Four … I think. They're right outside the front entrance, staying close to the wall."

"Link us to James."

The line crackles. James's voice erupts from the earpiece. "Blare, Rheema, on the count of three come out shooting. Marci, stay back until we've taken care of them." He doesn't wait for an answer. He simply starts counting. "One … two … three!"

Blare runs out toward the parking lot in a diagonal line. Rheema waits for a beat, then turns the corner and darts out, parallel with the building. Sparks fly from Blare's gun with each crack. I see her roll on the black top, making herself a moving target. She never stops shooting. New rapid fire joins in, sounding like some sort of machine gun. I can't see Rheema, but I can picture her pulling two triggers at blazing-fast speed.

The night explodes into what sounds like a Fourth of July celebration at Lake Union. Everyone is shooting. Bullets whiz by me and I press tight and low against the wall. I hope Rheema is okay.

Crouching here listening to the battle without doing anything to help my friends makes me nauseous, more than the fear of getting shot. I have to do something. I can't just sit here, hiding like a coward. Even if that's what James ordered. I'm *not* a coward.

But how can I help? They didn't give me a gun. They didn't trust … Wait, I shouldn't need a gun. I can move things with my mind. I just manipulated the intricate mechanism of a lock and allowed Blare to blow evil spawns into oblivion. As the idea finally clicks, every trace of fear slides off me like a silk garment. I walk out my hiding place, eyes piercing my surroundings, looking for anything that can be used as a weapon.

A quick reconnaissance reveals Blare squatting behind Rheema's car, her back pressed against the back bumper. I spot Rheema lying flat on the ground, hiding behind a row of bushes. Cross-shooting continues all around. No one notices me walking at a casual pace, taking in the building, the manicured front lawn, the direction of the oncoming enemy fire.

The cowards are staying well hidden, probably trying to prolong the confrontation until reinforcements arrive.

One of the guards peeks from behind a massive tree trunk. He takes several shots toward Rheema's car and in the process spots me. As I take another step, his eyes grow wide, surprised either by my nonchalant approach or by the fact that his head is now droning like mine is. He recovers quickly, adjusts his aim and finds me in his sight. Before I have time to consider exactly what to do, the guard falls limp to the ground, a bullet in his temple.

A shudder runs down my spine. I've never seen anyone get shot before. I'm about to get sick when I remember the man was a monster, an usurper cruel enough to condemn a human life to permanent torture. This is survival of the fittest and the fittest don't get sick to their stomach.

The barrage of gunfire intensifies by the building's entrance. Someone ... James ... runs out. He moves fast—though not as fast as he's capable of—spinning to the left and right as he shoots at the enemy. It must be infuriating not to be able to use the full range of his powers.

Suddenly, I realize I can't be out here, intending to move things with my mind, when James wants to keep what we are hidden from Blare and Oso. I freeze.

"Get down, you idiot," Blare screams. "You're going to get blown to pieces."

I remain motionless, my resolve dwindling to the size of a pea.

"Fine! Be my guest. I never liked you anyway," she adds before rolling away from the car and giving James some much needed backup.

Behind a large birdbath, a second guard rears his head and starts raising his gun toward James, who's just turned his back to shoot at a third guard. Blare's attention is on the same Eklyptor, while Rheema is dealing with a fourth. Oso is just coming out of the building, tentatively, like any brave yet cautious soldier would. He's no Symbiot. No super-human speed for him.

In that moment, everything comes into clear focus in slow motion. I realize that if I don't do something, James will get shot in the back of the head. Is he fast enough to outrun a bullet? Maybe, but not one he can't see coming.

I rush onward, desperately thinking of how to stop the monster from hurting James. My eyes jump around, trying to find something useful. On the ground, I spot a green hose, coiled next to the birdbath. I struggle with grasping a course of action. There is no time to ponder. I must act.

Time stands still as my brain goes into warp speed and my instincts kick into overdrive. Every ounce of who I am pours forward. I become hollow, long and flexible. I am the hose. I rear upward with vicious speed, like a striking cobra. I attack, sliding around the guard's neck, twisting into a noose, then squeeze. I stretch, reaching both toward the ground and the sky. I want to touch the stars before something stops me. So I squeeze harder and harder, even against the frantic hands that struggle to pry me away, and don't relent until a limp, heavy weight drags me down.

The echoes of gunfire ring in my ears. Someone shouts, but I can't make out what they're saying. I come to, blinking, completely disoriented. My body feels foreign for a very strange, very scary instant. My right hand is stretched, reaching toward the prone body by the birdbath. Gunfire has ceased and the blaring alarm is the only sound disturbing the night.

I take a look around and shiver. James is looking straight at me, while the others are coming out from their hiding places, seemingly unaware of what I've done. My eyes search for the remaining two guards. They lay on the ground and I don't even know how it happened.

Blurry with moisture, my eyes return to James, then to the limp body of his would-be killer. Did I just …? I shake my head. My lungs cease. I stagger forward as my knees go limp. My thoughts wade through the thick finality that clogs the air.

Death.

At my hands.

I fall to my knees, trembling. I killed a person. I just killed a person!

No! Not a person. A monster, I try to tell myself.

But … but it's not true. That man was innocent. Somebody's father. Somebody's son. A victim who never stood a chance against his agent, and especially not against the nasty little Symbiot who wasn't even supposed to be here. I wasn't meant to kill anyone. Oh God, what have I become?

I wrap my arms around my waist and choke on the thick wail trying to force its way past my tight lips. I can't fall apart. Not in front of the crew. Trying to gather myself, I think of James, only of James. I saved his life, the life of the man who's bent on saving everyone else and might give humanity a fighting chance, a life more important than anyone else's, more important than whatever remorse I feel, no matter how much it chokes me.

I saved him. I saved him!

"You saved me, Marci!" I'm on my feet, James shaking me. "You saved me," he says again, all in a low murmur that only I can hear. A mixture of gratitude and conviction bend his voice. "You did right by *us*." And by "us" he means much more than just him or our crew.

He means the world. The whole, wide world.

"More are coming. We need to get out here," he orders.

As everyone heeds his command, my feet refuse to move. James's words echo in my ears. I repeat them to myself. I did the right thing, by James, by IgNiTe, by all of *us*. Righteousness overtakes me, and I begin to run, thoughts jumping, erasing all trace of guilt for the time being.

I've almost caught up with the group when Aydan's voice pierces through my very confused brain. "Run faster. Reinforcements, at the gate."

"Where's Xave? Is he okay?" I ask in a hoarse voice. If reinforcements are here, it means he didn't succeed at stopping them. My heart hammers and, when Aydan doesn't respond, it hammers faster. My legs speed up and I pass Oso, Rheema and Blare. James stops to help them up.

"Aydan, is Xave okay?" I press, as I reach the wall, propel myself upward and jump to the other side. I don't wait for anyone. I keep running toward the van, indifferent to what anyone might think about my Olympic-quality jump.

I enter the van panting. "Where's Xave?!" I yell, as soon as I'm inside.

Aydan looks up at me and shakes his head, eyes charged with doubt. "I don't know," he says. "I lost communication with him."

289

Chapter 43

As I stand staring down at Aydan in disbelief, the rest of the crew piles into the van.

"What do you mean you lost communication?" I yell in his face.

He stares up at me, impassive, and makes no attempt to answer my question. I may as well be a gnat circling in front of him.

James points at the back seat. "Take your place, Marci."

No. I won't lose this face-off. Aydan needs to tell me where Xave is. Right now or I swear …

"Take a seat, Marci," James forcefully repeats.

I'm the only one still standing. Everyone else is sitting and Oso is already cranking the engine.

"We have to find Xave," I say.

Blare snaps on her seatbelt. "No, we have to get outta here."

I whirl, ready to explode all over the place.

James puts a hand on my arm but looks pointedly at Aydan. "Where's Xave?"

Aydan huffs and swivels his stool toward the computers, turning his back on James.

"I told her I lost communication. I don't know what else she wants to hear," Aydan responds.

"What about Clark?" James asks next.

"He went to try to find him." Aydan says this as if we're discussing a missing mutt.

"They should be okay, Marci," James reasons.

We're driving in reverse, backing out of the woods on the bumpy dirt road. I sway with the van through a few potholes, then decide it's best to take a seat. In his mad dash, Oso drives over underbrush and debris, rattling our teeth and bones.

"James, we can't leave them," I plead.

"They can take care of themselves."

When Oso hits the paved road, he takes a sharp turn and shifts gears. The sound of squealing tires and the raging engine echoes through the woods. We tear down the dark service road. Trees fly by to our left and a corroded metal railing on the other side is the only thing between the van and a sheer drop. Oso keeps his eyes straight ahead, while, in the passenger seat, Blare peers through the large side mirror, making sure no one's behind us.

After a minute, my heart slows down a bit, but not enough. I can't stop thinking about Xave. If he's hurt, I don't know what I'm going to do. And what if he's …

Panic strikes me and I can't even finish the thought. "Aydan, has Clark found Xave?"

"We're out of range."

There's so much contempt in his voice it raises my hackles. I'm an angry wolf. "What the hell is your problem?" I demand, feeling ready for a fight. "I'm getting sick of your bitchy, snooty ass."

"Why don't you just shut up. We're trying to escape here. In case you haven't noticed," he says in a calm, condescending tone.

291

"You know what? You're not worth my time, asshole," I say, flipping open my cell phone and dialing Xave's number. It goes straight to voicemail.

Blare's cynical laughter fills the cabin.

She's another one not worth bothering with. I ignore her and try to remember if I ever programmed Clark's number into my phone. I search for it, find it and dial. I get a message indicating the line is no longer in service. It must be an old number because I don't remember storing it.

I stuff the phone back into my cargo pants. Blare's still amused about something, letting out dry, jaded snorts. She probably wants someone to ask her to let us in on the joke, but everyone's attention is on the road. We're not far from the clinic and we're not out of the woods yet.

Oso takes a sharp turn and the side of the van scrapes a metal railing on the right.

"Watch it. I don't want to fly off the mountain," Blare says.

I look away from the chasm, feeling a surge of vertigo. Thumb jammed between my lips as I bite my nail, I tap a foot nervously. Images of Xave's bruised face dance in front of me. The knot in my throat feels like it's about to escape in the form of a desperate cry.

"Maybe they won't follow us," Oso says.

Blare points through the windshield. "You spoke too soon."

A set of headlights appears around the next bend. The vehicle is traveling as fast as we are. This service road is narrow. There's not enough room for two cars to get through. I reach for the seatbelt and buckle it. My forehead tingles. I have a bad feeling about this.

"Don't stop," James says.

Oso peers back through the rear-view mirror, his mellow eyes questioning, full of doubt.

"We won't stand a chance if we fight." James's tone is self-assured and erases all doubt about our fate if Oso doesn't heed the advice.

"Yes, sir," Oso responds as he steps on the gas.

We must be going close to ninety in a thirty-mile-an-hour area. The car approaching appears to be going just as fast. If nothing changes, we have a sure date with a head-on collision.

I clench my fists as my entire body tenses. We're going so fast that after only a few quick blinks the other vehicle's headlights are upon us, shining brightly into our dark space, making everyone look like pale, ghostly figures.

Desperate, I imagine the other driver turning the wheel sharply and smashing into a tree. Nothing happens. This would be a great time for my telekinesis to kick in, but it fails me. Maybe I need to be able to touch or see what I want to move, but all I see are stabbing beams of light.

Oso keeps his hands firm on the wheel, guiding the van right through the middle of the road. The driver of the incoming vehicle does the same. This is a battle of wills. The first one to veer off course is a rotten egg.

We're dead.

Dead!

As I feel my life in the balance, teetering between possibility and finality, something inside me cracks. I might be six-feet-under tomorrow, and what do I have to show for myself? A messed-up relationship with Mom, a twin brother I don't really know, and a friend I've pushed away because I feel I've nothing to offer. If I make it out of this alive, I'll shoot for the stars and fix all three. I will.

Sliding shaky hands under my knees, I grip the seat and hold on to the idea of fixing things with Xave—Xave who at this moment is with his brother unharmed and headed home. When I see him, I'll tell him how I feel ... I'll swear to him that I'll never push him away ever again ... I'll ...

"Hold on tight," Oso screams between clenched teeth as the incoming headlights swallow us whole. My head droops and my lids close. I let go of the seat and relax with a big, slow exhale that leaves my lungs empty. I gaze up and find James peering at me. Something passes between us and an instant later Oso jerks the wheel and our van swerves violently out of the way.

Oso lost. His will is merely human.

Except he was late. The tail-end of our van doesn't clear the road in time. The other vehicle clips us. The change in direction is brutal. My body wants to split in half. The crunch of metal is deafening, like a million soda cans crushing inside my head, like the world breaking into fragments.

We tumble and tumble and tumble. My arms are blades on a windmill, my spine the whip in the hands of a ringmaster. But the lion isn't tamed, it keeps roaring, crunching the van between its jaws.

No one screams, no one calls for mercy. We may as well be in hell.

Something sharp and heavy slams into my head. Warmth trickles down my cheek, my chest, my arms. Every drop down the drain, joining the muck I've made out of what should have been a good life.

Chapter 44

A sea of shadows swims in front of my eyes.

My heart thuds at the thought of having lost control of the agent, though the hammering in my chest lets me know I'm still alive. The realigning shapes in my vision, the scent of gasoline and motor-oil, the blissful sound of Blare's expletives ... all let me know I'm still me and I still have a chance to make things better. I blink.

My forehead stings, throbs, screams in pain. A chilled breeze hits my face making me notice the van's missing back doors. My seat is half out and half in, and I'm still strapped to it, dangling. I fumble for the buckle, push the button, and slide off the seat. I hit the ground with a *thunk*, and my face lands on cold, frozen weeds. The chill in the air is a blessing on my burning, aching temple. Red spreads over my vision. Pain bends my will.

I close my eyes and wish for the frigid temperature to numb me forever. If I never wake up again, it's fine by me. To hell with patching things up. Nothing is worth living through this agony. Not even redemption.

A loud sound brings me back from the cold arms of oblivion. It angers me, because it revives the pain. My side throbs in sync with my forehead, in sync with my heart. Something has gone through my ribs. The weeds tickle my nose with a strange scent. My stomach contracts and I want to vomit.

Then there's that sound again. I try to forget about the scented weeds and look up. Several yards away a bulky form stands out from all the other shadows. I blink repeatedly and wipe sticky blood from my eyes. The shape of the overturned enemy van comes into focus. It's laying on its side.

I flinch when a steady pounding from within the van literally makes it sway from side to side. I wipe my eyes again. The way the van's moving makes no sense. This has to be a hallucination. Very understandable after my concussion, because I have concussion, right?

The van stops swaying. The banging from within comes to a halt.

Yep. Just imagining things.

Then something explodes from the van and I catch a glimpse of a scrunched-up metal door flying up in the air. Hypnotized, I watch it reach the apex of its trajectory against a treeless, dark gray sky, then plummet behind the van without making a sound.

A movement from the gaping hole left behind by the disappearing door catches my attention. Two hands grab the sides, then a misshapen head pulls up followed by a torso. Soon the whole body is out and the van is swaying away, teetering somehow.

On all fours, the man, the *creature*, starts walking carefully on the side of the van. The figure is a dark, creeping shadow against sky. The van teeters precariously with each step the *thing* takes. A flattened head and body shuffle toward the back of the van. The way it moves with its stubby limbs and its fanning backside makes me want to start digging my own grave. It reminds me of something, but I'm not sure what. My primal instincts are sending me a warning that I can't fully comprehend.

A second creature pulls out through the missing door. Its elongated head takes forever to come fully into view. The van sways more fiercely. The first Eklyptor jerks its head back, makes a snapping sound. The second one opens its long snout and snaps back.

The small hairs stand on end throughout my body then my brain catches up with my instincts. Crocodiles! They're like freakin', deformed crocodiles! Grotesque in their half-human, incomplete state.

The beasts move more carefully in an orchestrated dance that keeps the van's wavering to a minimum. And then it hits me. Their vehicle is on the cliffside, vacillating between plunging over the side and clinging to the rocky edge.

The first Eklyptor is almost to the back of the van. Its gaze flickers my way, already anticipating its attack. Its protruding eyes reflect the light. A strange bitterness fills my mouth, and I have no doubt it's the taste of fear. Images of rolling waters, as predators dismember their hapless prey, flash with vivid detail in front of my widened, fixed eyes. Damn the Animal Planet.

I only have a few seconds before they attack. I try to call out a warning, but I can't get enough air into my lungs to muster more than a pathetic squeak.

God, I have to do something or I'm dead!

My bloody hand shoots up, aimed toward the teetering van. If I could only nudge it a bit, unbalance it just enough to make it tilt toward the overhang. My fingers shake, my body shivers with cold and exhaustion. It's too much. I don't have it in me. Exhausted, my arms fall limp to the cold ground.

I think of James and everyone else. I have to try harder for the others, if not for me. Even if my strength is dwindling to just scraps, even if it kills me. Pain is the only thing left, so I make it my focal point.

With every pulsing pang along my ribs, head, and spine, my blood-covered fingers reach out again. The first Eklyptor takes a leap toward the ground. A third one has exited the van; it walks upright, only its head fully transformed.

I tear my eyes away from the horror and concentrate. My eyes lock on the spot where the van's backside goes up and down like a seesaw, touching the ground for a second then moving a few inches away from it.

The first Eklyptor is on the ground. I hear it moving, but I don't look at it. I refuse to, because if I do, I will crumble. I ignore the fast shuffling of its thick, stout limbs, and the unnatural, inhuman laughter escaping through its short snout.

Forcing my terrified mind to pretend these creatures are not there, I pour my entire focus onto the van. If only one Eklyptor manages to jump off, James and the others can fight it. If all of them do, there's no hope.

When the van's backside leaves the ground next, I let the pain flow. My toes curl and my spine arches with a snap. An invisible extension of my hand, of myself, reaches out, slips strong fingers under the van and pushes up.

Two more shapes struggle to come out through the window. They fight in a frenzy to be the first to attack and tear us to pieces. Their weight helps further upset the balance. The long-snouted Eklyptor shrieks and starts sliding backward, crashing into the one behind it.

Claws run along the metal, making a screeching sound, like giant chalk pieces against a blackboard. As they glide backward, the burden becomes too much and the momentum shifts completely toward the cliff. In one interminable moment, the van hangs in the balance. Then it topples down the overhang and goes out of view in a strange and silent disappearing act.

When my eyes leave the empty space, my arm collapses to the frozen ground, lifeless. A short snout suddenly appears in front of my eyes. It gapes open, glinting with pointed, yellowed teeth two times taller than my wrist.

A foul smell, like ten pounds of rotting meat, inundates my nose. I shut my eyes, oblivious to what will happen next. I'm nothing but scraps as it is. I don't even feel the pain anymore. In the effort it's taken to tip the van over the cliff, I've lost myself and what's left of me isn't enough to put me back together. The hollow feel of my bones, the unconcerned quality of my thoughts, the absence of hope. I'm as good as crocodile bait.

Something like a thunderclap followed by an insistent voice calling my name brings me back from oblivion. My eyes flutter open.

I'm still here, on the frozen ground.

Really?!

Give me a break.

The one repeating my name over and over is James, I think.

I hear another loud *pop*, followed by Blare's loud curses. "Take that, you bastard!" A flash of silver catches my eye— Blare's large gun. I flinch as she discharges another round, gun pointed toward the ground. I glance over and catch a glimpse of something gruesome. Blood and splattered tissue.

I don't want to be awake. Nothingness is better than this. I try to tell James to let me be, but only garbled nonsense comes out. Pain is a ghost threatening to haunt me once more. I want it gone.

"Stay with me, Marci," he says.

Can't really go anywhere, can I? He won't let me, and even though something strong and blissful lures me, his rumbling voice has a stronger hold on me. My lips move.

"What, honey? What did you say?" James says tenderly in my ear. His voice shifts, changes directions. "We have to get out of here. Now!"

"I don't think we should move her," Aydan says in a feeble way.

"We have no choice," James says, as he picks me up in his arms.

Pain is definitely making a comeback. I groan.

"I'm sorry," James apologizes.

My head falls to his chest. The world turns, bounces, and jerks as James runs. Pain returns with a vengeance. I will darkness to take me away once more, and it doesn't take long to answer my call. The sliver of consciousness conjured by James is too weak to withstand this pulsating agony.

I'm sorry, James. I can't stay with you.

Chapter 45

"Say that again."

My throat, my mouth, my whole body feel dry, like a husk. I can't say it again.

"What did she say?"

"I don't know, but she needs to stop trying to talk."

"Is she in pain?"

"She shouldn't be. I gave her enough morphine."

"She has to make it."

"She will. She's strong."

Before I open my eyes, I become aware of my labored breathing, strained voices and shuffling steps. The word I've been trying to say sits like a practiced verse on my lips. It rolls off easily and this time I'm strong enough to make myself heard.

"Xave."

Someone squeezes my hand. "Hey, sweetie. Can you open your eyes?"

"Xave."

"Shhh, it's okay."

No, it's *not* okay. My eyes spring open. I want to know where Xave is.

Kristen stands over me. Other indistinguishable figures surround me.

"Xave," I repeat as forcefully as I can, which isn't saying much. Hot irons press against my ribs with the effort of saying his name.

"Calm down." James appears next to Kristen. "We're at The Tank. Clark and Xave don't know this place."

They don't know if Xave's okay. They still don't know anything! If I could scream, I would. I struggle, feebly. Yet it's enough to get a reaction.

"I'll go find him for you. I promise," James says.

"No, I'll go." It's Aydan. I must be in really rough shape if he's offering to help.

Kristen calls the shots. "C'mon, let's take her in for an X-ray. Then I'll hook her to an IV."

I slip in and out of consciousness. My lips move in a constant litany no matter whether I'm awake or dreaming. I don't know other words. Only Xave's name. In my semi-wakeful moments, the pain is just a dull, faraway thing. There's something on my face, but my hands don't obey me when I order them to fling it away.

How long have I been here? If they told me it's been five years, I'd believe them. If they said five seconds, I'd believe them too.

Suddenly, I'm awake, staring at James who is sitting on a chair next to me. He's still wearing the same clothes. There are scratches on his arms and a bandage on the side of his neck. I guess I haven't been out that long.

"Where's Xave?" I demand in a hoarse whisper. "You promised to find him."

James straightens from his slumped position on the chair.

"You look better," he says.

302

My tongue feels like sandpaper. I swallow a dry lump. "Where is he?"

"You are one determined pain in the ass." James laughs and walks toward the door. "I'll go get Kristen."

"You promised," I croak.

"Hey."

My heart skips a beat, then begins to thud at a higher pace. Slowly, I look to my left. Xave is sitting right next to the bed. A small smile tweaks his mouth, in spite of the concern brimming in his beautiful, hazel eyes. I exhale a thousand pounds of apprehension and inhale the peace of his presence.

"What happened to you? Are you all right?" I croak.

Xave gives an incredulous snort. "Am *I* all right? You silly goose!"

He hasn't called me that in a very long time. When we were little, I learned the endearment from Dad and used it on Xave. He used it back a few times and, apparently, still remembers it.

Something stings in my eyes. It must have something to do with the dull throbbing in my head.

Hesitantly, Xave takes my hand. An unearthly feeling prickles through my body till it collects in my core, making me feel like a smoldering ember inside.

He shakes his head, glaring at me. "What the hell were you doing in there, Marci?"

"They didn't explain?" I ask, unsure of what to say. The fact that he's here at The Tank raises a lot of questions. I don't know how much James told him.

"I just got here. I came straight to see you. Besides, it's a mad house out there." He gestures toward the door with his head.

"Why? What's happening?"

"Forget that. I want *you* to tell me why you went inside that clinic. You were supposed to be in the van, helping that pompous *jackass*. Next thing I know you're inside the freakin' building." The heat in his words, although subdued compared to what I'm used to, shows the same anger raging in his quick-tempered, hard head.

I clear my throat and make a big show of swallowing, which isn't that hard to do since I'm parched.

"Is there any water?" I look around the room.

With a frustrated sigh, Xave stands and pours some water from a pitcher on the side table. He sticks a straw in the white Styrofoam cup and puts it to my lips. I manage a few sips, but when my stomach threatens to send it back, I shake my head. Setting the cup back on the table, he sits and takes my hand, igniting me all over again. He glares at me.

We look at each other for a long moment, then I say, "It's hard to talk with all these bandages against my ribs. Why don't you tell me what happened to you? The others can explain why I had to go in. Or I can tell you when I feel better." Strangely, I feel as if I could break into a dissertation of my side of the story, but instead I wince and hold my side, pretending it hurts more than it does. I'm surprised by how well I feel, considering that just hours ago I thought I was going to die. My pain tolerance must be super low. What a wimp.

My bit of acting douses Xave's anger and replaces it with concern. It's wrong to worry him, considering how upset I was when I didn't know if he was okay, but I can't risk revealing something I shouldn't.

Xave humors me and begins his story. "That *jackass* kept me out of the loop."

I'm guessing he means Aydan, but I don't know why he keeps calling him a jackass. I mean, I know he's a jackass, but I don't know how Xave reached the same conclusion so soon. I resolve not to interrupt, hoping any questions I have are answered along the way.

"I had no idea what was going on. I sent Clark a text, telling him my earpiece wasn't working anymore, although at first it was receiving with no problems. He texted me back, said he'd let me know anything important. A while later, I get another text saying you'd gone in."

Xave squeezes my hand and stares at it, as if to make sure it's real. I squeeze back. He looks up, surprised, then tries to hide his reaction by jumping back into the story.

As I listen, I hold on tightly, wondering how to make things right between us and hoping to find the courage.

Chapter 46

Xave talks in a low voice. "When I saw that car speeding down the road, I warned Aydan about reinforcements. When he copied my message, I realized the earpiece was working all along and that jerk just thought I wasn't important enough to know what was happening."

That sounds like Aydan, all right.

"It's either that or ..." He trails off.

"Or what?"

"Nothing," he says, sounding like it's definitely something. "Anyway, I knew I had to stop them. I had to give you time to get out of there." The way he says "you" makes it clear he definitely means me and not everybody else.

"Trying to be a hero?" I want it sound like a joke, but it comes out like a reproach, which is what it really is. "You could've gotten yourself killed."

"Um, do I need to point out I'm not the one in a hospital bed?"

I roll my eyes. "So what did you do?"

"I chased them on my bike and shot out their tires."

My eyebrows jump up, but before I can ask, Xave answers what would have been my next question.

"Clark gave me a gun. Turns out I'm still a good shot."

Xave used to go hunting in north Washington with Clark and his father when he was little. I used to tease him and call him Yosemite Sam, using Bugs Bunny's voice. He hated it.

He continues, eyes fixed on our linked hands. "Their car skidded off the road and slammed against a tree. I waited to see if they'd come out. I wanted to make sure they wouldn't just run into the clinic. Next thing I know, three guys jump out and start toward me. I flipped tail and started driving away, but lost control of the bike. Got some pretty sweet road-rash on my back, but didn't feel it at the time." Xave cracks his neck and winces a little. "I feel it now, though." He gives an unamused chuckle.

"Has anyone looked at it?"

"Nah, everyone's more banged up than me."

"Still, you need to have it checked," I adamantly say.

Xave peers at me sideways. "Since when did you become so protective?"

"Um, I'm not. It's just … common sense. You know."

"A-ha." He's not buying it. With a satisfied smile he lets me off the hook and continues his story. "After I skidded along the road like an old piece of trash, I saw those freaks were still walking toward me, all cool and relaxed, as if they were chasing an ancient grandma. I was still clutching my gun, and they just kept coming. Something in their eyes … spooked me. I'm not embarrassed to say it," he adds in a hurry. "Those things are unnatural." He pauses, his hazel eyes dark and lost on a faraway spot beyond this room. "Evil," he whispers.

I shiver, remembering the glittering eyes of the half-crocodile beast that almost ate me. "Were they walking … normal?"

My question gives Xave pause. "Normal?" he repeats. "Yes, I guess. If walking all Terminator-like can be called normal. It was like they knew I would freak out, like they expected me to run even though I was armed.

"And I did. I took off into the woods like a mad man, trying to find a place to hide. I could hear them crunching leaves behind me. I ducked by a huge hollow tree and clutched the gun to my chest. It could've been a stuffed animal or something for all the good it was doing. I couldn't think straight." Xave shakes his head, smirking at his idiocy with incredulity.

"One of them laughed. He sounded like a freakin' hyena. That made me snap out of it. I wasn't about to just sit there waiting for them to flush me out like a rat. So I did what I thought they expected the least. I came out shooting."

"What?! Are you insane? You? Against three Eklyptors?"

"Yeah. Me. Against three freaks." The you-have-a-problem-with-that tone makes me doubt his sanity.

"You idiot," I say. "No one needs a dead hero."

"Sorry to point out the obvious, sweetheart, but I'm not dead."

I never knew Xave could smile with such sexy charm. And he's calling me *sweetheart*? In spite of how ridiculous it sounds, I find my face getting hot. What the heck? Am I blushing? *I* don't do blushing. He doesn't seem to notice, so I try getting it under control.

"And, in case you haven't noticed, I'm not the one wrapped up like a stinking mummy," he adds.

I put my hand on my torso, feeling for the bandages. I vaguely remember Kristen putting them on while I sat in a daze. She said I had a broken rib and would feel better once I was bandaged up. At first, I doubted anything would help, but it has.

"I don't stink," I protest, but I can't help wrinkling my nose a bit as I take in my own scent. Xave laughs. I do too, but stop when my broken rib starts to sing.

"Man, they were fast!" he continues his tale. "I kept missing, but all that experience shooting deer came in handy. I aimed ahead and two ran right into my bullets," he says, jaw twitching with intense feeling.

"The third one got smart. He almost had me. He jumped up in the air and sprouted freakin' bat wings. I'm not making it up."

"I know you're not." My own horrifying memories of the night come back to me and I have no trouble imagining what Xave saw. I know the underpinnings of this nightmare.

"Clark's the reason I'm still here."

"So yeah, you *are* an idiot," I say, holding his gaze. "Just a very lucky one."

He becomes all serious, props his arm on the pillow, and looks deep into my eyes. With his thumb, he smooths my eyebrow in a soft, shy caress. The room begins to spin, the bed becomes a weird, fluffy cloud. He's never looked at me this way—Xave with his stormy, hazel eyes and perfect lips. The temperamental boy who seems to have grown into a courageous man overnight and who risked his life to buy me a few precious seconds.

"I was so worried about you," he whispers, and he's so close that his warm, cinnamon breath grazes my cheek. "I panicked, started thinking that … I'd never see you again."

My throat tightens. I felt the same panic for him and hearing him talk openly about it—forgetting all our differences and clumsy attempts to communicate—cracks me open.

How could I ever pretend it was best to grow apart? Maybe he won't want me when he finds out what I really am. Maybe he will feel betrayed, revolted. But who was I kidding? I'd risk everything for just this moment.

"I thought I'd never get a chance to tell you …" His eyes are moist. I've never seen him like this. Ever. "To tell you what a pain in the ass you are." He fights a smile.

I mock-punch him and I open my mouth to reply, but he puts a finger on my lips for a fraction of a second. Heat seals my lips, makes me crave his touch.

"I've been dense, to say the least," he says.

"Yeah, a blockhead."

He gives me a sad smile. "That day at the arcade, I brought Judy to see how you'd react. I was shooting for Jealous Vixen, but got Cold Queen instead."

"What a genius plan," I say sarcastically.

"Hey, I'm just a plain old average guy. Yeah, it was stupid, but I didn't know what else to do. You'd turned away from me when I tried a different approach."

"Um, I did?"

"That time we ended up *this* close, remember?" He measures an invisible inch with his fingers.

"You did that on purpose? I thought that was an accident!"

He shrugs.

"Subtle," I say.

"Oh, I can be subtle," he says, then brushes his thumb along my jaw. I shudder.

"Let me finish, okay?" he says.

Who knew Xave could string more than two sentences together? Since he turned thirteen, I thought kicking Dumpsters was the extent of his communication skills. Of course I'm not about to discourage him, now.

"Well, Ms. Cold Queen, what I realized tonight is that I was being a coward."

"Mmm," I mumble, nodding in full agreement.

"Yeah, I admit it. But no more. Because even if you run for the hills after I tell you … well … I'll still feel exactly the same way. And I'll always regret not being braver. Besides, I can't run from it. Believe me, I've tried. It doesn't work.

'Cause it's you, Marci. It's always been you. And I've always known it, always been afraid that you would hate me and push me away. But I'm done with hiding from it. I'm crazy about you. Have been for a while."

He waits for me to say something, searches my face for a reaction. I'm not sure what he sees there, but I doubt it's helpful. My emotions are out of control, and maybe I expect him to say more. But short of the "L" word, there's nothing else he can say. Besides, I don't know if I'd be able to say it back. For that matter, I don't know if I'll be able to say anything at all, because that last thing he said … well … I'm dumbstruck.

"Um, you don't have to say anything," he says, staring at my mouth with more than just interest in the words that might come out of it. "I know it's hard and you may not … I mean, this may be too much for you right now."

I try to say something and only a puff of air comes out. How can I top what he just said when all I can think of is "Ditto, Xave, just kiss me already"?

He stares at the door in concentration, knits thick eyebrows and asks, "Do you want me to go? Let you rest?" He lets go of my hand and stands.

"No!"

Xave smiles, hopeful. "O-kay. I'll stay." He sits back down.

After a moment of awkward silence, during which I try to get my thoughts organized, Xave seems ready to try a new approach.

"Are you mad at me?" he asks.

"No, of course not."

"Okay. Not mad. That's good, right?"

We exchange smiles.

I push up on the pillow. "I'm just trying to … find the right words."

He gives a slow blink, straightens on the chair and widens the distance between us.

Man, I'm really screwing things up. That has got to be the stupidest thing to say at a moment like this. There can be no wrong words when you're giving your heart away. When you're about to break one, though …

"Get closer," I order him.

He stares at me confused for an instant, then scoots his chair toward the bed.

I take his hand back and his sudden vulnerable expression make me feel all warm inside. I can sense his expectation and doubts. I just hope that what I say next is as perfect as what he told me. No pressure, right? I take a deep breath and begin.

"I've been worried about you, too," I say. "You're my best friend."

Xave's body language tells me he would be sobbing if it wasn't unmanly. God, I might sob myself. I suck at this. Friend?! I want him to know he'll always be my friend, even if we become something else. Not going as planned.

"Wait, let me start again."

He rubs the back of his neck, and I wonder if he'll survive this conversation. "Look, I understand." He starts to pull his hand away from mine.

I tighten my grip, lock my gaze to his. "You're not going anywhere until *I* tell you how *I* feel about *you*. Even if it kills you."

"Are you sure? 'Cause it might." He puts a hand on his chest and grins.

God, why is the fact that he's able to joke about this so … so … hot?

"It won't," I say. "I promise you." My voice is low, flowing in a suggestive cadence that seems to come out of nowhere.

Xave's eyes widened, but he recovers quickly. "Is that so?" he asks, matching my tone.

"I was worried about you, too. Did they tell you I kept calling your name?"

"No."

"I *had* to know if you were okay, had to see you. That's why they came and got you."

"Aydan didn't say anything."

I shrug. Aydan doesn't matter. Whatever his problem is, he doesn't matter. Right now there's only Xave.

"If I acted that way at the arcade it's because ... it hurt," I continue. "It hurt like hell to see you with someone else."

Xave gets up from the chair and sits on the bed. Leaning in closer, he gives me a huge smile. "Jealous then?"

"Very," I whisper, staring at his mouth, which he's lowering closer and closer to mine at the pace of my thudding heartbeat.

"Why?"

"Same reason as you." I know it's a lame answer, but his mouth has hypnotized me. I can hardly breathe, much less think of a clever way to tell him how much he means to me.

Xave shakes his head. "Oh, no. I won't let you off the hook that easily. Why?" he asks again.

"Because ... because ..." Damn, this should be easy. All I need to do is tell him the truth. I take a deep breath. Okay, here it goes.

"Because ever since you showed up in my neighborhood splashing through puddles in those fireman rubber boots, I've thought about you every single day.

"Because you shared your Peeps with me every Easter, even though they were your favorites.

"Because you held me the day Dad died.

"Because I couldn't imagine my life without you."

313

His eyes seem to waver for an instant.

"Do I need to keep going?" I ask through the burning knot in my throat.

He shakes his head. "I always thought those Peeps might do the trick."

I sputter, trying to contain the laughter, the relief bubbling in my chest.

"You think I'm kidding?" he asks. "It was part of my master plan."

I feel *so* happy, so undeniably ecstatic that I think nothing else matters. Just this moment, just us. Not the world and this messed-up war we're in. Not Mom. Not Luke. Not anyone else.

He laughs and I try not to. Then we do it together, like we've always done everything, like it's meant to be.

"Can I kiss you?" he asks, stopping his laughter abruptly. "I've always wanted to kiss you."

A chill runs the length of my body and in the next instant I turn hot. My breaths speed up so much that my ribs begin to throb in sync with my heartbeat, but I don't care. Xave's mouth is only an inch from mine. His eyes are lighter now, a happy green. I've always loved the way they reflect his mood, revealing exactly the way he feels.

He licks his lips. Rumor has it he's a good kisser. Nerves grip me. I hope he doesn't find my kisses half bad. I close my eyes and wait to reach the sky.

"Oh, sorry." An intruding voice slams me back down to earth.

Really?! Could their timing be any worse?

Xave springs to his feet and smooths his shirt. "Hey," he says, wearing an innocent expression that makes him look seventeen again. And here I was thinking he was all grown up.

This business will *not* remain unfinished. I have to confirm if the rumors are true.

Chapter 47

Kristen strides in the room, wearing a stethoscope around her neck. Her white coat has her name stitched on the left breast pocket, and I wonder if this is from a previous job or if she's like James, living a dual life.

"How are you feeling?" she asks.

"I feel great." I look at Xave with a smile, knowing he's responsible for how surprisingly awesome I feel.

Kristen doesn't look happy about my response and gives me a disapproving glace.

She sets a long tube of cream on the side table to my right. "This is for your forehead. We'll change the dressing every day and apply this liberally on the spot. It will prevent scars." Her tone is clipped.

I blink slowly and take a calming breath. Kristen's attitude is stirring a bit of anger inside me, but I need to cut her some slack. It's not like she's ever treated me badly. She's actually been extra nice to me. She's probably stressed right now, with everyone here at The Tank and most of us injured. The thought makes me wonder how the others are reacting to meeting Kristen, especially Blare with her distrustful nature and bitchy personality.

"Xave, right?" Kristen asks, turning her attention away from me.

"Yeah, nice to meet you." Xave smiles.

"I'm Kristen Albright. It's nice meeting you, too." She pauses, then adds, "I need to check Marci's bandage, would you mind ... ?" She looks toward the door, subtly.

"Sure, no problem." He walks away. When he reaches the door, he gives me a backward glance that says it all. We'll finish what we started. I smile, until Kristen enters my field of vision, obstructing the view.

I wince while she checks the bandage around my ribs. "You're healing nicely. Make sure to wear this and the bandage on your head for a week or so."

Healing nicely? One week? That's it?! I must really be a wimp, thinking I was going to die, when all it'll take is one week to get better.

Kristen narrows her eyes, noticing my reaction. "You make sure you wear those bandages, okay? Especially around here," she says in an irritated tone.

"Huh?" What is wrong with her? "Sure, I'll wear them till I'm feeling better. No worries."

"No, Marci. Not *till you're feeling better*! I know it'll be a pain, but you need to wear them for at least a week. Longer would be *nice*." She says the word "nice" as if I wouldn't know nice if it crawled up my nose.

I can honestly say I tried to give her a break. I'm not thick-headed; I know it's been an awful day for everyone. But why has she suddenly become such a hag? I got injured risking my skin to save the day, while she sat here, all safe and prissy in her immaculate lab coat. I've had it.

"Hey, I don't know what's wrong with you today, *lady*, but you need to back off. Besides you're not making sense,

I'm injured. Of course I'll do what I need to do to get better. I'm not an idiot. I'll wear the stupid bandages." I'm amazed by my voice's resonance in the small room. Earlier, I could hardly breathe, now I'm practically screaming.

Kristen's eyebrows shoot up. "You don't know?!" she says in an amazed half-question.

"What?" I say defensively, my mind racing to figure out whatever she means.

"I asked you to wear the bandages for at least a week, because you'll be all better by tomorrow," Kristen says. "That's the one universal benefit of having an agent inside you." The way she says it suggests she thinks I'm dumber than a bag of bricks.

I blink in quick succession. As soon as her words sink in, I know they're true. All along I just thought I was healthy. I've had scrapes, a sprained ankle once or twice, stomach viruses and colds, but nothing has ever lasted for more than a few hours or a day at most. Even when everyone at school was laid out with the flu, I never missed a day due to illness. Suddenly, I remember Dad's jokes about how the fact that he was a doctor was wasted on me.

"I see," I say, staring at my hands, my voice void of all feistiness. "I'll keep the bandages for as long as you need me to."

Kristen goes through the motions of taking my pulse and blood pressure. She listens to my chest for what feels like ten whole minutes. But it's just me and this awkwardness I've laid out in front of us. Still, she has to realize she was being bitchy about it.

"Everything looks perfect," she says, taking three steps back.

I watch her as she stands there, looking hesitant. It's like she wants to say something else, but she's considering whether it's wise or not. Finally she says, "Perhaps I shouldn't *meddle*, but I don't think it's wise for you to … pursue your romantic interest in Xave."

My jaw drops. So this why she's being such a witch. How dare she? I didn't ask *Dr. Love* for her advice. What I do or don't do with Xave is my business and no one else's. She needs to butt out.

With the calmest tone I can manage, I say, "It's none of your concern."

"You're wrong. It does concern me and it will concern James even more."

I throw the sheets to one side and stand, putting the bed between us. "What is that supposed to mean?"

"Save yourself the heartache, Marci. It can't end well," Kristen says.

"And how would you know that?" I press the back of my stupid hospital gown together, trying to keep my dignity.

She nods, a sad, faraway gloom in her green eyes. "Oh, believe me, I know. But that's neither here nor there." She waves a hand. "This is work," she continues in a business-like tone. "What we do here is important, crucial to IgNiTe's success. You can't mix business with pleasure. It's a bad idea under normal circumstances. Under yours, it's a huge mistake."

"So what are you gonna do? *Fire us?*"

Kristen walks right up to the bed, locking her eyes with mine. "Do you love him?" she asks in a low whisper.

"Again, that's none of your business."

"My guess would be that you do. First love," Kristen says in a mocking, dreamy voice.

My bile stirs, the stainless steel water pitcher on the table shakes with a faint metallic sound. Kristen doesn't seem concerned by the telekinetic disturbance. But she would be, if she knew I'm considering dousing her with ice water.

"How long do you think you can lie to him?" She pauses, but I don't answer trick questions. "If you truly love him, do you think that's a good way to start a relationship?"

"He won't care," I say, yearning for it to be true. But the reality is, I don't know what Xave would do if he knew I'm a monster.

Kristen sighs. "Go on telling yourself that," she says bitterly.

I know what I'm about to say should probably never cross my lips, but she's asking for it. "Just because someone dumped *you* doesn't mean it'll happen to me."

An injured expression flashes through her eyes, but it's gone in an instant. "We're trying very hard to keep Oso, Blare and Clark from asking too many questions about The Tank, about me. We can't risk them learning what we are. There are other pods across the world also led by Symbiots, Marci. We can't have anyone in the ranks suspecting the leaders are the very creatures they're trying to destroy. We're dealing with something serious here, too much to risk on a mere teen crush. How much longer do you think you can keep up appearances? I wager not long, especially if you become romantically involved."

I hate Kristen for being right. It's been hard hiding things from Xave through the years, like the day I crashed Clark's bike. Mostly, I let him believe what he will, but I doubt that would work if we start ... dating. The idea fills me with giddiness and happiness, and in spite of everything, there's no way I would give up these emotions to keep James and Kristen from being disappointed in me. Maybe it'll be harder to hide my true nature from Xave, but I've done it this long. How much harder can it be?

I'll train harder. If I subdue my agent completely, Xave never has to know about it unless ... unless someone tells him. I stare at Kristen suspiciously. No, she wouldn't tell him. No one here would. She just said they're trying very hard to keep it a secret. All they can do is kick us out of IgNiTe. I can take that chance.

Once my mind is made up, I feel myself relax. The anger I felt toward Kristen dissipates.

"I will lie to Xave for as long as I have to. My personal life won't become an issue here. You have my word," I say. More tentatively I add, "If James feels I should leave, then I will." The way my voice cracks at the last word betrays my true feelings. I've finally found a place where I fit in. Leaving would be difficult.

Kristen's shoulders fall a few inches and a thin smile stretches her lips. "I've nothing against you, Marci. You're a brave girl who knows what she wants, and I admire that." She nods, walks to the door and before leaving she adds, "Just consider this, you have more than yourself to think about."

Her last words, although gentle, feel like a slap in the face. They echo inside my head over and over, an undeniable truth. She just called me selfish. The shoe fits all too perfectly.

Chapter 48

Just as Kristen is about to close the door, James walks up. He gives her a gentle smile.

"How is the patient doing?" he asks.

"See for yourself." Kristen slips past, leaving him behind with a puzzled expression on his face. I look at the wall straight ahead and try to get my frustration under control.

James walks in and closes the door behind him. "Something the matter?" he asks.

"No," I lie.

"Good." He sits on the chair to my right. "So, you feeling all right?"

I put a hand on my ribs. "Yeah, still a little sore, but not much."

"You gave us quite a scare."

"How bad was it? I mean, it felt pretty bad. I actually thought I was going to die, but I guess it mustn't have been that bad since ..."

"Oh, it was bad. Your lung was punctured. We got you here as quickly as possible. Kristen did a fantastic job putting you back together. She has experience with Symbiots and their injuries. She knows just how to take advantage of our healing abilities."

He sounds as if he's thinking about all the times Kristen has put him back together. A rueful smile stretches his mouth.

I nod, eyes set on the door knob, feeling ungrateful and rotten. James is too lost in his own recollections to notice.

He shakes his head and continues. "But only Kristen and I know how close you came to … you know. We've told everyone else it looked worse than it was."

"Are they buying it?"

"Everything happened too fast for them to really notice. Besides, they're too focused on asking questions about this place to worry about much else." James rubs his chin, looking preoccupied. "But they'll get over it. We just have to make sure not to slip up," he says, eyebrows raised questioningly as he tries to make sure I catch his meaning.

"No problem. I'll watch what I say."

"Good, good." James leans forward, hands on his knees. "That was some work you did out there. You … saved my life. I want to thank you for that."

"Oh, that was … nothing." I worry at a loose thread on the sheet. I don't want to think about what I did. That's the only way I've been able to deal with the fact I killed somebody.

He was a monster.

There was a human being in there, too.

No cure. There's no cure.

Yet.

I set him free from torture, from prison.

Keep telling yourself that.

James takes my hand in his. "You're going to make a hole in that sheet."

"Oh, sorry."

"Don't let remorse build up. You have to nip it in the bud. This is war, Marci. It's them or us. You understand?"

I swallow and clench my teeth.

"We may never find a cure," he continues. "And I feel we must operate under that assumption, because if we don't, any scruples we have about our enemies will mean the death of our race."

"I—I just …"

"*They* have no scruples. They won't think twice about destroying us. We have to do the same if we want to survive. I know you're too young for all this, but you have amazing powers and what you did out there was … necessary. I'll understand if it's too much for you, but I truly hope you stick with us and continue to fight."

James holds my gaze, waits for me to say something, but I feel overwhelmed by his request. He sounds as if he's counting on me, but it's not just that. There's something else. He sounds as if he actually *needs* me, like I've become indispensable. I wonder if he'll feel the same when he hears about Xave and me.

"Will you fight, Marci?" he asks when I don't say anything.

"I've no choice but to fight," I answer in a whisper. "I've lived through enough horrors not to let one more worry me."

James says nothing for a long moment. He looks regretful, as if he'd like to shelter me from this nightmare. But he can't. There are too many things in the balance and I'm the least of them.

"Did anyone notice what I did?" I ask, trying to dispel the awkwardness before it stretches beyond bearable. "You know, with the lock and … the hose?"

"You mean you didn't pick the lock? You used your powers to open it?"

I nod.

"Hell, I didn't even realize that myself." He looks genuinely surprised. "Amazing. Telekinesis and, I believe, some level of ESP. Think of all the things you could do."

"Um, ESP? What are you talking about?"

"Somehow you knew the code to the lab door had changed," he says.

"That was just a hunch. Not ESP," I protest.

"Are you sure about that?"

That's an unfair question. I'm not sure about anything these days.

James's eyes glitter with possibilities. I have the feeling he's laying out an intricate plan for my life at this very moment. I will become a tool in his hands. I'm not sure how that makes me feel.

James clears his throat. "Going back to your question. No, no one noticed what you did, and we're very lucky they didn't. Oso and Blare were too busy doing their job and trying to stay alive." He sighs. "It will be very hard to hide what we are, but we have to try, for as long as we can. We have to be discreet, Marci. Not to mention careful. As grateful as I am, stepping out into crossfire wasn't a good decision. Neither was using your powers in front of everyone. I know I sound like I'm contradicting myself. I want you to fight and use your powers, but you must do both wisely."

"I understand. I know what's at stake." Kristen made that all too clear.

"The fight will be more difficult from now on. Since this morning, the Eklyptors know we exist. You saw the size of that door they were ready to install. They're building vaults now, and after our attack and that of other cells, it will get worse. If we'd been one day late, we wouldn't have found the rudimentary security they had this morning. They under-estimated us and *we* got very lucky."

"Rudimentary or not, it gave us enough trouble," I say.

James lets out an unamused laugh. "That it did. But we had you."

He stands up and nods several times, looking proudly at me. A feeling of satisfaction floods my chest. At first it feels great, but then it scares me a little. Ha! I was already worried about letting him down before, now the pressure feels even greater.

"Rest now," he says. "There'll be much work to do. We have to reassess the situation and figure out where to strike next. For now, the most important thing is to safeguard our identities and our mission from others. I've already told you there are Eklyptor spies everywhere, and, after today, they'll only increase their efforts."

He walks toward the door and before he leaves he adds, "Not to mention those … dreaded meditation sessions." With a wink, he exits the room and leaves me.

Yeah, no pressure.

Chapter 49

I sleep for a while. I don't know how long. When I wake up, I look around, searching for Xave. I'm the only one in the room. After a few minutes staring at the ceiling, I grow restless, my mind swirling with everything that's happened. My thoughts keep going back to Xave and the sanity of my decision to tell him what I feel for him.

Nearly dying can seriously impair one's decision-making abilities. Before I almost ended up as crocodile bait, I'd decided I had nothing to offer him. One punctured lung and several bruises later, and I've spilled my heart out, putting us in a situation that could have devastating consequences for our friendship and even IgNiTe.

In spite of everything, I can't back down now. I won't. Nearly dying isn't that much different than actually doing so. Not when you're at war, and death looms like a hawk stalking prey. I won't miss the chance to be happy with Xave, not when it could be my last and only opportunity.

I'm sitting, staring at my hands, when there's a soft knock on the door.

Xave peeks in. "You're awake. How do you feel? Dr. Albright said you'll make a quick recovery," he says, walking in the room.

"Yeah," I mumble. My thoughts are jumbled. Xave frowns, probably puzzled by my hot and cold attitude. I brush aside my worries, knowing it isn't fair to him. I was the one who got us into this mess.

We exchange nervous glances and, if awkwardness was visible, we'd see a wall between us. The usual easy feeling of his presence is replaced by caution and doubt. We don't know how to be anything else besides friends. As I watch Xave fidget, I wonder if there are even more reasons that make this a mistake. Will we work out as a couple? Agent or not?

"Um, what's going on out there?" I ask. "I'm getting bored stuck in here." As wrong as it is, I'd rather have picked the conversation back up where we left it before Kristen interrupted us, but we have to start somewhere.

Xave eagerly jumps to answer. "You're better off in here. Believe me. Blare isn't making things easy for anyone."

"No," I say with mock skepticism. "Not Blare."

We both laugh.

"There's a wheelchair out there. You're sitting now. I don't see the difference. I'll roll you out, so you can take a look at this place. It's something."

"Yeah, that sounds good. I'd like to see it."

He leaves for a minute and comes back with the chair. I start to get out from under the covers.

"Hey, don't move," he orders.

I freeze, remembering I need to pretend my injuries aren't healing as quickly as they are. I don't think playing the helpless patient will come naturally to me.

Hesitantly, Xave puts an arm around my back, then slides another under my bent knees. My five-foot-five lean frame is nothing for his six-foot-two muscular one. I wrap shaky arms around his neck. He buries his nose in my hair and inhales. Xave's torso is hard and sinewy against the side of my body. I remember all the times I've seen him without a shirt and start feeling tingly all over.

As he sets me down on the chair and pulls his arm out from under my legs, goose bumps travel down my spine. He's close, with his left arm still around my back and his face next to mine.

Suddenly, he pulls me tight in a desperate embrace. "Thank God you're okay." His voice is a warm whisper beside my ear, his relief as real as the solid arms that envelop me, transporting me to the safest place I've ever known.

Xave pulls away slowly, grazing my cheek with two-day-old stubble. "Marci." He says my name like some sort of sacred vow. I never knew it could sound so beautiful and mean so much to someone.

From ear to chin, my jaw is electrified as his face slides along mine. He only pulls away when the corner of his mouth is about to touch mine. We gaze at each other. At this moment, his eyes are dark green with flecks of brown.

"I don't care who walks through the door," he says.

Slowly, he leans in and kisses me.

Xave's lips are gentle and slow at first. His cinnamon breath is almost edible, and I know that—from now until forever—a stick of Big Red will always remind me of him. His hands hold my face tenderly. He pulls away and looks me in the eye for two quick seconds, then kisses me again, this time deeper. I forget myself and forcefully press my mouth against his. His breath catches before he joins in with the same intensity. The world comes to pieces, disarmed by the force of the emotions surging through my body.

Suddenly I realize this is no mere kiss. A kiss is just a kiss until it becomes more than just two mouths pressed together.

A friend only a friend until the day you feel whole in his arms. A heart just a muscle until the embrace of a lifelong friend lights it on fire and makes you suspect you've never been truly alive.

I gasp. Xave pulls away alarmed, his gaze flickering to my injured side. He thinks he's hurt me, when what he's done is awaken a deep hunger within me.

"I'm sorry," he croaks and rests his forehead against mine, inhaling and exhaling deliberately, getting his agitated breaths back to normal. "Got carried away. I didn't mean to hurt you."

"You didn't," I blurt out, hoping he'll kiss me again.

Xave grazes my lower lip with his thumb. "That was ..." He shakes his head, words failing him.

"I know."

He pushes away, taking all the oxygen with him. I need him near me again. How I ever survived when he wasn't around is suddenly a puzzle.

"I need to take better care of you," he says. "I'm not being a good ... boyfriend." He searches my face for a reaction.

I smile, letting him know he can call himself whatever he wants. "No, you're not. You stopped kissing me." He smiles back, hazel eyes a lighter shade of green now.

Biting his lower lip, Xave leans in and gives me a lingering kiss, one that we both have a hard time pulling away from.

"I can't wait till you're all better." He sighs then straightens. "C'mon, let's tour the place, before we get in trouble."

Chapter 50

Xave rolls the chair forward. As we exit into the long corridor—the wheelchair making a rhythmic click as it rolls—Kristen's words ring in my ears.

How long do you think you can lie to him?

I bite my tongue. I already want to tell Xave that I'm all better, that he doesn't have to worry about me or be afraid of hurting me, that he can kiss me, crush me against his body and never let me go. I wish I could tell him everything.

"I think Blare's jealous," Xave says, as we pass closed doors on either side of the corridor. His words pull me back to the moment.

He's picking up the thread of our earlier conversation. I ponder for an instant, then catch his meaning. Blare must be jealous of Kristen, but I can hardly act like I know that. I'm not supposed to really know Kristen or the way she and James look at each other with such longing.

How Blare feels about James, on the other hand, is no secret to anyone. She's an open book to all. Well, except to James, apparently.

"Jealous of what?" I ask, playing my part.

"Not what. Who."

I pretend not to understand. "Huh?"

"Of Dr. Albright," he explains.

"You mean the doctor and James ... ?" This mock Q and A is actually kind of fun.

"Oh, I don't know, but Blare seems to think so."

"Funny," I say.

"Anything but. Blare's in rare form, demanding answers about this place and why we didn't know about it."

"Yeah, why didn't we know about it?" I'm curious to hear how James explained The Tank's existence.

"Well, James just procured the place and with the hit on Riverbend there was no time to bring it up," Xave explains, sounding as if he totally believes this explanation. James exudes nothing but trustworthiness, but still—"just procured the place"? With all that lab and computer equipment conveniently in one place? Hardly. And how about Kristen? How do they explain her away?

As soon as we exit the hospital wing, I get an answer to my first question. Jaw practically hitting my chest, I stare at The Tank, barely recognizing the place. The space where the pods used to be is empty. There's nothing in the middle of the vast open area, just polished wood floor and stark white walls. Even the oil paintings are gone. Cubicle walls are pushed against the wall and huge tarps cover lumpy objects, giving a just-moved-in appearance. Only James with his faster-than-light speed could have done this.

"It's big, isn't it?"

"Yeah," I say in a drawn-out breath.

"They call it The Tank because of those glass walls up there." He points upward, toward the elevator. "It's like a huge aquarium, I guess."

"So what is this? Why did James get a place like this?"

"He says it'll be our headquarters."

I nod. "Cool."

"Think of the kind of money the man has. Apparently he owns this building. Oh, you probably didn't notice when they brought you in, but we're smack in the middle of downtown, right under some fancy office building."

"Really?"

"Yep."

"Wow." The whole affair with James and his millions is still amazing to me, so I don't have to pretend to be surprised. "So where's everybody?"

"In the kitchen, getting lunch ready. Let's go. I'm starving."

Xave rolls the chair to the right, where the bedrooms, conference rooms and kitchen are.

"So how does Kristen fit in? Does she know about IgNiTe and Eklyptors?" I ask, trying to learn all I can about James's false version.

"Yes. From what I gather, she's not only a doctor, but also a biologist. Apparently, she's doing all kinds of research to figure out a cure."

"A cure," I say dreamily. "Do you think that's possible?"

"I don't know. I guess. If the infection is like a virus or something like that, it has to be possible."

"What if it's not?" I ask, watching the polished floor pass under my feet.

"I don't like to even think about that." Xave veers toward the kitchen.

"What time is it?" I ask, finally a question that makes sense.

"Um, twelve thirty. Are you hungry?"

"Not really." The thought of food makes my stomach queasy.

As we enter the kitchen, I rest an elbow on the armchair and prop my head on my hand. I think a bit of acting is in order.

"Hey!" Oso exclaims. "There's our girl. How you feeling?" He approaches me, wearing an apron over a wifebeater t-shirt and a pair of jeans. A gold watch squeezes his thick, hairy wrist. His eyes grow sad as if he's regarding an injured puppy. My acting is paying off. I take a quick look around the room and spot Kristen giving me an approving nod.

Oso pats my shoulder as Xave pushes me deeper into the large kitchen. The smell of grilled meat churns my stomach. I should be hungry. I haven't eaten since yesterday and I'm feeling better by the minute. The thought of food is unpleasant, though. Maybe it's nerves due to having a boyfriend for the first time, and under these circumstances.

Kristen stands by the long center island, slicing tomatoes. James is next to her, pouring wine into a row of glasses. He nods and smiles at me. I wonder if Kristen told him about Xave, if he disapproves. But, as he turns and passes Kristen a bowl full of lettuce, it seems I'm the last thing on his mind. They hold a quiet conversation, smiling easily at each other.

If they have a thing going, I don't know how they could object to my relationship with Xave. True, I've never seen any real evidence to indicate they're involved, but it seems pretty obvious. Do they hide an affair? Or do they hide their feelings from each other on principle? Either way, the sexual tension between them is palpable and—judging by the way Blare's staring at them, her eyes shooting invisible death rays in their direction—I'm not the only one who suspects something's going on between the boss and the doctor.

Perhaps the best thing Xave and I could do is keep things a secret. I mean, why does anyone need to know we're together? I make a mental note to discuss it with him, hoping he doesn't think I'm embarrassed to be his girlfriend. At that thought, I look behind me and smile.

"Girl, you look rough," Rheema says with a wink. Thick bandages cover her forearm, and she limps as she stands to move a chair out of the way.

Oso walks up to a large, chef-style gas stove, picks up a pair of tongs from the counter, and flips a large steak. "You gave us a real scare." His expression is stern.

"It looked worse than it really was," Kristen says.

"Yeah, you looked like shit," Blare says, snatching a wine glass from under James before he's even done pouring. Like Oso, she looks to have made it out unscathed. I guess all the loose surveillance equipment is responsible for injuring those of us in the back. "I even thought you'd croak, but I guess I'm no doctor," she adds with a nasty look at Kristen.

Xave pushes the wheelchair to a long dinner table, in the space Rheema cleared. Across from me, Clark waves and wiggles one eyebrow.

"'Bout time," he says in a low voice, then fake-zips his lips and throws away the key.

So much for keeping things a secret. I guess Xave already spilled it. I look away mortified. Xave pretends to be having trouble taking off his now torn IgNiTe jacket.

"You hungry, little girl?" Oso asks. "I've got a steak with your name on it."

Kristen looks my way. I clutch my belly and shake my head. "Thank you, Oso. But I couldn't stomach it." I don't have to pretend on this one.

"How about some juice?" Xave turns to Kristen. "Dr. Albright, can she have some juice?"

Kristen tosses the salad. "Yes, juice is fine. And call me Kristen, please."

As Xave walks to a battalion-size fridge to look for the juice, I notice Aydan sitting quietly at the end of the table.

One of his eyes is bruised and bloodshot, and a strip of bandage is wrapped around his head.

Xave returns with a glass of orange juice. "Here you go."

"Thank you," I say, my gaze still locked with Aydan's.

He narrows his eyes at me, then gets up from the table, pulls a beer out of the fridge and returns without giving me a second glance. I guess almost dying had no effect on him. He's the same jerk as before.

As if this was a family and they had done this a thousand times, everyone helps set the table in a matter of minutes— except Blare and Aydan of course. There's steak, salad, garlic bread and mashed potatoes.

The food gets passed around and everyone fills their plate. I sip orange juice, while everyone else eats with unsettling appetite. Clark teases Oso about keeping the larger steak for himself. After Oso cuts into it, he lifts the plate and offers it to Clark. The thing looks like it's barely been cooked. Clark waves a hand at the plate, and calls him a savage. Everyone laughs and my ribs don't hurt as much when I join in.

After a silent moment, James clears his throat. "To Marci," he says, taking me by surprise. "Because without her this whole operation would have been an utter failure."

"To Marci." Glasses go up and clink against each other.

Blare joins in, even if half-heartedly. Aydan crosses his arms and stares at his plate. His face is its usual sour flavor. I don't let it bother me for long. Not when everyone else wants to touch their glass to mine. Not when the celebratory mood is so contagious. It may be a small victory, but it's a victory nonetheless.

The disturbing reality of what the world has become looms like a terrifying phantom over my head. I take a deep breath and push away fearful thoughts of the future. I refuse to worry about it right now. I have a lot to be grateful for at the moment: Xave, new friends, the feeling that I belong. So I choose to concentrate on these things, even though the secrets I've uncovered are much bigger than I'd ever imagined.

The whole world depends on cells like this one, on people like us. The responsibility to defend our humanity hangs heavy in the air, a mass so sizable it seems to obstruct the view of our species' future. It's too much to take in at once. There are more immediate things for me to consider and accomplish, like getting my agent under control, so I focus on that.

I smile to myself, contemplating my new life. For the first time in years, I'm happy. The shadows feel distant, a small threat with a death sentence.

All I have to do to ignite them is flip the switch on my thoughts.

Click.

Epilogue

I've never been happier, even if the world as we know it is at the brink of collapse.

Not that you can tell when you walk the streets. Everything seems normal on the surface. People go about their business. They work, shop, party their butts off on Friday nights, walk their dogs and pick up their poop, kill each other. Some look content, others rather miserable. Same merry old world. But I know better. IgNiTe and each of its members know better.

And still … I'm happy.

If anyone had told me that my life would take a one-hundred-and-eighty-degree turn for the better, I wouldn't have believed it. Three weeks ago, my most likely guess about my future would have involved Mom—or some other concerned adult—committing me to the loony bin.

Instead, I now have a boyfriend, a miraculously tolerable mother, a brother, a definite hope to control my demons, a mentor I admire. In short, a life worth living, a life I'm more than willing to fight for.

I smile at my mocha latte and stir it with a wooden stick.

"I thought that was your bike," a familiar voice says behind me.

I look back, trying not to wince. I can't help but feel like I've been caught with both hands inside the cookie jar. But it's silly, I'm just a girl in a coffee shop. There's nothing here to betray the fact that I'm on my way to the underground headquarters of a secret organization.

"Luke! Hey, what are you doing on this side of town?"

My brother swaggers in, his blond hair resplendent under the track lighting overhead. "I was about to ask you the same thing," he says.

I'm supposed to meet James in ten minutes for a meditation session. I sip from my drink. "Library."

"Really? I was headed there, too. Let me get some coffee, and we can go together."

"Um, actually, I was just there dropping off some books."

"Oh, all right." He looks disappointed.

I feel bad and would go with Luke if I didn't have to meet James. "I would tag along, but I have to meet Xave."

"No worries." He walks to the counter and orders a double espresso.

I linger, staring at the cookies and pastries behind the display area.

"Do you want a cookie? My treat," Luke says with a wink.

I already turned him down once. I can't do it again. "I'd love one. Chocolate chip."

"A chocolate chip cookie for the lady, please."

After paying, he hands me a paper bag with my huge cookie inside. As I take it, the entrance door opens and my head begins droning. My heart hammers as I'm reminded of my encounter with Elliot. My eyes dart toward the door, all senses in high alert. A burst of adrenaline fizzles out as I see James pushing past the glass door. His eyes meet mine immediately, then he presses on toward the counter, pretending not to recognize me.

When I regain my composure, I realize I'm clutching the paper bag in a tight fist. I relax and look up to see if Luke noticed. The expression on his face takes me by surprise. A deep frown creases his forehead and his pupils are reduced to nothing, just dark pinpricks piercing his clear blue irises. Nostrils flaring, he looks past me, past anything laying in his field of vision. His attention is somewhere else.

He turns his head ever so slightly toward the counter, where James is ordering black coffee. Luke must have noticed my reaction, after all. Now he's worried about the person standing behind us.

"Well, um, I guess I'll get going," I say.

Luke turns toward the exit very slowly. "Okay, I'll see you later then." He spares one quick glance in James's direction, then walks beside me with firm steps, jaw taut and twitching. James looks straight at the cashier, chatting in friendly terms, ignoring me as if I was a complete stranger.

Outside we say goodbye, and I make time by checking my boots and putting on my helmet. Luke waves as he drives by in his SUV. I wave back and wait till he turns the corner, then start my bike. I'm so stupid. James warned me not to go in that coffee shop again. Aydan's brew is nasty, but that won't serve as an excuse for my screw-up.

After clearing all the security that leads to The Tank, I exit the elevator and look down through the glass. Rheema is the only one here, wearing greasy coveralls as she works on a dismantled engine. Noticing me, she waves, a genuine smile etched on her face.

I bounce down the metal staircase. "Hey, Rheema," I say, returning the smile. Her dirty blond hair is up in a tight bun, but two stubborn ringlets frame her face. "What you got there?"

"It's a Harley engine," she says looking back at the greasy pieces strewn on a long table. Switching a filthy old rag from one hand to another, she attempts to clean her fingers. It's a useless task.

I've discovered Rheema has a true passion for mechanics and now she has a helper in Xave. They make me wish I had a similar dedication to something I enjoy, but I'm afraid I still haven't found out what that is. I like computers and martial arts, but I don't think I'd like to make a career out of them. Anyhow, figuring out my life's passion isn't that important right now. Not when all I want to do is fight and wipe Eklyptors off the face of the planet.

"I'm going to fix it up for you," Rheema announces.

"You're what?!"

"For saving our sorry buns." She flicks me in the backside with her dirty rag.

"You don't have to do that," I say, but only half-heartedly, because I'm already getting excited about the idea.

"I know I don't have to, but I *want* to." Rheema sticks her tongue out at me. "There's one thing you have to do first, though."

"What is that? Whatever it is, I'll do it."

"You have to beat that bugger." She taps her forehead with a greasy finger, leaving a dark mark behind.

"You got it," I say. Meditation is still giving me problems, but it's getting easier with every session. James is still puzzled by my ability to move objects with my mind. Hell, *I'm* still puzzled. I can't even do it at will yet. Fear and anger are good triggers, but I can hardly fake those emotions. I've tried. It doesn't work.

I just wish I had a skill I could rely on, like Rheema with her deadly, incapacitating toxin. The one I found out she used on Dr. Schmitt that day at Riverbend. It's so totally cool that she developed fangs that can deliver the poison. Cooler yet is how she taught her body to manufacture the substance. Moving dry erase markers isn't quite deadly, unless you get really creative *and* desperate.

At the sound of steps, Rheema and I look up. James is coming down the staircase, coffee cup in hand.

"Marci, conference room," he orders in a stern voice, without even looking our way. He walks off at a brisk pace.

Rheema gives me a questioning look. I shrug—pretending I don't know what it's about—and follow James.

I curse under my breath. How could I have been so careless, hanging out close to our hideout again, buying mocha lattes and cookies? I feel like such an idiot. How can I expect him to treat me like an adult when I do childish stuff like this?

"Who was that?" he asks as soon as I step into the room.

"I promise you he doesn't know anything. I just ran into him by accident. I told him I'd just dropped off some books at the library. It won't happen again. I swear I won't go into that coffee shop anymore." My words stumble over each other like domino pieces speeding to a colossal collapse. I'm not even making sense.

James's gray eyes bear down on me. "You didn't answer my question."

My brain is slush and I have to muddle through the muck to remember the question. "Uh ... yeah ... the question. Um, that was Luke."

"And where did you meet this Luke?"

"Well, he ..." I swallow and take a deep breath.

I knew at some point I would have to explain this. It's something I've been meaning to do, but I haven't found the right time. This is definitely not it.

341

James and Kristen need to know about Luke. About the fact that he's not infected even though we're twins and we both came from one of those evil fertility clinics. My head doesn't drone in his presence. I think he doesn't have an agent inside him. My guess is that his embryo was just a perfect combination of human genes. But what if I'm wrong? What if he does have a parasite in his brain but is immune to it? If that's the case, that knowledge could propel Kristen's research to a whole new level. Suddenly, I feel callous for keeping this from them.

"I should have told you before," I begin.

James's gaze grows dark. He purses his lips as if he's trying to hold back a mean retort.

"Luke is my twin brother."

After a slow blink, James shakes his head. "Your twin brother?" He begins to pace in front of the whiteboard, gaze darting to and fro, as if looking at the floor, the walls, the beanbags will clear his confusion. I know he's wondering how come he couldn't sense Luke if he's my twin brother.

I press forward, glad that James isn't screaming at me yet. "It's a long story. I just recently learned that we're related. You see, he was kidnapped when he was a baby." I know it sounds like a soap opera, but it is what it is.

Pausing, James gives me his full attention. I'm glad to see he doesn't look skeptical given how ludicrous the story sounds.

"It's messed up," I continue. "The same doctor that performed my mother's insemination took Luke from the hospital the very day we were born. The man raised him like a father but was murdered a few weeks ago. My mom saw his picture on the news and that's how we found Luke. Funny thing is, he was there all along. He's been in my school since kindergarten. I've known him practically my whole life without realizing we were related."

The are-you-serious look on James's face shows me he is actually skeptical, after all.

"But you two look nothing alike," James says. "You look Hispanic and he's … well … a gringo, like me."

Man, I hate stereotypes. I excuse James's comment because I know him and realize he's only trying to make a point.

"I look like my father. He looks like Mom. We're not identical twins." I give him a mocking glare, after stating the obvious. "Starting with the fact that he's a boy and I'm a girl." This last part wins me a nasty glare. Okay, maybe I overdid it with the sarcasm.

I sigh and barrel through to the end of my explanation. "I didn't mention him before because I'd just found out who he really was and we weren't exactly getting along. You can only imagine the upheaval Mom and I were in when he showed up. I won't bore you with the details, but the thing is, I decided to wait and see what would happen before bringing him up. I thought you and Kristen would want to know about him, especially since he might be immune."

"Immune?" James looks at me as if I've gone crazy. "How do you figure that?"

"Well, you know. No weird feeling in the back of the head. I don't …"

I was going to say that I don't sense Luke, the way I can sense other Eklyptors, but James is shaking his head, looking very worried.

"I felt him, Marci."

"W-what?"

"Why else do you think I want to know what you were doing with an Eklyptor right outside headquarters?"

"He's not an Eklyptor," I say, shuddering worse than if he'd called Luke the son of Satan. "You must be confused.

Maybe it was the cashier you sensed." I know this isn't true, since I know the girl behind the counter isn't one of them.

James lifts his eyebrows to point out my pathetic excuse.

"Okay, not the cashier. Maybe you sensed *me*. Yeah, that's it!" I nod vigorously, convinced James just got it all wrong.

"No, Marci." His eyes are sad, then suddenly remote, as if he's searching his mind for an explanation.

My stomach becomes a wild, tumbling thing with a mind of its own. I keep telling myself that James is mistaken. There's no way Luke is infected. We've lived under the same roof for almost a month. I would know it if he had a parasite in his brain. I would have sensed it!

The heavy, sickening feeling settling in my gut tells me otherwise. James and I exchange glances.

"He could be a full-fledged Eklyptor, Marci. A spy," James says. "This whole tale sounds too convenient. And him coming out of nowhere just as you joined IgNiTe."

"No, no. He's my brother. They did DNA tests. They checked out."

"Those could be faked. You know they have their hands in everything." James rubs a hand across the back of his bald head.

"No way. He's the spitting image of Mom. They look so much like each other it's freaky."

"Marci, is he full-fledged? Has his agent taken over?!" James's voice grows loud as he takes a step in my direction.

"I ... I don't know." I rack my brain. I always thought he was healthy, normal. I never tried to look for signs to check whether he's an Eklyptor or Symbiot. And from what I can recall, I've never seen in him the telltale signs that indicate he may be fighting the shadows.

"This is not good, Marci." James takes his hands to both sides of his face and pulls back, stretching his eyes.

I feel sick, betrayed. If Luke is an Eklyptor, what is he doing in my house? Has he been planning all this time to infect Mom and I? Or worse, is he a spy working for Elliot, trying to infiltrate IgNiTe? Does everyone in this freakin' world live double lives, pretending to be something they're not?

And if he's a Symbiot, why hasn't he mentioned anything about the shadows?

I groan in frustration. My mind is whirling so fast, I'm not even making sense anymore. Of course Luke wouldn't mention the shadows. I haven't mentioned them to anyone outside of the Symbiots within IgNiTe. Not even Xave knows about them. Luke could be in the same situation I was in before I met James, desperate to figure out if he's crazy or possessed by demons.

This still leaves a huge, unanswered question, though. Why can't I sense him?

"Have you told him anything about us?" James asks.

"No."

"Do you think he followed you?"

"I ... I think it was a coincidence. He said he was on his way to the library when he saw my bike parked outside the coffee shop. I already told you."

"We have to find out what he is, Marci. You understand that, right?"

I nod.

James walks toward the door. "I think I need to post a few more guards in the parking deck."

"Wait!"

He turns and gives me a furious look. He looks as if he wants to yell and is trying very hard to hold his temper. His stance—with tight, quivering fists at his side—is intimidating, but I set my jaw and ask my question.

"How come I can't sense him?" There has to be an explanation and I'm hoping James knows what it is.

"How the hell should I know?" James's anger spills over, unchecked. His face is red, his voice a booming soundwave that slams against my face. I take a step backward. I've never seen him lose it like this.

Biting the inside of my cheek, I refuse to let his outburst hurt me. All on their own, deep, controlled breaths begin pumping my chest. My thoughts jump like fleas on a dog.

Remorse flashes in James's eyes, but it lasts only a fraction of a second. "*You* tell me why, Marci. Because I didn't know that was possible."

He walks off and his words ring in my ears like an accusation. I follow him, my own brand of anger surging to the surface.

"I wouldn't be asking if I knew," I yell at his retreating back.

He takes two steps at a time, headed for the elevator, ignoring me. I notice Rheema out of the corner of my eye. She takes a tentative step in my direction, looking dumbstruck.

"I can take care of this." I stand at the bottom of the steps, gripping the handrails, staring up at James. "I will find out what he is."

After mounting the last step, James stops. His wide shoulders rise up and down with each breath. He stands motionless for a long moment before turning.

"I'd prefer it if you stay away from headquarters until we figure this out."

"But ..."

"Sorry, Marci. *I'll* be in touch."

I let go of the railing and press my back against the wall. I wipe sweaty hands on my jeans and stare at the polished wood floor. Did James just ... kick me out of IgNiTe?

I replay our conversation, trying to see things from his point of view in hopes of understanding his decision.

Is he afraid Luke is a spy and will follow me here one day? Or does he suspect more than just my brother? Is it possible that he suspects me? But how could he? After all I've done? After the way I proved my loyalty?

It isn't fair. Whatever happened to trust? He asked me to stand by him by offering nothing but secrets, then just like that decides I'm not trustworthy?!

"What just happened?" Rheema asks, keeping her distance, looking concerned—whether for me or the team, I couldn't say. James's words still seem to echo through the expansive area, so I don't blame her for the caution and distrust written on her face.

I push away from the wall, roll my shoulders to see if the weight pressing down on them will fall out. It doesn't.

"I ... I really don't know."

My rubber soles scrape the metal steps as I climb my way out of The Tank. When I reach the top, Rheema is still standing there, scratching her head and looking back and forth from the conference room to me.

I really like Rheema. I think we could become friends. She must see something in my face because her expression softens.

"It'll be okay," she says. "Whatever it is, we'll figure it out."

"Thank you," I mouth and board the elevator.

Out in the parking deck, the sound of my bike's engine booms against the concrete walls. I rev it up, trying to drown the uncertainty that wraps its cold fingers around my neck. I tear out into the street, without a backward glance.

Uncertainty, helplessness … I thought I had shed them forever. It turns out it takes only minutes to conjure them back.

Just moments ago, I thought I had it all figured out. Most of my questions had answers and the ones that didn't I could stow away without panicking. I had IgNiTe's help, James's help, to give me hope. Now I feel I have nothing.

The sun hangs low in the sky, well on its way out of this crummy day. I drive past buildings left behind in the dwindling light. It isn't dark enough for the street lamps to switch on.

Shadows lurk in every alley.

I push forward, trying to leave them all behind.

Acknowledgements

To my mother for her support and patience. She's a lighthouse, a rock, a constant. To my father, for his stern talks and high standards, always sprinkled with plenty of love. To my husband, my first reader, my biggest supporter, my forever and forever and forever. To my kids, who give me smiles and heart palpitations and pride and the most unconditional of loves. You guys are the best—a mother couldn't ask for more.

To my agent, Beth Phelan, for her ideas, honesty and patience. To Natasha Bardon for believing in *Ignite the Shadows* and giving it a chance, and for helping get the story just right, along with Eleanor Ashfield and everyone at Harper *Voyager* UK who worked hard to get this out into the world. It is a pleasure working with such an amazing team.

To my friend Bret for all the pep talks, creative conversations, and for always reading my early drafts with patience and a keen eye. To Billie for always asking for more of my stories, for telling me I don't suck at this, and for believing I could get this far and telling me she wasn't surprised when I did. To Subu for his attention to detail and willingness to read all the wild things I write. To Katie French and Amy Trueblood for offering a critical eye when needed and for being such great teammates. You ladies are class acts.

And finally to all my readers whose support has been wonderful, so many enthusiastic people who have reached out to me and given me such encouraging comments and who, every day, make this author journey incredibly rewarding.

CPSIA information can be obtained
at www.ICGtesting.com
Printed in the USA
LVOW03s2058310317
529236LV00001B/3/P